The Red-Winged Blackbird

A Novel

The Red-Winged Blackbird

by Bob Reed

LITTLE BLUE STEM PRESS

ISBN: 978-1478373803

Title of novel and lyrics from "Red-Winged Blackbird" used with permission of author, copyright © Billy Edd Wheeler.

Excerpts from " 'Hope' is the thing with feathers" and "I'll tell you how the sun rose–" taken from *The Complete Poems of Emily Dickinson,* 1960.

Lines from *Macbeth,* Act IV, Scene III, taken from *The Complete Works of William Shakespeare*, 1980.

Speech by Mary Harris "Mother" Jones was given in a slightly different form, September 24, 1913, in Starkville, Colorado.

"The Battle Cry of Union" was penned by UMW Vice-President Frank Hays, 1913.

Lines from "Don't Go Down in the Mine, Dad" by Robert Donelly and Will Geddes taken from lyrics published by the Lawrence Wright Music Company, London, 1910.

Jacket art, James Galloway, David Alan Hall

Photography, James Galloway

Layout, Walter Webb

for Sandra
Bill
the miners
and the red-wings

COMMENCEMENT
1910

Give sorrow words. The grief that does not speak
Whispers the o'er-fraught heart and bids it break.
William Shakespeare, *Macbeth*

CHAPTER ONE
November 8, 1910

Of all the working mules in Delagua, Colorado, old Grady was number one. A Suffolk, bred to work, he was handsome, keen-nosed and predictable. Some mules would trick you. Stand there like a saw horse while you traced them. Turn your back, and they'd jigger around with a hind leg until they unhooked themselves, then trot away, grinning. Not Grady. Hitch him up, he stayed hitched. Holler, "Up mule," he pulled. Cry, "Whoa," he stopped. Never snapped, never napped, never farted. In the mines, where even a marginal mule was worth five men, an animal like Grady was worth ten.

Me and my brother were lucky enough to take him in at the start of our shift, instead of having to wait our turn for a mule later. That meant we could shovel coal all morning, uninterrupted. We'd found four timbers in case we needed props for weak spots in the ceiling or walls and headed for the entry. Had three cars hitched to the best mule in creation and a pile of clean coal waiting. Life was sweet.

We lit our headlamps. I grabbed Grady's reins and we followed him inside. What we called Numbers 1, 2 and 3 was really one big mine with three portals. Tunnels connected them all about a half-mile inside the mountain. It was *possible* to go in through one entry and come out another, but it would be a booger of wandering.

The main haulage-way just inside soon split into tighter tunnels. Jagged walls of granite and coal rose about four feet to support a pitched roof, tall enough at the high point for a mule or a working man to duck under. The tunnels were narrow, but you could walk beside your mule or train of cars in a few spots, if they weren't filled with unused props, rails or cones of rock and dust.

In a mine's silence, when the earth breathed and the timbers popped like a shotgun blast before they split or broke, you'd ignore the shit in your union suit to set another prop, right quick, before a cave-in. The walls and ceilings were held up by sawed timbers, logs and planks, wedged-in, nailed up, helter-skelter, as we dug deeper into the mountain. Shoring in these rat holes, done quick and half-ass to keep us from getting squished, looked like framing for a house thrown together by drunken carpenters.

Sidney's bandana hung on a bracing timber ahead to mark the turn-off for our station. The Victor-American Company wouldn't buy much new track or timbers, so, as we dug deeper into the mountain, we scavenged used rails and crossties, prying them up from rooms that were played out, toting them to the end of the line, coupling them up and spiking them to the floor.

Ten feet into the room, Grady stopped before big chunks of fresh coal. The day before, me and Sid had dug around and under the coal seam, separating and shoveling out shale and granite–"dead work" the company didn't pay us to do. Then we'd augured holes into the seam and set black powder charges for a shotfirer to blast overnight. The pile of coal in front of the mule was our gravy train this morning.

We crouched next to the cars, closed our eyes and listened for methane gas seeping through fresh cracks. If we missed that gas, the first spark from a pick or shovel could blow us into Lucifer's parlor. Satisfied, we used our picks to test the roof and walls for weak spots. I tapped and listened for the ping of solid rock or the hollow click of a pocket that might give way. Under a suspicious spot in the ceiling, we wedged in a timber.

Dust flecked the lamps' beams as we shoveled loose coal from the slag heap. Only thing that spoiled concentration and slowed the work was Sid's coughing, a wheezing hack that sounded like a cold engine gasping to start. He was just twenty, two years older than me. Pretty young to be coming down with the coal cough.

We had two cars' full and were about to start on the third, when Grady got restless. His ears perked. He jerked his head back toward the haulage and flared his nostrils.

"See what's up," Sid said. He took Grady's reins and sat on the nearest car, mopping his face with a bandana. "I'll take care of the mule."

I walked down the tunnel toward the entry. At a corner rounding back to the right, yellow flickers, like the end of a moving picture film, sputtered on the rough wall.

I crawled along the track and peered around the bend at the worst thing I could have seen. Inside a doorway fifty feet ahead a slag heap blazed. A feller up there was trying to beat out the fire with a shovel.

Suddenly, as if the area had been doused with kerosene, the walls, floor and ceiling around the pick jockey burst into flame. No way I could get to him.

Smoke stung my eyes and I couldn't draw full breaths. The teary light from my headlamp shot broken beams through the smoke billowing into the tunnel.

Expecting an explosion any second, I turned and ran back down the tunnel. Had to stop and stoop for air. More. More and more. As I sucked shallow breaths between coughs, my head cleared a little. After I'd wiped my eyes with a bandana and tied it over my nose and mouth, I got moving again.

Back at the station, Sid was trying to calm Grady, who brayed and kicked the car he was hitched to.

"Fire," I hollered. "We got to git."

Sid was coughing something awful, but I couldn't worry with anything until I got a drink. I found the canteen, gulped some water, coughed, spit, gulped more. Brother took a drink then slung the canteen over his back. From the lunch bucket I pulled a dry sausage and a hunk of cheese and slid them into my jacket pockets.

I held Grady while Sid unhooked him. Tugged his halter and whispered sweet nothins in his ear, trying to settle him some. Sidney shouldered his pick and a shovel then grabbed ahold of the mule's reins. I'd slipped on the pack just as Sid gave Grady his head. He dragged Brother down the track so hard we had to run to keep up.

A ways from our station, the tunnel forked. Track continued into the right passage, but was absent in the left. Grady stopped in front of the left header. He hooved the cinders like he wanted to go in. But he *didn't* go in. I'd seen this happen plenty, when you had trouble telling a side tunnel from the main one. And mules weren't much good in a predicament like this because they got so nervous about going through unfamiliar openings.

We pondered the situation. It made more sense to follow the curve of the tunnel and go right, but it might be a deeper room or even a crosscut. It was only a matter of time until the dust exploded. If we got sidetracked into a room, we'd be trapped.

Grady yanked on the reins, trying to get his head inside the tunnel.

"Knows where the air is," Sid coughed, pointing left.

After the mule sniffed around to make sure everything was okay, he started walking again. In another two hundred feet he pulled up in a circle of light beaming down through the dust. The mule had found an airway shaft and he held his nose high breathing from it. The rough hole was about two feet in diameter and over a hundred feet high. Daylight flickered through the blades of a dead fan at the top.

Me and Sid took turns drawing deep breaths from the shaft. I took off the pack, then we sat on the floor and waited.

A string of bad luck had hit the southern coal field lately and it seemed like every time you sneezed another mine blew. The Colorado Fuel and Iron mine in Primero in January. Another in Starkville, exactly one month before this disaster struck our Number 3.

"Trouble comes in threes," Mama always said.

Sitting in the pool of light, I mulled over the Tanner luck. Papa had told us how he survived a cave-in in Number 6 in 1905. Said he found a bratticed room with good air, laid low and thought pleasant thoughts.

For over twenty hours in the darkness, men suffocated outside his cloth wall. Papa said he could hear them gabbing, moaning and crying. He suspected that the strong had smothered the weak and he registered the passing lives by the growing stillness and the funk of sulfur and shit filling the hole. When he was dug out, his beard and eyebrows were green from the gases and daylight stung his eyes for a week.

I shivered at this and suddenly *I* could feel death gathering in the stillness. I asked for the canteen. Guess Sid could tell how scared I was.

"Allie, Papa was trapped like this once and he got out."

"Yeah. I was just thinkin' about that."

All of a sudden, Grady reared his head, sniffed and took off so quick neither of us could grab his lead.

A few seconds later we heard what sounded like gravel being rattled in a cigar box behind us and a gust of hot air rushed in.

"First blast," Sid whispered.

Explosion in a coal mine unleashed an odorless gas called afterdamp that would soon eat up the stale air. We knew the chances of being found in a forgotten tunnel were slim. And another explosion might close the airway.

Sid stood and peered at the dot of light at the top the shaft. I knew what he pondered.

"It's a long way, Sidney," I said. "What if we climb up there and can't pry the fan loose?"

"Ain't gonna lay here and suffocate, Alan. That fan is comin' off." Sid came out of his jacket, put a knot in one sleeve and dropped it at my feet. "Tie the coats together and I'll pull you up. Okay?"

"Well . . . you know I ain't keen on heights."

"Better than the alternative," Sid said.

"What if Grady comes back?"

"Alan, Grady's gone where the air is, just like he did with us. He'll be okay. Now, give me a boost."

I gave Brother a leg up. He pressed his hands against the shaft wall and lifted himself far enough into the hole to jam each boot sole into the rock and lean back against the opposite wall. By stepping, grabbing cracks or outcroppings and using his elbows and knees, he climbed higher to give me room.

"That don't look too easy," I called.

"You'll get the hang of it. Hang the canteen on the pick and hand 'em up."

Did that. He hung the water around his neck, pulled it behind his back. Slid the tool under one overall strap, so the handle crossed his back and the spike peeked over his shoulder.

"Tie the jackets together and throw 'em to me, Alan."

I stuffed the cheese and sausage into my bib, then followed his order.

Sidney caught the bundle. Pretty soon, he dangled a sleeve from the hole. "Be a miracle if that don't rip," he said, adjusting his stance. "Come on, grab ahold."

I snagged the sleeve, reached the knot, hand-over-handed my way up the jackets.

Sid coughed and pulled as I kicked and reached. Lost my cap and headlamp in the process.

"Grab my ankle," Sid said.

I did and hauled myself into the shaft. Sid caught my overall strap and held me while I pressed my soles into the rock and wedged my shoulders against the wall.

"I ain't in very good, chief . . ."

"Grab anything, scooter . . . ." Sid was winded and so was I.

I hooked fingers into the waist of his overalls.

"Can you climb any higher, Sid? I'm about to fall out."

Somehow, while holding onto my strap and lifting, my brother scooted up.

"Okay, I'm good," I said. "Got to blow a minute . . ."

"Me, too. Take your coat and the canteen back," he said, lowering them.

I chocked myself, put the jacket on, slung the canteen. "Can you climb with the pick like that?" I asked.

"Got no choice. You ready?"

"Yeah, I guess."

Aside from getting more jittery with each step, the hardest part of this chimneying was plastering my hands, knees and elbows into the rough wall. Hadn't gone more than a few feet before I was scraped and cut.

Before long, height got to me. My guts churned and I thought I might crap my overalls. The higher we went, the worse it got. I was breathing like a smithy's billows.

Sidney's light zigzagged above.

"Don't you need a break?" I called.

"Think I can make it. We're over halfway."

"Ain't feelin' too good, chief."

"Okay. Let's stop a minute."

We had wedged in and I was feeling better when the shaft started to spin. "Can't rest," I hollered. "Too scary."

"Deep breaths, scooter."

"Dizzy," I mumbled, pulling in all the air I could. Smelled smoke rising in the shaft.

"Grab my ankle again, Alan. Don't pull. Just hold it."

I latched onto his boot top and, pretty soon, the spinning slowed.

"Guess I'm ready," I called after a few minutes.

We ooched upward, stopping from time to time. After what seemed like hours, we reached the top.

Now, Sid had to deal with the fan, a defunct original that hadn't been replaced by one of the new squirrel-cage rotaries. The blade turned in the draft, but it wasn't running.

Sid slid the pick out of his overalls and banged on the motor, to see if he could dislodge the machine. Blades bent, but the cage didn't give.

Sid started coughing and had to rest. "Gonna have to dig it out."

"Want to trade places?" I asked.

"I'm okay. It'd take more wind to climb around each other than I've got. Don't look up till I say. I don't know what's gonna come loose when I start messing with this piece of shit."

"Will do." I bowed my head and gazed into the darkness, until I felt sickly and closed my eyes.

As Sidney chipped, pried and banged, rocks and dirt rained on my shoulders, the back of my head and neck.

Head spun. Fingers, knees and toes slipped.

"Goddamn right," Sid grunted, still pounding. "Got an edge, Allie. Just hang on."

Bang-grunt. Bang-grunt.

"Don't look up yet. Still ain't good loose."

Dirt and rocks pelting. "Sidney . . . I'm about to fall," I heard myself holler.

"Hold on, Allie. It's . . . almost . . . there . . ."

"SIDNEY . . . I'M GONNA FALL."

I felt the pick handle slide down and rest on my shoulder. "Grab it, Alan. Don't pull, now, just hold it. I'm here and almost done. Take deep breaths and relax."

"Okay," I whimpered. Closed one hand around the handle and drew the deepest breaths I could.

"Better?"

"A little, yeah."

"All right. Move your hand to my closest foot. Don't pull. Just hold it like you done before."

I jumped my hand up to his ankle again. "That's better, chief. Thanks."

"All right. I'm takin' the pick back up. Just hold on a little longer."

Dizziness slowed and I let go of his ankle.

Sid hit the motor again and again and again, gasping for breath, until another edge opened. He kept at it until he could push the housing over like a trap door.

"I'm throwin' the pick outside."

Heard it clunk the ground.

Sidney stepped higher.

"Don't leave me in here by myself, Sidney, goddammit."

"Okay. Calm down, now, Allie. You already done the hardest part. You got three . . . maybe four steps left."

I didn't say anything.

"Can you manage one step right up under me?"

"Yeah, I think." I did that.

"Okay. How about one more?"

"All right."

Suddenly, he climbed out and I followed, two lost souls escaping hell's innards. We stretched out on our backs, huffing. Heart pounding, sweating and freezing, I got the shakes. You know how sometimes, after a really close call, your mind starts playing "the what-ifs" and you're six times scareder than you were going through it? That was me.

The sun had dropped into a bank of low, milky clouds that hinted snow. Gusts from the north tormented the craggy hillsides, stirring up dust, rustling the junipers, pinyon pines and whisker weed. A red-tail burst from the crown of a cottonwood and flapped into the canyon, sailing in ever-widening loops. A crow caught up, pestering the bigger bird until she escaped in an updraft. I wondered how Mother Nature could go on with men fighting for their lives in her belly.

Our papa used to bring me and Sid up here to school us on the bleak terrain.

"Looks worthless, don't it?" he'd slap the ground and lecture in his high-pitched voice. "Won't grow nothin'. But right here, under our feet, God put the richest bituminous coal deposit in the West. When I shine my lamp across a face, the coal twinkles for me like diamonds on black velvet. The whole world operates on coal, boys. Men will kill for it. That makes a coalass pretty damn powerful."

This god-forsaken countryside was our inheritance.

I propped myself on one elbow and looked at Sidney. He was a little taller, little heavier than me. Lot smarter. Did arithmetic in his head. See a problem, plan a solution, right quick, no hem-haw. Could recite the alphabet backwards, fast as a zipper. Match the letters with their numbers, too.

"What letter's number 15?" I'd ask, right out of the blue, to take him by surprise.

"*O*," he'd snap back, all cocky, like I was a pinhead.

"8?"

"*H*."

"Backwards from *Z*, what's 17?"

He'd crack up. "*J*. Ask me somethin' hard."

"Frontwards . . . letter *L* divided by *F*."

"Easy . . . *B*."

Good-humored for the most part, too. Always grinning, playing pranks, poking fun at stuff he didn't care about. Criticize one of his passions, though, and you were in for a tussle.

In daylight, I could see teensy bits of glass sparkling in the coal dust ground into his face, hands, jacket, cap, overalls and boots. Breathed that ten hours a day, six days a week. No wonder he coughed.

I threw a pebble at Sid's cap.

"What?" he asked without looking up.

"You gonna tell everybody I wee-weed out down there?"

"Ain't decided. You're on probation."

I studied the wrecked fan housing lying upside-down.

"Couldn't have got up that thing without you," I said.

"Yeah, I made it easy, didn't I, knocking that rock down in your face."

"I'll get you back."

When black smoke belched from the shaft, terror knotted my belly again. If we had stayed below, we'd have suffocated. I hoped Sid was right about Grady.

"Hey, chief," I called. "How much you think Victor-American's gonna charge you for tearin' up their fan?"

CHAPTER TWO
November 8, 1910

I halved the wedge of cheese and hunk of sausage and handed the pieces to Sid. We ate and shared the last of our water, looking down the hill at town.

An edgy calm filled the coal camp. Operators had shut down the winches that pulled coal cars coming from the mines across the great trestle spanning the canyon. Center of this bridge sat a deserted tipple house where rows of loaded cars waited to be weighed and dumped into boxcars sixty feet below.

When a mine blew, routine ceased. The day shift would come out of the other mines to help with the rescue and the night shift wouldn't go in. Along with lunkers from neighboring camps, company swells, ink slingers, doctors, undertakers and coffin builders would come up. We'd be newsworthy, like Primero and Starkville.

Folks scurried about in the streets, with some already climbing the hill up to the mines.

"Notice they ain't goin' to Number 3?" I said.

"Fire was close to the front," Sidney said. "Blast probably closed off the entry and rescue will come through 1 and 2. Guess we better go, huh? You ready?"

"Yeah."

On our way down the hill to the portal, we got discovered by our buddies, greeting us with shouts and slaps on the back. All worked the night shift except for Delagua's mayor, Andrew Jackson McKintrick. He was around fifty, tall with thick arms and broad chest. A thin, painted-on-looking mustache pulled your eye to a nose mashed long ago in bare-knuckle bouts–or so he bragged. Orated so much Sid speculated he'd been vaccinated with a phonograph needle.

To hear him tell it, McKintrick had done about everything interesting and dangerous a man could do and still be kicking. Fought Comanches and Kiowa, mined silver, deputy-sheriffed, play-acted, reported for newspapers.

Wrote dime novels in his spare time.

Like the tales of almost everybody I knew, McKintrick's wild deeds were tough to verify. Around here, an acceptable life story depended more on the entertainment value of flannel flapped than facts proved.

We'd all heard the yarn. Upon arrival in Delagua, Jack had distinguished himself within that breed of schemers whose job it was to take money from slag monkeys and swells alike, in exchange for left-handed merrymaking. As his circle of investors expanded, McKintrick's purchasing power and political influence increased. If you needed something–and were willing to pay–Jack could get it. As a result of his persuasions and timely monetary contributions, McKintrick's enterprises were not simply tolerated, but encouraged. He'd been mayor for six years.

Jack called his bankrollers "The Chamber of Commerce." Street noise fancied them as rich, powerful businessmen from Trinidad, Walsenburg and Pueblo. These investors remained so tight-lipped, we wondered if they even existed.

Wherever his money sprang from, Jack always seemed to have cash for development. He built a saloon to compete with Paine's and Merkel's rat holes. Staked whorehouses and bars in Chinkville and Hastings. Sweet-talked Elma Von Raven into selling him the controlling interest in her ramshackle brothel in Delagua.

Providing both sides of the street with soothing staples that kept minds off troubles and complaints, The Chamber gained the heartfelt gratitude and trust of diggers and company swells. Victor-American liked us lubricated.

As our friends overran us, the mayor celebrated. He hugged everybody. His hands flew around like nosey ravens. His eyes widened and narrowed. He tittered. He cried. He threw his fedora into the air.

While Jack described in painful detail every single thing he'd witnessed that day and what it meant to humanity, Fred Giotto picked his nose, Charlie Costa squeezed a sore on his hand, Mack Persons and Tommy Merryweather tossed rocks, Sid scratched his balls and stared at the sky and I thought about falling down that air shaft.

Every so often, coalasses passing by would shout a greeting, shake our hands, slap our backs. Felt kinda good being the center of attention.

When Jack gassed out and ran back to retrieve his hat, I asked Mack about my neighbor Cockeye Bastrop and his buddy Barba Tostakis, who were digging closer to the front than me and Sid.

"Don't know," Mack said. "Explosion brought down the ceiling at the first tunnel junction. Blew out so hard, flyin' rocks and timbers killed three slag monkeys standin' outside."

"Buried three pit bosses, the superintendent and his assistant, too," Tommy added.

Mack ticked off names on his fingers. "Peterman, Browder, Carlton."

"Pit bosses," Tommy threw in, like we didn't know.

"Potts and McConnaghue," Mack added.

"The supers," Tommy concluded. "Went in to fight the fire with a water hose."

Sid whistled. "We gripe about them guys, but it feels bad to think they're dead."

Mack nodded. "I know. It'll take a week to ream out that haulage. Rescue's gonna happen through Number 2."

"That's where we was headed when ya'll popped up," Tommy said.

"If Potts and McConnaghue is buried, who's in charge?" Sid asked.

"Assistant Superintendent from Hastings," Mack said.

"About thirty years old," Tommy added. "Could be thirty-one. Got him a beard."

Delagua had its share of oddballs and Mack and Tommy were two of the oddest. They'd known each other all their lives and had come to Colorado's southern fields to escape troubles at the coal mines in Thurber, Texas. Tommy tended to echo or throw light on everything Mack said. Tall and rail-thin, Tommy had a hard time fitting in tight places, so he worked on his knees a lot.

The brains of the twosome, stubby Mack, scurried in and out of holes and under coal seams like a mole, but couldn't shovel or load near as much as Tommy, who was a lot stronger. These buddies held the record for the most cars brought out in a single shift. Twelve.

On the landing outside Number 2, women milled around with miners, swells, guards and mules. The wives had brought up food, coffee and blankets. But with no information coming down about their men in the mine and nothing to do but wait, I knew they'd grow panicky.

So different underneath, the women looked pretty much the same wrapped in old overcoats covering sack dresses, shawls tied over their heads. All wore those high-buttoned shoes that could kick the shit out of a stray dog or a lazy man.

Although most kept their long hair piled up and pinned like their mothers, a few had it shorn and curled in the new way the Italian girls favored. Their skin shrank and stretched with heat and cold, like the ground beneath them. Up close you could see the crazes on their faces and hands from hours spent outdoors.

Each told her version of the same story about keeping a family fed and clothed on meager wages. They took in laundry and cleaned house for swells.

Cooked mush and beans and, when that ran out, boiled prickly pear pads and cattail roots. Made dandelion and watercress salads. Raised chickens and rabbits. Some trapped game.

Every month they paid down on a past-due account at the pluck-me store. On his first work day, when her man had picked up pack, black powder and fuses, auger, cap, carbide lamp, pick, shovel and lunch bucket, the account opened with debt. And it seldom closed, even if he died.

To stretch the wage, the women mended holes in overalls and dresses. When the cloth around the stitches rotted, they sewed patches over that. If they were scared or sad or bored or angry, they learned to stuff it. Because, above all, they had to bolster a fickle and moody knothead who might go on a bender or run off or get himself trapped in the mine. The working man was the hub of their wheels and they weren't about to wait long for news about his well-being.

By far the loudest and most persistent complainer was Ida Bastrop, shrieking like a goshawk. A gabby, squat-bodied, hard-shell Baptist, Ida tracked like an Indian and quoted scripture better than the company preacher. Though she clutched the good book always, she could spout all day without opening the cover. Her husband William Ernest was my best friend and occasional drinking partner. Called him "Cockeye" because his left eye had been fixed skyward when a chunk of coal fell on his head years ago. The Bastrops had lived next door to us for seven years.

Homing in on Ida, we located Mama. She held both of the Bastrop babies and was trying to calm their mother. Me and Sid did our best to reach her, but Ida headed us off.

"Tanners," she wailed. "Have you heard anything about my William Ernest? Him and Mr. Tostakis must be trapped. Nobody will tell me anything."

"Ain't heard nothin', Mrs. Bastrop," Sid said.

We skirted Ida to give Mama hugs and kisses.

"Are you hurt?" she asked. "How are your eyes?" Tears tracked the dust on her cheeks, but she brushed them dry quick as she could. Mama couldn't abide taking on in public.

The Bastrop tykes tuned up in the squishing they got from our hugs.

". . . Oh, Lord, I foresaw this disaster in scripture," Ida proclaimed, leafing through her tattered, marked-up Bible. "It's God's punishment for the iniquity that surrounds us . . . ."

"We're all right, Mama," Sid said, coughing some. "Little wheezy from the dust and smoke."

Ida's finger found her passage and she read, " 'Now is the end come upon thee, and I will send mine anger upon thee, and will judge according to thy ways, and will recompense upon thee all thine abominations . . .' "

"Ida," Mama interrupted. "You have to calm down, now. You're scaring your children and everybody else's. I need to talk to my boys."

"I'm speaking the words of the Lord, Ethel. 'I will do unto them after their way . . .' "

The Bastrops' oldest kid sat on a timber with his chin in his hands.

"Sloan," Sidney hollered, "come here."

The kid shambled over.

"Take care of your mama, son."

With a withering look, the youngster glanced from Sid to his mama and back.

"Boy . . ."

"Yes, sir." He grabbed Ida's coat and pulled her away, like he'd had practice. Only ten years old and having to manage his loony mama, who kept quoting.

" '. . . and according to their desserts will I judge them; and they shall know that I am the Lord!' Boy, will you quit?" Ida swatted at the kid, but he kept hauling.

Mama still held the babies. "Take Colby, Alan. My arm's giving out. Bounce her around a little. She likes that."

The whiney infant was wrapped up like a loaf of fresh bread against the cold. I uncovered her face and cooed a little mule talk. The soapy baby smell reminded me of our little sisters, Griselle and Mary. I was sixteen when they passed.

I told Mama how we'd escaped and she shook her head at the miracle. Reminded her of Papa and the explosion at Number 6, I figured.

"Did you boys give thanks? You were awfully lucky."

"Yeah, we did," I said.

"Weren't you scared climbing that high?" she asked me.

"He was rock solid," Sid offered. "Couldn't have done it without him."

Sidney got us sandwiches and coffee and we walked away from Ida's caterwauling.

"Why won't she point those verses at swells instead of us?" Sid asked.

"Yeah," I stuck in. "What did we do?"

Mama tried to stare some guilt into me. "I'm sure you've done something, sonny boy. A reformer like Ida can smell it on a person."

"Yeah, well, she's an unaimed shotgun, as far as I'm concerned," Sid said. "You're just tryin' to be nice."

"She wants to know what's going on, like the rest of us. Worried about Mr. Bastrop. The young super from Hastings took a search party into Number

2. They're trying to beat the afterdamp."

More women moved around the landing, carrying kids or dragging them along by hand. The company sawbones, Dr. Shay, shouted instructions at flunkies who were putting up two tents and hauling in cots for a make-shift hospital.

Around four o'clock, the first load of ink slingers motored up to Number 2 in a Model T. Few of us had seen an automobile up close. Gawkers closed around the car and Jack greeted the men who climbed out like they were old friends.

A photographer set up a three-legged camera box. The other news hounds sniffed around, trying to get somebody to talk. If anybody on the landing knew anything about the rescue or what had caused the explosion, they weren't likely to tell a legman.

Mama caught sight of McKintrick heading our way. "Oh, here comes that awful man. Where can I hide?"

You know how a dog will sidle up to the person who hates dogs the most? The mayor trotted straight to Mama.

"Ah, Mrs. Tanner, holding a tot, I see," he said, doffing his hat. "The rescue seems to be progressing. So glad your boys got out." He cleared his throat. "I must say, you look lovely today. That scarf complements your eyes."

Sidney elbowed me. He believed McKintrick was interested in our mother. I just figured the mayor sweet-talked all pretty women.

"You're full of dookie, Mr. McKintrick," Mama said. "I look the same as everybody else. Common and ugly."

"*Au contraire, madam.* You are an orchid among brambles."

Mama fanned him away like a pesky insect, took Colby back and walked off.

"You ain't gonna get on her dance card, thataway, Mayor," Sid said. "Head ain't turned by compliments."

"I assure you I am not attempting to turn your mother's head in any fashion, Sidney. I was put here on this earth to acknowledge and admire beauty and refinement wherever I observe it." After Jack watched Mama disappear, he turned his attention to the photographer who was taking pictures of anybody who'd pose for him.

"I know that young man from my days as a reporter for the *Chronicle-News* in Trinidad. Back when Bat Masterson was sheriff. His name is Louis Dold. I think you two should have a photograph made as the first men to escape. I'm sure your mother would like it."

Having a photograph of us with our clothes near blowed off appealed. People might not believe it if we didn't have a picture.

The mayor introduced me and Sid to the photographer like we were famous. While the man prepared his works, Sid asked him if he wasn't a little nervous about guards busting up his equipment. The photographer shook his head.

"Victor-American and CF&I like to have me around taking pictures sympathetic to their position. Those I sell to company newspapers." Dold winked at Sid. "When the companies aren't looking, though, I tell the coal miners' stories with pictures I keep hid."

Two wagons filled with new timbers arrived and fellers started unloading and stacking them. It had been a long time since I'd seen fresh props in bulk, the creosote shining in sticky splashes all over. When there weren't any used timbers to scavenge, we had to cut birch trunks. I figured V-A wanted to put on its best face for the rescue team.

Dold stood us up against a timber bale. He slipped under a black drape to look in his camera, came out holding a rubber ball attached to a long tube. Told us not to smile, not to do anything but stand there with our arms around each other. Said me and Sid were about to become a part of Colorado's history and I believed him.

* * *

"Darlin' on the line! Stiffs comin' out."

A mule pulled three cars loaded with wounded and dead into the light. Dr. Shay moved down the line, trying to figure out who needed attention the most. After immediate treatment for those right there, he had all but eight carried into a tent. We laid the new bodies on tarps next to the guys who'd died outside 3 and covered them with canvas sheets.

Before Dold could get pictures of the dead, the guards ran him down the hill.

"Some walkin'."

Strings of lunkers drifted out of Number 2 and a hullabaloo of joy and disappointment swept through the hopefuls. The diggers were dusty and beat to hell, but they were alive. Several of the jokers–rescued and rescuers –collapsed as they stepped outside. Some sat in the dirt and bawled; some prayed. Others babbled like lunatics. A few said they were done and hiked down the hill.

Women scurried among the survivors, screaming names, sobbing, in relief, when they found their somebody–or in grief, when they didn't.

Ida sniveled as she walked back where Mama stood, watching the kids. Still no Cockeye. And no Barba.

Some women were giving food and drink to those who'd just walked out when the assistant super from Hastings climbed on a timber bale to talk. Even though he was a stranger, that man had earned instant respect by leading the rescue party into a mine filling with afterdamp. Still dressed in a company man's working clothes: trousers, a tweed overcoat with tie and dusty shoes. The only difference: in place of a derby or fedora he wore a tunnel cap with its lamp burning. His face was coal-smudged and his clothes were scuffed and filthy.

It puzzled me why swells insisted on wearing their best duds, even around mines. They lived in a coal canyon. They knew how nasty it was, just walking around town, but they all dressed the same. Guess they didn't want to be mistaken for coalasses.

Swells didn't have a thing to worry about. Telling the difference between a company man and a digger was a snap: just look at his hands. A swell's got smooth, white hands with nails trimmed like a woman's. No blisters or callouses, crooked or missing fingers. Look at the hands of a slag monkey and see black wedged forever under his fingernails and ground into creases and whorls. Might get him a bath on Saturday, scrub himself red-raw. Still every pore and pockmark is full of black. No way you'd mistake a swell for a coalass.

The super had a strong voice and spoke simply. He said a prayer then dished the news.

"My name is Miles Edgerton. I've been assistant superintendent at the Victor-American mine in Hastings for just over a year. I was asked to come up here to oversee the rescue.

"Day shift workers in mines 1 and 2 didn't hear the explosion–didn't even know anything out of the ordinary had happened until miners from 3 showed up in their tunnels. That's a good sign. We're certain there are more men, alive and waiting for rescue, but we can't get to them right now because of the damp. I want you to know that we went back as far as we dared, then the rescuers got woozy and the mules balked. We found just over fifty men wandering around inside before we had to pull out."

The super got applause for that.

"If your man hasn't come out yet, don't lose faith. We phoned CF&I in Pueblo this afternoon and their new rescue car is on its way. Trained and well-rested professionals with oxygen masks and special tools will take over and go where we can't."

"When will it get here?"

"Early evening. We'll keep sending in crews to search for stragglers, but they can't go as far back even as we did. It's just too dangerous. Right now, I need for everyone who's not directly involved in the rescue to go down the hill. That means *all* the women and children."

Moans and sobbing.

The super raised his hands. "This is for the good of everyone. It's going to be a cold night and you'll want to be at home. We can't do much more until the rescue car arrives. Then it will take time for the professionals to search the tunnels. In the meantime, we have to clear the landing and keep it clear for medical personal and rescuers. The guards will cordon off the area. Please stay down the hill and be patient. We'll send runners to your houses with updates. If you don't hear anything from me, you'll know I have no new information. In the upcoming hours, take care of each other. And pray hard. Pray with all the strength you have, because you know our Lord and Savior will carry us through this travail."

"Amen," Ida called. She and some of the other women were still upset, but they seemed to trust the super's religious zeal and the grit he'd shown in the mine.

After me and Sid gave Mama a kiss and hug, she and the other women and kids trudged down the hill.

Something told me they wouldn't stay put for long.

*   *   *

The train pulling the rescue car arrived in Delagua around seven. It took four wagons four trips from the depot to get men, equipment and pine planks for coffins up to Number 2. McKintrick greeted as many of the new arrivals as he could.

Armed guards strung ropes around the outer edge of the landing. Lanterns were hung from nail and stub. Edgerton gave orders for the news hounds to stay down the hill with the women.

Four doctors joined Shay. The undertakers started in on the bodies.

The wagon load of lumber and tools was parked far over to the side, across the landing from the tent hospital, and the carpenters set to building coffins.

Jack was having himself a regular conversation with one of two derbies who'd just arrived. I figured these dudes were company muck-a-mucks, come down from Pueblo to check on the youngster. When the assistant superintendent shooed the mayor away and latched onto the newcomers, Jack just stood there, gazing around like a lost kid. Finally, he sat on a railroad tie and mopped his face with a handkerchief.

After the rescue bosses powwowed with the new swells and Edgerton, the crew unloaded their gear, donned breathing tanks and masks with head lamps. Along with their tanks they carried picks and shovels–over forty pounds' worth total, I heard. Even had three shot-firers, who put on masks and tanks, too. They started entering Number 2, a few at a time, just after nine o'clock.

With the helmet men gone, the mucks carried their bags around the railway bend to their encampment–a tent that had been set up for them between portals 2 and 3.

Me and Sid walked over to Jack and sat on either side.

"Who're them derbies you was talkin' to?" Sid asked.

"The younger man is a 'deviation overseer.' When a mine goes up, the companies send an official like him to determine what happened."

"What's he gonna find in a plugged mine?" I asked.

"Oh, he'll sniff out problems," Jack said. "Or manufacture them."

"What about the geezer?" I asked.

"*That* is Charles Garvin Edgerton, vice-president of the Victor-American Company."

Sid whistled. "Never heard of a big dog comin' to a disaster-in-progress," he said. "He related to that kid?"

"His father," Jack offered. "And Billy Potts is his brother-in-law."

"Family business, eh?" I asked. "Ain't he afraid of gettin' them clothes dirty?"

The mayor shook his head. "C.G. has dust in his pockets."

Sidney cut his eyes at me.

"You're stringin' a whizzer, Mayor," I said.

"No, I am totally serious, Young Tanner. Garvin Edgerton isn't some rich, panty-waisted company man. He commenced as a digger almost forty years ago. Worked his way up to pit boss and climbed the company ladder the hard way."

"Sounds like you know him," Sid teased. Jack claimed to know everybody.

"I do. Or did, I should say. Garvin was superintendent of mines in Lafayette, where I opened my first imbibery. He pretended not to recognize me, just now, but I reminded him of our indubitable connection."

"And that is?" Sid probed.

"C.G. and I had a dispute over the future Mrs. Edgerton, a young woman I employed as a singer and actress. A dazzling creature, really, crazy for me, as you might expect. But Garvin turned her head."

"You boys duke it out?" Sid asked.

"Let's just say that in the battle between passion and security, security won." The mayor sighed and smiled. "Like so many things in my life, I surrendered her too easily."

"Darlin' on the line. Stiffs comin'."

A mule pulled three cars full of bodies outside and we stood to help unload them. The three of us sadly carried Black Otis. When an old-timer got the chop, lunkers shuddered at the bad luck.

"One of the last ones left who worked with Papa," Sid remarked.

"I am ambushed by despair," Jack said, as we trudged back for another corpse. "The first thing Garvin wanted to know was how many mules were trapped. He didn't even inquire about Potts."

Last body we hoisted was our neighbor, Baldy Cuminetti, who'd been found leaning against the wall of a little grotto, his jackknife by his side. Had cut his throat rather than suffocate. Done a damned good job of it, too, stabbing deep under one ear and slicing across to the other. With eyes and mouth open, his face looked like the white underside of a fish.

Thought I might puke. This wasn't the guy who'd bounced kids on his knees and played practical jokes on everyone, the guy who'd drink his wine outdoors and make as much racket as possible poling Cissy on Sundays, just to stir up Ida Bastrop. This was butchered, stinking meat.

"Too much, ain't it?" Sid said.

"Just about," I replied.

Jack pulled his flask, took a swig and offered us a taste. "This is a sad, sad day for Delagua, gentlemen," the mayor said and we agreed.

CHAPTER THREE
November 9-18, 1910

The stench filled Number 2's haulage and reeked onto the landing. As the rescuers discovered bodies inside, they toted them into the safe zone where mask-less drivers and their mules waited to cart the remains outside. The dead had trickled out all evening. But when the rescue parties punched into the first rooms and grottos around midnight, a caboodle of corpses emerged.

Except for two engineers, a doctor and cook who manned the Pullman, the helmet men were lumpies like us, Americans from the coal mines up north, specially trained in Pueblo. Said our disaster was the worst they'd ever worked. They discovered bodies huddled with their arms wrapped around each other. Found 'em alone, some with their hands folded in prayer. Came on ones who'd scribbled goodbyes on scraps of paper.

Sid organized a crew to tote and cover the dead. We draped faces stretched in terror and faces calm as a sleeping baby. Faces smashed so bad you had trouble telling they were faces. We laid out men whose fingers were bloody stubs from trying to dig out.

Alongside diggers, we sardined nippers, electricians, motor men, track layers and shot-firers. The smell and the grisly sights got to me, at first. But after hauling so many stiffs, I didn't notice.

Among the dead was Willis Evans, one of the rescue engineers. He had given up his helmet to save a joker overcome from the damp, then kept working, unprotected, until he suffocated. His twin brother, Wallace–the other engineer–sobbed as he helped unload his brother.

Sunlight warmed the landing when the remains of Superintendent Potts, his assistant Homer McConnaghue and two pit bosses were carried out. The tunnel had exploded right in their faces and their pancaked, twisted bodies–with a hand sticking out here, a foot poking out there–marked the results. What was left of their heads looked like a rhubarb pie dropped on the kitchen floor. Shreds of the third pit boss, identified by process of elimination and location, had come out in a tow sack.

We shucked our caps and I felt sad. It wasn't that these swells were great guys or anything–like old Edgerton, they cared more about the welfare of the mules than diggers. And we cussed them every day. But they were our bosses, for better or worse, direct links to the company that gave us work. Nothing could happen in a coal camp without them. And they'd died trying to put out the fire.

The undertakers immediately turned to these five. The carpenters abandoned the coffins they were building and started on boxes for the pit bosses. After their embalmings, the two superintendents would be loaded in a wagon and taken to the company office so their wives could view them in private and arrangements could be made for fancy coffins, funerals and burials.

When they heard that the bosses had been brought out, the Edgertons returned to the landing. First time I was close enough to C.G. to notice that he smoked non-stop and coughed constantly. His words, squeezed in among drags, hacks and gasps, discharged in rapid-fire fits and starts.

While the old man lit a cigarette off the one he was finishing, his son grabbed a corner of the sheet. "What are these piles here?" he asked just before getting a picture and a whiff of putrid gore.

"Holy Christ." Young Edgerton choked. He dropped the coverlet and heaved up his breakfast. "Holy fucking Christ."

"That don't sound very religious, does it?" Sid whispered to me.

"Guess he's never seen a dead man," I returned. "Takes some gettin' used to, for sure."

Mack and Tommy came over. "Super-puker, huh?" Mack observed.

Tommy nodded. "That boy's callin' them buffaloes."

The old man seemed irritated by his son's reaction. "Goddamn, Miles. Sit on those timbers, there. Put your head between your knees and take deep breaths," he instructed, never taking his eyes off the corduroy of dead men.

Sheet-white and holding his hand over his mouth, the younger Edgerton sat as he was told. He blew his nose then dry-heaved, like a cat hacking up a hairball.

The old pit boss threw back the canvas to examine the dead up close. Must have stirred some memories inspecting that dusty carrion. He looked over at the young super. "Here's Evans, Miles," he coughed. "Didn't you go to school with him?"

"Yeah. Willis and his twin, both. Drop that damn canvas, please." He heaved again.

My brother approached the old man. "Excuse me, Mr. Edgerton."

The muck worked his way down the line without responding.

"Name's Sid Tanner. I just want to tell you how much we appreciate you comin' all this way to help with the rescue. I heard you were a digger early on. That true?"

The old man pulled the sheet over the bodies and looked at Sid. "What . . . do you want?"

"I figured you'd been through somethin' like this and might have some advice."

"You have a complaint . . . and you're wasting my time getting to it."

"Yeah . . . well, okay. I was hoping you'd let us bring up a few women at a time to check these bodies."

"Have you witnessed truly hysterical women before?"

"Yes, sir, I have," Sid responded. "It's hell when they can't get information about their loved-ones, ain't it? Kinda like rebellion with a side order of panic and grief."

"Victor-American has an identification protocol that avoids confusion. You'll wait for instructions." The muck looked at his son. "Miles?"

Miles raised his head.

"Come on, boy." The boss stepped over, clutched his son's arm and pulled. "Buck up."

Sid caught the old man's sleeve as he passed. "You ain't gonna wait till all them coffins get built, are ya? That'll take days. The women got a right to know, now."

C.G. coughed hard while jerking his arm away. A guard approached, but the swell held up his hand to keep him back. When Edgerton turned, his face burned and his eyes were hoops of anger. "What . . . did I . . . just tell you, nipper?"

"For us to wait for instructions, but . . ."

"But nothing," the old man gasped. "If my son hadn't gotten you people organized, you'd have . . . no . . . bodies to identify . . . or get . . . hysterical . . . about."

C.G. pulled a bandana from his pocket and covered his mouth. His wheeze and red face vouched that the old man was barely checking the hack.

"Be thankful . . . for your bounty and . . . leave . . . us . . . alone," exploded from Edgerton in a fit of coughing, gagging and spitting that continued until the muck pulled a bottle from his inside pocket, uncorked it and took a couple of swigs. When he was breathing easier, the swells disappeared in the direction of their camp.

"Well," Mack said. "Guess he told you."

"Cut your water right off," Tommy threw in.

"When I need you twos' opinions, I'll knock 'em out," Sid said. "Wonder what he was sippin' that stanched that cough?"

"Darlin' on the line!"

We backed up, expecting a regular mule pulling more cars full of bodies. What we witnessed, instead, was a miracle: Grady lumbered out, just like any old work day, with Cockeye, Barba and two Mexicans holding onto his tail. When they stepped into the light, the men shielded their eyes. One of the Mexicans ran up, seized Grady's halter and covered the mule's eyes with his hand. All four diggers and the animal were green as juniper berries from the damp.

In the haze of surprise and gratitude, shouts erupted. The roughest pick jockeys hugged the survivors and our sweet, magical mule.

I grabbed Cockeye, who swiveled his head like a jay-bird having trouble focusing his good eye on me.

"It's Alan, ya goozie," I said, throwing my arm around him. "Thought you was a goner."

"Well, gol-dang, boy. Me, too." He started crying. "We was some lost sheep, I'll tell ya . . ."

"I was never lost, Tanner," Barba broke in. "Wasn't even scared."

"Then why'd you let us wander around like that, dumbass?" Cockeye asked, his voice cracking.

Routine for these two. Bosom buddies one minute, mortal enemies the next. Ordinarily, they'd grab each other, maybe wrestle. Too exhausted for that malarkey today.

"Bastrop . . . I will be cutting off your nuts and killing you, soon," Barba said. "Saving your white ass make me more tired and I got to sit."

Cockeye watched the Greek walk away. "Stupid ouzo. He was just as scared as the rest of us." He wiped his eyes on his sleeve. "Where was I?"

"You was lost sheep," Sid answered.

"Oh, yeah. We *was* lost *and* wore out. Ran out of water, of course. I swear I fell asleep walking. Seemed like we was doubling back on ourselves, over and over, gettin' woozier all the time. So we sat. By and by, here come Grady with the Mexicans attached. Good greasers, them two. Shared the last of their water with us."

The Mexicans were still stroking the mule and whispering in his ears.

"Dang mule understands spic to boot," Cockeye observed. He stepped over to shake each man's hand before they left.

I called the mule's name and went up to him. After some sweet talk and petting, he let me take his halter.

"Hey, boy, look at you." I hugged the old mule's neck and thanked him proper for saving all of us. That's when I noticed how cloudy his eyes were. I passed my hand back and forth in front of his face. Even made a punching motion, trying to startle him. No response. Grady was blind as Homer from the gas.

The mayor reappeared, his mood brightened by these walking survivors. He welcomed the four back to the surface like he'd done with me and Sidney. Jack also decreed that Grady would live in the lap for the rest of his days. Everybody cheered. The mule was a lucky charm and one of the few bright spots in the cruel ordeal.

"Baldy's over there," I told Cockeye and pointed to the tarp. "Cut his own throat."

"Oh, Lord, no." Cockeye let it sink in. Everybody liked Baldy. "Why would he do that, Alan?"

"Quicker than smothering, I guess. Baldy wasn't a patient man. Couldn't stand just laying there in the dark. Might have been too afraid. Sure was messy."

"You seen Ida?"

"Yeah."

"Bet she's carryin' on, ain't she. Quoting scripture."

"She's nervous, like all of them," Sid said. "Swells ain't lettin' nobody come up or go down."

"Well . . . I got to find her."

Me and Sid was following Cockeye down the tracks when we heard singing.

It was hard to believe what I saw—a gang of women walking up, with Mama, Ida, Cissy Cuminetti and Cedi Costa, arm-in-arm, at the front. Reporters marched behind them.

"What the hell do they think they're doing?" Cockeye said. "Ida's too frail to be in on somethin' like this."

Frail as a wolf, I thought.

"Figure *they* can force Victor-American's hand when us men can't, I guess," Sid said. "Seems pretty risky to me."

The women stopped.

"We've come to see Mr. Edgerton," Ida called, hoisting the Bible. "Christ Jesus marches with us. Any God-fearers up there better let us through. The wrath of the Lord is swift and absolute."

Cockeye fidgeted. "Goldang, I got to go to her. She don't know I'm alive." He waved his arms. "Ida? It's me up here. I'm all right, Snowflake."

Ida screamed and I feared she was gonna break loose.

The guard closest to us brought his shotgun up and crossed Cockeye's midsection with the barrel.

"Man . . . that's my wife crying. I got to go to her." And with that,

Cockeye busted through the line and ran down the tracks.

The guard raised his weapon.

"I'd think twice before using that thing," Sid coughed out. "If you kill him, them reporters is gonna see the whole thing, so you'll have to shoot them, too."

I swallowed. "It's gonna take a lot of explaining if you guys open up on these people."

Cockeye clattered down through the rocks with everyone watching, the gaggle of diggers and guards up here, the women below. But never a shot was fired.

The Bastrops hugged and disappeared into the crowd.

"We've come to see the boss man," Mama hollered.

"Ain't here," the guard said.

"You'd better find him, because we're coming up," Mama called and the women started walking again.

"MAMA, HOLD ON," I screamed and looked at Sid.

"You'll have to talk to Edgerton, scooter," he said. "I shot my wad with him."

I turned to the guard. "That's our mother leadin' the way, mister. You already showed you want to do the right thing here and I'm beholden. What if I get Mr. Edgerton to straighten this out?"

The guard said okay. "You let them women know what's goin' on," he said to Sid. "I'll tell the boys to hold fire."

"Mama, Allie's goin' after Mr. Edgerton," Sidney hollered, "but I'm stayin' right here. Be patient for a little while longer."

When I turned around, McKintrick stood behind me.

"I'll come along, if you like, Young Tanner," he said. "I might have influence with Garvin."

"Think I'd like to do this on my own, Jack. I'm obliged for your offer, though."

He nodded. "I understand. But . . . may I give you some advice? Garvin Edgerton is a husk of the man he was once. Silicosis. He longs to be flinty, but he has no strength. Remember the paroxysm of coughing when Sidney confronted him? Go at him again. He won't like it when another working man challenges him. He'll get exercised and the cough will do the work for you. The son will cave in. Just remember: those two sit to crap, the same as you. Look them right in the eyes and have your say."

"Yes, sir," slipped out like a bad habit. I surprised myself.

With the guards occupied, I had no trouble hiking around to the mucks' camp. The two Edgertons and the overseer sat in folding chairs outside a tent. The old man had the bandana folded on one knee and was smoking.

When he saw me coming, the overseer hurried away, like I'd caught him doing something fishy. Guess he didn't want me thinking he had time or inclination to chat with the people he was supposed to be investigating.

"Stop right there," Garvin wheezed. "What the hell . . . do you think you're doing?"

I didn't know which Edgerton to speak to, so I aimed at both. "Women are marchin' up the hill. They're worried because they can't get no information about who's alive."

"They'll have to wait until coffins are ready and they can identify their men in an orderly fashion," Miles said. He still didn't sound too steady. "That's Victor-American's policy."

Garvin kept hacking, regular as a ticking clock.

I stepped closer. "How important is that really, Mr. Edgerton, when your guards are thinkin' about shooting women? Reporters are everywhere and they're gonna see whatever happens." With time a-wasting, I could feel my fuse burning shorter.

Old Edgerton called for Potts' little suck-ass clerk, Abercrombie, who seemed to appear out of nowhere. "Go get one of the guards, Carl."

"Hold on, Abercrombie," I said. "Mr. Edgerton, a guard sent me to get *you*, sir. He wants to know what to do about the women." I was dead tired and out of patience. I hadn't crawled out of that air shaft to let two Vics in slick soles stifle me. "Just because the company don't want reporters gettin' stories and pictures don't mean it ain't gonna happen."

Garvin clutched the bandana. "That's enough. Carl-get-a-guard." He coughed hard into the rag.

Abercrombie scurried off like the rodent he was.

Miles turned to his papa. "I'm not giving orders to fire on women, Daddy. Coming to Delagua as a favor to you didn't include that. This kid might as well talk."

"That's . . . where we've gone . . . wrong for years, letting trash like this talk. I didn't come . . . to argue with . . . *miners*, Miles." Garvin hocked up a wad of black crud and spit it out. The old man took another pull on his medicine, drew the deepest breath he could, lit a cigarette. "You're a . . . goddamn bleeding heart, boy . . . like Billy was. Whole . . . situation could have been avoided . . . if he'd handled it right . . . from the start. I hate . . . goddamn appeasement."

"Mr. Edgerton, there's no time for all this," I said. "The women have come up as far as the guards will let them . . . ."

"You want a job tomorrow?" the old man asked me. I could tell he was dying to beat me senseless, but his body wouldn't let him. Instead of attacking, the old man kind of shrunk back into himself, like a flour sack being emptied. Jack had predicted this. Edgerton's face got more wrinkled. His eyes watered. His lips quivered as he hissed, "Then . . . get . . . away."

He coughed again and the little bottle fell to the ground. I bent to retrieve it, noting the label: *B.J. Meyer's Liquid Heroin.*

"Give me that," the muck snapped. He slid the bottle into his coat pocket.

Face and neck on fire, couple of deep breaths, again not sure which swell to address. "The women got a right to know who's dead and who ain't. Your men are gettin' nervous with their shotguns."

Abercrombie returned with a guard who started yakking as soon as he was in ear-shot.

"Excuse me, boss, but before you deal with this guy we got to decide about them women. They've topped the hill."

The old man gathered what little steam he had left. "Tell . . . damn women to disperse. They refuse, do what . . . you were hired to do."

"Okay, but . . ."

"But, what?" Garvin panted.

"We didn't sign up to shoot no women, Mr. Edgerton. I'll pop this kid off for you right now, just to show my appreciation. But the boys'll walk if you order them to shoot women."

The boss's sinking spell seemed to rally Miles. He stood and stepped over to his father, laid his hand on the old man's shoulder and pressed his fingers and thumb deep into the suit coat. Hacking into the bandana, Garvin looked up at his son, attempted to fidget out of the grip. The younger man held on, eyes bulging. "Buck up, Daddy," he said and capped the treatment with a good, long pinch.

Miles turned back to us. "What's your name?" he asked the guard, who, like me, looked dumb-struck by what he'd just seen.

"Uh, Dub, sir. Dub Hollister."

Miles watched C.G. light a cigarette. Just before the old man took his first drag, the young super bent, flicked the weed out of his papa's fingers. Sonny-boy's mouth squirmed into a thin smile. "How many women do you estimate?" he asked the guard.

"Around fifty," he answered.

"Okay, Dub. Let them come up a few at a time. Are you serious about nailing this kid?"

"Well . . . yeah." The guard grinned. "Sure."

"Good," the super said. "If any of those bitches give you trouble, shoot him."

*　　　　　*　　　　　*

Victor-American had to bring more funeral people up from Trinidad for the burials. Flunkies split a dollar a grave, digging in the softer earth west of town, wagoning the full coffins out to their resting spots.

Each family and their pall bearers got five minutes with a loved-one before the lid was nailed down. For two days, burials commenced at noon and lasted until midnight.

Six of us carried Baldy. We set his coffin beside a hole and waited with Cissy and her kids for our turn to view the body.

"Emilio Cominelli," the little suck-ass clerk, Abercrombie, called out. The gravediggers removed the lid.

Baldy looked like a one-eyed taxidermist had got hold of him, even rouged and powdered, with a white shirt and tie pulled up high. I could still see dried blood in the jagged, whip-stitched crack in his throat.

Cissy sucked in her breath when she saw her husband. But she made her kids get a good look anyway. "Is Emilio," she whispered.

The company preacher used the same words for each body: "The Lord giveth and the Lord taketh away. Next."

Cissy laid a rosary and a tintype of the family on Baldy's chest.

The preacher asked Abercrombie the name of the dead man and the clerk checked his manifest.

"Cominelli. Emilio Cominelli."

"Our name is Cuminetti," Cissy corrected.

Abercrombie cut his eyes toward me, like I was going to sympathize.

"Say it right, suckass," I said.

The clerk smirked. "Cuminetti." Then he called out, "Constantine Dellades."

As we walked away, the carpenters nailed down the coffin lid.

CHAPTER FOUR
December 5-12, 1910

The explosion in Number 3 was worse than the blasts at Primero and Starkville and an inquest was arranged at the courthouse in Trinidad. An independent state official would be coming from Denver to conduct the hearing and a panel would lay blame. The company encouraged us to attend the show. Guess Victor-American figured that inviting coalasses was a way to demonstrate its good intentions and prove it had nothing to hide.

Sid, me, Mama, Cockeye, Cissy Cuminetti, the Costas, the Giottos, Mack and Tommy planned to go hear the testimony. McKintrick was providing two Chamber of Commerce wagons and coming along for the ride.

Corralling the freight hauling business was Jack McKintrick's most dazzling feat. As Delagua and Hastings grew and the sin trade boomed, demand for all kinds of goods increased. Jack had discovered that, while the mucks supported The Chamber's venture, they didn't want entertainment staples carted around in company wagons for all to see. And the Chamber had no interest in moving its valuable cargo in the broke-down vehicles V-A owned.

After McKintrick convinced the higher-ups that he and his partners could transport light freight cheaper and better than the company while keeping the merriment stores hidden, The Chamber bought ten new Gestring wagons and twenty mules, hired ten Mexican skinners, built barns, opened yards in Delagua and Hastings and arranged for one-way drop-offs with a livery in Ludlow.

"I wish that awful man wasn't going," Mama offered. "He annoys me."

"He's got wagons and free passage to and from Ludlow," Sid said. "You want to stay home because you don't like somebody?"

"*Somebody* is a gambler, an alcoholic, a whore monger and a loud-mouthed show-off," Mama said. "I don't like you and Alan hanging around him. And I certainly don't like being around him myself. He nauseates me."

"Yeah, but he's got a great vocabulary," Sid said.

Me and him thought that was the funniest thing we'd ever heard and about fell over. Mama didn't crack.

"Aren't I fortunate to live with such gifted comedians? Listen: loquacity does not denote erudition, any more than wind builds windmills." Mama snapped her pocket book shut. "I'll ride in the wagon with the Costas and Giottos while you regale your comrades with that dazzling wit."

"We got a dictionary in this house?" I asked.

"One in the back by my bed. Under the Emily," Mama said. "Why?"

"Tired of people using words I don't understand."

When I went to get Cockeye at 4:30, Ida followed him onto the porch. "Mr. Tanner, I say 'Fie' to this pilgrimage with Satan McKintrick to the Sodom and Gomorrah of Southern Colorado."

I didn't know what to say. The women sure were down on the mayor.

"Fie!" Ida called again, stomping inside and slamming the door.

"Bye-bye, Snowflake," Cockeye called. "Let's go before she gets the Bible. Been listening to the book of *Job* since 4 o'clock."

Our plan was to take The Chamber's wagons to Ludlow then catch the "Red Eye" into Trinidad, so we'd have time to look around town before the hearing started.

We walked to the wagon yard, toting a load of blankets to cover up with. The Thanksgiving snow had mostly melted, but it was still cold at that hour of the morning.

Mama wasn't happy to find the Costa wagon already filled. She'd have to ride with McKintrick after all.

Jack stepped out of the livery shed, decked out in plaid top coat, bow tie and derby for the city. "Good day, fellow travelers. What a beautiful morning. Brisk and clear. Look to the east." He pointed. "The stars are aligned on our behalf."

A line of stars climbed the inky sky.

Jack pointed. "The brightest is Jupiter. Next Venus. Above her is the cluster often mistaken for the Little Dipper, the Pleiades. Now look down to the right. Those three stars form Orion's belt buckle. My fellow travelers, this celestial rarity bodes well for a fantastic journey."

Jack sashayed over to Mama, while me, Sid, Tommy, Cockeye and Mack snuck into the wagon bed and covered up. "Mrs. Tanner. You're looking exceedingly comely this morning."

"Mr. McKintrick, it's pitch dark and you can't see doodlum-squat."

"I beg to differ. Beauty radiates both light and heat. May I call you Ethel?"

"Mayor," Sid hollered. "Let's get a move on. It's freezin'."

Jack and Mama turned to the full bed.

McKintrick grinned like a monkey. "Well . . . it appears that we're loaded. Guess you'll be riding up front with me, Mrs. Tanner. May I assist you?"

"I can get up there by myself, thank you." And she did. "Hand me one of those blankets, scallywag."

I passed some cover to her.

"Will the Greeks be joining us?" Jack asked, climbing up.

"Ouzos walked to Ludlow last night," Cockeye said. "Might have traipsed all the way to Trinidad, for all I know. They're too good to come with us."

"Very well. We're off." Jack got the team up and we wheeled away.

"Mrs. Tanner, I hear you are a devotee of the Belle of Amherst . . . Miss Dickinson," Jack said. "Is that true?"

"True."

"I find her fascinating. Did you know the words 'Called Back' are etched on her tombstone? I have visited her gravesite and toured her home."

"Please avoid that ditch, Mr. McKintrick."

"Ah, yes." Jack corrected the mules. "Would you like a recitation?"

"Mayor," Sid hollered. "Could you just kill us all now and get it over with?"

"Naw," Mack piped up. "Let's hear the poem first."

"Then you can kill us," Tommy added.

"Perhaps Mrs. Tanner should decide," Jack suggested.

"Press on," Mama said. "It'll pass the time."

"Very well." The mayor cleared his throat and recited.

"I don't know that verse," Mama said, when he'd finished.

"It is entitled, ' "Hope" is the thing with feathers.' What edition of her poetry do you own?"

Mama sighed. "*Poems of Emily Dickinson* is all I know. My sister gave it to me when I left home."

"I would surmise that it's the 1890 edition, so well received that another came out in 1891 and a third in 1896. I shall loan you my copy of the '96. Should we have another recitation? How about . . ."

" 'I'll tell you how the Sun rose–' " Mama interrupted, " 'A Ribbon at a time–The Steeples swam in Amethyst–The news, like Squirrels, ran . . .' "

When she finished, we clapped.

"That is one of the four poems she sent to Higginson in 1862," Jack commented. "Astounding. Could you render another? Your voice is so melodious."

It continued like that for the hour it took to get to Ludlow, with Jack and Mama trading lines. Though I didn't understand much of what they had to say, it did pass the time. And it was melodious.

* * *

From the depot in Trinidad, we crossed the bridge over the Purgatoire River and hiked into downtown. On Main Street, red-brick buildings, some with canvas awnings, rose on both sides of the street. Trolleys rumbled by. Here was the McCormick Building, there the Columbian Hotel, farther down the Hotel Toltec, First State Bank and Masonic Lodge. Signs advertised: **Pool and Cigars . . . Hardware and Tack . . . Uncalled for Suits at Half-Price . . . Chinese Laundry and Seamstress . . . Las Animas Mercantile and Notions.** One store had three gold balls dangling over its door. Another sported a hand with an eye in its palm.

We mingled with bankers, shopkeepers, snooty ladies in bustle dresses and big hats, Mexican farmers, wops, chinks, two niggers and a gaggle of flatfeet in uniforms and bell caps.

The shops pulled at the women, so we decided to split up and meet them at the courthouse at 10:30. That gave us an hour to kill. Jack steered our brood straight to Church Street.

I never saw so many whorehouses and bars in one place, all open for business at 9:30 in the morning. Jack said the sporting women in Trinidad worked a day and a night shift, like we did at the mine, and the bars stayed open around the clock.

When we came to a joint called Maybes, a bunch of girls on the porch screamed, "Uncle Jack."

"I'll be joining you gentlemen at the courthouse," he said. "I must visit my nieces." The mayor disappeared inside with the whores surrounding him.

"Won't see him till dark, I bet," Sid said. "If then."

We walked on. You'd think the cold weather would've made those floozies cover up, but there they were, about to fall out of their nightdresses and underwear, calling us over to have a taste.

I, personally, had not yet poled a whore. But I knew Sidney visited Elma Von Raven's in Delagua and my time was drawing nigh. If Mama hadn't been roaming around, I'd have been tempted to dip the stick that morning.

I guess I'd lagged behind, gawking, because I lost sight of Sid and the boys. Figured they'd gone in a bar and I missed them. Worries over separation dissolved when I noticed four whores about my age sitting on a bench at the edge of the boardwalk, swinging their feet like little girls. They were wrapped in blankets. Thought the older whores must be more cold-natured than the young ones. Then they threw off their wraps.

These half-naked chirpies looked at each other and giggled. Guess I had cherry sucker written all over.

"You want flicky-flicky, cowboy?" a cute little Jap with a pigtail and skinny legs asked. "Cowboy got a big ying-yang."

They all giggled again.

"How about a juicy slice of raw tenderloin?" a blond, with the tops of her titties sticking out, cooed.

"Oooh, tenderloin," they sang.

I felt my face and neck heat up.

"Go around the world for a dollar."

Man, they were pressuring me. I felt a woody rising and reached in my pocket to make an adjustment.

"No reason to play pocket pool, little man." The blond stood, stepped into the street and laid a hand on my tummy. Her arms and shoulders had goose bumps. She licked her lips. "Take care of that thing 'round the corner for fifty cents."

I was about to cave in when somebody grabbed my coat collar. "Come on, ying-yang," Sid said.

The blond had slid her fingers behind my belt buckle and held on so it snapped back as my brother dragged me off.

"Goddamn. I guess you'll be feeding me my baby bottle next, huh?" I said, pulling away.

Sid sniggered and coughed. "Might do it."

I followed him into Masterson's Saloon, where our remaining members had settled. The place kinda reminded me of McKintrick's. Bar along one wall and tables scattered around. Picture windows across the front. Piano, of course. Pool table. Somebody was cooking in the back and a few jittery locals were rushing through their steak and eggs. Figured they were uncomfortable surrounded by coalasses. The Greeks already had a card game going. Barba told me once that they were born shuffling a deck.

I got me a beer and paid. "You Masterson?" I asked the barkeep, as Cockeye walked up.

"I'm Munson. *That's* Bat Masterson," the barkeep said, pointing.

Over the doorway hung a big picture of a cop in a black bell cap with chin strap. Cockeye got excited and bounced over to have a closer look.

Guess Munson thought I'd know who this Masterson was. Seemed like Jack had mentioned knowing him, but I couldn't remember anything pertinent.

"U.S. Marshal of Dodge City, Kansas? Wyatt Earp's buddy? Pretty famous," Munson stressed.

Still nothing from me.

"Sheriff of Las Animas County for a year before his brother took over," Munson said. "Owned several sporting houses and bars in Trinidad. This one among them."

"Never heard of him," I said.

Cockeye had taken out a scrap of paper and the pencil stub he always carried in his shirt pocket and was copying down a saying written under the picture. When he finished, he walked back to the bar.

"What's it say?" I asked.

Cockeye took the paper out and read: " 'Every dog, we are told, has his day–unless there are more dogs than days.' W.B. Masterson."

I looked back at the picture and smiled. "I like that."

The locals skedaddled and we had the place to ourselves. When talk turned from the abundance of whores and saloons in Trinidad to what caused the explosions and what good a hearing would do, Cockeye joined the debate.

I ordered another beer. "Let me ask you somethin', Mr. Munson. I heard them whores work a day shift and a night shift. That true?"

"Depends. They're out this morning because there's so many miners in town for the hearing."

"You sayin' we're easy marks?"

Munson shook his head. "Not at all . . . not at all. You boys just don't get to the city much, is what I'm saying. When you do come, you're more . . . eager than the local yokel, who has this finery at his disposal all the time. The number of miners who came to the hearing after the Primero disaster took the entertainment district by surprise and a lot of places were closed. We swore it wouldn't happen again. Tourist trade is our life-blood." The barkeep grinned and wiped the counter. "Where you from?"

"Delagua . . ."

"Yeah, where the mine went up. I bet you know Jackson McKintrick."

"Sure do. He come with us. Visiting his nieces presently." I winked.

"No shit? Wish he'd drop by. Always has too much to do when he's in town. You know he was one of Kentry Milbank's deputies, don't you?" Milbank was the high-sheriff of Las Animas County, bound to be present at the inquiry.

"Heard he'd been a deputy," I replied. "Didn't hear where."

"Right here, in 1901." From under the bar, Munson pulled a worn-out book called *The Hunt for Black Jack Ketchum* by McKintrick Jackson.

I took the copy. The cover showed a drawing of two men having a close-up gun battle on horseback.

"Guess McKintrick Jackson is Jackson McKintrick, huh?" I asked.

"Yes. That's Jack's version of catching Tom Ketchum. He ever tell you that story?"

I leafed through the book. "Heard about it, but we all thought it was guff."

"It's bully," Munson said. "Black Jack's gang had stopped the train south of Walsenburg, intending to rob it, when a fireman shot Ketchum in the arm. In the confusion, the train pulled away and Ketchum's henchmen abandoned their boss. Train came into Trinidad and got word to Milbank who took a posse out to investigate. McKintrick was with him. They only had to beat the bushes a little to find Ketchum, because he was wounded pretty bad. They took him to the hospital here in town, where a doctor amputated his arm."

I looked up from the pages. "That all in here?"

"Yeah. But it's slanted, with lots more gunplay and courageous daring-do by the hero. That picture on the cover never happened. Jack drew that."

I laid the book on the bar. "So what happened after they cut off Black Jack's arm? They hung him?"

"Well, not immediately. When Ketchum got well enough to travel by train, Milbank sent Jack and three other guys to escort him to Clayton, New Mexico for trial. He was found guilty and hung there. The weirdest thing happened when the bandit dropped through the trap door in the scaffold. Ketchum was fat, the rope had too much slack and his head popped off like a chicken's. After they mopped up the blood, the sheriff in Clayton said for somebody in the Trinidad crew to get up there and sew the thing back on. And Jack done it." Munson picked up the book and pulled out a picture post card that I'd missed, stuck in the back. "That's Ketchum's body," Munson pointed, "and right there's his head." Munson inched his finger to a mustachioed feller kneeling beside the body. "Who you think that is?"

I looked at Munson. "That's Jack, ain't it?"

"That's him, the feller who sewed Black Jack Ketchum's head back on. Can you believe they sold picture post cards of that?" Munson snickered, sliding the card back inside the book. "Listen, tell McKintrick Dick Munson said hello, will ya? Threw away the mold when they made that guy."

"I couldn't agree with you more," I said.

The more the knotheads drank, the louder and more prickly the opinions got. Sidney played peacemaker and kept things pretty civil until Cockeye and Barba got into it. Cockeye said static sparks from hair-combing could make coal dust explode. Barba called him an idiot. Cockeye called Barba "ouzo." Barba shoved Cockeye. Cockeye shoved back. They grabbed coat fronts, danced around, turned chairs over, threatened to kill each other the way they did at home.

Munson came around from behind the bar with a stick, just like our barkeep did when patrons got rowdy.

I didn't come all the way to Trinidad to hear these two bone-pickers argue, so while Sid was preoccupied with the skirmish, I slipped out. Figured I'd find Mama and go to the courthouse a little early.

The whores threw off their blankets and hawked their wares again as I walked by. I grinned and tipped my cap, but kept moving. Even if I was just another wad of dough to the girls on Church Street, it felt pretty nice having them take an interest in me.

Turning back onto Main was like stepping out of the circus tent, mid-show. Suddenly, I didn't feel so chipper. This was sure-enough derby and suit territory and, walking along all by myself, I stuck out like a cockroach in a swanky cafe. Seemed like everybody was staring at my faded, rolled-cuff trousers, cracked boots, filthy cap and threadbare overcoat. Even felt like I must be moving against the foot-traffic on the boardwalk, so I stepped into the dirt.

Guess I figured the courthouse would just appear if I walked around long enough. But I didn't see any promising signs. I looked up and down the street, feeling even more stupid and out-of-place.

That's when a cop appeared. Thought he was going to roust me for loitering. Instead, he asked if I needed directions to the courthouse. Said I did and he pointed to a cross-street opening into Main. "That's First right there. Down five blocks, corner of First and Maple."

I thanked him and stepped off again. Was about to turn the corner when I saw Mama across the street, staring at a dark green dress and matching hat on a dummy in the widow of a dressmaker's shop. When she went inside, a little bell sounded.

I was crossing to the shop when the door tinkled opened again and Mama stumbled onto the boardwalk. The door slammed behind her and the latch fell.

Mama was in a snit.

"What's wrong?" I asked.

"A rude clerk is what. I expected with a bath and powder and my nicest coat, I could go into that shop and look around. Open my mouth and out comes the soot, I guess. That shrimp said, 'Now, where on earth would a girl like you wear a dress like that?' 'Girl,' my hind end. God, I wanted to slap his face."

"You look fine to me in the dress you're wearing, Mama."

"Oh, hush, Alan. That's not the point. I didn't go in there to buy that dress. I went in to browse. Not every woman who goes in a store buys something. Said I just wanted to look around and he had to make a crack. Couldn't let me look. Fixed up, I could be as pretty as any dame prancing around these streets."

"Mama, you look just fine. Prettiest woman in town." I almost threw in, "Jack sure thinks so," but saved myself at the last second. I gave her a kiss and a hug, which seemed to calm her down a bit. "Someday we'll come back and buy any outfit you see. And if a rude clerk horns in, I'll flatten him. Or, I could bust in and kick his patootie right now, if you like."

Mama laughed. "Where's your brother?"

"Talking business. He'll meet us."

She took my arm and we strolled to the corner of First and Maple.

* * *

Even if Victor-American ordered it, Kentry Milbank didn't like the idea of letting working men and women into the courthouse and he filled the place with flatfeet. The sheriff hollered specific instructions about keeping our mouths shut, about not moving around–not even leaning forward–or we would be thrown out.

"You see McKintrick anywhere?" I mumbled to Sid.

He raised his eyes to the balcony. High in the back, up by the windows, sat Jack. The way his derby tilted forward it looked like he was asleep.

"Guess his nieces wore him out," Sid whispered, as a few more onlookers took seats.

I smiled and nodded. "You know the mayor was one of Milbank's deputies, don't you? That could save us some trouble."

A detailed map of Number 1-2-3 hung on a tripod at the front of the room. It was interesting to see the mountain top peeled off so you could find every artery and vein of the tunnel system. I tried to pinpoint where me and Sidney had been digging and the airway shaft where Grady had taken us, but I sat too far away to be sure.

Six men in suits sat at a long table off to one side. One of them, a tall, skinny dude with a beaked nose and bug-eyes, rose to address the congregation.

"My name is Cecil Clark, Deputy Assistant Commissioner of Coal Mines for the state of Colorado. On the morning of November 8, 1910, one of the worst mining disasters in Colorado history occurred. Mine Number 3, owned by the Victor-American Company, exploded, destroying more than 2610 square feet or about four-and-a-half tons of coal. Damage to company property has been assessed at just over $100,000. Eighty-two miners and twenty mules perished. Among the dead are Superintendent William Potts and his assistant Homer McConnaghue.

"Upon learning of the tragedy, Governor John Shaforth ordered our office to appoint a panel to determine the cause of the fire and subsequent explosion, to assess culpability and, most importantly, to make recommendations that will ensure safety and security in Colorado's mines. That panel, seated here before you, consists of five representatives from our state's most prestigious colleges. These men were chosen for their knowledge of coal mining, their inquiring minds and their impartiality. We are glad that so many employees and their families could join us this morning. More than likely, you will not agree with all that you hear today. That is expected. What we are all interested in is a fair and respectful hearing. The rules of conduct that Sheriff Milbank enumerated will guarantee orderliness. I encourage you to heed his directives."

The deviation overseer who'd come up with old man Edgerton was questioned first. For starters, Clark asked him his name and title.

"Silas Griggs, Chief Deviation Inspector, Colorado Mining Association."

"How long have you been inspecting mines and investigating accidents?"

"Twenty-three years."

"Have you inspected the mines in Delagua before?"

"I have."

"When did you last inspect?"

"Six months ago."

"Did you file the customary report for that inspection?"

"Yes."

Clark handed the inspector a folder. "Is that your report?"

"It is."

"What is the date?"

"April 7, 1910."

"Is that your signature?"

"It is."

"Upon what did you base your conclusions in the report?"

"Visual and tactile inspection of the mines, plus the records kept by Superintendent William Potts, Assistant Superintendent McConnaghue and their pit bosses. I supplemented and confirmed my findings during our recent investigation conducted on November 9, the day after the explosions."

"That document is twenty-six pages in length. The panel and I have read the report. To save time this morning, would you read from your summary?" Clark pointed. "Please start here."

" 'The Victor-American Company owns six of eleven coal mines in Delagua, Colorado. In spite of extenuating circumstances cited above, these mines function safely and efficiently. Dust and debris are removed and tunnels sprinkled in a timely fashion. . . .' "

Somewhere in the crowd a knothead moaned.

" '. . . Miners have been thoroughly schooled on methane gas detection methods and check for its presence daily. Most of the outdated steam-driven ventilation fans were replaced this year with twenty-two electric fans at a cost of $165 per fan. The new fans are more powerful than their predecessors, so they disperse dust and any gas that might seep in more effectively. They can also be reversed to pull out gas or dust particles in an emergency.' "

Thank God Victor-American overlooked the broken fan in our shaft, I thought.

"Were the fans reversed during the rescue at Number 3?"

"They were. And where the air flowed freely, they saved lives."

Two groans. Cops surveyed the horde, tapping nightsticks on their palms. While they were looking the other way, chatter seeped.

"We'll have order in this room," Milbank hollered, "or I'll have it cleared."

Clark waited for the gallery to quieten, before he continued. "Mr. Griggs, you preface your conclusion with the phrase, 'In spite of extenuating circumstances cited above.' Rather than going back and reading from the report, would you just discuss those circumstances for us?"

"Certainly. First and foremost are the forces of nature in Southern Colorado. Geology and weather create unassailable risk in mines. The rock surrounding coal seams shifts, constantly. What seems solid one day might crumble the next. Even carefully shored ceilings or walls give way for no apparent reason. Low humidity at higher altitude is another challenge. Coal mines in Appalachia have their problems, but low humidity isn't one of them. The risk of a fire like the one in V-A 3 would be increased in dry weather."

"Is that why the mines are sprinkled?"

"That and to keep the dust down. As I've testified, Victor-American's mines in Delagua are sprinkled frequently and the dust is removed as necessary."

Me and Sid traded looks. The investigator was either lying, had been tricked or bribed. We never hauled out dust or sprinkled unless we got word that an inspector was coming. More "dead work" we didn't get paid to do.

That's when the coughing commenced. The hack was contagious and I knew Sid must be struggling.

"Did you find evidence of sprinkling and dust removal on November 8?" Clark asked.

"Water stood in the haulage and tunnels."

"It rained the night before, Mr. Sir," a lunkhead yelled. "Water always seeps in."

One of the laws caught the surprised upstart by the sleeve, pulled him up, cracked him on the shoulder and pushed him out. Chairs slid back and women yelped. Mama tried to stand, but Sid pulled her back. Her face was red and sweaty.

"We're about to vacate this room," the sheriff called.

The flock settled some, but the coughing persisted. Sounded like a silicosis convention.

Mama squirmed. "This isn't right," she whispered.

Clark looked flustered, but he continued. "Are there other circumstances, Mr. Griggs?"

"Yes. Since the disasters at Primero and Starkville, the southern field has been short-handed. Like most superintendents, William Potts had to rely on foreign-born workers with little or no mining experience."

More coughs and scattered grumbles. A smattering of sighs.

"Few speak English. They either don't know or understand rules–or choose to ignore them. Especially regulations concerning smoking in the mines." Griggs pulled something from his coat pocket and handed it to Clark.

The Deputy Assistant held up a tobacco pipe and some in the herd snickered. Two more were driven out.

Griggs pressed on. "I found that pipe in the main haulage in V-A 3. Something has to ignite dust or methane gas. It doesn't just spontaneously combust. Smoking could have caused the fire and subsequent explosions."

More grumbling and hacking.

"Anything else?"

"No matter how many laws are passed as safeguards, coal mining remains dangerous. A miner must be cautious, observant. He needs years of experience. Unfortunately, haphazard, careless work habits seem to be the rule rather than the exception in these mines right now."

"Could you give some specific examples of carelessness?"

"Insufficient shoring is one. Timbers placed incorrectly or in the wrong spot, another. Explosives set improperly . . . mules mishandled and frightened . . . runaway coal cars . . . habitual drunkenness. The list goes on and on."

"Pit boss come in drunk every morning," Ricky Morales bawled. "We have to prop him up." He and Lupe stood near the door and, when the sticks went after them, they beat a hasty getaway.

When that commotion died, Clark addressed the audience. "We encouraged miners and their families to attend this hearing so you could hear for yourselves how the state of Colorado is working on your behalf. Perhaps we've made a mistake."

Loud fart noise followed by titters. Sidney let the hubbub cover coughs he poured into the crook of his arm.

Clark turned back to his notes. "Mr. Griggs, findings from Primero and Starkville pointed to excessive dust as the culprit."

When the inspector cleared his throat, it set off a mess of throat-clearing.

The flatfeet scanned the room like hawks browsing a prairie.

"You can't mine coal without generating dust," Griggs said. "Miners are responsible for brushing back–for removing the dust and loose rock. The companies shouldn't have to nursemaid these men."

Widespread groaning, snorting, throat-clearing and wheezing. One unidentified *hoo-ha* from the balcony.

Clark's face was pale. "Mr. Griggs, in your opinion, what was the cause of the fire and explosions?"

"Aside from the ungovernables, I'd say carelessness, ignorance, a shortage of skilled miners . . ."

Groans belched and the sticks beat and dragged out three more. A woman screamed when blood speckled her frock and she was removed.

"Go ahead, Mr. Griggs" Clark urged. You were about to state another cause."

"A source of ignition, of course," the investigator said. "For the fire."

"Are you including dust and gas as 'ungovernables'?"

"Inspectors customarily consider dust, gas, friable rock and climatic conditions as ungovernables. The explosions in V-A 3 can't be attributed to dust. Some gas possibly in the second blast. Very little gas in Delagua's mines, though. Fairly stable rock. In my opinion, whoever or whatever ignited the doorway in the crosscut caused the explosions. That's why I stressed carelessness and ignorance."

Groans and mumbling. Loud fart noises from the east side and the balcony.

Griggs was rattled. "I was assured these proceedings would be serious, Mr. Clark."

"They are, sir," Clark said. "Can your officers handle these distractions, Sheriff?"

"We goddamn sure can," Milbank called, grabbing an innocent who was sound asleep and shoving him toward a deputy. "Take care of this rat," he commanded.

The investigator forged ahead. "When the doorway caught fire, smoke accumulated and oxygenated. Ordinarily the safety fans pull or push air two miles through the mine. The burning door created a short-circuit in that flow, a sudden draft that provided more than enough air for smoke and gas to explode."

"Thank you, Mr. Griggs," Clark said. "You may step down."

The only surviving pit boss from Number 3, Moss Browder–the one who'd got dug out–spoke next. After the same kind of opening questions that he'd asked Griggs, Clark served the red meat.

"Have you found smoking materials in mine Number 3?" Clark asked.

"Yessir. I've found pipes, cigarette papers and tobacco hid in socks. It's got to where me and the other bosses have to frisk them guys before they go on shift. They're too ignorant and hard-headed to follow rules."

Barba jumped up and pointed. "Is you who is ignorant, sombitch."

Two sticks hacked through the audience to get to the Greek.

"You ungrateful bastard," Barba hollered. "We save your ass and you spit on us."

One of the laws bulldogged Barba as the other clubbed the Greek. Two of Barba's cronies mounted the cops' backs and two more sticks beat them. It was a rodeo, with the Greeks riding the laws bareback. More sticks joined in, knocking the violators unconscious, then dragging them out. When the pistols and sawed-off shotguns came out, the commotion ceased.

Browder looked at the panel. "See what we have to put up with? Foreigners break every law in the books. It's because of them that my good friends are dead." The pit boss teared up and his voice broke. "We just couldn't be in enough places."

The deputies let a few moans get by. The coughing had stopped, but Sid was barely holding back.

Last to come up was Miles Edgerton. He looked spent, with dark circles under his eyes and stooped shoulders. I figured the cough had laid his daddy low, because the young super appeared to be on his own.

"Superintendent Edgerton, you've heard Mr. Griggs' evaluation and conclusions," Clark said. "You've asked to make a statement. Is that correct?"

"Yes."

"Go right ahead."

"First of all, let me say how deeply saddened I am about the deaths at the mine. One of those deceased was my uncle, William Potts. He believed in a simple principle: if you treat your employees right and give them the freedom to work, they will be happy. I adhere to that principle also."

Sid coughed.

"My uncle, God rest his soul, was in charge when the last inspection and evaluation took place, so I can't speak to those findings. But I organized the rescue at Number 3 and . . . I understand these camps. We at Victor-American and those at Colorado Fuel and Iron, I might add, have always tried to find the safest and most efficient ways to conduct mining operations in Colorado. I grant that extenuating circumstances exist. Yes, there is low humidity. Yes, some miners are incautious, even reckless. Some smoke on the job, that is true. We've tried every way we know to stop this practice. But, as Mr. Browder has pointed out, we can't be everywhere.

"Ask any of the men sitting out here and they will tell you they like digging in Southern Colorado because they are independent contractors whose wages depend on their initiative. When these men come to work for us, they assume a certain amount of risk and agree to extraneous work for the privilege of bringing out as much coal as they want."

Edgerton cut his eyes from Clark to the panel and back.

"The fact is, gentlemen, Victor-American and its employees and independent contractors did the best they could on November 8th and those terrible days that followed. Eighty-two of our brothers reside in the company of the Lord. We mourn their passing and will care for their families. But we celebrate the fact that over two hundred men were saved. The newly-trained rescuers with their masks and heavy oxygen bottles strode the tunnels of death to dig out trapped miners. One of their skilled engineers sacrificed his life to save a poor miner. These men are true American heroes. We celebrate our modern ventilation system whose fans pulled the poison from the air, so that those who were trapped could breathe until rescue crews broke through. We also praise those stalwart women who made sandwiches and coffee and kept vigil. Most of all we commend Delagua's miners who risked their lives to help their threatened brothers.

"As Investigator Griggs noted, coal mining is dangerous work. Every day, I have the honor of standing shoulder-to-shoulder with these brave men who bring the coal that this country depends upon out of God's good earth. If discoveries made as a result of our disaster–and the disasters at Primero and Starkville–can advance the science of mining safety, these brave souls will not have died in vain."

Suddenly, Sidney exploded in a fit of coughing. Mama stood. Holding her palm up to stop the deputies, she took hold of Brother's arm. I joined her and we guided him through the back door, with Cockeye, Mack and Tommy following.

A smattering of flatfeet loitered outside.

Soon after we left, lunkers exited the courthouse and I figured the session was over. Jack lumbered out and Cockeye approached him. After they talked, my neighbor shoved through the crowd and caught my sleeve. "Time's our train?"

"Six."

"I'll meet you," Cockeye said.

"Where're you goin'?" Sid asked.

"To find Barba," Cockeye answered.

"Since when did you get so palsy-walsy with McKintrick?" I asked. "Ida finds out and you'll be sleepin' in the privy."

"Well, she won't find out if certain people button their lips. Jack's got pull with the sheriff and we aim to use it."

"Why don't you just let Barba stew?" Sid asked. "He got himself into that fix with his loud mouth."

Cockeye looked hurt. "That's cold-hearted, Sidney, to leave our friend here like that. He got beat pretty bad."

"This morning you wanted to kill him," Mack said.

"Thought you was about to," Tommy opined.

"Some people can't understand friendship and loyalty," Cockeye said. He turned to join McKintrick and the Greeks who were waiting.

Sid crowed. "Greeks, Cockeye and Jack McKintrick. Talk about deviation."

"Wonder if the state has an inspector for that?" Mack asked.

"If they don't, they need to get one," Tommy offered.

Our merry mood petered out and we strolled through town without talking.

I mourned Baldy and the others who'd gotten the chop. But after listening to Edgerton's slant, I felt confused. If the panel ruled against the company, we'd get strapped with a bunch of state regulations and never get coal dug. Like Edgerton said, diggers knew what the risks were. And we had to work.

Mack broke the lull. "How about that pipe? I nearly busted a gut. Investigator could have bought that thing anywhere."

"Coulda bought it today, even, right over there." Tommy pointed to a tobacco shop.

"I don't care where he got it," I said. "He made his point. You know there's smoking in the mines all the time. Some of you do it. That could have sparked the fire."

"Or," Charlie Costa interrupted, "coulda been combing the hair, like Bastrop say. I find a pocket comb once, on the floor of Number 3."

We laughed.

Sid held back a cough. "None of this matters. Sloppy habits and bad luck'll get the blame."

"You know, Edgerton sure offered a high opinion of us," Mack said. " 'Standing shoulder-to-shoulder with brave men' and all that flimflam. Made me want a dip of snuff."

"Made me want a cigar," Tommy spouted.

I snorted.

"Did Edgerton seem nervous to you all?" Sid asked. "He sure cut his eyes around a lot?"

"I noticed that," I said.

"He's not nearly as confident as he puts on," Sid said. "Bet he's our next super, though. His old man must've coughed up a lung not to be here."

"Edgerton's and Browder's stories were sad and noble, though, weren't they?" Mama said. "Pitiful bastards."

A surprised quietus ruptured in laughter.

Sid laid a hand across his chest. "Mother, my goodness . . . you curse like a coalass."

"I am the proud mother of two coalasses and widow of a coalass, boy. How else should I curse?"

"Hell, yeah," Cissy Cuminetti said.

At the depot, we were relaxing around the stove, waiting for our train, when a paddy wagon pulled up. Jack, Cockeye and a few of the Greeks got out. While they helped Barba shamble inside, the mayor chatted with the driver. They seemed pretty chummy. Just before Jack came inside, he took a roll of bills from his pants pocket, peeled off a few and gave them to the copper.

The Greeks deposited their countryman on a bench and sat on either side of him.

Cockeye ambled over. "He's still pretty woozy."

"Ain't so cocky now, is he?" I asked.

"You're a hard man, Alan Tanner," Cockeye said.

Jack came in, stone silent, lay down on the floor and went to sleep.

"Oh, I about forgot," Cockeye said, pulling two little bottles out of his pocket. "Jack got these for Sid. Said it was the only thing worth a damn for the coal cough. He's gettin' it stocked at the pluck-me."

B.J. Meyer and Co. Liquid Heroin. It was the same medicine C.G. Edgerton sipped.

*　　　　*　　　　*

A skim of pink etched the mountains out the train's window. Seemed like we'd been gone a month. My day in the city had been an eye-opener, but I didn't know what we'd accomplished by going. I felt pretty confused about the hearing. If the panel ruled against Victor-American, our freebooting days were over.

The inquest went on, in closed sessions, for two more days, with helmet men and surviving twin engineer, Wallace Evans, testifying.

A week later, the professors concluded that smokers, dry air and fate caused the explosions. Just like Sid had predicted.

The panel also noted that the companies had gone out of their way to accommodate our needs and create as safe a working environment as possible, considering the circumstances. The *Chronicle-News* called the Edgertons great Americans who were doing good Christian work in spite of foreigners who couldn't speak English and wouldn't follow rules. Victor-American agreed to install an alarm whistle, hire additional guards and post "No Smoking" signs printed in several languages.

To show the world that its heart was in the right place, the company established a relief fund of $66,000 for the miners killed. Families of swells got between $1500 and $2000, in cash. Coalass families got $1000 worth of company scrip, which could only be spent at the pluck-me, one of the saloons or Elma's whorehouse.

The next Monday, we went back to work.

PART ONE

"Oh, can't you see that pretty little bird,
Singing with all of his heart and soul?
He's got a blood-red spot on his wing,
And all the rest of him is black as coal."

"Red-Winged Blackbird"
by Billy Edd Wheeler

CHAPTER FIVE
October 5, 1912

Sid's coughing woke me. It was so bad in the dry weather, he had to lie on his back with his head propped on a rolled-up quilt to fall asleep. When he could spit up, he spat coal bile. He'd been fighting the hack for over two years with steam, the whiskey and lemon concoction Mama mixed and the *Heroin*, but the wheeze was winning.

In the gray light, he hunched up on his knees, head down in the covers, trying to muffle the hack so it wouldn't wake Mama. She slept behind a flimsy wall twenty feet away. If she heard him coughing like that, she wouldn't let him go to work.

Sid's cot squeaked. Before rummaging for his clothes, he snagged a bottle of *Meyer's* and drained it. Then he padded out of our room. The front door scraped the floor when he opened it. As he pulled it to, I heard Brother gasp for fresh air.

I hunkered down, hoping for another forty winks. Static sparks crackled in the blanket, stinging my face. With my late night at Elma's, I hadn't had but a two-hour nap. Came home drunk, fell on the cot, still wearing my shirt and overalls.

Outside Sid wheezed. The hell with it. I threw back the covers, swung my feet to the floor and sat for a second on the edge of the cot, rubbing my neck and shoulders. Somewhere in a whiskey haze hid Clara, my favorite. Got to pace myself better on the drink. What was the use of going to the whorehouse, if I couldn't recall pleasure next morning?

Before going outside, I pulled up on the knob so the door wouldn't drag and disturb Mama any more than Sid already had. Brother roosted on the porch steps, with a blanket thrown over his back, trying to pull on his boots.

"You're gonna break a rib with that hack," I observed. "Why don't you go on the mend for a few days?"

"What good's that? I can go to work and cough and make my wage, or stay home and cough and make nothin'. We can't afford for me to take off."

"You sound more like old Edgerton every day. Seems worse this morning than regular."

"Nah, it ain't. It's just this dry weather. And I run out of medicine. I'll catch my breath in a minute, if you'll quit asking questions."

"Mama ain't gonna let you go to work hackin' like that. You couldn't hold a pick."

"She won't know if you'll shut up so I can get goin'."

The floor in the shack next door creaked with movement inside and lights flickered against the window glasses. Soon, the yammering commenced. When Cockeye stepped out to set his gear on the porch, Ida was right behind, quizzing him about the night before. He had to keep watch all the time or she'd catch him sinning and pin his ears back.

"Cockeye drank with me at McKintrick's until I got my time with Clara," I told Sid. "If Ida wears him down and he yaks, she'll tattle and I'll catch hell. Ida wouldn't keep a secret like that, even if Jesus begged her."

Brother nodded, barked and spit.

The door rasped behind us, with Mama standing just inside. "Sid-ney . . . put some medicine in that throat."

"Aw, me," he whispered, "I was hopin' she wouldn't wake up."

There was no escape for him now. "You made too much racket hackin'," I said.

He reached out from under the blanket, slapped my head and wheezed again.

"Sid-ney!"

"Drank all of it, Mama . . . don't have any more."

"Well, come back in here and get in bed. You're not going anywhere today, coughing like that. Allie . . . are you out there?"

"No ma'am."

"Sass-mouth. Bring in some wood, so I can stoke up this fire." Mama shuffled across the floor and clinked open the stove's door.

"You want some help standing?" I asked Sid.

"I'm breathin' easier out here. Just let me sit."

I grabbed some kindling from the pile on the porch and took it inside. Mama had lit two lamps and was bent over, blowing the coals in the firebox. She wore one of Papa's old woolen shirts over her nightgown and a pair of his brogans underneath.

When I laid the sticks next to her, she sighed and rubbed her eyes with the back of her hand.

"Seems like somebody could take it upon himself to stoke up this fire for his poor, sick brother."

I rested some pinyon twigs across the slender flame. "I know, Mama, I should've done it. I'm miserable and unworthy."

"No call for sarcasm, Mr. Smart Aleck." She fed in bigger pieces of juniper. "You going back to bed?"

"No. I'm tryin' to find my boots. They were right here with my pack, where I took 'em off last night."

"This morning, you mean–and in the wee hours of it. I moved them to the corner over there, because they stink. Let's get some steam going for Brother."

I filled the kettle from one of the buckets, set it on the stove, retrieved my boots and sat down to put them on.

"Oiled Sid's last night," Mama said, "and I bet they're comfy as house slippers. You could get yours seen to if you stayed home some. I'd think a man's feet would split wearing those things." She stood, grabbed my chin and pulled my face into the lamplight. "Let me see that eye. Uh-huh, just what I suspected." Released. "Smells like somebody mopped the barroom with that shirt of yours, too."

I touched a lump below my left eye, saw myself taking a swing at somebody who'd bad-mouthed Clara Dawes. "I ran into a low-hangin' branch in the darkness," I said, boosting the flame with more sticks.

Mama grunted. "Handsome young fellow like you could attract a nice girl if he didn't spend so much time drinking and sporting with trash."

Pointless to rebut yet. Mama was primed for a lecture. Afterwards, she'd want me to chew on her wise observations. Sooner or later she'd ask, "Well, don't you have anything to say for yourself?" Then I'd explain. Letting her tap off steam gave me a chance to rally a defense for the whole infraction, instead of trying to explain each part a little at a time.

Mama chunked a few lumps of coal in and got the stove and the room hot as a smelter, boiling that water. After she put coffee on, she poured milk over flour and eggs in a bowl. Took the big wooden spoon out and raised it toward me like it was her finger.

"You know, it's dreadful you stay out all hours of the night, doing who-knows-what and here's Brother can't do anything but work and come home these days."

Mama had locked her arm around the bowl, pulled it under her bosom and beat the lumps out of the batter like she was running off of a battery. Some strings of hair had fallen down across her face and they danced with each rotation of the spoon. Wavy, dark tresses with only a few gray streaks. Button nose, cow-shit brown eyes, wide mouth, straight, white teeth. Unlike most coal camp women her age, Mama kept her youngish shape and soft skin. Before going to sleep, she'd rub her face, neck and hands with lotions. Papa had prized her as the town beauty and she was still handsome at 44. After him and the girls passed, a few hopefuls lurked around with wildflowers and candy, but she ran 'em off.

She'd let a suspicious amount of time lapse between complaints. Figured I'd run a dodge. Two of her passions–food and family–were almost foolproof for distraction reliability. Get her talking about one or both and you might escape. Had my opening when she set the molasses can on the table alongside a cup of coffee for me.

"Somethin' smells good. Whatcha cookin'?" I asked.

Mama poured out three cakes that bubbled and popped on the griddle. "As if you didn't know. Got sausage, too, but you're too puny to eat any. Sid and I will have a feast."

"You know I can't resist those cakes." It was true. I could eat my weight in 'em. "Can of molasses made me think about the time you and Papa were fussin' and you totaled up all the meals you'd fixed and wrote the number on the wall so us kids could sympathize with you."

"I know what you're up to, buster brown," she said, turning the cakes.

"Papa said it was your lot in life to cook and clean and . . ."

"And I hid the silverware and refused to cook," she interrupted. "Not my proudest moment."

I chuckled. "We got so desperate eatin' Papa's cold-water cornbread and molasses with our fingers, we begged him to say he was sorry."

"He held out for two more days, just to let all of us know who was in charge. Lloyd was just like his daddy that way," she said. "He'd never admit it, but he was."

"What way?" Like I didn't know.

"Hard-headed, stiff-necked. Only one way to do everything. Like other somebodies I'm acquainted with." Mama pointed to a sign hanging between the tintype of us kids on the horse and Dold's picture of me and Sid outside Number 3. "There's the proof."

She was referring to Papa's list.

THE FOUR RULES

1. ***Keep your mouth shut and your eyes open.***
2. ***Use your head for something besides a hat rack.***
3. ***Put everything back where you found it.***
4. ***Use it up, wear it out, make it do, or do without.***

"Papa painted that thing just before we moved to Delagua," I said, stomping my feet into the boots. They were a bit on the shabby side and when they dried out between wearings, it took thirty minutes of suffering to loosen them up. Most working men had two pair, but I had better things to spend wages on than new boots. A perfect example of Rule 4.

"Lloyd didn't paint that, Alan. Grandpa Tanner did. It hung in his kitchen." Mama scraped off the cakes and poured on four more. "Here, start on these. SIDNEY . . . BREAKFAST. Lloyd took that sign when we all went to see Grandpa the last time. I thought you knew that."

I poured molasses over the cakes and picked up my fork. "Must have done it while me and Sid looked for somethin' to do. Papa told us he hated farming and hated Grandpa Tanner, too."

"He never said *hate*."

"Called him a miser and a skinflint. Told me and Sid he got a beating one time for leaving a screwdriver out in the rain. You said Grandpa treated his family like farm equipment to be kept up and repaired, stored in their proper places until needed. Sounds like Papa had plenty to hate." I was inhaling those cakes like a fat boy at the flapjack fair. "Why would he steal a list of rules made up by somebody like that?"

Mama flipped the cakes, laid out sausage patties in the cast iron. "You believe in the Tanner luck, don't you?"

"Yes, ma'am. It's what brought me and Sid out of Number 3 alive."

"Lloyd thought good fortune sprang from those rules."

"Even if they were made up by a crazy man?"

"Yep. People are funny like that, Alan. They'll spend a lifetime trying to convince themselves and everybody they know how much they despise something; then, when they have the chance to let go, they cling to it. Lloyd criticized his papa for almost everything he did and I will say the old man deserved most of it. He was flat mean. But Lloyd thought his daddy had the best luck of any man alive."

"Papa said Grandpa could run a stick in the ground at night and have leaves on it the next morning," I said between bites.

Mama nodded. "He was a good farmer. And he had foresight. One of the first to produce melons for profit in Rocky Ford. But he was obsessed with efficiency and hard work and his well-oiled human machines rebelled. Your grandma ran off with a seed drummer. Lloyd's sister and two brothers just vanished–your papa never knew where. Lloyd stayed till that Mexican family moved in and Grandpa took up with one of the daughters. That was the last straw for him."

"Why'd he hang around so long after everybody else left?"

"Grandpa Tanner believed that good fortune came from following those rules and he presented his farm and its bounty as proof. That made sense to your papa. He figured that if he left, he'd be tempting fate. Plus, Lloyd hated to give up on anything, even his papa."

I considered the list again. "Well, they are good rules," I said. "Kinda strict. But good."

"Your papa thought all of us–himself included–ought to be reminded of them every day. That's the reason he hung that sign. SIDNEY . . . COME EAT."

"He's likely asleep." I syrupted two more cakes and started on some sausage. "That medicine makes him drowsy. Cranky, too."

"I know. But it's the only thing that helps," Mama said. "Only supposed to take it twice a day, but he sips on it like sarsaparilla." She'd crossed her arms and I could feel her watching me eat. "You've always liked griddle cakes, haven't you?"

I forked the last of the batch and shoved them in. "Yes ma'am. Could I take a few to work?"

Mama put four cakes and two sausages in the lunch bucket and divvied the rest of the batter across the griddle. "Don't you have anything to say for yourself?"

Shit. "About what?"

"You know about what."

"Aw, Mama. You act like I'm the only man who ever stretched out."

"You're still a kid, Alan. You do a man's work, I'll grant, but you act like a kid. Stretching out is your name for reckless abandon and irresponsibility, two things I can't abide."

Started to argue, thought better. I'd been outfoxed by the master. Last hope: my shame-grin might calm her down. Got that tactic from Papa.

Mama rubbed my cheek. "Need a shave. That spot under your eye hurt?"

"Nah."

"Such a handsome boy not to take better care of himself. Got your papa's blue eyes, don't you? You shouldn't be so stiff-necked."

"Came by it natural, from both sides of the family, you always said. Granddaddy Sanger was stubborn, too." Like you, I almost threw in.

"True. He was." Mama turned the cakes. "Go see about your brother."

I filled the canteen, picked up my lunch pail and pack and stepped onto the porch.

Mama had told us that her papa was as hard-headed as Grandpa Tanner, in his way. Said Granddaddy Sanger believed that black clouds followed most people–especially his family–and misfortune lurked around every corner. According to him, the truly wise man couldn't be too cautious or observant. When bad luck struck, he called it God's will and tried everything he could to make amends. Mama said he spent so much time watching over his shoulder and praying, he missed what was in front of him. That made him accident-prone, which led to more superstition, more prayer, more misfortune.

Two brands of luck influenced our fortunes, the Tanner and the Sanger, the good, to celebrate, and the bad, to beware of. We never knew which would win.

Leaning against a porch round, Sidney was sound asleep, nesting in his blanket. I shook him and he stirred.

"Mama's got some griddle cakes, sausage and a bucket of steam for you, chief. You cleared up a little? I ain't heard you hackin' in a while."

Sid uncovered his head. "Med'cine kicked in. Been dozin'. Cockeye come by. Said he didn't blab. I tried to stand, but too weak. You're right about me holding a pick."

"It's okay. A couple of days off and you'll be a wild man again. Let me help you up." His arm was just skin and bones. Sidney might not be digging coal for a long time. "I'll stop by the pluck-me directly and get more *Heroin*."

"Slow you down. Mama can go after 'while. She don't have nothin' to do but feed them chickens, wash the floor and do laundry."

I sniggered. "Sounds like a dang holiday, don't it? I'll get Mack and Tommy to bring it up. They'll be having a beer at McKintrick's."

"Way we set them charges yesterday evening, it's gonna be a gravy train today. Bet you don't even use the pick till noon."

Mama came out carrying my pick, shovel and lunch pail. "Here." She handed me my stuff. "Don't forget Brother's medicine."

"He won't forget," Sid said, leaning against the pillar again.

"Somebody's a little cross." She put her arm around him. "Think you can find a man to help you work, Alan?"

"Aw, yeah. The boss'll assign me somebody. I'll get us three cars out, at least."

"You won't do anything dangerous without Sidney there, will you?"

"We did all the heavy work yesterday," I said. "No need to worry."

"Just taking care of my boy," Mama said.

"I enjoyed our chat," I told her. "And I'll take everything you said to heart."

"In a pig's eye, you will," she said.

I kissed her and gave her a hug. Then I picked up my gear and scampered down the hill into town.

CHAPTER SIX
October 5, 1912

Rising up in the cleft where the hills sank to the plains, the sun blinked a little of the morning chill off the hillsides and ravines.

After I stopped at the pluck-me for the *Heroin,* I went by McKintrick's. Like I figured, Mack and Tommy stood at the bar. Said they'd be glad to deliver Sid's medicine.

At Number 3, I fished in a bucket full of brass checks until I found mine. The disk would hang on the station board until the end of my shift when I'd throw it back in the bucket. That way, the bosses would know who was working where. We'd started this system after the explosion.

Every time I entered the mine I thanked the Tanner luck that me and Sid had escaped. But two years after the disaster, the stench of death lingered and memories waylaid. Some days, hauling out mangled bodies haunted me. Others, I brooded over sham burials and the pointless hearing. That morning I fretted about new pit bosses, jittery guards and a stand-in for my brother.

Timbers, some whole, some split or twisted from the explosion, still lay scattered around the landing. Up ahead, 3's boss, Chesterfield, doled out coal cars from a string of empties parked on a side track. When it was my turn, I reminded him of where me and Sid had been digging the day before and I hung my disk on the board.

The boss checked his manifest. "Where's your brother at?" he asked.

When I told him Sid was sick, it set off a row of bellyaching from the lumpies behind me. They thought it was going to slow down the line, but the boss grinned and held up his hand.

"Hey, I got just the bird for the occasion. A Greek, straight from the old country." He motioned to a guy standing by the empty coal cars.

The ouzo was a little taller than me, stout, with a round, smooth face. Atop his head tilted one of the new metal hardhats nobody wanted to wear because of the weight, a greenhorn fit if I'd ever seen one. Some of the dumbbells tittered when he stepped up, cradling a shovel and pick like they were babies.

"Nicholas Kistos," the guy said, "twenty-five years."

Just what I needed, a dummy to nursemaid.

"Yeah, still hot from killing Turks, ain't you? You hump it today, Tanner, you might get three, four cars." Chesterfield grinned. "If your buddy don't cut your throat."

We loaded our gear into the first empty car, coupled up two more and pushed them up the grade.

"Sava, English?" I asked and he held up five fingers and smiled. I had no idea what that meant. "You're just a temporary, here. I want you to know that."

The dummy smiled, nodded and shook my hand, like he'd been paid a compliment.

The track leveled off for about fifty feet before dropping again into the mine. Me and the newbie stopped along the way, picked up four timbers and loaded them into the cars.

We filled our headlamps with carbide and water, fired the wicks and pushed our little train into the main haulage. Several tunnels entered left and right and light from lamps flashed off the walls. A mule brayed from a dark entry and the Greek jerked. I grinned and pulled him along. Boneheads got hurt sometimes, surprising a mule that way.

"Easy, baby, look at you," I said, aiming my lamp. Light caught the animal's eye, making it gleam. The mule shook its head in the light.

We ran with our cars, building a head of steam to push into another tunnel. After the turn we rolled along for a ways, ducking under a header. The walls were close and the Greek kept bumping his head and shoulders against the tight squeezes.

Sid's bandana hung on a timber up ahead and I spragged a wheel to slow the cars for the junction. At our station, I showed Kistos how to check for gas and weak spots. Everything seemed safe and solid.

The Greek turned out to be a good worker and we shoveled fast. We filled two cars before using the picks then spelled each other, one breaking the larger chunks, the other red-handing the pieces into the cars. Every once in a while, we shoveled some slate and granite away from the coal. By noon we had three cars' worth.

I made the sound of a mule braying and pointed toward the tunnel.

The Greek nodded. "*Moulari*," he whispered and started loading the fourth car as I left the station.

In the main haulage, I was surprised to find crews shoveling dust instead of working their coal faces. Then I noticed veins of water running across the floor and puddling in spots. A water car sat at a tunnel junction and a crew was spraying the floors. In spite of C.G. Edgerton's grand promises to the state, shoveling dust and sprinkling still never happened unless the superintendent got wind of an inspection.

Digging and hauling coal seemed to have stopped in a flurry of housekeeping. Outside, shovel jockeys were dumping loads of dust and slate wherever they could find bare spots in the yard.

Down the rails, Chesterfield was talking to Edgerton. A mule lumbered up behind me, so I stepped off the track to let three cars filled with dust pass. Cockeye, covered with mud, drove a jack named Oscar, foul-tempered and flatulent. Barba walked to the side, away from any outbursts from the mule.

"Hey," I hollered at Bastrop and stepped in beside him. "You slip down?"

"No, I didn't slip down. The crew on that water truck upside from us flushed out without givin' no warning. I was layin' on my back all the way up under the seam, undercuttin', when about a foot of water poured in on me. It's a wonder I didn't drown." He wiped his bushy eyebrows with the heel of his hand. "Can't count on ouzo here to warn me about nothin'."

Barba chimed in from the rear. "Boss come in and say for us to forget coal and shovel dust. I tell Bastrop this morning we should get coal out before we dress the face, but he want to do hard work first. Now, we get nothing again today."

"Always 'I told you so,' ain't it?" Cockeye shot back. "You don't know everything there is to know about everything. When that water come in on me, you just stood there."

"I been knowing plenty that you never imagine. Ever since five years, Tanner, this man want to argue. Such as now, you is passing a spot to dump."

Cockeye reined the mule. "Well, I can't concentrate with you yakkin' all the time."

"I got the mule," I said, taking the reins.

Still arguing as they grabbed their shovels and threw dust onto the pile, only a few feet away from Chesterfield and the superintendent.

About to ask if I could use Oscar after Cockeye and Barba finished with him when the mule shook its head and farted.

"Been doing that all morning," Cockeye said. "Bad news back in them rooms. Wonder if a mule's gas could explode? That'll be the next thing."

I fanned the air. "Goddamn, it's awful. Just hangs there, don't it? They're feedin' 'em too much green hay." I grinned and shook my head. "Was thinkin' of borrowing him, but now I don't know."

Barba threw a shovelful onto their growing pile. "You ain't moving no coal, Tanner, any more than us. Me and Cockeye is believing that state inspector come to . . ."

"Take us by surprise," Cockeye filled in, tossing his shovel into the last empty car. "Edgerton come rushing up here, ordered shovelin' and sprinklin'."

"That *would* be a hell of a note, wouldn't it?" I said. "Got three cars full and an inspector shows up."

I was mopey until I imagined Clara, lying around down at Elma's, all perfumed in her floozies, waiting for me to come by. An early off and a quick run down the hill and I'd be in her twat before anybody else could lay a black hand on her.

Cockeye unhitched Oscar, but when he reached up to grab his halter to turn him around, the mule snapped. Cockeye recoiled, as Barba slapped the animal on the flank with his shovel. The mule shook his head and farted again.

"Won't do no good to spank him." I held my hand up so Oscar could see it before I grabbed his halter. "You don't never put your hand on a mule's face without showing it to him first. Only ones that won't bite are the big drafts. Oscar don't have an ounce of draft mule in him. You're just a tiny one, ain't you, buddy? More donkey than mule." I pulled Oscar's head down and whispered a few sweet nothins in his ear.

"Dang, Alan, you talk to them like they was people," Cockeye said. "You could be a teamster."

I did like mules and donkeys and I'd been spending some of my time off helping Machito at The Chamber's livery. Gave me a chance to visit with old Grady, too.

I coaxed the mule around to the other end of the train of cars, reasoning with him the whole time. That's the way with a mule–he won't do anything unless he thinks it's in his own best interest. Crack diggers work for years around mules and never figure that out. Instead of talking and coaxing, they beat an animal or lock him up without food, trying to make him work. Mules remember and the next time that guy gets ready to trace the animal, he gets the noodles kicked out of him.

Chesterfield stopped me before I reached the mine entrance with Oscar. Dust sparkled on the pit boss's shirt, face and cap.

"I need this mule," I said.

"Yeah, and I need a new hat, coaly," Chesterfield said. "You're lucky you got to dig all morning, while these other goozies hauled dust. Superintendent's closed the tipple till further notice. Everybody's got to be out in fifteen minutes."

"Inspection," Barba blurted.

Chesterfield stink-eyed the Greek.

"Is what we guess, me and Cockeye. What you think, that inspection write us a letter?" Barba grinned and coughed.

Chesterfield's cheeks reddened. "No, grease bag. It seems fishy to me that you just guessed out of the blue sky. When this inspector showed up, we was thinking that somebody wrote him a letter. You do something like that?"

"Come on, boss," Cockeye said. "Barba can't write his name without help."

"I will cut your throat, soon," Barba barked.

"I'll be waitin', ouzo." Cockeye turned back to Chesterfield. "Boss, why would a lunker do somethin' to knock us out of our wages? We need to work."

"We're watchin', boys," the boss said. "Ain't nothin' like what's happenin' up north gonna happen down here. If I find out anybody's organizin' or informin', I'll run 'em down the canyon, fast." Chesterfield glared at us before walking away.

"Delagua is home," Barba said. "Boss can't just drive me out. What he mean, union? I can't figure."

"Shut up, Barba," Cockeye said. "You said all you're entitled. Got us on the shit-list is what you did."

"You might as well take him back," I said to Cockeye, placing Oscar's reins in his hand.

The buddies shouted insults at each other as I took off down the tunnel to our station. Didn't care about loss of work, now. If I could get out of the mine and down the hill before every other horny dick, I might have a shot at Clara while she was fresh and frisky.

But my hope flagged when I found Kistos lying behind the last car, unconscious. Passed out from breathing the dusty air. Had happened to Sid before. Been lightheaded a time or two, myself. I got the canteen and spirits of ammonia from my pack and knelt over him. When he came to, I offered sips of water. I hung Sid's bandana again and helped the Greek shamble into the tunnel.

"Sit," I ordered. The big man sank onto a timber. I pulled his knees up and forced his head between his legs so he could breathe deep. When the Greek made signs like he was better, he tailed me into the main haulage.

Out there we met a shadow, back-lit from the rectangle of light at the portal. The man took quick, short steps along the track, and, when he heard us coming, shined a flashlight. "Edgerton said you were out," Flashlight remarked, all irritated, like we'd been hiding in there just to aggravate him.

Me and Kistos passed him without explaining and the inspector followed us back to the entry. Edgerton and Chesterfield waited, just outside.

"Morning, boss," I said, as we passed.

When we had found out Miles would be the new superintendent, we'd hoped to deal with a swell who understood the working man a little bit, one we could read. After all, when 3 went up, he'd led the first rescue party and took the women's side against his papa–even if he had threatened to have me killed in the process. And he talked like he knew how to connect with us when he testified to the commission.

But two years in Delagua had done him in. You saw it in his sunk-back, shifty eyes and early graying hair, sensed it in his windy sway. Guess he thought we'd stay scared shitless and cooperative just because he was C.G.'s son. Hadn't worked out that way. These days he mostly stayed in his office and let the new pit bosses run things.

"Are you sure these are the last two, now, Mr. Edgerton?" the inspector asked.

The superintendent looked at Chesterfield, who said we were the last.

The inspector re-entered the mine. I jerked my disk off the board, dropped it in the bucket and lit out for Elma's.

CHAPTER SEVEN
October 5, 1912

I ran down the hill, with Kistos right behind, juggling his gear. Who knows what cleared his head. Maybe he could sniff out pussy like a rooster. But he stayed with me all the way into Elma's yard.

Von Raven's Rooming House was a spiffed-up two-story frame that sat across the street from McKintrick's Imbibery and Domicile of Chance. Once a rickety flophouse filled with full-time dipsos, scabby whores, lumpy mattresses and rats the size of a small dog, Elma's now stood as grand testament to her partnership with Jack and The Chamber. The building that scared us as kids had been stripped to its frame, shored up and fancified. The fresh clapboard siding was pink; the porch, stretching half-way across the front of the house, pale blue. Atop the porch was a balcony with yellow railing.

Inside, the hallway and living room were decorated with shiny furniture, glass trinkets, rugs and lace curtains. Each of the ten bedrooms bore the name of a flower and was spruced up to fit. Elma invited in the grimiest and horniest men in Colorado then raised hell when they scraped the wallpaper or threw up on a rug. It didn't make sense because, under all that icing, Elma's was still a whorehouse. But fancy and formal was her way and we went along to squeeze the tenderloin.

Lumpies were already sitting around under the cottonwoods or stretched out in the sunshine, drinking from pails of beer, waiting their turns with a whore. Barba was playing boccie with the other Greeks so I left Kistos and my gear with him. Shit. I'd have been first in line, if that dummy hadn't passed out.

A bell tinkled when I opened the door. Before I could step inside, Elma called from the front room.

"Lester?" She rushed into the hall and stopped when she saw me. "Where's Lester?"

I shrugged. Lester was Elma's bouncer.

"He was outside just a few minutes ago. He's supposed to get you kids to dust off and clean your boots. Did you wipe your feet? Hell, no, look at them." She pressed her fingers against my chest and pushed me back onto the porch. "Didn't anybody outside tell you to dust off?"

The lunkheads under the cottonwoods crowed.

"Buffoons," she hollered at them. "This just slows everything down. Ignorant, ignorant, ignorant." Elma stepped to the side of the porch and yelled for her bouncer.

Lester ambled around the corner, carrying his bat. "Chasin' off them wops from under Clara's window. They was throwin' rocks and raisin' hell." He sat down in a chair by the door. "My feet's killin' me, Elma."

"The masses took us by surprise." Elma turned back to me. "Move farther out in the yard to dust off, son. What did you boys do, wallow in it? Remove those nasty boots, too, before you come back in. They stink." The glass door rattled when she slammed it behind her.

I sat on the porch, pulled off my much-maligned boots and stored them in the flower bed. "What's the deal, Lester? She's finickier than usual."

"Aw, Elma's jumpy because the mine inspector's stayin' here tonight."

"You're kiddin'."

"Nope. Edgerton sent word about a half-hour ago. Elma's tryin' to turn as many meatballs as she can before he comes down, I guess." Lester wiped his face with a grimy towel hanging around his neck. "About to run me ragged."

Inside, Elma held a feather duster like it was a bouquet of flowers while she cranked a victrola in the front room. The curtains rose and fell with the breeze sliding in through an open window. After she got the music going, the old whore pointed to a tablet lying on a table in front of the sofa.

"Shoot, is these all for Clara?" I couldn't believe it.

Elma pranced over and stared down at the table top. "Pick up that tablet." She jiggled the feathers where the paper had been. "See what I'm saying? I just dusted in here." She looked up at me. "All the girls got a list today, not just Clara. Some aren't as long as hers, though," she said, turning the pages. "There's six ahead of you, counting the fellow Clara's with now. I'd say you'd get in around four, four-thirty. The girls are having to clean filth up after everybody. If Jack would just get me that bath house built."

I was pissed. I'd never been lower than third for Clara. By the time she got to me, she'd be dirty, smelly and worn-out. Still, a dirty and worn-out Clara was better than a clean and rested anybody else. I wrote my name down and went back outside.

A few of the disappointed were organizing a ball game and tried to get me interested. But I was too horny to concentrate on anything but my girl.

Kistos was tossing the boccie balls now and he straightened when I walked up. The Greek reached to shake my hand, as he blathered something to Barba.

"Nicholas say you save his life," Barba said.

"All I did was give him a whiff of ammonia and push him outside. He just needed fresh air."

"Don't matter," Barba said. "Kistos don't have the language yet, but he is glad for what you done. He chase you down the hill, try to thank you, but you run too fast." Barba nodded. "When a man is square with a Greek, a Greek don't forget it. He will like to buy you a drink."

"Well, sure." Barba handed me a pail of beer.

Kistos stood there, with his hands in his pockets and a stub of cigarette burning in the corner of his mouth.

"Where's his?" I asked.

"He don't stand strong drink or whores. But he don't judge neither. When he get the language, you watch out."

I raised the present toward Kistos, grinned and gulped.

* * *

The Greeks made the wait a little more tolerable. We consumed vinegared eggs and beer from McKintrick's and I even took a turn tossing the wooden balls. The wops humped and gyrated under Clara's window, until she soaked them with the soup from her slop jar.

By the time Lester called my name around five, I was wobbly. I staggered onto the porch and pulled off my boots again.

Elma waited in the hall. She took me by the shoulders and turned me around. "You got crabs or lice?"

"Every time I come in here I tell you I ain't."

"What about open sores? Got any of them?"

"No."

"Okay. Clara's just had her break and she's waiting for you in Columbine. Two lines for the girl and two for the room. Mind that wallpaper as you go up. An ox just scratched some off."

I paid my scrip and climbed the stairs.

The floorboards sagged on the second floor as I walked down the hall. Seemed like a miracle that the old frame held up under the traffic. Someday this house was sure to collapse, the victim of the banging and bumping that had gone on inside it.

* * *

My time with Clara was a disaster. No woody. No matter how hard I tried to get it up, nothing. I even paid what little scrip I had left for Clara to try a few special whore tricks on it. But it just laid there, a dead lizard. First time *that* ever happened. Booze and the long wait must have done him in.

I came downstairs all hangdog. Elma looked at me kind of sympathetic as I left. Guess she'd seen disappointment like that before. Was sitting on the porch lacing up my boots when somebody under the cottonwood beckoned. It was Kistos, minding my gear. I shuffled over. He shook my hand again, chattered something, handed me the pack and tools.

Knowing the Greek didn't care for drinking and hoping he'd take a hint and go off some place to sleep, I turned away and crossed over to the saloon. I didn't want a drink. Just needed to kill some time and get this guy off my tail.

McKintrick's bulged in manufactured glee. With curses and cackles, the reek of stale beer and sweat, the blackened mob of working men and whores coming and going, the saloon marked the prime spot for news-gathering, liquor swilling and boredom relief in Delagua.

Monroe Purvis's music waged war against the din. A piano player in a mining town saloon had to beat the hell out of his instrument to be heard, which was no problem for Monroe. He was the champion piano pounder in town. Jack had him brought in special. Had the strongest hand I ever shook.

The mayor cruised the room, demanding peace and harmony, while his Mexican bouncers sat in high chairs, ready to pounce on trouble-makers.

I wasn't in the mood for socializing so I turned away. Kistos waited under a street-light halo, his hardhat tilted on his head again.

"I like the way you wear that hat," I said.

The dummy smiled and nodded.

At the edge of town, we ran into Tommy and Mack, hot for news about the inspection. When they found out I knew nothing, they couldn't resist needling my new buddy.

"Carries them tools funny, don't he, Tommy?" Mack snickered.

"Yeah. Like a pinhead," Tommy answered.

For some reason, Kistos couldn't get onto balancing pick, shovel and pack on his shoulders. So, he cradled the tools again and wagged the knapsack in the crook of one arm. When he stopped walking, his helmet fell off.

"Dumbass looks like he's been put together from spare parts, don't he?" Mack said.

"From the junk yard," Tommy inserted.

Both of them gassed so hard I thought they'd piss their britches.

"Oh, like you two halfwits was perfect your first day." I dropped my gear and pushed the Greek into better light so I could help him. "This guy dug more coal today than you two could in a month. Kept his mouth shut doing it, too, unlike some I know." I snagged the hardhat and perched it on the Greek's head once more, rehung his pack, balanced the pick over the shovel and fixed the handles in his left hand. "Now, don't let none of that slide, ouzo." I patted the bundle, hoping he'd understand.

Kistos nodded and grinned. He shook hands with me, turned to Mack and Tommy, shook with them and rattled what I figured to be his introduction.

"You should of kept to olive pickin'," Mack said, withdrawing his hand.

"Back in olive-picker city," Tommy tacked on.

Both looked at each other and broke up again.

From his trouser pocket, the Greek pulled a cloth bag of tobacco and held it in his teeth. Brought out a paper, which he laid on the flat handle of the pick.

"You want some help with that?" Mack asked.

"I'll hold them tools," Tommy offered.

Kistos concentrated on his task. He filled the paper with a pinch of tobacco, yanked the drawstring on the bag with his teeth and put it back in his pocket. Picked up the project and rolled it around between his thumb and fingers. When it was satisfactory, he licked the edge of the paper and held up a perfect cigarette.

A grin spread across his face. "You want?"

We shook our heads.

"You done it," Mack said.

Tommy nodded. "You smoke it."

Kistos hung the rollie on his lip, produced a match, snapped a flame with his thumbnail and lit the damn thing.

The Greek blew out a gust, dragged again. "Is okay. I see you friends another day," he said, as plain as any American, before he hiked off into the darkness.

I traded looks with the knotheads. "Coulda sandbagged me with that 'no-speakie' bullshit," I said. "Them foreigners love to do that."

"Never seen nobody roll a weed like that," Mack said.

"Done it one-handed," Tommy pointed out.

"He seem different to you?" Mack asked.

"Seemed different to me," Tommy answered.

"How do you mean?" I asked.

"I don't know. Just different. Us makin' fun didn't even faze him," Mack said.

"Happy as a meadowlark," Tommy muttered.

"I like that," Mack declared.

Tommy agreed.

The chuckleheads said adios and headed for town and I struck out for home. The aroma from Kistos' cigarette lingered. Funny how quick his breezy manner had turned those two around.

I heard the crash of shovel and pick as they hit the ground ahead.

"Hey, ouzo," I hollered into the darkness. "Wait up."

CHAPTER EIGHT
October 5, 1912

Night had fallen clear and warm for October, with a fingernail moon holding water in the east.

Away from town, music and the smell of meat roasting drifted out of the sheet-metal shacks and lean-tos of Greektown. First time I'd ever got this close. A fire blazed ahead. Three guys played funny-looking instruments while the rest danced in a line, their arms around each other's shoulders. All wore blouses and puffy pants with scarves tied below their knees and each one took a turn hopping around by himself. Sure seemed happy.

Kistos turned to me, jabbering and pointing, like he was trying to explain something. When I didn't say anything, he shook hands, again, and said, "Tanner, I see you another day." He turned and clattered off to the fire.

My new buddy dropped his gear and joined the line of dancers, keeping time, swaying in and out as the music quickened. Soon, Kistos pranced into the center, jumping and slapping his boot soles. Different. I watched until he rejoined the group, then I headed for home.

I found Sid roosting on the porch where I'd left him, still wrapped in his blanket. Mama had set one of the big coal-oil lamps next to Brother and its buttery light played across his chest and face. Lips fluttered as he snored. He jerked awake when I dropped my gear in the yard.

"Well, if it ain't baby bruddah. Drag your lazy ass on up here. Bastrop already told me you got the day off . . ."

"For an inspection."

"I know for an inspection. Let me finish."

I waited, but he didn't say anything. "You picked a good day to lounge around," I said. "Edgerton had us shovelin' rash instead of coal."

"He'll just pay that asshole off, like all the other times," Sid commented.

"I guess. Got three cars loaded. Was on my way after a mule when they shut us down."

Sid scratched himself beneath the blanket then pulled the wrap tighter around his shoulders. "Shoulda took two out when you had the chance."

The *Heroin* was talking and I didn't like it. "Yeah, I wish you'd a been there to tell me exactly what to do."

"Gettin' your back up, huh?"

"Ain't. You hear I got a Greek buddy?"

"Yup. Bastrop told me," Sid said. "He do anything 'sides sleep?"

"Oh, yeah," I said. "Works faster than a one-armed paper hanger and holds his peace. Why ain't you in bed?"

"I'm sick of goddamn bed. Breathe easier out here." Sid's eyes closed. "Bring any more medicine?"

"Just what I sent this morning. Seems to me like you had enough already."

"Tell you when I've had enough, scamp." He tried to stand, fell back. "Fuck it," he said, scratching himself again.

"What?"

"Said, 'Fuck it.' You and Mama don't understand this cough."

"Well, if we don't, nobody does. We're the best you got." I yawned, stretched, rubbed my butt and thought about a bath. "She in bed?"

"Yeah. Ain't asleep, though. Light's on. Lookin' at a goddamn magazine she's already read fifty times. Or her Emily." He coughed some, took a swig of syrup. "Somethin' eatin' you?"

" 'Side from your bad mood, ain't nothin'."

"Is *somethin'*. You lettin' that goddamn whore turn you upside-down?"

"No . . ."

"Can't get her off your mind or your cob out of your hand, can you? I been there. Brain's in your ying-yang, cowboy, right where she wants it."

I smiled, thinking about Sid pulling me off those kid whores in Trinidad two years before.

"Is not. We're just on the outs. She's got too popular, chargin' high prices for favors she used to give away. Actin' like a princess 'cause she's got the longest list. Forgets she's a whore."

"But you're in love, ain't you?"

"Am not."

"Are, too. Dedicated customer like you keeps whores in business. Whore's a piece of perishable property. Got about . . . ." Sidney dozed off.

"YOU'RE ASLEEP, DIPSHIT."

Eyes opened. "Ain't too 'sleep to kick your ass."

I ignored his crack. "Whaddaya mean a whore's perishable property?"

"She's got about five good years, if she can stay healthy and in demand. Still pretty? Still talented? You lope your mule all the time, thinkin' about her?

If she can keep you comin' back, everybody's happy."

Mr. Know-It-All even had prostitution figured out. Had to admit it made sense, but I wouldn't say it. I needed to shift the subject a little. "You know what Cockeye told me? The company makes Elma pay seven dollars a month, per whore. Goddamn Victor-American's got their fingers on everything up here, even pussy."

"Let me tell you . . ."

Pain in the butt, this chat was. "Tell me what, Sidney?"

" '*Tell me what, Sidney,*' " he mocked. "Mr. Smart Ass, McKintrick arranged that bribe to keep the superintendent's nose out of his business. He calls it a 'protection tax'."

The music picked up louder from Greektown.

"Listen to that racket," Sid said. "The fuck they got to celebrate?"

"Same as the wops, spics and bohunks. Happy to be diggin' coal with us smart white boys." I snickered.

"What's funny?" Sid asked.

"Your hair." I yawned. "Looks like a hoorah's nest."

Sid stifled a cough. "Your gear's layin' there, next to that dog."

"What dog?"

Sid pointed. "That one. There."

"Well, get him to watch my stuff, would you?"

Inside, I stoked the fire and put the big kettle on to heat some water. Banged around because I was mad.

"Sidney?" Mama called out. "What do you need, son?"

"It's me, Mama." I peeped around the door jamb.

She let the Emily fall onto her chest and sat up. "Are you sick?"

"No, I'm not sick. Just came in from work and thought I'd take a bath."

"A bath? It's not Saturday, Allie. You wash too much and you'll take cold. What brings this on?"

"Nothin'. Just feel like havin' a bath."

She threw off the covers and got out of bed. "Mr. Bastrop said they closed the mine. I didn't have any idea you'd be home or I'd have held supper. There's fried chicken under the drape on the table. Biscuits and gravy, mashed potatoes."

She wrapped up in papa's shirt and followed me into the big room. We moved the table out of the way so I could bathe up close to the stove.

I spread the tarpaulin on the floor. "Didn't intend for you to get up, Mama. Go on back to bed, now."

"You'll make a mess, Alan. Sit down and eat and I'll get you some more water. Let me put on my shoes."

"I'll go for the water, Mama."

I picked up the two well buckets and went outside.

Sid dozed on the porch and only stirred a little when I passed.

By the time I got back from the well, Mama had turned the wash tub on its side and rolled it onto the tarp. Waiting for the stove water to get hot, I sat down to eat.

"Let me heat up that food for you. You can't eat potatoes cold like that."

"They're fine, Mama. Sit down or go back to bed, now."

She eased herself onto a chair. "It's no trouble to heat it. You want some more bread?"

"That's all right. Tell me what you did today."

"Took care of Brother. Mended the wire on the coop. Washed the floor. Boiled the laundry and hung it out. Everything got dry in this warm weather. Worked out good for your bath, now, didn't it? Fresh union suit and overalls in the wardrobe. You boys sure do need some new work clothes. What you got is threadbare. I wish we could get to Ludlow. Things aren't so expensive down there. Got to have cash, though." She sat with her thoughts, watching me eat. "I'm worried about Sidney, swilling that medicine all day."

"You raised Cain this morning because he ran out."

"I know . . ."

"Didn't you hound me to get him some more?"

"Allie, why are you so upset?"

I took a deep breath and let it out. "I'm sorry, Mama. Sid's hard to take when he's sippin'. I wanted to punch him just now, the way he was yammerin'. He say ugly stuff to you?"

"No. I'd take it, though, if his cough got better. The medicine helps some, but he takes too much. When he's not sleeping, he talks wild, slurs his words, hallucinates. Wish we could get him a good doctor."

"Needs to go to Carbondale for the cure," I inserted.

"Oh, Lordy, we can't afford that, especially now with him not working," Mama said.

"I got me a regular man, if Sid can't come back. A Greek."

"That splits our wage, if you dig with somebody other than Brother. Still, the way he's coughing every other breath and crazy on the syrup, he's no good for digging, is he?"

"Naw. But *nobody's* gonna be diggin' with this inspection goin'. When they let us go back to work, I'll double up. Till then, Jack'll let me do odd jobs around the livery. Pays good."

"I hate for you to work for that awful man. Maybe Sid can get an outside job. Or I could take in washing and ironing."

Maybe, maybe, maybe–our favorite word. *Maybe* we'll make some wages soon, *maybe* the dust won't explode, *maybe* it'll hail nickels.

The water on the stove was steamy. I poured cold bucket water into the tub and mixed it with hot from the kettle. Stripped to my long johns and knelt to scrub my hands and face.

The water turned black.

"You're streaked, Alan. Let's pour that out and get you some fresh to bathe in."

Mama helped me dump the dirty water outside. We refilled the tub and I scrubbed some more.

"Wash your hair while you're at it," she said, pulling a chair up so she could instruct in comfort. "That place on your face hurt? It looks bad."

"Hurts a little. The way I been rubbin', I'm gonna wash it off. Face ain't . . . hasn't been this clean in a long time."

"Will you let me give you a shave? Lloyd always liked that after his bath."

"You can't see good in this light, Mama. How about tomorrow?"

"Just thought you'd sleep easier with smooth cheeks. I'll help you refill the tub, so you can finish in peace."

When we carried the water outside, Sid stirred and coughed.

Mama stayed outdoors with Brother and I closed the door. I fixed another hot tub, peeled off the underwear and lowered myself into the water, ass-first, legs outside. If Clara was here right now, she'd be scrubbing my back, pouring me a glass of whiskey, pulling off her floozies, straddling the tub. Got a woody thinking about it. Now, the damn thing was raring to go.

Sid was coughing harder, now. It sounded like a dull saw being pushed through a plank. Thought I'd get used to hearing it, but I didn't, because it wasn't a regular, constant noise. It made my chest sore to hear him.

The front door scraped open and Mama hurried in. "Brother can't get his breath. We got to steam him." She poured the kettle full of hot water into the bucket, covered it with a towel and ran back outside.

Jammed down in the tub so low, I had to pry myself out. I put on the fresh overalls, buckled one shoulder and went outside.

Mama had Sid down on all fours over the steaming bucket, towel thrown over his head. She held his forehead with one hand and patted his back with the other. But he kept coughing.

"Calm down, son," she said. "You got to breathe. Grab him around the waist, Allie. He's not getting any air."

I wrapped my arms around Sid and lifted, then let him back down onto his knees.

"He's gonna pass out if you can't get him to breathe."

Out of frustration, I jerked up on his stomach and Sid heaved into the bucket. After that, he breathed easier and we pulled him back to sit on the blanket.

"Hand me my med'cine," Sid whined.

Mama poured out what little bit remained in the bottle and threw it into the bushes. "You're out," she said. "It's back to whiskey and lemon for you, buster brown."

"That shit's no good," Sid said.

"Well, it's all you're getting here from now on," Mama said. "You want to sip, go somewhere else to do it." The foot had come down. "Henceforth, *Meyer's Liquid Heroin* is banned from the premises," she threw in for good measure.

I went in the house to get a shirt and socks. By the time I got back, Ida had dragged Cockeye over to see what the commotion was about.

I noticed that Cissy Cuminetti, the Giottos and the Costas all stood on their porches, looking our way. Privacy was scarce in Coalass Row. You couldn't fart in one house without somebody smelling it next door. Cockeye held a lamp and Ida went right to work, fretting and scripturizing.

" 'Come, and let us return unto the Lord, for he hath torn, and he will heal us; he hath smitten, and he will bind us.' "

"Let the boy breathe awhile, Ida," Cockeye said. "He can't concentrate right now."

But the woman was hard at it. She stooped to peer into Sidney's face. "The demons is pourin' out in his perspiry," Ida called. "Pile on the blankets, Ethel. Stoke up the fire and read scripture all night. Demons is what's makin' this boy cough. Got to drive 'em out." Ida looked from Cockeye to me. "Other sinners present best take heed."

Sidney leaned forward and puked on the busybody's button hooks.

"Oh, the end of days," Ida called, pointing at the vomit. "See what I told you? Demons erupting, from just that teensy bit of scripture."

"Time to go home, Snowflake." Cockeye tugged on her arm.

"Let go of me, man, 'less you want to sleep in the privy." Ida turned back to Mama, her eyes ablaze with conviction. "You want me to spell you, reading the gospel tonight, Ethel? I know verses just right for driving out these particular demons. Had to do it for my daddy."

Mama rose, damp and weary. She pulled the shirt down around her middle, raked strings of hair away from her face, spoke in little more than a whisper. "I'm much obliged, Ida, but I think we're capable of taking care of our own, here. Why don't you and Mr. Bastrop go on home?"

CHAPTER NINE
October 6, 1912

The fit of coughing, swilling medicine and soiling Ida's shoes must have exhausted Sid because he slept through the night and into the morning. Mama didn't wake me, either, so I got up late. She fried eggs and gave me a shave. By the time I mended some shingles that had come loose on the side of the house, fixed that scratching front door, ate lunch and then played catch with her, it was almost two o'clock. Hoping to divert any suspicion of my lusty intentions, I took my ball glove with me to town.

One thing coalasses in Delagua could do besides dig was play baseball. Games after work, all day on Sundays or days off. During down times in the summer, we played as long as daylight allowed. If you thought about what a miner did all day long–swing a pick or a sledge–you'd know why we could hit so good.

Almost as many women showed up for games as men. Mama had played softball as a little girl with her mama and sissies. In high school, she led her team to the state championship, two years running, as their star pitcher. Mama's most notorious pitch was "The Windmill," named for the rotations she'd take before firing at a batter. And it wasn't just speed that bamboozled. Since hitters never knew how many rotations Mama was going to make, they never knew when the pitch was coming.

When me and Sid were kids, Mama would throw the pitch only to Papa. After he died, we learned to catch her; but it cost us lots of sore hands, even wearing padded mitts. Everybody loved to watch her throw the pitch, warming-up. But the knotheads in Delagua refused to play with her if she threw "The Windmill" in a game.

I should have gone straight to the ball field or to McKintrick's, because I missed Clara completely. Couldn't have said howdy even if I'd got down there at the bust of dawn. Somebody had bought her for the whole day and took her off some place.

Out at the ball diamonds, two games were in full swing, with no openings for late-comers and not enough spectators for a third match. I watched for a while, hoping somebody would get tired or pissed off–or more stragglers would show–and I could play. But it never happened, so I went to McKintrick's. Being horny all the time spoiled everything.

I stepped inside the imbibery, looking like a king. Old King Coal, that was me. Only problem, my queen was out getting poled by some dude with more scrip than me. Bet he didn't look or smell as good, though. Bet his cheeks weren't shiny and smooth.

Everybody was working hard to float their boredom. A low ceiling of smoke hung just above an orgy of flailing arms and howling. Whores too scabby to work at Elma's fanned themselves and meandered, hoping to stir up some interest in going out back to a crib or at least buying them a beer. McKintrick dealt faro. And Monroe pounded the piano.

A new mahogany bar ran along the side wall. It had been arriving in pieces from Denver for over a year and just this week stood complete with brass boot rails and spittoons.

Jack's soap flunky, Charlie Delveccio, moved up and down the counter, swabbing, pulling off empties, serving beers, talking to customers along the way. A short, rambunctious wop with a handlebar mustache, waxed solid, and a white shirt with the sleeves rolled up over thick arms, Delveccio had been with McKintrick since the place opened. If you made trouble, Charlie had you removed, without regard for what part of your anatomy hit what part of the establishment in the exit. Kept a billy club under the bar and a knife in his boot in case of big trouble.

Cockeye slouched over the mahogany, staring into his mug and I wondered how he'd slipped out from under Ida's supervision. He could usually get away with a few beers at the end of a shift; but the risk of getting caught on a day off was so great, I was amazed he'd chance it.

Up front by the piano, Kistos sat straight in his chair, arms folded on his chest, smoking and visiting with Barba and some of the other Greeks. He looked different in a white shirt and tie with his hair slicked down.

A place at the bar opened up when the guy next to Cockeye poured beer on his other neighbor then smacked him with the empty mug.

Charlie threw himself across the counter, raised the billy and swatted the slugger until he went down. Both customers lay on the floor, out cold.

"Sombitches from Paine's rat hole," Charlie said, returning the billy. "Beer and a shot, Tanner?"

I nodded.

Two Mexicans appeared to drag the troublemakers outside.

"Ain't that curly-haired galoot the one you got into it with over Clara?" Cockeye asked.

I looked down at the feller who was sliding away. "Can't rightly say. I had a bad flu that night."

"I recall. 'Bout as sickly as I ever seen you." Cockeye grinned then cleared his throat. "Uh, Alan . . . you know . . . Ida . . . last night? She's like a music box. I just have to let her run down, sometimes." He paused. "By-gones?"

"Course," I said. "Mama's the same way . . . only different."

We snickered.

"Why ain't they perfect like us?" Cockeye asked.

"I can't figure that out."

Charlie pulled mugs of beer and poured shots of some swill McKintrick had got a deal on.

"Earl Bombat's Yukon Jack Sipping Whiskey," I read out loud.

Charlie nodded. "Jack buy 100 cases this week. So, drink up."

I kicked back the oily shot, winced and swigged my beer to mask the taste.

Cockeye teared up and hacked from just a sip. "Gol-lee, it's smooth, ain't it?"

Charlie grinned. "Can be used also to remove paint."

I chuckled while my neighbor wheezed. Pulled out a line of scrip and laid it on the bar. "How are the relatives in Italy?"

"*Bene, grazie*," Charlie said. "First sister write she have another baby. Make five." He wiped the bar. "You get down here too late for *scubata*, yes, Tanner?" Charlie smiled. "Pit boss take your tenderloin for a picnic."

"Which . . . that fuck, Chesterfield?"

Charlie nodded.

"Goddamn, I quit. How'd you know that?"

"Seen them leave town in a buggy. They look very sweet together." Charlie shook his head. "Love is hell, ain't she?"

Before I could respond, Charlie slid away from us.

"That cutlet's gonna break your heart," Cockeye said.

"I ain't in love with that whore, dammit," I said.

My neighbor grinned.

"You heard anything about work?" I asked.

"Inspector'll finish today, I bet."

"Eleven mines in a day-and-a-half? Ain't possible," I said.

"Skipping around. Seen him go into Number 9 first thing this morning."

"Shit, Cockeye, with that haywire eye, you see guys in two places at once."

Cockeye pinned me with the steady peeper. "You know, that ain't very neighborly, Alan, makin' fun of the afflicted like that. I say the inspector's almost finished. We'll be goin' back to work in two days at the most." He perked up a little. "Bet you a line of scrip." The idea of a wager always cheered Cockeye.

"Hate to disappoint you, buddy. Only got enough for a few drinks."

"Spent all your entertainment allowance at the poontang palace, didn't ya? You're headin' straight for heartbreak junction, my friend."

"Could you just keep your big honkin' nose out of my business?"

Cockeye smiled. "You hear that the inspector stayed at Elma's last night? I can just imagine him tryin' to sleep."

"Might have got some tail on the house, though," I said. "You have any idea what Kistos is doin' in here? Barba said he didn't drink."

"He plays some kind of fiddle thing," Cockeye said. "Performed for the Greeks last night and they convinced him to come up today."

"Think they might be funnin'?" I asked. "You'd know if anybody would." Greeks loved playing tricks. Barba threw a lit fuse in on Cockeye one time down at their station and Cockeye shit his overalls. Thought a stick of dynamite had been flung on him.

Cockeye watched Kistos. "Can't say for sure. But if your Greek's one bit suspicious, he ain't lettin' on."

"Kind of makes you feel sorry for him, don't it?" I said. "Looks like he's goin' to a funeral."

"Might be his if he ain't no good," Cockeye said, as Charlie slid back up to us. "That ain't no run-of-the-mill instrument, neither. Even if he can play it, who's gonna know what they're hearin'?"

Monroe climbed onto his bench and called for everybody's attention. Some guys hooted and wads of tobacco hit the piano player in the face and chest.

When it became obvious that Monroe wasn't going to stifle anybody, Barba rose. "Shut up, gumboots," he hollered. "We have a gift, if you would shut up."

This request didn't rest too well with some, but others were curious enough to listen. While the supporters shouted down the hooligans, Kistos took out his instrument.

Monroe encouraged the Greek to climb up on a chair, but he wouldn't have any of that. Stood up there with a fresh cigarette in the corner of his mouth, holding his music gizmo in front of him.

Cockeye was hot for a wager. "Bet you a line of scrip that somebody kicks that olive picker's butt soon as he draws a note."

Before I could remind him about my monetary shortage, Barba raised his hand and called, "You. Attention. Nicholas Kistos just come from Greece and he play this lyra last night. Can he play today, here?"

Seemed kind of silly to me, asking these morons anything like that. But guys hollered for the Greek to proceed.

Barba nodded. "Okay. This guy will play, now."

Kistos propped a foot on the chair that Monroe had offered and rested the lyra on his knee. First, he pulled the bow across the strings, drawing out some long, low notes. Next, he screeched some long high notes. I was jolted by how still it had gotten, like just before a frog-strangler. Shit, here comes a boot or a beer mug, I thought.

Kistos stopped the bow and looked around, like he was daring somebody to holler or throw something. When his eyes reached me, he nodded.

Music shot out in sparks. The tune spun, wild and fast, while Kistos's hand jigged across the instrument. He bent over for a little while, jig-jig-jig, snapped up straight, jig-jig-jig, finished with the slow melody he'd started with.

The lunkers detonated. Fellers clapped and hollered. Boots stomped and mugs clanked on the tables.

Kistos bowed, waved the bow over his head, played two more tunes, lit another cigarette and packed up. Men slapped his back as him and Barba sashayed through the rabble

Delveccio grinned. "Is a moment, by God. I get McKintrick to hire that sombitch."

"He don't drink, Charlie," I said. "Might not want to have anything regular to do with a sin-den like this-here."

Delveccio frowned. "You think an artist will not want to play where men can appreciate? I wager he can organize us a band."

Cockeye took the bet straight away. With the distractions gone, he sank back into the mood he'd been drinking himself into. The more he drank, the more pitiful he got. He whined about the strain not working put on our families. He slobbered about what good women Ida and Mama were and how we shouldn't be down here drinking up the last of our wages. Said again how sorry he was about Ida's behavior, but that was just her way. When he lit into me about whore mongering, I told him to hush.

The saloon began draining and I knew something was up.

Me and Cockeye walked over to the table where the mayor sat behind his stack of chips. A lunker parked next to him, filling out an IOU for his night's losses. When the unfortunate gamester left, we stepped up.

"Evening, Young Tanner, Bill." Jack picked up the deck and fanned it with one hand then closed the fan. "Your inspector has just entered the boarding house."

Cockeye got all smart-ass and I-told-you-so when he heard that.

"Just because he come back to the whorehouse don't mean nothin'," I said. "Maybe he's just tired."

"Bet you a line of scrip," Cockeye replied.

"*I* would not take that bet, Young Tanner," Jack inserted. "Abercrombie has gone for my John Deere to take Mr. Turnbull to Ludlow."

"I knew it," Cockeye said. "Why couldn't I get nobody to bet me? Let's get over there, boy. We don't want to miss nothin'."

I itched to cross the street, but was too hot for information from the mayor. I had an idea to check out.

"You go on, Cockeye. I'll be there directly."

He took off and I turned back to the mayor.

"Did you enjoy the recital?" Jack asked.

"Kistos? Pretty good, I guess. Don't know nothing about that particular instrument."

"Mystical . . . singular . . . ancient. Orpheus soothed savage beasts with a lyra. Think your compatriots would like to hear that Greek on a regular basis? I could hire him."

"Expect so, based on what we just seen. I'll be glad to introduce you two. Right now, though, I'd like to talk about something else. Got a minute?"

"Of course."

"Well, I don't think that clerk knows nothin' about mules, Jack. Why ain't one of your boys takin' the inspector?"

"Most scattered like ravens when they heard the word *inspection.* Lying up inebriated, somewhere, no doubt. I can't spare my bouncers."

"If Edgerton's little suck-ass ain't up to the chore, how would you feel about me takin' the inspector to Ludlow in your wagon?"

"Splendid, Young Tanner. What's mine is yours–you know that. But why would you want to assume that risk?"

I smiled. "Money-money-money."

"All right. Allow me to attend to a few matters here and I will join you across the street shortly."

Outside, I found Cockeye bobbing like a cork in a stinky sea of angry drunks. Abercrombie had pulled the wagon up in front of Elma's and the flood tide had him and his team engulfed.

You could tell right off the mules hitched to the John Deere might be trouble. Two small grays, always risky paired up. Experienced working men are leery about taking them into a mine. Grays are so naturally nervous, they tend to kick and bite worse than other breeds. Guys who don't know better get hoodwinked by an animal's size. Think that a cute little mule won't harm a fly. Shoot, they'll kick your ass into next month. Whoever traced these two didn't know anything about mules, didn't have much mules to choose from or was pulling a joke.

Two guards with shotguns in their laps sat on the porch at Paine's, but they didn't seem concerned about trouble brewing. Me and Cockeye pushed our way up to Elma's porch, where Kistos stood with Barba and the other Greeks.

"Inspection is finished, Bastrop," Barba hollered.

Cockeye nodded. "McKintrick told us."

When the inspector and Edgerton came outside, the herd closed in tighter and the uproar increased. The inspector lit a cigar and took in the bug eyes and besotted voices of Delagua's working men.

"Our babies are starvin', mister."

"We don't get paid for cleanin' up . . . we got to work."

Inspector stood with hands in his pockets, puffing and scrutinizing like an innocent bystander instead of the main attraction.

"Work, work, work, work," the chant went up, all spouting the same language for the first time.

Inspector closed his eyes and nodded understanding.

Edgerton flew off the porch and ran around the crush. To fetch the guards, I figured. In his sprint, the super almost collided with McKintrick who was crossing from the other direction.

"Work, work, work, work."

Throughout the protest, drunks had been shouting insults at Abercrombie. Several Greeks rocked the wagon wheels back and forth and the mules stirred up dust. The little suck-ass ordered the men to stop, but they kept right on. When a rock hit Abercrombie in the shoulder, he jumped down and scrabbled off, like the vermin he was.

"One, two, three, four . . ."

I could see the mischievous hand of Machito in this mule mismatch. Jack's hombre had jinxed the little suck-ass good and proper with these two.

". . . what's this damn inspection for?"

"They roughhouse too much and them mules is gonna get skitterish," I hollered at Cockeye. "Especially that littlest one."

"Work, work, work, work."

I stepped over to the team, holding up my hand so they could see it before grabbing a halter. I'd call the lead mule Maud and the other one Annie. They might have been called that before. You hear more mules with the names

Maud and Annie than anything else.

"Hey, Maud, look at you." I pulled down on her halter. "Ain't you a pretty one. And you, too, Annie. Prize-winners. Up now."

I led the team and wagon away from the turmoil just as the inspector yelled, "This is all for your own good. It's state law."

Boo. Hoot.

"I piss on state law," Barba shouted. "We have to clean and for no wage. Now, you say close down because of dust. You shit on us, you think we give you a party?"

"Work, work, work, work."

Shoving commenced from the rear and it looked like the inspector might be washed away by a wave of stumbling halfwits when something smashed into the street.

On Elma's balcony, two whores hung over the railing, whooping and crowing about the jar full of piss they'd just dropped.

The eager-beavers at the front knew another jar was coming and tried to retreat. But the pushing continued and fists flew.

McKintrick sauntered up. Guess he figured he could just make an appearance and the seas would calm. As he prepared to speak, a waterfall of piss drenched him. Then a pot came down. If he hadn't been wearing that marble-crown derby, he might have been killed.

Jack dropped like a lodge pine, anyway. Some howled. The rest tussled. The inspector backed up but stayed on the porch.

After the trial runs, the whores had a ball, running across the balcony, pouring out their soup and flinging pots. Every one of them seemed to have a jar to donate, too, because at one point it hailed crockery.

Meanwhile, I whispered sweet nothins to the mules.

The piss party drowned the uprising. By the time the law and Edgerton arrived, Elma and Lester had lugged the mayor inside and the mob had thinned. Seemed catastrophe had been avoided, when a shot gun went off. Guess the guards figured it was a waste of valuable butt time to get up from their chairs, cross the street and not fire their weapons. So one knucklehead had cut loose.

Roused by the shot, the gray closest to me brayed twice and kicked the floorboard out from under the wagon's seat. Maud's eyes looked crazy and I fought to pull her head down so I could flirt.

"Hey, baby." Head reared, socked my chin, rattled my teeth. I pulled again. "Maud . . . *Maud* . . . look at you. Look at you. You're calm, now, ain't you? *Look at you.*"

The little gray's head bobbed. She hooved, but stayed in one spot. The other mule shied a little.

"There, there, Annie. Maud's calm and pretty, ain't she? Yes, yes. Be calm, now. Look at *you."*

Cockeye crept closer. "You know you missed your calling, Alan," he hollered. Then he pointed at the superintendent and the guards. "Edgerton is sure strutting around with them guns to back him up. I ain't ever seen them guards so active."

"Likely offered 'em a bonus to get up," I said, stroking Maud and whispering to her. "Who's *Bill*?"

"Aw, that's what they called me growin' up," Cockeye said. "Jack picked up on it."

Edgerton and the two guards surrounded the inspector. The lunkers who were left looked around to see what others were going to do. A standoff like this could go either way and I planned to haul ass in the wagon if gunplay flared.

One of the guards hollered for us to clear the street.

"We have to dig and get our wage," Barba called.

Kistos jabbered something to Barba–just like me whispering in the touchy mule's ear. Barba turned and jabbered something back at Kistos. Kistos jabbered another thing. Barba looked at the inspector, then at Edgerton, then back at Kistos. Kistos stood there, calm as a deacon, holding his lyra case under one arm and smoking.

Barba mumbled something to the Greeks. Some grinned and nodded, then they started walking away, two or three at a time.

"You see that?" Cockeye called. "Your buddy is a goldang magician. Broke up a riot. I ain't never seen anybody calm Barba down without throwing a punch."

Before disappearing into the shadows, Kistos looked back, fixed me in his gaze and raised a hand. I waved and grinned.

The new world had arrived in Delagua disguised as an olive picker. Worked like a mule, said little. Won over hard cases, not with rough talk or muscle, but with friendliness, good humor, reason and neat feats. Played the lyra like a demon, to boot.

Like Barba said, watch out. When that man gets the language, he'll want to take over.

CHAPTER TEN
October 6, 1912

While the inspector stepped inside the boarding house to get his bags, Edgerton waited with the guards.

I gripped Maud's halter with one hand and stroked her forehead with the other. Cockeye said he needed to get home before Ida got too suspicious, but I planned to hang around.

"Jack said I could take this wagon to Ludlow if the suckass didn't work out. There might be some scratch in this, if Edgerton believes I'm a mule man."

"What are you gonna do?"

"Ain't sure, yet." I looked around for something that might rile the mules again. "Could you hold onto Maud's halter for a little while?"

Cockeye showed the mule his hand then slipped it under the leather strap as I pulled mine free.

Long pieces of livery straw lay scattered in the wagon bed. I picked up a bundle and sauntered over to talk to the superintendent.

"Hey, Mr. Edgerton. Remember me? Alan Tanner."

No response.

"I'm the guy you told that guard to shoot if the women didn't cooperate."

"I remember," the super said.

"Since your clerk took off and Jack's conked out, how you plan to get the inspector down canyon?"

Edgerton stared at me. "Why is it any of your business?"

"If that guy wants to leave and you ain't got a driver who can handle these mules, I might be able to help you out."

"Just let me deal with that, all right?"

"Guess he'll have to ride the coal train tomorrow, huh?" I asked.

"Oh, no. He's leaving tonight, in this goddamn wagon. He's ready to go and I'm ready to have him gone."

"With these mules?" I asked.

"Why not with them?"

"They ain't wagon mules, for one thing. And they're agitated. If they run with that rig down our road, that little J.D. will fly apart. And you'll only find pieces of your inspector."

"Let one of them chili-munchers take him," a guard piped up.

"McKintrick told me they're on strike," I said.

"How hard can it be to drive a wagon down to Ludlow?" Edgerton asked. "One of the guards can do it."

The laws gave each other sour looks, like the super had suggested they cut off a nut or something.

"Wouldn't let just anybody drive these-here mules," I said. "They got trouble-eyes."

Edgerton studied the grays. "Carl said they were the only ones the livery boy could spare. They look harmless enough to me."

Edgerton aimed to pat Maud's head. She pulled away from Cockeye and snapped at the superintendent. He jerked like she'd bit his hand off. The guards hid their chuckles.

"Goddamn, Mr. Edgerton . . . you okay?" I hollered, grabbing Maud's halter again and jerking it down. "Can't you hold onto this mule, Bastrop? I just got her settled."

Cockeye had fallen into the dirt, play-acting like a Denver hambone. "They're too much for me, Tanner."

With Maud calmed once more, I looked back at Edgerton. "See? Even an experienced man like Bastrop can't handle these two. They're cute. But cute can trick you."

"Yeah, Mr. Edgerton," Cockeye chimed in, getting up and dusting himself off. "They're dangerous."

"You're gonna need you an awful good and experienced mule man for this job," I said. "I could take the inspector out of town for fifty dollars."

Edgerton looked like he'd been hit with Lester's bat. "Fifty dollars? I wouldn't pay fifty dollars to get Senior Rockefeller out of town."

"Suit yourself."

The inspector emerged from Elma's smoking a fresh cigar. He dropped his bags in the bed of the wagon and joined us next to the mules. "So, who's taking me to Ludlow–this kid?"

"Just tellin' Mr. Edgerton I'd be glad to do it," I said.

"So, what's the holdup?"

"He wants fifty dollars," Edgerton answered.

The inspector gave me the once-over. "What makes you so special?"

"You fellers ain't never heard of 'Mule' Tanner?" Cockeye butted in.

"Best skinner in Delagua. Need you an inside man who knows his way around mules *and* a guy them immigrants trust. Think about it: in this situation, you got your ornery mules, your rickety wagon *and* your drunken Greeks and wops," Cockeye pointed into the darkness, "waitin' out there."

"Yeah," I took up, "them immigrants is pretty sneaky, slippin' around with knives and clubs. Bushwhacks around every corner. I'll be glad to transport the inspector down canyon for fifty real dollars–not scrip. Just give me a note to get us through the gates at Hastings and past any guards we might meet on the road and we'll be on our way."

The super studied me. "Looks like a smart boy like you would be nervous that some of those immigrants might slit *your* throat."

Cockeye interrupted again. "Shoot, Mr. Edgerton, Tanner knows Greeks almost as good as mules. That guy who pulled the lead hot-head off the inspector just now? Tanner saved his life yesterday up at Number 3. A Greek don't forget. Won't nobody touch a hair on this goozie's head. If we didn't already call Tanner 'Mule,' we'd call him 'ouzo'. This boy's your best bet, gentlemen–only bet, really. That's why he's worth fifty dollars."

Edgerton pulled the inspector aside.

I turned to Cockeye and whispered, "You laid it on pretty thick, there." Afraid he might have queered the deal.

"Just helpin' my neighbor. What you gonna do now?"

"Hide and watch. I got me one risky tack, in case they balk." I rolled the straws around in my fingers, getting them ready in case we hadn't been persuasive enough.

"The offer is ten dollars and a note," Edgerton said.

Slid my hand lower on the halter and made a little show of pulling Maud's head down–like she was being unruly again–then jammed the straws up her nostril.

The little mule screeched and bucked. Cockeye stumbled backwards. Edgerton and the inspector climbed on Elma's porch. The guards ran away, howling.

"Was afraid of this," I hollered. "Everybody stay back."

Maud kicked and bucked so much Annie got stirred up. At last, I got Maud's head down. When she tried to pull away, I jerked on the halter. We went on like that, with me jerking and Maud nodding, until she settled a little. Every time her head came down, I reasoned with her, working hard to show these guys that I was fit to control unruly animals.

Jerking and the soothing words did the trick with Maud and directly Annie took her cue.

The inspector was convinced. "*I'll* give you twenty-five dollars, myself, to get out of this hell-hole."

"You're crazy to take these mules any place," Cockeye called, sounding serious, now. "What riled 'em like that?"

"That stingy offer insulted her," I said, stroking Maud's nose. "Need another twenty-five from somebody. As you can see, this could be a tough job."

"Goddammit, Edgerton, pay him," the inspector thundered in a cloud of cigar smoke, "or I'll tell C.G. you held me hostage in a whorehouse."

"It's *you* holding *me* hostage, Turnbull," Edgerton said. You could tell by the way he stalled that he was licked. "I'll have to go to the office for cash."

I volunteered to give the superintendent a ride up, but he didn't want any part of me or the mules.

The inspector sat down on Elma's steps and smoked, while me and Cockeye comforted the team.

We hadn't been waiting but a few minutes when someone hollered from the shadows over by McKintrick's. It was Ida, calling her husband by his Christian name.

Cockeye trembled. "Dang, it's Sittin' Bull. Snuck up on me in the dark. Thank the Lord we wasn't in the bar."

"Yeah. Just standin' in piss-puddles in front of a whorehouse," I said.

"William Ernest," she shouted again, waddling into the light. "Why ain't you home?"

"Snowflake, we're in the midst of a crisis here. Why ain't you home with the children?"

"Ethel is watching them. You're gonna find out what a real crisis is if you don't come along. Bet you got liquor on your breath, too. Heed the Word: 'Be not among the winebibbers . . . for the drunkard and the glutton shall come to poverty . . .' "

"Ain't drunk no wine, Ida."

The little woman crossed the street, hand raised, spouting scripture. " 'Who hath woe? who hath sorrow? who hath contentions? who hath babbling? who hath wounds without cause? who hath redness of the eyes?' "

"Woman, will you hush-up." A defeated man, Cockeye looked back at me. "It's one of her favorite passages. Got it memorized."

" 'They that tarry long at the wine,' is who. Ethel's worried sick about you, too, Mr. Tanner."

"Got me a little moonlight job, Mrs. Bastrop. Taking the inspector to Ludlow. Be much obliged if you and William Ernest would tell my mother I'll be home tomorrow afternoon."

After Ida sniffed to see if she smelled a lie, she assured me she'd deliver my message. She marched Cockeye away, quoting scripture the whole time.

"That woman can't stand for a man to have any fun," I said to the inspector, trying to be friendly.

The feller stared up at the night sky, puffing his cigar like a locomotive climbing a steep grade.

CHAPTER ELEVEN
October 6, 1912

A breeze whistled up the canyon, as the inspector lifted his collar and settled in, rocking to the mules' gait. The wagon creaked down the narrow road, lit by one grimy carbide headlamp. My passenger fired up another cigar, puffed out a cloud of smoke, reached into his bag, found a bottle, uncorked it and took a swallow. Rude bastard didn't offer me a sip.

Made sense he'd be distracted, since he'd come close to getting his ass kicked or worse. But I saw no signs that he was rattled.

Halfway between Delagua and Hastings, we passed the lights of Chinkville up a side canyon.

"Up there you can get your liver carved out and your buddy might have it with his eggs for breakfast, next morning. I stay away from that place." I stuck out my hand. "Name's Alan Tanner. You're Turnbuckle, right?"

"Turn-*bull.* Gus Turnbull."

"Proud to meet ya."

Balls of fire flickered like cats' eyes in thirty coke ovens lining the bottom of the hills in Hastings. The inspector asked me to stop at the first saloon so he could buy another bottle of booze.

The smoke from the ovens stung my eyes. Bigger than Delagua, Hastings was a five-saloon, three-whorehouse town with eighteen mines. Clara could have come here for her day off. She might even be inside the joint my passenger had gone into. If she looked out the door, she wouldn't recognize me, white-faced from my bath and all wrapped up against the cold.

When Turnbull climbed aboard once more, he offered me the bottle and I took a swig, making the liquor bubble.

Familiar fumes rushed into my nose. I teared up, coughed and snorted. It was *Yukon Jack.*

I got the mules moving again without any trouble. The gates at the mouth of Hastings rose ten feet with strands of barbed wire stretched across the tops. Barbed wire, twisted in long, loose spirals, surprised you in the weeds on the perimeters. The companies didn't like having diggers roaming around or leaving a camp whenever they took a notion and the wire set a snarling trap.

The guard at the gate shined a light and called for identification. He read Edgerton's letter and waved us past.

We were crossing a plank bridge away from town when something rose from the railing and sailed off into the black pinyon. Me and Turnbull both started so hard the mules roused and gave me a little trouble reining them. The inspector was taking a drink and he leaned forward now, coughing and snorting.

"A dang owl," I hacked. "Scare you to death every time."

Turnbull barked awhile then wiped his nose on his sleeve.

"Gee, mules." I snapped Maud's ass with the reins and the mules stepped off again.

"Little grays," Turnbull observed. "Not worth a damn with a wagon."

"Tracin' them two was a joke, I imagine," I said. "You know that dude who got beaned, Jack McKintrick? This is his rig. His livery man paired these two."

"I recall an *A. J.* McKintrick who owned a saloon in Lafayette. Two-bit actor, known for Shakespearean scenes performed with a girl who worked for him. Big fish in a very small pond." Turnbull lit another cigar. "Getting hit with a chamber pot like that would have killed most men."

"Looked like a glancin' blow, where I was standin'," I said.

"That straw-up-the-nostril move was chancy back there, kid. I wouldn't have tried it."

"Noticed that, huh? Didn't concern you too much, I guess, since you're ridin' with me."

"I needed to get out of town and you seemed like my best hope," Turnbull said.

"That near-riot make you a little nervous?" I asked. "Them lumpies wanted blood."

"Nothing I haven't seen before," he said, "nor couldn't handle."

"Had you a rough couple days, though, huh?" I asked.

"I've had worse," the inspector said.

"Mm-hum. How was the stay at Elma's?"

"Better than most holes superintendents stick me in. Like a gingerbread house. There's furniture worth some money in there. You know the old tart who runs the place?"

Said I did.

"Proud in her way. Stuck me off in the back of the house, separate from the action. That's a regular tactic, putting an inspector up in a nanny shop."

"How'd we do on our inspection?" I asked.

Turnbull took a drink. "You tell me."

"You serious?"

"Sure. Go ahead."

"Okay." What did I have to lose? "Let's see . . . we're still careless and still smoking, ain't we?"

"Yep. Found butts and tobacco wads. Edgerton has them." The inspector held up the bottle and I took it.

"The weather's bone dry and the rock's crumbly and our luck's about to run out," I added.

"Right again. What about dust?"

"Gobbed so thick in every room, the mules could barely pull a car through. Could go up any second. All it needs is a source of . . . ignition."

"Very good. You're not sprinkling enough, either. Got a D- on housekeeping."

I took a swig and handed the bottle back. Figured he was gettin' about four pulls for every sip I took. Okay, though. I couldn't afford to get shit-faced with these particular mules.

"So if things are the same as they were two years ago and it's clear they ain't gonna change, why does the state waste its money on inspections?"

"It's the law."

I sniggered. "You saw how that proclamation went over with the lunkheads back there."

The inspector puffed his cigar. "Let me ask you something," Turnbull said. "Do you want things to change?"

He caught me by surprise. "Well . . . not really. I need to work."

"And you believe that without regulation you could work as many hours as you wanted, shoveling all the coal you had the gumption to go after. Isn't that true? Freebooting lives."

"Yeah, but . . . we keep gettin' slowed down or stopped by outsiders."

"You ever shovel rash on your own?"

"Sure, to get to the coal."

"What about when the mules can't pull cars through?"

"Yeah."

"That slows you down, doesn't it? What if somebody's foot gets run over by a car or a mule kicks him? Do you just let him lie there and keep shoveling?"

"No, of course not, but . . ."

"Helping somebody slows you down, doesn't it?"

He had me.

"How about an explosion that kills eighty-two men, a rescue, burials and an investigation. That doesn't just slow things down. Everything stops."

"Got it all figured out, ain't you?"

"I've been doing this a long time, Mr. Tanner. When my recommendations are heeded and conditions improve, mining is safer, laborers work more *and* America gets her coal."

"In what world, Mr. Turnbull? You think the Edgertons give a rat's ass about the recommendations you write? They hate inspections worse than we do."

Guess I had *him* because he shut up for a while.

The grays pulled us along at such a nice pace, I got drowsy. When the inspector took up the conversation again, he had to call my name to get my attention.

"Yes, sir?"

"I asked you how long you've worked in the mines."

"Seven years, inside. First dug with my papa when I was eleven. Before that, I worked part-time at the washer house."

"Your dad still alive?"

"No. Just me, a brother and mother, now. Was two sisters, but they and my papa died from the typhoid." Wondered if I was blabbing too much to this stranger.

"I'm sorry," Turnbull said. "Mind if I ask how your family ended up in Delagua?"

Deep breath, let it out. "Mr. Turnbull . . . what the hell do you care?"

"Just curious. Talking with working men, finding out what they're thinking, what their history is helps me do my job. Seldom find anybody who'll talk or has the time to do it. Tonight's different. You got opinions and aren't afraid to share them. And we got this long wagon ride."

"I ain't for the union, if that's what you're drivin' at. So, don't go back to Denver and tattletale me."

"You got everything ass-backwards, son. The state realizes that unions are a fact of life in Colorado. You have a labor secretary, now, and the governor sees the workers' side. UMW's headed this way, whether you like it or not."

"Well . . . I don't like it and I don't like your noseying around in my business."

"Hey, that's just fine. It's no skin off my ass."

I watched the mules' rumps and thought about the situation. Seemed like this guy was on the level, without any reason to use what I told him against me or mine. Tanners liked to talk and, I had to admit, it would feel good to unload some. Here was an opportunity to jaw with an official who might give me some valuable information and I was acting like a suspicious knucklehead. If nothing else, yapping would pass the time.

"Sorry for the outburst," I said. "Never met an outsider interested in us."

"It's okay. Most lumpies feel the same way. I don't blame you if you don't want to talk."

"No, I'd like to. Could I ask you a couple of questions first?"

"Sure."

"How'd you get into this line of work?"

"I grew up in Golden and my dad was superintendent at the CF&I mines up there. I went to college at Colorado School of Mines and got work with the state inspecting."

"You married."

"Not anymore."

"Were once, though, huh?"

"Twice. No kids."

"What happened?"

"To the marriages? My charm and great wealth weren't enough to keep the ladies at home." Turnbull took a drink. "I'm married to this job."

"How old are you?"

"Forty-nine."

"I'm twenty, a coal miner from birth. My folks came to Hastings, first, in 1890, the year my brother was born. Mama read about this new kind of coal town in *The Pueblo Chieftain.* Said that piece made Hastings sound like a worker's paradise."

"I remember. Big promotion in lots of papers that first year, even in Golden," Turnbull said. "Your folks lived in Pueblo?"

"Mama's family did. Papa grew up on a farm near Rocky Ford. You know where that's at?

"Yeah. Melon country," Turnbull said. "About 60 miles east of Pueblo."

I nodded. "Papa got fed-up with farming, so he stole grandpa's mule and rode it to Pueblo. Only job he could find was at the CF&I mill. My mother's pop was his boss."

"I've been to that mill a lot. What was your granddad's name?"

"Emanuel Sanger. They called him 'Preacher'. You know him?"

"Actually, I believe I did meet him one time. A kettle boss?"

"Yeah."

"So, your dad was a hurler," Turnbull said.

"He was." I laughed. "You know about that?"

"That is the *worst* job in the world, throwing in sacks of coal and shoveling manganese under cauldrons to boil the shank out of raw iron. It's a wonder those guys didn't catch fire." The inspector took a drink and gave me the bottle. "Just shows you what men will do for a paycheck."

"Yeah, for twelve hours a day, six days a week. Got paid by the number of sacks they threw in. Papa said coal mining was a sugar tit in a clean handkerchief compared to hurlin'. When me or my brother got in dutch or bellyached about somethin', Papa would threaten to send us to the CF&I." I took a swallow and handed the bottle back. Not much left.

"Some of the first mine inspections I did were in Hastings," Turnbull said. "Boy, was I green. Scared to go around a corner." The inspector puffed. "There weren't any saloons or hook shops up here. If a man wanted a drink, he had to dress up, go to the men's club and pay for the privilege of having *two* whiskeys. Of course, bootlegged liquor and sporting women could be found in the darkness."

"Mama said most things described in the newspaper was true, at first. Cute little houses, all in rows, flowers growin' in the dooryards. They had a baseball team made up of pick jockeys *and* swells. Women played, too. Victor-American gave picnics, ice-cream socials and dances. Traveling museum collections passed through. Even had a circus, one time."

"Actually, the company was called Victor Fuel then," Turnbull said. "A Trinidad businessman named Delos Chappell started the operation to compete with CF&I. Chappell thought if the company treated miners and their families right, they'd be happy and work harder. And wouldn't think about a union."

"That was before the strike in 1903 changed things, wadden't it?"

No response. *Yukon Jack* must have stupefied the inspector because he slumped forward all of a sudden. I caught him before he fell into the mules, but he dropped his cigar and the bottle of whiskey.

I reined and braked the team, carried the inspector around and flopped him into the wagon bed. Coat flap got pushed up and I saw a pistol, grip out, resting in a holster strapped to his left side. Get in a bind, shoot a few lunkers and the rest would scatter. Reason he was so calm in that stormy sea.

There was only one sip of whiskey left. I swallowed it, then flung the bottle into the weeds. Aboard the wagon once more, I roused the mules for the last push to Ludlow. With no questions to keep me yakking, I had to slap myself to stay awake.

Pulled into town just after ten, stopping in front of a saloon that advertised dollar rooms. Planks of light from the windows reached into the street. I expected a party with good-looking whores who would run out, drag me off the seat and have my overalls down before we reached the darkness.

But the railroad bump dozed on the prairie, with a piano sleep-walking and stray voices floating.

I had a time waking Turnbull, but finally he sat up, stretched and yawned. He pulled himself and his bag out of the wagon bed. "Mush obliged," the inspector said. "Get a room in here?"

"Yeah. It's awful peaceful, ain't it?"

Turnbull gave the town a quick glance. "Suits me just fine . . . ready for bed."

The inspector stumbled into the bar. I grabbed Maud's halter and walked the team to the livery stable.

CHAPTER TWELVE
October 7, 1912

Turnbull monopolized the bed and snored like a rooting pig most of the night. I slept on the floor, wrapped against the cold in dusty curtains I pulled down. When the first sprigs of dawn flecked the wall, I got up.

In the street, the smell of coffee and something cooking pulled me to a bakery. A little feller who spoke pretty good English ran the place. Seemed glad to have a customer and yammered like an old friend who needed to catch me up on things. His name was Harry Pagonia and he bragged about being the only baker ever run out of a coal town.

"Everybody is griping so I say make a union. Ruffians catch me on the way home from work and lay a pipe against my head–pop. So, I come here."

The bakery was bigger than it looked from the outside, with about twenty tables scattered around the deep room.

"Nice place," I commented.

"Is a café for lunch and dinner, too. You come back."

I looked over some cookies he had cooling on a metal rack.

"These is baklava–honey, thin pastry, walnuts. Delicious. You want some?"

"How much?"

"First one, free. Then you buy four more for fifty cent."

"We'll see about that." The doodad was tasty, but sticky. I bought four and a cup of strong coffee. The baker loaned me a mug, which I promised to bring back. Sipping coffee and nibbling a cookie, I walked to the depot.

From the platform you could see where the road disappeared into Delagua Canyon, west. Due south rose the gray and black mountains of Raton Pass. Northwest, in pastures across the tracks, cattle loped in fingers of sunlight, opening in a big hand across the hills.

I sat on a bench. Folks needing to get to Hastings or Delagua in a hurry would be coming up on the "Red Eye" from Trinidad and they wouldn't want to wait around for the noon train. A wagon ride would be dirty and chilly, but it would beat the train by over two hours. Be nice to have a rider or two to keep me company on the trip back home.

A whistle sounded a ways out of town. Soon, the cars appeared with a thin cloud of smoke trailing.

The train coughed up the grade into Ludlow station. The brakes screeched in wispy billows and the first passengers got off–company guys, probably, in suits and derbies. I'd need to call out to attract a rider, but yakking with swells still made me nervous. Lumpies stuck out like boils on a baby's rump around those dudes.

One of the last passengers to get off was a skinny girl, carrying two cloth bags and a hat box. In her flimsy dress, wide-brimmed hat and oversized brogans, she looked like a kid dressed in grownups' hand-downs. The girl clomped over to a porter, who was sliding a ragged trunk out of the freight car.

"Excuse me, sir," the girl said to the porter in some kind of foreign accent. "That's my only possessions. Some of the contents are very dear and fragile. Please take care."

The boy looked up, like he didn't care for her picky drift, then he eased the trunk onto a dolly.

While she searched her handbag for a coin, the girl asked about catching a train to Delagua.

"Coal train's the only thing runs up there and it ain't fit for a woman," the porter said.

The girl looked to be in her early twenties–about Sid's age–but it was hard to tell. She had milky skin and freckles across her nose and cheeks. Crimpy orange hair clung like cobwebs to the underside of the hat brim. This could be the perfect passenger to keep me company. I got up and stepped closer.

Porter gave me the once-over. "What do you want?"

"I work in Delagua. Got a wagon and I'm heading back up there this morning." I could tell the boy wasn't too sure about this girl going anywhere with a coalass.

I put my hand out. "Name's Alan Tanner." She had a sandpaper paw.

"Caitlin Broiles, Mr. Tanner. I'm going to Delagua to meet my husband. I'll pay a dollar for the ride."

"You can keep your money. It'll be nice havin' company. Got to get some things from the dry goods, first, then fetch the wagon. Make yourself comfortable here and I'll be back directly."

"Well, thank you, Mr. Tanner," the girl said and sat down.

Crossing the street to return the Greek's mug, I ran into Turnbull on his way to the station. He looked pretty ragged in the daylight, even walked with a limp. Had a cigar going already.

"Mornin'," I said. "What do I owe you for the room?"

"Not a thing. Charged it to my expense account." Turnbull smiled and glanced at the train.

"Well . . . okay, then. Don't want you to miss your ride."

"Walk to the station with me," Turnbull said, puffing his stogie. "You know a shit-storm is brewing, don't you? Your buddies in Delagua seem to."

"Aw, that was just drunks blowin' off steam. Won't amount to a hill of beans when we go back to work."

"You called it a 'near-riot.' I'm seeing that sort of thing in every mining camp I enter. I know everyone's opinion of me and what I do. But it's my job and I do it the best and fairest way I can. Here's the nut: things are changing all over and they're changing fast. And what I write down or what the companies think about it doesn't really matter. What matters is, do you lunkers give a good goddamn about yourselves, your families and friends?"

"Well, sure."

"Then you'd better make plans for what you'll do after the last straw leaves the broom." The train whistle sounded and Turnbull put out his hand. "You're a good kid, Tanner. The story you told about your family's struggles makes my point. You got a right to dig coal safely and make a good wage doing it. I hope things work out for you."

"For you too," I said. And he limped up the depot stairs.

Goddammit. Here I was with a pocket full of jack and a red-haired girl to keep me company and that bastard had stuck me with a new batch of worries. Wished I hadn't run into him.

The girl was sitting right where I left her, smoking, and she caught my eye and waved. "Is everything all right?" she called.

I worked my way down the platform. "Sorry, Mrs. Broiles. I ran into a friend. Give me a little while longer. Or . . . you could come along."

"I'll stay with my trunk. Take your time."

The dry goods store was cool and dark inside. A lady raising window shades at the far end of the room said to let her know if she could help.

I'd got so used to being treated like trash at the pluck-me, hospitality made me suspicious. I figured that when the lady saw a slag monkey standing in her store, she'd tail me like a copper on a crook. But she only came up after I'd filled her countertop with treasures.

Six pairs of overalls, six shirts, twelve pairs of socks, a sack of oranges, a *Scribner's* and *Century* for Mama, a pound of peanut brittle, a pound of licorice and some new boots. Two cans of tomato juice, a wedge of cheese and a tin of crackers for lunch. Even got some cloves for sour mouth.

"Will this be all, sir?" the woman asked, wrapping my purchases in brown paper. Her face and hands were sun-dark and leathery, odd for a shopkeeper.

"Yes, ma'am. I need to try on the boots, though. You got a box for the food?"

"Right back here, I believe. You can sit over there to try the boots."

A tight fit, the new boots might give me blisters if I wore them too long. But I wanted to make a good impression on my passenger, so I left them on. I tied my old boots together and hung them over my shoulder.

The woman had lunch boxed for me on the counter. "Boots okay?"

"Kinda stiff. You know how it is."

The woman came around from behind the counter and knelt to check the fit. Brown hair in a bun. Wide back, narrow waist. Gingham dress. Pretty little chain around her tanned neck.

"Can you wiggle your toes?"

"Yes, ma'am.

"Do they slip on your heels when you walk?"

I stepped across the room and back. "Left one some. Ain't too bad. Just tight in places."

She stood. "Seems like a pretty good fit. If you're in a hurry to break them in, my dad says, 'Get 'em wet and wear 'em till they're dry.' Patience isn't his strong suit, though. It'll just take some time. Can't bring them back if they're scuffed up."

I nodded. "What do I owe you?"

"Forty-seven sixty."

The cash came out of my pocket, magical in its green crispness, floating between me and this town lady. The swift exchange dizzied me. No haggling about what a particular line of scrip was worth, here. In Ludlow, a dollar was a dollar and the man who carried it was treated with respect.

"Two dollars and forty cents is your change. Come again when you're in town." The lady smiled and I grinned back.

Foot and wagon traffic had perked up on Main Street. The train whistled twice to call its stragglers and a couple of guys with little suitcases held their hats and hurried along. A kid on a bicycle shot out of an alley and nearly ran me down. Back home, he'd have got his ass kicked for that.

Hobbling to the livery with my booty, feeling so good in spite of the tight boots and the conversation with Turnbull, I waved at the engineer when the train chugged past.

Gabey's Horse and Mule Barn sat between the railroad tracks and the Ludlow road, north of town. Worn out and half-asleep the night before, I'd broken down the team, wiped off and stalled my mules in dim lantern light without paying any attention to the size or shape of the place. But now I could see the operation.

The livery man took me back down the path between two long rows of painted stalls. Mules or work horses filled most of them and a perfume of shit, wet hay and animal flesh hung in the air. Reminded me of Machito's.

Most of the animals were awake and rattling around. They shook heads and swished tails, brayed and whinnied, pissed and farted, brushed up against walls and gates, hankering to go somewhere and do something.

Behind the barn a dozen wagons sat in two rows. This had to be The Chamber's drop-off and pick-up station.

"Got you a fine place here, mister."

"Thank you. Actually belongs to Clement Haddock." He pointed across the tracks to the pasture land I'd been admiring from the depot platform earlier. "That's his spread out yonder. I'm Oliver Gabey. Mr. Haddock lets me run this place."

"Proud to meet ya, Mr. Gabey. Alan Tanner here. You know Jack McKintrick, by any chance? Figured them wagons out back might be his."

"Yeah, I know him." Gabey replied. "Leases the space from us. He still have that good-for-nothin' blind mule?"

"Old Grady. He's our good-luck-charm. Saved at least six lives in the explosion."

"Waste of stall space, if you ask me," Gabey said.

Some of the other beasts' friskiness had rubbed off on Annie and I had trouble leading her out of the stall. She shook her head and stepped away when I tried to halter her. Then she moved sideways, pinning me in a corner until the livery man came inside, turned her all the way around and led her out.

With the mule harnessed, I tied a length of rope to the noseband and walked her around in the yard, in case she needed to let go with a buck or two before we hitched her to the double tree. After three approaches and three balks, we got her into the traces.

Maud, on the other hand, came out calm as a nag on a flying jenny. When we hitched her to the tree, though, Annie brayed and kicked a few more splinters out of the footboard.

Gabey pulled down on Annie's halter, whispered in her ear, then looked back at me. "Mojito trace these two?"

"Yeah. Done it as a joke on somebody, I think." I gave Gabey my last two dollars and climbed aboard. "They ain't too bad once you get 'em moving. Just takes patience."

"You'll do. Up, mules," the livery man hollered. "See ya next time, kid. Tell Jack I said don't take no wooden nickels."

Back at the depot, we loaded the trunk and bags, then I helped Mrs. Broiles onto the seat. "Sorry this wagon don't have much of a footboard. Got a couple of nervous animals. We can rest our feet along the ledges here, if we're careful. Up mules." I snapped the reins on Maud's ass and we were off.

The girl sat up real straight. With some fattening up, she might have a nicer shape. I asked her where she was from.

"I grew up on the seacoast in Cardiff, Wales. My husband and I came over three years ago. We lived in Boulder. The union was taking over and he heard the freebooting was better down here. So he came ahead of me. You might know him–John Broiles, a tall man with long, curly black hair and a beard. Loves to gamble."

"There's eleven mines with day and night shifts and about four hundred diggers in Delagua," I said. "I don't know half the guys up there. Why didn't you come down with your husband?"

"I had some things to take care of."

"Like what things?"

"Aren't you a nosey little bleeder?"

"Just curious."

She didn't say anything for a while. "Johnny abandoned me is why. Woke up one morning and he was gone. It took me three months to pay off our debt to the store. But I wanted to find my husband. They got payrolls in Trinidad and he was listed in Delagua at Victor-American's mine Number 11."

Pretty smart of her finding him this way, I thought. "That's the one way up in the hills. Like another little town, up there. I wouldn't know him if he works at Number 11."

"Johnny's eel-slippery. He might escape again before I can nab him."

"What if he ain't up there no more?"

She shrugged. "There's always jobs for a girl in a mining camp."

"Yeah. I'm sure you could get on washing coal."

She giggled. "Well, you're quite the flatterer, aren't you?"

My face burned. "Sorry."

"It's all right–I know what you meant. I *did* wash coal when I was a girl and could do it again. I'll worry about all that after I find Johnny Broiles."

She dug in her pocket book and pulled out a ready-roll cigarette, struck a match, cupped her hand around it to block the wind and lit up. "Have a smoke?" she asked.

"Never took it up. You won't see too many women smoking cigarettes in Delagua."

"Watch the road there," she pointed, ignoring my comment. "You're heading for a rut."

"Haw, Maud." The mule pulled left.

This girl was feisty, interesting. I wondered what might lie ahead of us if she didn't find that husband.

CHAPTER THIRTEEN
October 7, 1912

It was highfalutin, bringing this pretty girl into town. Didn't any of the knotheads on the street have to know right then that she was married and not my little private slice, come-by in Ludlow. I could get a girl like her if I wanted.

I steered the wagon to the west end of town, where the railroad looped back on itself and the Victor-American building sat. The red brick two-story housed offices, a ballroom, the pluck-me store and the Edgertons' upstairs apartment.

I reined the mules under a cottonwood and jumped down, intending to come around and assist Mrs. Broiles. But the girl reached the ground before me.

"Could you guide me to the lavatory?" she asked.

I tied the team to the tree. "Lavatory?"

"Yes," she answered looking around. "You must have a public facility of some sort. I need to piddle."

I grinned. "There ain't no lavatory. Women don't go where men do up here."

"And where do men *go*?"

"Over there," I said, pointing to Paine's bar. "There's three privies behind that building. But women ain't . . ."

She marched away.

". . . allowed."

"So," Cockeye called as he ambled up. "You're back from bigtown. You see the elephant?"

"Missed him." I walked toward Paine's rat hole, figuring it would be a good idea to keep a lookout for the girl. Cockeye accompanied me.

"Stepping kinda careful there, ain't you? Them new kicks?"

"Yeah, if it's any of your business."

"They're so pretty and shiny, ain't sure I'd wear 'em in a mine." Cockeye pointed at the outhoues. "Found you a sage hen down there, huh?

Taking up the sportin' life?"

"She ain't no whore, Cockeye." The girl had reached the first outhouse and gone inside.

"Needs to broaden up that beam if she intends to spend any time on it. Ain't got no titty bumps, neither, that I can see."

"You won't never find out. She come up lookin' for her husband."

"Uh-huh. Using the gentlemen's johnny to boot. You tell her that's against the rules?"

"Tried to, but she's a hardhead and you can't tell a hardhead nothin'. Where do women do their business, anyway?"

"Slop jars in their rooms, I reckon," Cockeye said.

"What if they need to go out in public?"

"Just hold it, I guess, Alan. Never give it no thought."

"Me, neither, till just now."

A lumpie came out of the bar and headed straight for the girl's shack.

"Hey, that's occupied," I hollered.

"Why's it your business?"

"My brother's got the runs and he asked me to keep a watch-out. I wouldn't go openin' that door if I was you."

The feller found an empty and went inside. Couple of minutes later, Mrs. Broiles came out.

When she reached us, I introduced her to Cockeye. She shook his hand then turned to me. "Would you be so kind as to watch my belongings while I go inside?"

"You ain't gonna just walk right in up there, ma'am," Cockeye said. "There'll be a guard."

"We'll see about that," she said and pranced off.

"This could be good," Cockeye said.

We followed the girl through a gaggle of rubbernecks. Just as we reached the steps at the V-A building, Sloan staggered around the corner toting a box of groceries. When the boy saw his papa, he reeled over.

"Goddern, there's that caretaker," I said. "Just wasn't out where I could see him. Hiya, Sloan."

"Hi, Mr. Tanner," the boy mumbled. "Papa, I got to tie my boot."

Cockeye took the box, advising me to mind my business. "Let's sit here a little while, son, and watch this lady. Might be a scuffle."

The kid seemed interested.

The girl was almost to the porch, now. The batch of nitwits closed in around us and waited at the bottom of the stairs to see what she was up to.

"You better stop your kewpie doll, Tanner," Mack hollered. "She's about to get in trouble."

"Tryin'-to-go-in-the-front-door kind of trouble," Tommy expanded.

"She ain't a goddamn kewpie doll." I pushed through the lunkers and started up the stairs.

The girl turned around. "What is it?"

"Thought you might like some company."

"I'll handle this myself."

"Come on, now."

"Are you deaf, son?"

"Suit yourself," I said, but stood fast about mid-way up.

Mrs. Broiles went through the front door and was brought right back out by Edgerton's little suck-ass clerk, Abercrombie.

She jerked her arm away. "I'm just looking for my husband, tiny. Let me go."

Reference to his size in front of us low-lifes didn't suit Abercrombie and he reached for her again, figuring that she'd be moved along with a little push. But before he could touch her, she cuffed him so hard in the jaw his glasses flew off and hit the wall.

Whoop . . . whoop!

Abercrombie grabbed the girl's wrist and she kicked his shin. The suck-ass hollered, let go and rubbed his leg. Mrs. Broiles circled around, but the clerk caught her around the waist.

Get him, cupcake!

I climbed the steps.

Let 'em fight, Tanner!

The pair was a tangle of slapping and cussing and I reached them just as Edgerton came outside.

"What is this?" he hollered.

I grabbed ahold of the girl's arm. "Could you pull off your man, here, Mr. Edgerton?"

Let 'em fight!

The superintendent scowled as he grabbed the clerk's coat collar. "Carl, let go. Let . . . go."

We got them separated, but Mrs. Broiles shook me off. A sleeve was torn away from her dress and her hat was smashed. Hair had uncoiled and strings of it clung to her face.

The clerk covered his bloody nose with a handkerchief. He pointed around the super at Mrs. Broiles. "I should kill you, bitch."

"Kill your grandma, tiny. You ruined my hat."

Whoop!

Abercrombie lunged at her, but Edgerton pulled him away, again. "All right, that's enough. Get out of here, for Christ's sake, Carl."

Go home, you little suck-ass . . . you're whupped!

Mrs. Broiles advanced. I pushed her back and she slapped my hand away. "I told you this isn't your affair."

That made me mad. "Why don't you calm down, little girl?"

Boo-o-o-o!

Thought she might hit me, but she just spouted off. "I came up here to find my husband and I can't get in because I don't have the snooty airs and clothes of a company lady to come in the front door. That little bastard nearly tore my dress off. And now you're pestering me."

Tell him!

"You're a hard person to be friends with, Mrs. Broiles." I snatched the hat, poofed it out and handed it to her.

"Where do you come into all of this?" Edgerton asked me.

The girl didn't let me answer. "I needed a ride up from Ludlow and he offered. My name is Caitlin Broiles. My husband is working in mine Number 11. Help me find out where he's living and I won't bother anybody anymore."

Edgerton hustled us inside.

Boo . . . boo-o-o-o!

It was the first time I'd ever entered the building through the front.

"Um . . . come to my office where we can talk. I don't have much time. Officials from Victor-American on their way."

No wonder he was in such a hurry to clear his porch. Wouldn't want the mucks to happen onto a rumpus. "Is the vice-president comin' back?" I asked.

"Uh . . . no . . . I don't think so." Edgerton acted like he forgot I'd met his pop. "You put Turnbull on his train?"

"First thing this morning."

"You know, you had me over a barrel or I never would have given you that money. I hope you spent it on something worthwhile."

"Whiskey and dope in Chinkville."

The girl snorted.

Edgerton glared at me, then turned back to Mrs. Broiles. "You said you know where your husband works?"

"He's listed as John Broiles, at Victor-American 11. Been up here for at least three months. He doesn't know I'm coming, Mr. Edgerton. I need to find out where he's living so he doesn't slip out on me again."

"All right," Edgerton said. "I'll have to look on a pay manifest and guess who has it in his office? The fellow you just had the fight with. I'll go check it. Take a seat there. I'll be right back."

Mrs. Broiles sat, fiddled with her torn sleeve, then looked at me. "You got to perform sometimes to get your way."

I wondered if her easy-going ways and nice manners, in Ludlow, were just flapdoodle to get what she wanted from *me*.

Edgerton seemed even more agitated when he returned. "We have a problem, Mrs. Broiles, so I'll get right to the point. No other way around it. Your husband is dead. He was killed last month. The body was found in the hills, outside the perimeter. He'd been stabbed."

"Oh, my God," Mrs. Broiles sighed and, real or fake, started crying. She pulled a hanky out of her handbag, sniveled, dabbed for a little while, then tilted her head back and drew a breath. "Any idea who did it?"

"None. Things like this happen in coal towns."

"I'm not surprised, really. Johnny could be a scamp. Quick with a mean word or a slap, always in fights." Her eyes were still wet but her voice had steadied.

Edgerton took a seat behind his desk. He pinched a loop of string and turned it around on his fingers. "Your husband was something of a rabble-rouser."

Caitlin nodded. "He liked to scrap. Some he got on with, some he didn't."

"Was he a union man in Boulder, Mrs. Broiles? We have reason to believe that the union is being brought into the southern fields from up north."

"Johnny? No, sir. We left Wales in the first place because of the strikes that had been on for over two years. It got so nobody could go to work anymore. In Cardiff we heard about the coal in Colorado, how you could dig all you pleased without the threat of strikes or union regulations. We came to Boulder and soon the same thing was happening up there–men beating each other up instead of digging coal. I woke one morning and Johnny had run off. I found out from one of his friends that he'd come down here to freeboot. My husband was a deserting louse, Mr. Edgerton. But he wasn't trying to import a union into Delagua. He hated unions."

"I hope not, because that's a *very* serious thing. We're trying to avoid the kind of trouble down here they're having up north. Violence and property damage follow union men. When they say they care about you people, that is hogwash. What they want is anarchy–to overthrow the government of this country. And if they ruin good jobs and destroy property in the process, well, even better for them."

Edgerton was killing two birds with one stone now, giving me a little warning that I'd carry back to the slag flunkies *and* dunking for the girl's opinion.

"I understand exactly what you're saying," Mrs. Broiles said. "I've known my share of union men, Mr. Edgerton, all of them lazy bums."

"Well . . . this boy here will take you to the cemetery. Then, I suppose you'll be on your way?"

She wiped her eyes. "I'm nearly broke, sir. By the time I pay John's burial expense, I won't have a thing left. I couldn't even buy a ticket out of town on the coal train."

"No one here expects you to pay for John's burial expense. Victor-American has already taken care of that."

"That's so kind of you, sir." She dabbed her eyes again. "I'm not one to take a handout. But I'm going to need some work, even if I don't have to pay for . . . Johnny."

Edgerton studied that string like it was going to tell him what to say next. "Perhaps we could make a deal for a position. You're pretty lively, Mrs. Broiles. If you can hold your temper, I'm sure you'll make friends fast. And it sounds like you can sniff out union men. If you see or hear anything, you think you might let me know?"

She blew her nose. "I'll do what I can to help."

"My wife has been looking for someone to clean and do chores for almost two years. We don't get too many clean, white girls through here. I'll talk to her and see if she'd like to meet you."

"That would be very nice, Mr. Edgerton."

"What will you do about a place to stay?" the super asked.

"Well . . . we have room . . . I think. Have to check with Mama, first. But I imagine she'd be glad to have a boarder."

Mrs. Broiles patted my arm, sniffed and wiped her nose. "This began so awful, finding out about Johnny and all. Now, I might have a job and a place to stay. I feel terrible about rough-housing on your porch, Mr. Edgerton. I need to watch my temper."

The super rose and came around his desk. "Didn't hurt for Abercrombie to be taken down a peg. Frankly, I got a kick out of it." He patted the girl on the back and his hand lingered a second. "Help me out and I'll do what I can to return the favor."

Mrs. Broiles smiled and thanked him again, then Edgerton ushered us out the back door.

CHAPTER FOURTEEN
October 7, 1912

After we visited her husband's grave, I took Mrs. Broiles home. Mama had the old brown hen cornered in the pen and she didn't notice us at first. She caught the bird by the neck, jerked quick, spinning it, popping off the head. The carcass sprinted, blood spurting.

The girl wore a funny look.

"You never seen a chicken's neck wrung?" I asked.

"Plenty of times–by *my* mum."

Mama looked our way, shielding her eyes with her hand.

"She'll need a few minutes to digest your arrival. Just wait here."

I pulled the wagon under our cottonwood for shade, then got down, tied the team and walked to the pen. On the way, I pondered what to say. The girl would be paying room and board. With Sid sick, it made sense that she should come live with us right now. But it wasn't *Mama's* idea. I could already hear her scolding me for putting her in a "position" where she couldn't say no. I'd need to act stupid, sad and sorrowful.

"Very nice boots, sonny boy," Mama remarked. "You throw your old ones away?"

"No, ma'am, they're in the wagon. I bought these with the money I earned takin' the inspector down. Didn't Ida tell you where I went?"

"Told me. I was just commenting. You get a good fit? Don't want to hear any bellyaching about blisters."

"They fit okay. Bought overalls and shirts and you some goodies, too."

"Get that girl at the dry goods store?"

"Yessum. Hanging on a nail. Mama, she's just found out her husband was killed up near Number 11. Now, she's all alone. Thought a boarder might be a good idea, since Sid's not working."

"A female boarder."

"Yes, ma'am."

"With you two roosters pecking around."

I stared at the ground, putting on my pitiful face.

"You are pathetic, son."

"Whaddaya mean?"

"Expecting me to swallow that baloney about a boarder to help us out. You want that girl close so you can sniff her out. She might take a shine to Sidney, you know."

"Listen. Me and that girl don't agree on much of anything. Got that straight already."

"*That girl and I*, Alan," she corrected.

"Dang. I'm just tryin' to earn us a little money. If it's gonna hairlip the governor, Edgerton can deal with her. Not squat to me."

The hen had played out. "Looks like this old girl's ready. She just quit laying, all of a sudden." Mama picked up the carcass and walked back to me. "Would have been nice to have a warning so I could think about it. You know what position this puts me in, with her already here, don't you? You should have asked me about this first."

"When was I supposed to do that?"

She pointed the hen's feet at me for sassing. "Just remember in the future."

"Mama, dern it. I got to make some decisions concerning this family sooner or later, don't I?" I pulled back a corner of the chicken wire so she could step out of the pen.

"Don't have to be cheeky about it. She looks real skinny. Could have a disease or anything. You don't know."

"Want me to take her back to town?"

"You can't do that. You've got us into this, now. What'd you say her name was?"

"Mrs. Broiles is all I remember."

"Well, bring her to the porch and we'll talk."

* * *

By the time I got back from returning the wagon, a pot of beans was cooking and the house had a nice, steamy pork smell to it. Mrs. Broiles had plucked the hen and cut it up, while Sid peeled potatoes.

After Mama put the chicken in to bake, she made coffee and I laid out the bounty from the dry goods. Everybody sampled the candy and Sid tried on one of his new shirts. Mama and Mrs. Broiles scanned the contents of the magazines. I harnessed all my story-telling talents to make my trip to Ludlow come alive. While I gesticulated, mimicked voices and sounds, sketched vivid, hilarious pictures of the adventure, the girl pitched in tidbits about our meeting and my kindness. Neither of us mentioned the fight with the clerk or the deal with Edgerton. Did tell Mama that Turnbull had met Granddaddy Sanger, though. Said she wished she could have spoken to the inspector about it.

When the food was ready, we all ladled beans over slices of cornbread. Mama put the plate of baked chicken and fried potatoes on the table and we sat down. I figured we'd start eating right off, but Mama got back up.

"What is it?" Sidney asked.

"I have an onion. Ida gave it to me this morning. It'll be real nice with the beans." She came back with the onion and a knife, which she laid on the table. But she didn't sit down. "Does anybody need anything else? Doesn't seem like we're having much."

"Sit down, now, Mama," Brother said. "You're making me nervous."

"Well, I was just trying to get everything right, Sidney. Please return thanks."

After the blessing, we passed the pans.

"Certainly looks tasty, Mrs. Tanner," the girl said.

"I'm Ethel," Mama said. "Mrs. Tanner was my mother-in-law."

"And I'm Caitlin," the girl returned with a smile.

"What's it like living in Wales?" Sid asked.

"Cold and rainy . . . windy and briny on the coast. Up north, there's mountains and green, rolling dells with cattle. Mum said it used to be that way in the south, too, until they found coal and iron a hundred years ago and stripped everything bare to get to it. My pa was a collier up the Rhondda River Valley in Caerphilly. The only time we saw him was when he ran out of money or suffered remorse and went on the wagon. Pa would shave, put on his suit and come down on the train. He liked the seacoast. Said the air was good for his lungs."

"Sidney needs him a seacoast," I said, through a mouthful of chicken.

Mama shot me a look that said, "Don't talk with your mouth full."

Caitlin smiled. "When Pa came home, my brothers and I would dance around the room till the windows fogged. Mum would ask him if he was home for good. He'd hug us all and say nothing lasts forever. Due time, he'd get restless, you know, pinching mum for a shilling so he could go to the wharf bars. He'd get worse and worse, slouching home pissed and bruised every night. Soon, he was slapping us for any little thing. There would be a row and sometimes the brothers got into it. He'd disappear, back to the mines. Mum lived like that for at least ten years, with him going and coming."

"And your family is still in Wales?" Mama asked.

"Yes. Mum and my two brothers live in Cardiff. She sews for a little money. One brother is a sailor and the other a bookkeeper for a shipping line.

My pa–his name was Walter–he got killed in the Tonypaddy Riot in 1910, just after . . . Johnny . . . ," voice quivered and her eyes filled with tears. She sniffed and dabbed with her napkin. ". . . after Johnny and I came across. Union troubles."

"I'm so sorry," Mama said.

"It's all right, Ethel. I don't mind talking about it. It's pretty interesting, really, seeing what men will go through to get some rights."

"What rights?" I asked, sopping up bean juice with my cornbread. "All a union's good for is gettin' guys hurt. We tried it before. Doesn't work."

Mrs. Broiles tilted her head, like she didn't exactly agree with me. "My pa used to say God gave the rich the coal and the poor the union."

"Same as here," Sid broke in. "We have to scratch for every little thing. A union might be the only way to get any respect. Alan's got other things on his mind."

Mama gave him a "hush-up" look, wrinkling her eyebrows and frowning.

"What?" Sid asked her.

"Supper table isn't the place."

"No place is the right place," Sid said. "Things aren't just gonna change by themselves."

"We're not discussing it now, Sidney," Mama said.

* * *

After the dishes were done, Mrs. Broiles brought out a music box and wound it. A tune tinkled. "It's called 'Cockles and Mussels.' Mum gave me the box when we left Cardiff."

Me and Sid listened to the music like real appreciators. When the box finished, she wound it again and, this time, sang the words. Had a pretty voice.

"Where'd you learn to sing like that?" Mama asked.

"From my mother. You can soak up all kinds of music in a wharf town–church hymns, folk songs, sheet tunes, even opera. Puccini is my favorite."

"Would you sing opera for us?" Mama asked.

"Ethel, I would be honored."

This time, Caitlin cranked up the volume, hitting high notes that made the loose window glasses buzz. Sang in Italian, so I had no idea what she was saying. But something about hearing it made me feel serious and smart.

When she finished, we clapped. Then, Mama shooed me and Sid so Mrs. Broiles could put her things away and get ready for bed. She and Mama would have to sleep together till we found another cot.

Outside, I lit into Sidney. "You think your hooey's gonna impress that girl?"

"What the hell are you talking about?" he asked.

"That shit about a union gettin' us rights and respect ain't gonna raise her skirt."

"You're the one dragged her up here, Alan."

"I dragged her up here because you ain't workin', idget, and we need the money."

"You really don't think we need a union?"

"I'm doing just fine with the way things are," I answered.

"A pinhead can see they ain't fair."

"Remember what Mama says about *fair*?"

" 'Fair day comes but once a year. And that's not today,' " Sid said. "That never settled you down none, as I recall."

"Well, I'm older and wiser now."

"And a lot more stiff-necked. A union for the southern fields ain't such a far-fetched notion. Only way to fight back is organize."

"Fight back with what–sticks and words? Didn't you hear what that girl said? Her papa was killed in a union riot. Her and her husband come across the *ocean*–then left Boulder–to get away from the damn union, up north. The husband gets killed in Delagua and the first thing Edgerton wants to know was Broiles tryin' to import a union down here."

"Don't mean it ain't the right thing. Wouldn't be unions nowhere if they didn't make things better. Why are you so closed-minded?"

"Papa tried organizing. Spent a year in a tent–six of us. He had the same complaints you do and nothin' changed–except most of the Americans left and we got surrounded by foreigners."

That was 1903. I was 11, Sidney, 13, both done with school, both mucking stalls and currying mules, both working in the mine sometimes with Papa. It was cold and cramped living in that tent with only baseball and exploring to keep us occupied.

"Seems like we got two choices," I said. "Mine coal the best we can or pull out."

"That strike was nine years ago, Alan. Lot's changed. The union's stronger, with more members. People in state government are on our side. Governor even has a secretary of labor who travels around and knows the score."

"Governor and his secretary might as well live on the moon with the state inspector, Sidney. Papa told us the union makes promises it can't keep.

Why put your faith in somethin' that won't deliver?"

"Papa didn't *always* feel that way," Sid said.

"Shit, you can't argue with a hardhead."

Couldn't say whether we paused to gather more ammunition or if we were talked out, but me and Sidney quit squabbling long enough to notice Mama sitting on the porch steps.

"How long you been over there?" Sid asked.

"Seems like hours, days. Long enough to hear the King's English brutalized. But don't quit on my account. No, sir. Keep flapping till you get it all out."

We glared at each other like desperados.

Mama snickered. "Oh, come on. Just when it was getting good and I thought you were gonna fist-fight, you go mumsey."

Her dose of sarcasm stunted our belligerence.

"You're both so stubborn. Come here and sit," she said. Felt a scolding brewing.

When we were kids, Mama gave us our whippings. If she caught you doing something wrong–or she was even suspicious–you might as well take off your belt and hand it to her. Wearing overalls? Didn't matter. Go on and cut a juniper switch and bend over because your butt was about to get beat. After you dried up from crying, you had to thank her for the correction, then give her a kiss and hug.

Nowadays, she relied on guilt and remorse to rein us in. But she still expected hugs and kisses to show our appreciation for putting us back on track.

We stomped over and settled on either side of her.

"Alan, state your brother's side, without using the word *but*."

"Aw, Mama, we're too old to be . . ."

"State."

I did, with her prodding.

"Now, Sidney, you give his, the same way," she said.

He did. Just like when we were kids.

"My darling knuckleheads. You'd get along fine if I was there to referee you, every minute of the day."

"Yeah. I'd give anything for that," I said.

"So, Mrs. Referee, which one of us is right?" Sid asked.

"Gonna say *both* and *neither*, aren't you?" I said.

"Yessir. One of you thinks he can be happy with things just like they are and hates change. Other believes conditions could always be better. One settles *too* much and the other never has enough. Both have a lot to offer the other, but they're not trading information. They're wasting listening and gathering time thinking up come-backs to draw blood."

I knew we ought to stop jack-jawing right then and act mature, like her preaching had made some sense. But I couldn't shut up.

"Did Papa say the union was trouble or not?" I asked.

"Lloyd did come to believe that, Alan," Mama said.

"Then why'd we go on strike?" I asked.

"Got no choice if everybody else walks, numbskull," Sid interrupted. " 'less you want to scab and get beat to death."

"Shut up talkin' to me, buttinsky," I said.

"Enough," Mama said. "Everyone had to go out, that's true. But the UMW was like your papa's religion back then. Even when he got beat up and thrown in jail. Even when hooligans hauled strikers off by the wagon-load and kicked them out in the middle of nowhere. Even though men got shot, Lloyd held fast. When the companies offered diggers up north an eight-hour day and a little raise per ton, the union caved in. Americans in Hastings and the other camps pulled up stakes and the strike fizzled. That's when Lloyd lost his faith."

"Why didn't we leave when everybody else did?" I asked.

"Would have, I guess, if V-A hadn't just incorporated Delagua," Mama said. "They needed experienced men to teach newbies. Lloyd got a raise and the company offered families like us and the Bastrops material to build houses and own them after they were completed. Mostly, Lloyd loved mining and the skill it took. No interest in being a pit boss. And he didn't want an outside job when it was offered. He loved to dig coal. Was a proud hardhead who'd seldom admit he'd been wrong."

"If I loved this canyon like Papa did, I wouldn't give up on it either," Sid inserted.

"What? Like I would?" I shot back. "I care about all this as much as you do."

"Hush, now. You'd know why he liked Delagua if you stayed very long in Rocky Ford," Mama said. "A table top. Wind out there could blow the snout off a pig. And dust? Clouds of it. Two o'clock in the afternoon, you'd think it was midnight, sometimes."

"It was nice in Rocky Ford that time we went," Sid said.

"Yeah," Mama said. "That was in the lull between the end of the strike and us moving to Delagua. We went to Pueblo on the train and visited Mother and Daddy. Lloyd said as long as we'd come that far, we ought to go see his papa. Took all day in a borrowed wagon."

"Had watermelon under a tree, I remember," Sid said. "Then we went inside where Grandpa was propped up in bed, asleep. We sat around while that Mexican lady came and went. Finally, Grandpa woke up and glared at

Papa. 'Well?' he said. 'Well, what?' Papa answered. 'Well, nothin',' Grandpa came back. Then we got up and left. That was all they said to each other the whole time we were there."

We laughed.

"Had the tintype taken on the horse at the county fair during that trip," I said. The picture hanging next to Grandpa Tanner's *Rules* showed Papa and Mama standing on the ground holding the lead; us four kids sitting on the animal. "Sidney had his nostrils flared."

"Imitatin' that nag." Brother giggled.

"That was a good time, wasn't it?" Mama said. "All of us together."

"*That* was a *fair* day," Sid said, grinning.

"Comes once a year," Mama returned. "And it's not today." She looked toward the Bastrop house where a dispute was in progress. "Growing up in Pueblo seems like a million years ago, on another planet, to me now. Mother and my sissies had it rough, but they would've keeled over if they'd had to boil cattail roots for supper."

"Aunt Franny and Aunt Lulu still live in Pueblo, don't they?" I asked.

"Yes, as far as I know," Mama said. "Old maids. I haven't heard from either of them in so long. Another thing I need to do is visit. Can't escape though." She sniffed.

Sid put his arm around her. "All this family talk makin' you blue?"

"I suppose." She dabbed her eyes on the hem of her dress. "You realize it'll be four years next week since Lloyd and the girls passed?"

That wee reminder took me back to our month of sickness, isolation and terror. Seemed like an ordinary fever with headaches at first–surely something Mama could handle. Then came the bloody noses, swollen stomachs and pea-soup scoots, the shaking and picking at the bedclothes. Papa and Griselle had the red spots. The fever broke after three weeks and we thought they'd get well. Doctor knew better. Before they died, the oozing sores and screaming fits plagued them. Griselle went first, then Papa, finally Mary.

We sat in silence, listening to Ida badger Cockeye. Their bickering and Ida's scripturizing could drive you crazy. But, during the sickness, they'd left food and Bible verses on the porch every morning. Burned the soiled bedclothes Mama threw outside and brought more when we ran out.

Mama patted our legs. "I can't make you two get along. But I can keep you from upsetting our guest. If you can't agree a hundred percent on a thing, find what you can agree on and build from that. You've always done well sticking up for each other. That'll be really important in the days to come. Life-saving important." She stood. "I'm going to bed."

We gave her hugs and kisses, then watched her go inside.

"Remember us looking for the red specks on our bellies every day?" I asked my brother.

"Yeah, I sure do. Scared shitless, weren't we? Things went downhill fast when them specks appeared."

"I barely recall what the girls was like, Sid. Remember Papa, but can't feature Griselle and Mary."

"That's sad," Brother said.

I nodded. "Seems like me and you are having a hell of a time agreeing on anything these days. Think she wants us to compromise?"

"That's asking for a shit-load, ain't it?"

"Yeah, it is. Completely beyond reason," I said.

"A violation of our blood-line," Sid said. "Might have to give you a rinktum, if you don't start seein' my side." That cracked us up.

Papa's ultimate wrestling tactic. He'd get you in a headlock then rub his knuckles across the top of your head, fast and furious, till you hollered, "Give." Rinktums hurt. I'd start crying and Papa would tease me for being a baby. That made Sidney mad because he always took up for me. Then we'd fight Papa for real.

Clamming up for a minute, we listened. Cockeye was offering his defense, when Sid piped up.

"Alan, I'm goin' for a job outside. You've got a good man . . ."

"Ain't you. He's just a fill-in till you get better."

"He'll have to do. I can't take the dust no more. Feels like I got a boulder on my chest all the time."

"Well . . . if I get stabbed, it's your fault."

"I'll be proud to speak at the funeral," Sid said.

Like Mama hoped, me and Brother had got it out, at least for that night. Guess our opinions were beside the point, anyway, because it seemed like we were stuck on a conveyor.

Fact was, Father Time had dragged Sister Change to our party. And whether we wanted to or not, he'd make us dance with her.

PART TWO

"Of all the colors I ever did see,
Red and black are the ones I dread.
For when a man spills blood on the coal,
They carry him down from the coal mines dead."

"Red-Winged Blackbird"
by Billy Edd Wheeler

CHAPTER FIFTEEN
August 23, 1913

In the hills above Delagua, you could hear the snarl of cables, the clank and squeal of coal cars being pulled across the bridge to the tipple. You smelled crushed sage and juniper, tasted the sour cloud of dust and smoke that always hung over the canyon. Electric lights pooled in the streets and were scattered like white beads upon hillsides and flats.

But in the dark away from town, you couldn't tell stranger from brother. It was a good night for sneaky doings. Thievery, murder, unionizing.

With the new superintendent and his detectives, organizing was riskier than it had been with Billy Potts or Miles Edgerton and the Keystone Kops. George Slatter was a veteran of strikes up north and none of us doubted that he would have his goons fire on anybody.

I'd lost sight of Sid now, slipping between the pinyons and junipers, so I followed the sound of his boots, clattering up through the rocks and crumbling shale.

Instead of visiting Elma's or having a drink at McKintrick's, I was climbing this stupid hill, because Nick and Sidney wanted me to meet an organizer from Pennsylvania.

We topped the slope, then crawled under a slab of sandstone jutting out of the hillside, to wait for Nick's signal.

Kistos had come a long way in a year. He was smarter and more ambitious than I had figured. Caitlin had spent considerable time working with him on his English–and everything else, I reckoned. Nick said English gave him power and he went a little crazy soaking up the language. He was like a dipso itching for another bottle–except the dipso would drink himself to sleep sooner or later. The more English Nick spoke, the wider awake he got.

This guy I'd once called "dummy" now shook his fist at diggers, trying to get them to demand shorter work days or pay for dead work. He'd get all red-faced and excited when he couldn't persuade a victim. Seemed more likely that he'd teach mules geography than get Delagua's working men interested in the union.

But he kept on, and over time, more and more listened. He'd been serious from the first day in the mine. Now, he was bold and cocky, to boot. Some of the Greeks said he'd turned *xeni*–foreign. Said he wanted to be Anglo-Saxon, with his Anglo-Saxon words and his Anglo-Saxon girlfriend. Said he thought his shit didn't stink anymore.

"*This* Greek will learn to play the system fast," he told me early on, tapping his chest. "He will not stay at bottom of pile."

It got so union was all Nick wanted to talk about. Convinced I wouldn't budge, he recruited Sid to pester me, like the club just couldn't make it in Delagua if Alan Tanner wouldn't join. I didn't know whether they really believed that something could be accomplished or they just craved excitement.

So, to shut them up, I said I'd come out there to listen to John Lawson. But I didn't give a flyin' fuck about the union. Just wanted to see for myself what Sid was up to.

"You here on business?" Nick cawed from the shadows below.

"No, we're here on vacation," Sidney answered and Nick stepped out from a clump of juniper and waited for us to come down. Then he took us to a clearing where we joined other guys standing in a circle.

"Here is the man I tell you about, John," Nick said. "Alan Tanner."

Lawson shook my hand, said hello to Sid and turned to the small assembly. "Thanks for coming tonight," he said. "What you're doing is dangerous and courageous. I appreciate it. I want to ask you a question: can you trust Victor-American to make your life better?"

Nobody said anything, of course. The union man knew we couldn't depend on the company for much more than letting us have access to its mines.

"Victor-American beats you every way, don't it?" Lawson asked. "At the tipple, at the company store, at the infirmary, at church, at the whorehouse, even."

Several knotheads chuckled.

"Never having a say frustrates a man, robs his dignity. The coal miner in the southern fields is hardly better than a chattel slave. He has no power on his own. The United Mine Workers gives you power, through bargaining and, if necessary, strikes. When you join and you work, things change."

One feller asked Lawson if there would be a strike.

"We'd like to avoid it. You all know that things are never the same afterward. A strike costs money and time off the job."

"And lives," I added.

"Yes, lives," Lawson said. "But what is a life lived on your knees? Lunkers up here have been living on their knees for so long, they've forgot how to stand up. I've been organizing for over ten years in Colorado, north and south. My dad was a union man in Pennsylvania. I've been shot by a mine superintendent and my home in Denver was bombed. When beatings and shootings and bombings didn't work, Victor-American offered me a healthy bribe not to come south. But here I am."

A few mumbled words of admiration.

"So, some of you have felt the lead pipe beside your ear before, huh? Right now, you're getting your head cracked for nothing. When you're working for the union, you get your head cracked for something."

Morons chuckled.

"For decent wages and hours, for medical care and a check-weighman at the tipple, for the right to protest and ask questions and shop where you please with real money and not a handful of worthless scrip.

"Did you know that those things are already state law in Colorado? But the southern field is not considered a part of Colorado by the coal companies. It's their private slave state. Now, no slave ever broke his chains by himself. He did it with help. And once the chains break, watch out."

Nick came in. "We ask you men to come here because you are leaders. We want 100% union membership. Organizers are everywhere in southern fields, tonight, to sign men up. Is a dollar a month."

"And what does a man get for his dollar?" a guy asked.

"Representation, unity," Lawson said. "Encouragement and support to stand up and fight."

"Delagua and Hastings ain't like camps up north," I said. "We're under armed guard, surrounded by barbed wire. Everybody lives in their own little cage. Don't speak the same language, don't understand each other's ways. Reason we fight half the time."

"You're making my point, Tanner," Lawson said. "Without a union, we're just a lot of frustrated individuals with no focus or concentration. The union pulls all that individual energy into one powerful machine. It's amazing when it comes together. You don't realize it day-to-day in the camps, but I see from the outside. Thousands of men ready to put their lives on the line."

Nick interrupted again. "We have a list of demands to present at a convention in Trinidad. If they ain't met, we strike. And if the union strike, everybody leave, union or not. Unless you want to scab. Me, I will rather leave as a proud union member already, than be shamed later on."

"We own our house," I threw in. "They can't just kick us out."

"You don't own the land house sit on," Nick said. "Company will evict."

"Look, we know that all of this is risky," Lawson said. "But, like I said, change can't happen unless we're united. We can win if we're organized. I know it, I've seen it. A union is the only way you're gonna get any power."

I'd had a snoot full. "Power to do what? Companies got the guns and the money. That's where the power's at."

Sidney spoke up. "Alan, you're wrong. *We* are the power, just like Papa used to say. We can refuse to work until our demands are met. The UMW will help us with wages, if we walk out. If you don't think the companies fear the union, why are they tryin' so hard to keep it out?"

Nick came back in. "One year ago, sixty-nine Greeks walk out at Frederick. Next day, all but three diggers join the Greeks. They come back when things change. There is no reason we cannot have the same power here. We will try something tomorrow to test. A stack-up at all tipples in the southern field, to compare miners' figures of how much they dig with what company scale show. Spot-checks already estimate it take 2400 and 2600 pounds of coal to make a ton, depending upon the tipple. We think Delagua scales weigh very light."

"If we don't have a man inside the weigh shack with the scale flunky, it's just our word against the company," I said. "That ain't any better than what we have right now. It's a waste of time. We can shovel three more cars' worth in the time it takes to stand in a goddamn line."

"The companies want to avoid a strike," Lawson said. "Want it bad enough to follow state law and let us have check-weighmen in the sheds."

"Startin' when?" a feller asked.

"Starting tomorrow morning," Lawson said.

"But can we trust the check-weighman?" I asked. "You know the company pays them guys off."

"*I'll* be the check-weighman, Alan," Sid said. "I'll be watching the scale and keeping a record."

"That makes you the biggest dumbass chump of all, Sidney," I fired back. "These guys have got inside your head."

"Come on, Alan," Sid said. "I hear you bellyachin' all the time about gettin' rooked at the tipple. This is a good thing and worth payin' for. I brung a dollar for you, right here."

"Don't sign my name to nothin', Sidney, you hear? I'll wait for you up the hill."

I trudged away from the group, but Sid stayed with the others Lawson was signing up. Brother had got so blamed opinionated working outside, I had trouble being around him. When he took a job as a cable man, I reckoned it would be a good thing. If he wasn't sipping, Sidney was always the friendly sort. Greeting jokers and coupling their cars so they could get pulled into the tipple house gave him a chance to gab with everybody. But the farther away he got from digging and loading cars–and the more he gassed with piss-offs–the more unionized he got. Now, he was taking a chancy job and counting on the union for wages.

I figured in a perfect world where you wouldn't get your ass shot off for going against the company, a union might be okay. But right now it seemed like a shitload of trouble and pain with Slatter, the hired guns and the new rules against every little thing.

Nick had crept up on me. When he spoke, I bucked.

"You're a very nervous man, Alan. You should pick a better fight with your brother than this thing. The union is good."

"I know how you feel, Nick. Now, I'm asking you to mind your own business."

"You are my business, because you are my friend. Always remember that, no matter what I say in anger or what happens."

I didn't respond.

"What is it you need, Alan? More time? Time to go home and think? Time to see more men suffer? 'The woman who don't wish to bake bread spend five days sifting flour.' Soon you will be left by yourself, sitting on your fist and leaning back on your thumb."

"This ain't no game, Nick. Somebody's gonna get killed."

He put his hand on my shoulder. "There is always a fellow who want someone to fight his fight, then get benefit of the blood. We have a word in the language for men who will not stand up and fight–*analatos*. It mean 'no salt.' Men who think too much lack salt. I do not want to insult you, Alan, but I wonder how much men have to suffer before they act like men."

"You sound like Barba." Nick wanted to make me mad and he was succeeding. "You independent birds who weren't around for the last strike is so quick to talk about what it takes to be a man. Does a man just chunk his family in the bucket and walk off the job? Does he buy him a gun and get hisself killed for a union that can't do nothin' to help noways? Ask Sid what it's like to live six-in-a-tent for a year."

"Alan, I know you. And I hear what you say. We cannot do this thing with passion alone. We must have help from men who have doubts and can reason on both sides. Men of great courage."

"Okay, Nick, we understand each other. Now, leave me alone."

"Will you dig with me and go to the tipple tomorrow or do you have to think about even that?"

Nick knew he had me, because I *had* to go to work. But I felt like letting him have it. "The hell with you, Nick, and the hell with your union. I think you troublemakers want somebody to get hurt, just to prove your point.

Edgerton warned me about this last year. Said guys like you don't care about nothin' except tearing everything up then crowin' about it."

Nick was silent for a few seconds and I could feel anger coming off him like heat from a radiator.

"Go home to Mama, then, Alan. Get drunk and hide under the covers with your whore. Lick Slatter's boots when he come by. We don't need *analatos* like you."

CHAPTER SIXTEEN
August 24, 1913

Like the other holdouts, I soon realized that I couldn't avoid union activity, even if I didn't join. Didn't matter that I thought the stack-up was dangerous or pointless. Showing up for work got me involved.

A car chockablock with bitty slag was supposed to weigh 3000 pounds and diggers were paid fifty cents a ton. But we could get rooked at the tipple in many ways. The scale could just be fucked up and weighing wrong. If the scale wasn't busted, the weigh boss could record less weight and the company would get a bunch of free coal at our expense. If the boss thought the coal had too much rash, or he was pissed off at the diggers, or he was just in an ornery mood that day, he could reject all or part of a car's load. Those cars got dumped on the ground where flunkies sifted the dregs. And what did the working man get for his effort? A corncob up his ass.

With Sid as our check-weighman, we promised to load the cleanest coal possible that morning. That meant fewer cars coming out and less wage, because separating rash ate up a lot of time.

During our shift, Nick said nothing about our tussle the night before and little about anything else. Guess he still had his feathers ruffled. We loaded three cars and coupled them to others being pulled to the entry. But instead of taking more empties back inside, as usual, we gathered under the great bridge to eyeball our cars on their way to the scales.

Inside the tipple house, the scale boss would record the weights for each car, while Sidney watched over his shoulder and wrote down what he saw. What Victor-American was offering each team–and what Sid recorded–would be posted later in the day at the weigh shed on the ground.

Electric winches pulled two rows of loaded cars from mines on either side of the canyon across the trestle and up to the scales. After the cars were weighed and their coal dumped through a trap door into a boxcar, the empties rolled into a line that could be taken back into the mines. Cars rejected for too much rock or dirt would roll, lickity-split, through the tipple to be dumped into rash piles at each end of the bridge. Diggers marked their first car with a flag so they could keep up with their day's work as it was hauled across the trestle.

A growing pack of slag monkeys congregated outside the weigh shed, eating lunch and killing time until their cars passed through. Nick caught sight of Tostakis and Cockeye near the front of the cluster and we worked our way toward them.

"I worry about what will happen with these two," Nick said. "They are not careful when digging. And Barba will argue with his trousers."

Tostakis had insisted on digging and loading in a rush so his and Cockeye's cars were seven ahead of us. Me and Nick reached the mule heads just as their first car rolled through the tipple, too fast.

"Goddamn," Barba hissed.

The second and the third cars came out. All three rolled past the trap door and hit the rejects, chock-full.

Barba turned to Nick. "Kistos. They never weigh these car. Sombitch send straight to dump."

"I kept tellin' you to slow down," Cockeye hollered. "We loaded a mess of crud and got nothin' to show for it, stupid ouzo."

Barba shoved his buddy. "You never say that name no more to me, Bastrop. I am through with white-bread games."

Cockeye looked sad, like Tostakis had really hurt his feelings. "Okay, Greek. Get your butt shot off and see if I care. I'm done with *you*."

A guard picked his teeth and watched from a folding chair at the bottom of the stairs.

As Cockeye walked away, two wops caterwauled when their cars got chucked.

Pretty soon, me and Nick's cars rolled straight through and bumped against the other cast-offs. Nobody fussed over a load more than Nick. We expected at least 5500 pounds of credit. We got zero.

Sidney clomped down the stairs and posted his weights on the shed wall next to the boss' allowances. The jig was clear: all the Greek and wop teams, a few greasers, plus me and Cockeye received corncobs. American buddies got credit for the weight they'd figured and sauntered off happy.

Boos and insults erupted. Barba shambled up to my brother. "Why you let sombitch reject my car?"

I paced over and stood beside Sidney.

Nick joined us and the remaining lunkers closed in. "Is what we expect, Barba," Kistos said. "What would you have Tanner do?"

"Grab that sombitch and shake him," Tostakis hollered. "Throw him off the bridge. We work goddamn hard for good coal. Scale boss pick on Greek. And we didn't need no check-man to prove it."

"I didn't get nothin' either, ouzo," I yelled. "And I ain't no goddamn Greek."

Sid swept me aside. I'd fought Brother and watched him fight all my life. The cough had slowed him, for sure. But Barba was skating on thin ice.

Sid pressed his fingers into the Greek's bib. "You best button up."

Barba knocked Sid's hand away, but Brother snapped it back.

"Hold up, Sidney," Nick said.

Brother held Barba's gaze. "Tell this bastard to hold up, Kistos," Sid spat.

Nick stepped forward. Looked like a fist-fight coming, when Brother started coughing, a full-blown fit that dropped him to his hands and knees, gasping.

Barba watched with fists balled.

When the spell tapered, I reached to help Sidney stand, but he brushed me off and rose slowly. "All right, Barba, put 'em up."

Barba turned and walked away.

Sid dusted himself off and retrieved his hat. "I'll–get-word . . . to-John . . . about-the . . . rejects," he said to Nick, then lurched through the parting mob. His halting speech reminded me of old man Edgerton. I figured Sid was still sipping, just not where me or Mama would see. We'd found out it was hard to give that syrup up once you got started.

Barba milled through the lunkers, working hard to stir them up.

The scale boss probably saw trouble brewing and picked up the telephone, because five of the new detectives showed up. Another outfit who favored suits and fedoras as working clothes, some carried sawed-offs; some, rifles. All had their coats pulled back over strapped-on pistols. A few wore two hand guns, grips turned out.

Victor-American had hired Baldwin-Felts agents from West Virginia to keep order and ferret out union activity in the southern field. The detectives specialized in handling testy coalasses.

Under our former supers, guards and town cops had been an irritation to tolerate, like black flies or poison ivy. Every so often, they'd lock up a mean drunk or try to enforce some stupid rule few were violating. Mostly, they were just a gang of dumpy lie-abouts, easy to butter-up or hoodwink.

But these Baldies were different. Rumor had it that most of them were three-dollar-a-day gunmen, free to use any tactic to keep the mines open and us behaving. A few loudmouths had had run-ins with them already.

Barba was still yammering when the dicks snuck up. Two jerked the Greek's hands behind him and a third manacled him. A professional arrest.

"Why you do this?" Barba whined.

" 'Cause you're the goddamn union anarchist ringleader," the boss dick said.

"Ain't true." Barba found Kistos. "You tell."

Nick moved toward the detective. "Is just a loudmouth. I will take him."

The Baldwin whipped out his revolver. "You ain't doin' shit, boy."

Nick and the immigrants followed the coppers from a distance as they marched their prisoner away.

* * *

Figured a trip to Elma's might steady my nerves. I was strolling into town, when I heard men's voices. Turned a corner and saw Greeks and Italians, standing in front of the office.

The men held their packs, picks and shovels and the clank and rattle of equipment mixed with their loud talk. Many of the Greeks had on the loose pants and shirts I'd seen them wearing on their special days. Each man had tied a red bandana around his neck and some of the ones I knew clapped me on the back and shook my hand, like I'd come to join them.

Nick stood at the front, making sure the workers stayed off the porch steps. I asked him what was going on.

"The super fire Barba. Said if he ain't out of town before nightfall, he will keep in jail. I call a meeting and we vote to leave. Come to draw our pay."

I whistled at the size of the decision. Figured this was the plan from the beginning, to walk out. Sid just provided a written excuse.

"Guys in other camps walk, too," Nick said. "Now, there is organization."

While we gabbed, detectives rounded the corner of the building and spread out in front of us.

As the Baldwins settled, George Slatter stepped outside. Stocky feller in sweat-stained hat, working jacket and a tie. Had his pants tucked into scuffed boots. He was followed by Abercrombie, now Slatter's little suckass clerk. The lead dick who'd drawn on Nick came out last and closed the door.

This gunslinger walked half-way down the steps and sat, letting his eyes linger on me. Probably curious about an American's presence among all the foreigners.

The superintendent walked to the edge of the porch and most of the gumboots got quiet.

"We want no trouble, Mr. Slatter," Nick shouted. "We come here to draw our time. If Barba Tostakis cannot work for Victor-American, Greek and

Italian in Delagua or Hastings won't either."

"That's fine and dandy, Kistos," Slatter said. "You understand that if your boys go out today, they'll never work again in Colorado?" Slatter waited for some response. When none came, he told Nick to take his men around to the pluck-me door. "Keep them in a single file and have them come in, one-at-a-time. They'd better have every piece of gear we issued, or they'll get no pay. If anybody gets contentious, we'll run the ones left standing down the canyon without so much as a washrag. Be sure that there's somebody around the whole time who can translate everything into English."

Nick and a wop I didn't know delivered the instructions and the coalasses and guards began to move to the side of the building.

I caught Nick as he was walking away. "Well, you did what you said, didn't you, ouzo? Iron's in the fire, now."

Nick put his hand on my shoulder. "And you are the hardhead you always complain about. I see you another day, Alan, and you join with us because you can never be a scab. Soon you come to hate scabs worse than this union." Before joining the immigrants, he shook my hand.

The detective sitting on the steps stayed behind. "Those olive pickers are some oily bastards, ain't they?" he called to me.

I didn't say anything.

"Hey, dummy, you speakie?"

I felt my face redden. "Yeah, I speakie."

The man smiled. "My name is Delores Paul Hawkins. I'm wonderin' what white bread is doin' hangin' out with Greeks. Some of them are union boys." The man stood, walked down the stairs, stepped onto the ground and moved toward me. "Union boys stink. I smell somethin' on you. Can't tell if it's union shit or chickenshit."

Hawkins came so close I could see the veins in his eyes. He drew his pistol and I felt its barrel creeping up my leg. It lingered at my crotch, then slipped under my chin.

I was wringing wet.

Hawkins held the gun in place while he found my pecker with his free hand. "There it is. You like this little thing, boy, 'cause if you don't, I'll cut it off right now and stuff it in that gap-toothed mouth of yours. Let those other cocksuckers watch you bleed, just as an example." He squeezed me a little. "Let's do it right now, motherfucker. A moron like you in Paint Creek sucked his own dick for over an hour before dyin' in the street. You can't believe the blood when a guy's pud gets lopped. Pretty messy, with his wife and kids watchin', but it got the message across. It's the agency's guarantee, you might say. NO. MORE. TROUBLE."

He let his hand rest on me a few more seconds. "You're eager to do somethin', right now, ain't you? I wish you would."

To give me the chance to jump him, I guess, he put the pistol away and lit a cigarette. My face and neck were on fire. If I hit him, he'd kill me.

"Listen. For me not cuttin' off your dick today, I want you to do me a favor. You tell your suck-buddies that Baldwin-Felts Detectives do not play games with stupid rednecks like you all. We ain't gonna say, 'Pretty please,' before sendin' your asses to hell."

The company's Model T pulled around and stopped in front of the office. I figured the Baldwins were going to escort the Greeks down-canyon.

"I'm comin'," Hawkins yelled, then looked back at me. "You had it easy up here with that dumplin' Edgerton. I hope you're not too dense to get what I'm sayin'. Stay out of trouble, boy, or we'll be on you faster than shit through a goose."

I turned away. If I ever felt dumber and weaker, I didn't remember it.

John Lawson had talked about men living on their knees. For the first time, I understood what he meant.

CHAPTER SEVENTEEN
August 24-25, 1913

Desire had shriveled and there was nobody around for a ball game, so I decided to have a drink and jaw with Delveccio. The saloon was empty, except for Monroe Purvis and Rolf Levy, playing double solitaire. Levy was an electrician who sometimes strummed guitar with Cait, Nick and Monroe.

Charlie was washing glasses. "You look wore-out, Tanner. Want a beer?"

"I sure do. In fact, run me a tab." Determined to have a normal conversation with the bartender, in spite of my mood. "How are the relatives in Italy?"

"*Tuto va bene.* Mama write it has been very dry. The grape, she is puny–no bigger than baseball this year." He cackled, pulled a beer and set it atop the bar. "You want to talk about what is wrong?"

"No, I do not." I took a sip. "You got anything salty?"

"Just today, I get pickled pigs' feet and boiled pullet eggs in vinegar."

"Fix me a little plate, please, sir."

Charlie lifted the top from a jar that sat on the bar, stirred around with a wooden spoon until he captured one, then another, of the eggs. He rolled them onto a plate next to the pink knot of pigs' feet he'd already put there. "So how is the coal business?"

"Shitty. I guess you heard the Greeks and wops went out. There's talk of everybody leavin'." I gnawed the flesh from a pig's foot, wiped my mouth on my sleeve. "What do you think about the UMW, Charlie?"

"Some say good, some bad. I am hearing about much organizing. You gone to a meeting?"

"Not me," I lied. "If there's a strike and the immigrants get much more stirred up, there's gonna be gun-trouble. Some of them Greeks is beggin' for a fight." The episode with Hawkins ran through my mind. "One wrong move and them new dicks will give us somethin' we can't handle."

Charlie coughed and nodded. "Well, maybe this union ain't so bad, what with things like these. With Mr. George Slatter and his detectives in charge, I hear more customers talking membership."

"Funny," I said. "Instead of Slatter and the thugs slowin' down the union, they're becoming its best recruitment tool."

I was rolling one of the eggs around on the plate with my finger, sulking about the run-in, when two Baldies flapped the saloon doors and sauntered among the tables. One of them stooped to say something that didn't sit too well with Levy.

"I see the law has arrived," I said and popped the egg into my mouth.

Charlie leaned in, spoke soft. "These two is big customers. They try to drink this bar dry, then go off and molest some poor woman on the street. Do you know them?"

"Naw. But I had a talk with their commander just now. A man name of Hawkins. Got a woman's first name."

"Delores . . . I know him," Charlie nodded. "Worst of the bunch. He talk rude to you?"

"Yes, and he insulted my occupation, too. I put him on my dance card for later. Give me a refill, please, and a couple more of them eggs."

The dicks took seats at a table behind the card players and kept hassling Levy.

"These men is real asshole," Charlie muttered, rolling two more eggs onto my plate. "The tall, skinny fellow is Willy Crimmons. He get money and favors from coalass wives and girlfriends. If the woman put out, her man can stay in town. The other is Choice Grabble. Pistol-whip a man yesterday for ignoring the rock-throwing law."

I snickered. "I ain't heard of no rock-throwin' law."

"It is one. The fellow that throw the rock, he know it, now, too, so you better not throw one, even if you need to. These is not men to toy with."

While his buddy continued to hassle Levy, the other traipsed up and leaned against the far end of the bar.

"They is after Rolf," Charlie said. "I see trouble for them three."

I barely knew the electrician. "Why are they pickin' on him?"

"Don't like Jews, I think."

Grabble pulled out a coin and pecked on the mahogany.

This got the saloon keeper moving. "*Si fermi*, man, you will scratch the wood. I am coming."

Charlie served up two mugs and Grabble carried them back to the table. Crimmons let up on Levy just long enough to share something funny with his buddy and swig his beer.

I guessed the Jew had had enough abuse, because he scooted his chair back, stood and hurried out of the saloon. His face was red and wet and he left his hat behind.

"Ain't that just like a kike?" Crimmons hollered. "Leaving without saying excuse me or nothin'."

A few idlers came in and Delveccio busied himself with them.

A little while later, Levy returned, carrying his guitar. Caitlin busted in right behind, greeting those who'd straggled in. She'd shucked her washerhouse duds in favor of an outfit I'd never seen: red bloomers, a yellow sweater, and plimsols. Reminded me of a clown.

Choice Grabble got into a poker game with three hang-arounds. At the table next to him, Crimmons had passed out. When Monroe hit some piano keys so the guitar player could tune up, Crimmons raised his head for a moment, then dropped it back onto his arms.

Caitlin warbled as she marched up to the bar. "Good evening, Charles. Let me have four pints."

"You sing from *Madame Butterfly,* Caitlin, and I will run away with you this evening."

"I'll go in a wink, Charlie, but we have to drag this grump along." Caitlin nudged me with an elbow. "Allie, the grump. Why are you so glum? Sorry your playmates left?"

"Them Greeks? Left a couple of years too late as far as I'm concerned." I mustered a smile. "Where'd you get that outfit?"

"Angelina Hernandez picked it up in Trinidad when she went to visit her mum. I want the other girls to get these so we can start an exercise club."

"I'd like to see Mama in one of them things."

"Ethel has one ordered."

I shook my head and smiled. "You gonna try for housekeeping with the new super?"

"I've already talked to him," Cait said. "He's not interested."

Charlie set the mugs of beer on the counter and Cait paid.

"You try bawling, like you done with Edgerton?" I asked. "Seemed to melt *his* heart."

She frogged my arm. "You'll never let me live that down, will you? That family was pleased to have a perfectionist like myself cleaning their apartment. When Miles had his breakdown, Marvinia was really glad I was there. Said she couldn't handle it without me. After talking with George Slatter, I'm not sure I'd like working for him. All hands."

"It's just as well. You didn't bring much information."

"You can't report what you don't know, Alan."

I took a swig of beer. "You gonna miss your fiddle player?"

A sad look flashed over Cait. "Yeah . . . our band was getting pretty good."

"That's what everybody says. Have a drink with me?"

"After we practice, I will. We can't all just sit down and mope, Allie. We'll see the boys again."

"Who's mopin'?"

Monroe and Levy ran through a piece of some tune and Caitlin grabbed her beers. "Got to go. Thanks for the service, Charlie." She winked at me and joined the musicians.

I'd been living in the same house with that girl for over a year, peeking at her when she bathed, ducking under her underwear hanging around the house when it rained. I'd seen her puke, heard her fart, caught her wrath first thing in the morning and last thing at night, smelled her when she came home funky from the washerhouse or drunk from McKintrick's. I knew her. And I still felt queasy when she came around.

"The *gabbaruss* make a man wobble, don't she?" Charlie said. "I never seen a girl flirt so much and not get into trouble. Wouldn't you love to be her bar of soap?" The barkeep grinned. "How can you live in a house with her? I would burn up."

"Who . . . Carrot Head? She's like my sister."

"Don't try to shit me, Tanner. Why you don't go for her? You was once the bantam rooster of Delagua. 'Young wood make the hottest fire.' You sick or something?"

"Caitlin makes me nervous–like that last carful of slag you want to get before the roof caves in. There it is on the floor, yours for the shoveling, but the timbers are cracking and you can't decide what you're willing to risk to have it."

"You is philosopher, Tanner. The philosopher of mules and women." Something caught Charlie's eye and he turned away from me.

It was Crimmons, stumbling around. I figured he'd be leaving, but he ordered another beer. Pulled his chair out into what little aisle remained between his table and the bar.

Monroe tinkled a gentle introduction on the piano. Cait climbed on a chair and trilled some opera. The singing stopped everything–the service, the talk, Crimmons' drunken carrying-on. Clear and cold as wintertime air, that voice could take you a long way from a hot summer day of mining and contention. I noticed tears on Charlie's cheeks when the song ended.

The rabble clapped and hollered for more. Caitlin took a long swig from a mug handed her. "I'd like to dedicate this lament to our friends who left today." She cleared her throat and sang my favorite with Levy strumming:

Don't go down in the mine, Dad;
Dreams very often come true;
Daddy, you know it would break my heart
If anything happened to you;
Just go and tell my dream to your mates,
And as true as the stars that shine,
Something is going to happen today,
Dear Daddy, don't go down in the mine.

Caitlin smiled at the applause and was about to offer another tune when Crimmons stood. "That's your last fuggin' union song today." He walked up to the chair. "Get down."

Caitlin didn't move.

"Easy, Willy," Grabble said, folding his cards. "I think these people are about finished anyway, ain't you all?"

Charlie put his hand on my arm. "Whatever happen, now, Tanner, take care of the girl. Do not worry about the other thing. You hear?"

I nodded.

"I don't want no trouble in here, Mr. Crimmons," Charlie hollered. The blood had drained from his face and he had a hand under the bar. Holding the billy, I figured.

"You just shut up, prince," Crimmons called. He didn't sound too drunk to me. "I'm in charge right now and I want this skank off that chair."

When Caitlin still didn't move, Crimmons yanked her. She part-stepped, part-fell to the floor.

At the same time, the air exploded, the guitar whanged and Levy tumbled backwards in his chair. Grabble had shot him.

Guys ran for the doors–Monroe Purvis with them–but I stayed put. The Jew lay on his side, holding his belly, squirming a little in the puddle of blood spreading under his coat.

Caitlin took Levy's head into her lap. His teeth were clinched in a weird smile, his face pale and wet.

"Goddamn, Cait, it hurts," the guitar man whispered.

Crimmons sneezed twice. "Gun smoke. It's an occupational hazard." After he blew his nose, the detective pointed down at the guitar player with his bandana. "You gut-shot this fucker, Choice. He's hurtin'."

"Stomach wound is the worst a man can get. Messy, too, ain't it? Would you look at all the blood? Won't last long in that shape." Grabble stood over Caitlin and Levy. "He was goin' for a gun. Look here, Willy." He kicked the guitar out of the way, pushed the flap of the Jew's coat with the toe of his boot, reached down and pulled out a pistol.

"Well, I'm goddamned. A .45 automatic, just like mine," Crimmons said. "That's a considerable weapon."

"Saw its grip when he sat down. Son of a bitch wanted you dead, Willy." Grabble weighed the pistol, aimed it at the lights.

"Don't fire that thing in here," Crimmons said. "My nose can't take it."

"I ain't." Grabble lowered the pistol. "I was just testin' the weight. Wonder where he got this thing? Looks new."

"Why you not get Rolf a doctor?" Charlie called.

Grabble walked over to the bar. "Far as I know, there ain't no union doctor in town, prince. That yid wouldn't want just anybody diggin' out that slug." The detective turned back to his crony. "You think this wop's touchin' that billy club, Willy?"

"Bet a silver dollar he is."

Grabble laid the .45 on top of the mahogany and gave it a spin. "You all had yourself a nice little operation, here, didn't you, wop? Willy and me knew it was gonna be just a matter of time till you fucked up."

Charlie kept his hand under the bar and said nothing.

"You touchin' that club, Charlie?" Grabble asked.

The saloon keeper didn't answer.

"When I ask somebody a question, I appreciate an answer." Crimmons spun the automatic again. "Why don't you just put the billy up here. Willy's nose won't take no more gunplay."

Charlie glanced at me, then did as he was told.

"There's that persuader." Grabble hoisted the club. "This thing could hurt a feller." The detective slammed the club into Charlie's elbow. "You see him go for that gun, Willy?"

"Sure did, Choice. I bet that hurt real bad."

Charlie leaned against the back shelves holding his left arm.

Grabble whacked the edge of the bar, denting it. "With this stick I can teach these wops some manners. Yeah. This'll be my wop whomper."

Crimmons sneezed again and blew his nose. "Goddamn, this is awful. Why don't we go outside?" The Baldy gestured toward me and Cait. "You two pick up this bastard and carry him out. He might like to die in the fresh air. You comin', Choice?"

"You all go ahead. I need to ask Charlie a few things in private. I'll be out directly."

I got Levy under the arms and Cait lifted his legs. When we picked him up, he moaned that we were hurting him.

"I know, Rolf," Caitlin cried. "We have to move you."

It was like carrying a torn gunny sack with butchered meat spilling out. Levy stank.

"It's hurting, Cait. Don't hurt me," Levy whined.

Crimmons waited for us on the porch.

A few jumpy rubbernecks had bunched up at the edge of the street. Elma and the whores watched from the balcony and their windows. None of the ladies would drop chamber pots today.

"Goddammit, shoot me!" Levy hissed as we passed the detective. "You fuck your mother's asshole, you fuck."

"That ain't a very nice thing to say." Crimmons followed us into the street. "Drop him right there, if he's gonna be so rude. That way, all these brave men can watch him die. Your tummy hurtin', Jewboy?"

Me and Cait set Levy down and knelt on either side of him. When he tried to speak, he coughed up blood through blue lips.

Cait turned his face to one side, patted his cheek. "Tanner and I are right here, Rolf."

A fracas kicked up inside the saloon. Glass broke, furniture scooted. Heavy footfalls, thuds and smacks, muffled groans and curses.

"Somebody's gettin' a run for his money in there," I muttered, glancing up at Crimmons, who was listening to the commotion himself. "Wouldn't want to mess with Charlie's secret weapon."

"Choice . . . ," Crimmons hollered, "quit jackin' off and get out here."

Levy clutched Cait's sweater, arched his back, coughed and relaxed. Cait closed the Jew's eyes and lowered his head into the dirt. It was the first time I'd seen somebody die, close-up.

We stood as Grabble gimped onto the porch, face swollen, hatless, body twisted. He held his side and looked down at blood leaking between his fingers. "Fugger stuck me, Willy." The detective leaned against the jamb for a second before toppling backwards through the swinging doors.

When Crimmons ran inside the saloon to see about his partner, Cait bolted. I was about to follow when someone hollered at me from down the street. It was McKintrick, hoofing it

The street-rabble seeped closer, with Jack's Mexicans fronting.

McKintrick pulled up. "Young Tanner . . . what in thunder is going on?"

I told Jack what I'd seen.

The mayor bent over Levy and felt his throat for a pulse. "Dead?" He looked up at me. "He's dead, by God. Where is Charlie?"

I pointed at the imbibery.

McKintrick sighted his head Mexican, made a quick "circle-around" motion with one finger, then barreled through the doors. A few brave souls stepped out of the crowd, picked up the body and carried it away.

This ruckus had me juiced up. Figuring I was trapped already and might as well witness, I followed Jack onto the porch and peered over the doors.

McKintrick swept through his saloon, glanced behind the bar and disappeared into the back room. I heard the storage closet door and the rear entrance door open and slam. The mayor reappeared, cantered across the floorboards and stopped in front of the detectives. "Where's my man?"

Crimmons had pulled Grabble out of the doorway and crouched next to him, trying to slow the blood with a bandana.

"I asked you where Delveccio is," Jack called.

"Just a goddamn minute, ass-wipe," Crimmons said. "Choice?"

The wounded detective opened his eyes.

Crimmons moved his buddy's hand to cover the bloody bandana. "Press hard, right here."

Crimmons stood. "*You* tell *me* where Delveccio is. That motherfucker stabbed my man and got away, scot-free."

"What is your name, sir?" Jack asked.

I couldn't believe McKintrick was being so nervy. Figured I ought to skedaddle, but my feet were glued to the porch.

"I'm Detective William Crimmons, ass-wipe."

"You'll address me as 'Mayor' or 'Your Honor'."

I'd seen Jack mess around like this before, but never with a pistol-packer.

"I'm addressing you as ass-wipe."

"Mr. Crimmons, you are a coarse ruffian with no more regard for law and order than swine . . ."

The dick swung. Jack blocked the punch, jabbed Crimmons' belly with a right, then round-housed with a left. The detective's head spun and a gob of blood and teeth spewed as he went down.

The herd rushed the porch so hard I was turned sideways and had to struggle to get my view back.

Three of Jack's Mexicans had come in the back door and stood behind the bar. And McKintrick knelt over Crimmons.

The mayor held up the detective's pistol and the porch lunkers around me got quiet. Jack twirled the .45 on his trigger finger, Tom Mix-style, before tossing the weapon to his closest Mexican. The greaser had just hidden the gun when Slatter and three Baldies rammed through the swinging doors. Three more spics followed.

The superintendent got a funny look, realizing, I guess, that him and the detectives were surrounded by six pepperbellies who answered only to the mayor of Delagua.

"Mr. Slatter," Jack called, "please look around. This establishment is in shambles. A gifted musician lies dead in the street and my proprietor is missing. Furniture has been smashed and my beautiful bar is ruined. I have a contract for certain services that the companies require. I understand the need for law and order here. As you well know, I contribute to it generously. But this is unacceptable."

"These saloons have become hot beds of organizing and recruiting," Slatter said.

"You could have apprised me of that before defacing my property, terrifying my clientele and attacking my employee," Jack said.

"Like you didn't already know?" Slatter was mad. "There was no *attack*. Our detectives were conducting an investigation. Levy was a suspected anarchist."

"Mr. Slatter . . . you are letting thugs ruin your relationship with the business community and the citizenry in Delagua and Hastings."

I felt a hand on my shoulder and I jumped. It was Sidney.

"You missed it," I muttered. "Jack just knocked out Willy Crimmons."

"Always bragged about being a boxer," Sid commented.

"Cait took off, Sid, and Charlie's disappeared."

A few of the lunkers gave us "shut-up" looks and we complied.

Back inside, Crimmons was coming around. A bloody tooth clung to his cheek. One of the Baldwins gave him a bandana to suck on.

"Watch this," I whispered.

Sitting up now, face purple and swollen, Crimmons reached for his pistol, which, of course, was gone.

Some nitwits cackled.

The detective winced as he spoke. "Thum-one in thith fuckhole . . . hath my weapon."

"What does it look like?" Jack, the cat, asked the mouse.

"Ith's a .45 automathic, thit-head." Crimmons made a pitiful try at spitting out a wad of blood, but the mess just drooled off his chin. "You thstole it," he moaned.

Dr. Shay pushed into the saloon, spied Grabble and went to work.

McKintrick gibbered to his Mexicans. The spics looked at each other and shrugged.

"They have seen no pistol," Jack said.

Crimmons looked up at the super. "Slather . . . I want theeth men therched."

The super scrunched his eyes and ran a handkerchief over his bald head. "You go right ahead and search 'em, Willy."

"Excuse me, Mr. Slatter," Dr. Shay interrupted. "I need your men to carry this fellow to my office. I can't work here."

Hemmed in by Mexicans, eyeballed by coalasses, the super fidgeted. He told two of the detectives to help with Grabble. As they carried their buddy out the front doors, the super turned back to McKintrick.

"My agents will find your man, tonight, Jack. And when they do, we'll get to the bottom of this."

Jack stood. "You're goddamned right we will, George."

The flock started to thin out. Sid snagged my pack from the bin in front of McKintrick's and I shouldered pick and shovel.

"The Baldies ain't gonna let Jack get away with that," I said. "You think he needs us?"

"Goddamn, Alan, he's got the Mexican army in there. And there's only one good detective left with Slatter. I'd like to take a look around back for Cait and Charlie, though. They're the ones who might use our help."

We'd just rounded the corner of the imbibery when a team pulling a Gestring rumbled down the alley. Me and Sid stepped back. Slatter's little suckass, Abercrombie, drove. The wagon was full of stuff covered by a tarp.

Me and Sid searched the alleyways while the sun set and it cooled off. Inside a crib, a whore was beating the shit out of a bare-ass with pants around his ankles. Another girl watched from a corner where she was taking a piss and smoking a cigarette. Three dogs fought over wet garbage. A victrola in need of a crank moaned through an open window. Stumpy Smith, who'd lost both legs in Number 3's explosion, dragged himself through the dust, heading for his cup-shaking spot on Main Street. A floating crap game rattled on in the washhouse. Lights from the mines and the squealing tipple winch told us that some on the night shift were working.

No Charlie; no Caitlin.

On the east end of town, we happened onto Abercrombie in the wagon again. He was just starting down the hill toward Hastings as the company automobile motored up. The Baldies were drunk, hollering and singing. Swerving from ditch to ditch, they almost smacked into the mule team.

"Get-the-fuck out of the way, you little suck-ass," the driver hollered as they rolled past.

I snorted. "Even the company dicks give that dude shit. He must be the world's greatest clerk, though, workin' for his third superintendent."

"Abercrombie's got him a pound of dirt on the mucks and they all know it," Sid said. "Guess we might as well go home, huh?"

"You know what I'd like to do on the way? Go by the livery and see Grady. I ain't done that in a long time."

"Okay," Sid said.

Victor-American had no use for a blind mule and McKintrick had bought him for a dollar. Under Jack's orders, the livery Mexican took special care of Grady, currying him every day, letting him walk in the wagon yard and roll in the dirt all he wanted.

The old mule was grayer at the muzzle, his eyes more clouded. But his ears perked up when he smelled our hands and felt our cheeks.

"Look at you," I said. "Still ready for work, huh?"

Grady nodded.

We fed the animal carrots and whispered sweet nothins in his ears. He was happy.

Sid pitched me one of the curries and we took sides, brushing dust clouds from the mule's flanks. "You notice all the teams is gone?"

"I ain't." I looked around the corner into the yard. "Ever' one. Never seen that. Hey, Machito? . . . *donde esta los wagones*?"

The Mexican was sitting in a chair, whittling a wooden chain. "Ludlow. First-of-the-month pick-up tomorrow. Hastings teams gone, too."

"First of the month's a week off," Sid mumbled.

"Jack send 'em all at once, *hombre*?" I hollered.

"You is now a detective, Tanner? Only four was here this morning. *El suck-ass pequenyo* take *la ultima*," Machito answered.

"He's talking about Abercrombie," Sid said.

I grinned. "*El suck-ass pequenyo.* I'm gonna remember that."

We took Grady for a walk, put him back in his stall and started up the hill for home.

* * *

Rifle shots woke us in the middle of the night, scattered pops from the west end of town. Soon a barrage kicked up, town-center. More commenced at the bottom of our hill.

As blazes from the gunshot sites lit the sky, folks in Coalass Row stirred. Some peered through windows, stood on porches, climbed on roofs or meandered in their yards. A few had already dressed and were on the run with buckets and axes. Stragglers coming home from Paine's and Merkel's headed back to town.

Me, Mama and Sid threw on clothes and boots. Buttoned, cinched and tied them outdoors.

Word spread that the Baldwins were burning the Chamber out. They'd shot Jack's guards, set fire to his house, the imbibery, whorehouse and mule barn. Fire in a town full of frame buildings was as scary as fire in the mine. The night shift let out to fight the blazes.

As we approached the livery, I saw flames swirling from the stable. Machito's body lay in the yard.

We ran around the barn to where we thought Grady's stall was and chopped through. Flames lapped out but no mule.

"Come on, Alan," Sid hollered. "He's either burnt up or got out. We can't do nothin' now."

McKintrick's and Elma's had burned to the frames by the time we got there. Some of the early birds had tried to fight the fire. But we just stood with our empty buckets, watching.

The pump wagon sat to the side, with firemen ready in case flames leapt to company buildings.

Six of Jack's Mexicans had been killed at the imbibery and two at Elma's. Four whores broke legs jumping from second-story windows. The rest escaped, terrified, but unharmed. Dr. Shay was gonna be working late setting bones.

After failing at fighting fires, saving Grady, or finding Jack, we couldn't do much but gawk at the ruination as we plodded through town.

While Sid and Mama yakked, my mind raced over the events of the day. The more I pondered, the more I worried. And the more I worried, the angrier I got.

"What's wrong?" Mama asked me. "You're not talking."

"Rolf Levy got shot because those detectives thought he was a union man. The Jew was totin'. I saw the pistol. Was he usin' Jack's place to organize, Sid?"

"I don't know," he responded.

"The hell you say. Cait ran off. Guess that means she's involved. What about you?"

"What-about-me what?"

"Are you union organizin' in town?"

Mama stopped. "You're not, Sidney. You can't be."

"What if I am?"

"You could get us all killed, is what, you nitwit. They're closing in on you guys. And if the Baldwins would burn out Jack and kill his Mexicans or torch Elma's with girls inside, why wouldn't they come burn *us* out? Be the fastest way to rid this town of trouble-makers."

"Shut-up interrogating me," Sidney squawked. "If the Baldwins were gonna do something, they would have done it already,"

"You can't know that," I said.

"Hush, both of you," Mama commanded. "You're crying over spilled milk. What are we going to do right now?"

"It's not too long before daylight," Sidney stuck in. "Why don't we go up the hill right here and keep an eye out? If goons show up, we'll ring the fire bell."

"I suppose that's best," Mama said. "What do you think, Allie?"

"I think the damn union's gonna get us all killed," I mumbled as we started climbing.

"You best shut-up, scamp," Sid uttered.

Hadn't gone very far when someone called from the outcropping above. "Business or vacation?"

"Vacation," Sidney answered, startled.

"Who goes?" another voice hollered.

Sidney told him. "That you, Tommy?"

"Yeah, me and Mack. Why?"

"Just checkin'. You think we're safe enough to come up?"

"Come ahead," Mack said.

"Watch your step," Tommy added.

We climbed through the rocks until we reached the Texans.

" 'Bout time you showed up," Mack muttered.

" 'Bout missed it," Tommy added.

"What's going on?" Sid asked.

"Neighborhood watch party," Mack said. "People all the way around, on the hillside. You can make 'em out if you look hard."

Sure enough, shapes emerged in the moonlight.

"Nobody's in their houses, near as we can tell," Tommy said.

"Baldwins come up here, they gonna wisht they hadn't." Mack offered. "Ever been hit with a pipe?"

"Pipe can hurt cha," Tommy reflected.

"Put you boys on a list for guard-duty rotation," Mack whispered.

"Everybody's gonna have a night and a time," Tommy added. "So we ain't out here all at once. Unless you work the night shift already like me and Mack and can't stand guard."

A few more folks joined us on the hillside. Soon, we were all quiet, even the kiddies. Nothing to do but watch, listen and deliberate. Or sleep.

Scanning Coalass Row for hostiles, I grew mindful of my breathing, not just hearing and feeling it, but giving in to it. In its coming and going, I sensed the comings and goings of breaths around me. And the longer I mused, the more I felt that we were no longer a mass of isolated souls gasping at different paces, but a single soul taking in the night air.

In the first light of day, Ida offered scripture as we gathered our belongings: "This come from *First Thessalonians*, Chapter 5, Verses 4 and 6: 'But ye, brethren, are not in the darkness, that that day should overtake you as a thief. Therefore let us not sleep, as do others; but let us watch and be sober. Prove all things; hold fast that which is good.' "

Folks made their way back home. Along with blankets, food buckets and babies, they carried crude weapons–ball bats, planks, pinyon clubs, axes, shovels and picks. Mack and Tommy hefted their lengths of pipe.

"Hey, Sidney," I muttered, "right there's your union."

CHAPTER EIGHTEEN
September 17, 1913

For weeks after the mayhem, Delagua remained a stirred-up ant bed, with people crawling over each other, not knowing which way to go.

If you multiplied the goings-on in our town by twenty, you'd have a good idea of the sorry situation in the southern fields. Hastings, La Veta, Prior, Rouse, Green Canyon, Aguilar, Empire, Forbes, Coal Creek, Starkville, Berwind, Tabasco, Primero, Segundo, Florence, Tollerburg, Majestic, Sopris, Rugby and Walsenburg. Each camp could tell a miserable tale, with working men run out of town or killed, private property damaged or destroyed, gunslingers unleashed. Inspector Turnbull was right: we needed a plan.

McKintrick was still missing. No bones or trinkets appeared when they combed the ashes at Jack's house or at the imbibery. Guess he might have skipped town, but I couldn't imagine him leaving the Mexicans to defend his property all by themselves.

The troubles in Delagua, Hastings and Chinkville had left everybody I knew fed-up and jumpy. Some families had even pulled out.

Violence and destruction in coal towns, a growing shortage of diggers and the threat of a strike had caught the state's attention. And pressure applied from above persuaded Victor-American and CF&I to ease up on us.

Sidney continued as our check-weighman and now fewer cars were rejected. Because we were so short-handed, the mines operated with day-shifts only and everyone who showed up got a full-day's work. The pluck-me put things on sale and there was even a rumor of a wage increase.

We stood guard at night, dug coal during the day and got paid regular. Paine's and Merkel's rat holes stayed open and a few whores slinked back into town to conduct business in tents and cribs.

Best of all, the Baldies slipped into the background. You'd still see 'em, but they'd quit bedeviling citizens. Hawkins took Grabble and Crimmons to the hospital in Trinidad–and stayed–so those three troublemakers were out of the picture.

Union organizers got bolder, passing out leaflets on the street and signing suckers up in broad daylight. The UMW had opened offices in Aguilar, Walsenburg and Trinidad–actual storefronts with United Mine Workers painted on their windows. We even heard that 135 diggers from the Radiant Mine in Coal Creek had walked out to join the union, with C.G. Edgerton right in the middle of a speech. Bet that caused a coughing fit.

As a result of the bedlam, a goodly number of out-of-towners visited Delagua. First came the news hounds. The morning after, our gang was walking through town on our way to Number 1 when a Model T pulled up. Four reporters and Lou Dold piled out.

The photographer started setting up in front of the imbibery's ashes. The rest of the leg men approached us, all palsy-walsy.

"Heard you boys had some trouble last night," a fat ass, with a shaggy brown mustache full of dried tobacco juice, said.

"None that *I* know of," Sid said.

"Home readin' my Bible," Mack said.

"Book of *Revelation*," Tommy added.

"Turned in early," I said.

"Watching the children," Cockeye piped in.

"You're wasting your time on those halfwits," Dold hollered. "All Helen Kellers."

"Guess you ain't got an opinion on the strike coming, either, huh?" another gasbag shouted as we walked away.

With Nick and Barba gone and Sid working at the tipple, I started digging with Cockeye, a true test of patience and friendship. Being left-handed–and cockeyed–he did almost everything wrong. Insisted on taking care of the dead work *before* shoveling any coal, for example. Liked to eat lunch, mid-morning. Cooed, "Easy now, darlin' girl" into a mule's ear instead of whispering, "Calm down, now, look at you," like a normal person. Rolled charges up *before* augering. His ways just didn't feel right and I would have told him, if he hadn't said the same thing about mine first.

In spite of the arguments, near-fist-fights and re-dos, me and Cockeye eventually got cars loaded and weighed.

Official word of a strike came into town with our duly-elected UMW representatives Mack and Tommy. On the union's nickel, they'd traveled to Trinidad, September 15, for the State Federation of Labor convention and returned from Ludlow in one of the Chamber's Gestrings. They brought a list of demands that the companies would have to meet to avoid a strike. These included recognition of the union; a ten-cent raise in wages; an eight-hour work day for all classes of labor; pay for dead work; an elected check-weighman; the right to trade in any store, pick a doctor and choose a place to live; enforcement of existing Colorado laws and abolishment of the criminal guard system.

Sporting red bandanas, just like the Greeks on the day Barba got fired, Mack and Tommy drove the Gestring around town, announcing the strike and handing out flyers. On both sides of the wagon hung big signs that read:

ATTENTION MINE WORKERS
Emancipation Day is upon us!
UMW walkout coming September 23!
Wagons for rent, cheap, while they last in Ludlow!
Free rides with Mack and Tommy!
Don't miss out!

The day of the burn-out, some inkling of the coming misfortune had prompted McKintrick to transfer the Council's wagons from Delagua and Hastings to Ludlow, a few at a time. That way, the superintendents wouldn't be suspicious and commandeer the teams. Now, if the companies wanted anything hauled in or out of the coal towns, they had to rely on the old wagons they had abandoned when the Chamber got involved or pay the sky-high price that Oliver Gabey demanded.

I figured the mayor had no feeling one way or the other for the UMW. Didn't matter to him who he gambled with or who sampled his whisky and whores. I *had* seen him talking to John Lawson a time or two–and he was friendly with Nick, Rolf Levy and Cait, of course. But Jack gabbed with everybody. No. Taking the wagons out of Delagua and Hastings allowed McKintrick to stick his thumb in Slatter's eye, even from the grave.

I knew Jack. If a strike came and families could use those wagons to carry their belongings out of the coal towns, even better. We'd just have to trek to Ludlow to get them.

The day the Texans brought the strike news, I'd told Sid I'd meet him at Paine's. By the time I got to the rat hole, the union wagon was parked in the street out front of the saloon.

Inside, Mack and Tommy held court.

"If them demands ain't met, we strike," Mack said.

"Stickin' point is recognition of the union, state-wide," Tommy added. "Companies done already said it won't happen. So, I guess you know what that means."

"You boys ever hear of a woman name of Mother Jones?" Mack asked.

"Old lady, 'bout 90," Tommy added.

A couple of lumpies had.

"Spoke at the convention," Mack said. "Said she stuck her finger in a machine gun barrel in West Virginia and told the guards they better not fire."

"Said if us men was too scared to fight, they was enough hot-headed women to beat hell out of ever'body," Tommy chirped. "Kistos and Mrs. Broiles was on stage with her."

"Cait?" I interrupted. "Where'd she come from?"

"Out of the audience, I guess," Tommy answered.

"No, I mean, where's she stayin'? How'd she get out of Delagua?"

"I didn't talk to her," Mack said. "You talk to her, Tommy?"

He shook his head. "Said 'howdy' and tipped my cap. Tried to talk to Charlie, but he's loony from that beatin'."

"Charlie's alive?" Sid asked.

"Yep," Mack answered.

"But loony," Tommy added.

"I can't believe it," I said. "How'd he and Cait get away?"

"Kistos'll fill you in," Mack said. "He come up here today with Lawson and the governor's secretary of labor in the union's new touring car. Four state militia followed in a regular Model T. Come to have a sit-down with Slatter."

"You can't miss that car," Tommy threw in. "It's red, like a fire wagon."

"How about Jack?" I asked.

"Didn't hear nothin' about Jack," Mack said.

"Bet he burned up," Tommy tacked on

I found two autos parked in front of the V-A office. Tommy wasn't kidding about the union car's bright color. Two soldiers were sleeping under the cottonwood, with their rifles at their sides. A third leaned against the tree trunk, smoking and watching. It was so hot, all had unbuttoned their shirts and taken off their hats.

I was looking inside the car when the awake soldier hollered, "Can I help you?"

I crossed my arms and leaned against old red with one boot heel hung on the running board. "Naw. I'm waiting to see Kistos and Lawson."

The trooper stood. Looked to be about my age. As he marched toward me, I got primed for another law-and-order hassle. This one I could handle.

"You ever see such red in all your life?" he asked, finishing his smoke and mashing it into the dirt with his boot heel.

I shook my head. "Looks brand new, don't it? Know how long they've had it?"

"Two weeks, I heard. Bought it off some greasers in Pew-eblo." The kid cracked up. "You a coal miner?"

"Yeah."

"What's that pay?"

" 'Bout sixty dollars a month," I answered. "Depends on how much we dig."

The kid snickered.

"What's funny?" I asked.

"Oh, nothing," he said, smiling like a pin-head.

"How about I knock that fuckin' grin down your throat?"

Still smiling, the kid looked down at his boots, then up at me. "You could try."

I'd seen uneasiness and this kid's gray eyes showed some. He had blond hair and gapped teeth, like mine. His smooth white skin was spoiled only by a smear of pink, back of his neck, where the sun had blistered him that day.

I pulled one of Sidney's old tricks, unfolding my arms, real quick–like I was gonna throw a punch–but reaching up to scratch my ear instead.

The kid batted his eyes, flinched and put up his dukes. He was frowning now, ready to throw down.

I showed my palms and grinned. "Easy, General Custer. I was just playin'."

The kid lowered his fists but kept them clinched in case I sucker-punched.

"What's the army doing down here?" I asked.

"We escorted Brake, in case of trouble."

"That the governor's secretary?"

"Yeah. Of labor. He's trying to avert a strike," the kid said. "Spoke at the union convention in Trinidad, now he's touring some camps. He heard about your . . . problems."

"Guess the governor thinks it's too dangerous for his secretary to travel alone down here, huh?"

"I guess."

I looked around. "Yeah . . . this whole damn place is a death trap. Oughta live here. You like bein' in the army?"

"National Guard. Good part-time job. I go to school. In Denver."

"College-puke?"

"We're not going to be friends, are we?"

"Ain't decided." I looked up at the office doors. Still closed. "What're ya gonna be from college?"

"A lawyer, maybe. I just started this year." After he looked back at his buddies who were fast asleep, the trooper pointed to the portal at Number 6. "That where you work?"

"Sometimes."

"Can you take me inside?"

"What . . . so you can cackle some more? I ain't here for your amusement, sonny."

"Look . . . I've never been inside a coal mine. I'm just curious." The kid glanced back at his friends. "Sorry for being an asshole. My name is Jim Rubin." He put out his hand.

"You ain't afraid I'll rub off on you, Jim Rubin?"

"It'll wash off."

I grinned and shook his hand. "Alan Tanner. We *might* be able to go inside, but we'll have to play a little trick. Up top, there'll be a certified asshole, who won't let me take you in. But, if you was to tell the goober that the state secretary gave you direct orders to have a look and I'm the man that got picked to show you around, we'll be in like John D. You game?"

"Okay," Jim Rubin said.

"Better button up, put on your hat and carry your rifle."

"Sure. We have a flashlight under the seat in the Ford. Want me to get it?"

"Yeah," I said.

Jim Rubin stepped over to where his buddies were napping and got his gun. They never stirred. He nabbed the flashlight from the auto and we were off.

"What are you, a sergeant or somethin'?" I asked as we walked.

"A private. First class."

"What's 'at pay?"

"Hundred dollars a month. Part-time."

I swallowed a "Goddamn-are-you-shittin'-me?" comment and changed the subject. "It's hotter down here than Denver, ain't it?"

"Considerably. And dryer."

We left the flat and climbed the tracks.

"I ain't never been to Denver," I said. "Pretty big, with a lot of whorehouses and saloons, I bet."

"If that's what you're looking for. Got a semi-pro ball team, music halls, moving picture theaters, restaurants. Museums, too. I grew up there."

"Okay, we're gettin' close. You got your story straight?"

"Yep."

We topped the hill and found a deserted entrance with no guard.

"Humph." I looked around. "Might be inside and he'll be armed. Just stay ready with that made-up."

Jim Rubin banged the flashlight against his hand until it lit good and we went inside. I told him about how we laid track and set props. Explained the rash cones rising here and there.

"This big room we're in right now is all played out. See them pillars of coal along here? That's what we leave after taking what's safe to dig. That gets hauled out for you to burn in your heaters in Denver."

Jim Rubin shined the light around the room. "And the pillars hold up the ceiling as you go deeper. Pretty ingenious."

I was impressed by Jim Rubin's interest and quick understanding. "Let's go down to a station so you can see the operation."

The working seam was a little ways in. I knew we were pushing our luck, time-wise, but we were having fun and Jim Rubin was learning something valuable.

When we stepped inside the first work station we came to, the soldier bumped his head.

"Shit, just crouch down here, Jim Rubin. Shorties like me have an advantage. My buddy Mack's so stubby he almost never has to work on his knees–'less he's under a seam–like right here." I pointed to a deep trench cut under the wall of coal.

Jim Rubin shined his light across the face. "What are these pieces of rope running out?"

"Fuses. Diggers got an auger to drill holes and fix black powder charges. After the shift is over, shotfirers come in and set-off the charges."

"And the next morning, you have a pile of coal to load," Jim Rubin said.

"Yeah. You better separate out the granite and shit before you fill your cars, though, or the whole load'll get rejected."

The coal sparkled in the soldier's light. Jim Rubin ran his free hand across the face. "It's like another world in here. Don't you get claustrophobic?"

"Jim Rubin?"

"Yeah."

"Speak English."

Jim Rubin laughed. "I mean, it seems awful cramped. Would give me the creeps." Before we went back outside, he picked up some chunks of coal and slipped them in his pocket for a souvenir. Still no guard.

As we walked back down the track, the kid kept yapping.

"I can't figure why you guys fight to do this work, considering how you say the coal companies shit on you and how dangerous your working conditions are. No offense, but it seems to me you'd want to get a better job out in the world."

I snickered. "The world of mollycoddles? No offense. I always wanted to dig coal, Jim Rubin, just like my papa. Never thought of doing nothin' else. It ain't no pink tea in them mines, that's for sure. But it's honest work and you've done something after a day in the hole. If you love it, you take the risk."

We gassed until we ran out of subjects. I was plenty curious about the life Jim Rubin lived in Denver. But I kept mum, not wanting to show my ignorance. When we got back to the office, the two troopers, Lawson, Nick, Slatter, a head soldier I hadn't seen before, all the reporters, two strangers in suits and two Baldwins awaited us. Lou Dold stood ready beside his camera.

"We might have fucked up, Jim Rubin," I said.

"Yep," the soldier agreed. "But this'll give us a chance to practice our powers of persuasion, won't it?"

When we strolled up, the reporters had their pencils cocked over those little pads and everyone closed in.

Slatter and the head soldier were the kind of red-faced-hopping-mad that couldn't hear our explanations for their yelling. They said we had no respect or sense of responsibility. Didn't appreciate the seriousness of the situation. Were security threats. Acted like children.

Clearly the new super didn't recognize me from the night of the burn-out. "What do you have to say for yourself?" Slatter asked. Sounded like Mama.

"I was showin' off for the college-puke," I said. "That's why I took him up to Number 6. Cross my heart and hope to die, he didn't steal nothin' or make no drawings."

"This guy doesn't speak for me," Jim Rubin said. "The tour was my idea. *I* asked *him* to take *me* up there. Curiosity got the better of me."

"Bein' proud of our work, I was happy to show him around, too," I said.

"And it helped me see how the other half lives," Jim Rubin said. "Like you always say, Cap, 'Know your enemy.' "

With that wise-ass mouth on him, Jim Rubin reminded me of me. Guess the captain didn't appreciate the kid's crack because he got even redder. He motioned for the private to follow and before they'd walked ten feet, you could hear the commander shouting.

Slatter turned back to me. "Anarchists attacked this camp last month, boy. They assaulted two detectives and burned private property. Today, you lured a trooper away from his post. That's interference with an officer of the government. You think this is a game?"

I looked at the ground, tempted to spew, "Yeah, I think it's all a big game, you asshole, and we'll never win." Instead I muttered, "No, sir."

Jim Rubin was still getting tongue-lashed.

"You want me to take care of this piss-ant, boss?" one of the Baldwins asked.

"No. I want to hear what he has to say for himself," Slatter said.

Bobbing their heads to watch, listen and scribble, the reporters resembled feeding vultures.

"Mr. Slatter, I come up to the V-A office this afternoon to see my friends Kistos and Lawson–and hoped they'd introduce me to the secretary of labor. I got to talking with this kid and we had a look into Number 6."

"George," the suit I figured to be the secretary, interrupted, "what exactly *is* wrong with this boy showing the trooper around, except that it's a breach of company protocol?"

"Protocol, my ass," Slatter said. "It's against the law."

The other suit broke in. "You didn't answer Ed's question. What *is* the problem?"

"The problem is this boy . . ."

"Name's Alan Tanner," I said.

He poked a stubby finger at me. "That *YOU,* Alan Tanner, weaseled your way past a guard and went inside unauthorized."

"Weren't no weaslin' 'cause there weren't no guard, Mr. Slatter. Neither when we went inside nor come out. Weren't nobody around at all. We just walked straight in."

"No guard? Goddammit . . . ." He eyed his remaining detectives. "Anyway, it's a stupid thing for you to do, a thing that could put *you* under suspicion."

Jim Rubin joined the other soldiers standing at attention under the tree and the captain walked back to the group.

"Suspicion of what?" Second Suit asked.

"Anarchy," Slatter spat.

"WHAT?" Brake hollered.

"No, Ed, I get it," Lawson interrupted. "The superintendent's already told us he thinks the UMW promotes anarchy and what he has in front of him is a clear example. In an effort to overthrow the government of the United States, Tanner and his cronies burned a private residence, a saloon and a whorehouse, then worked half the night to put the fires out, to throw the law off scent. It all makes sense, now."

Nick smiled. "Yes. And to trick us more, Tanner act like he come to see me and Lawson, but he is really meeting another anarchist–that trooper–so he can pass the secret about mine 6."

"Ingenious," Brake said, smiling.

The commander saw nothing funny. "Private Rubin used poor judgment. But he's certainly no anarchist. What's the matter with you people?"

"Nobody's saying the *trooper* is an anarchist," Slatter whined.

"Then what are you saying?" Captain asked.

I jacked up my nerve and interrupted. "I ain't no damn whatchama-callit–anarchist–or a union man or a Mason or Catholic or nothin' else except another dumbass tryin' to make his wages, take care of his family and have a little fun. I see, now, what a big mistake I made takin' the soldier inside."

Nick looked at the super. "This Baldwin here call me a goddamn redneck inside your office and I am proud to be one. If my friend Alan Tanner is anarchist, I am anarchist."

"And I'm their leader," Lawson said.

Slatter stared at them. "You smart-asses aren't above the law."

"All right, now, George," the secretary interrupted. "I've got a pretty clear idea of the situation. And some recommendations for Governor Ammons that should prevent further trouble. If I can use your telephone once more."

Without answering, Slatter marched up the stairs with two news hounds on his tail. The Baldwins stayed put.

The secretary looked me over. "What did you say your name was, son?"

Told him. Figured I was in for a lecture.

"I'd like for you to know that the state of Colorado cares about you and your family," Brake said. "We'll remain involved."

"Well . . . I appreciate that," I said. "But what's took you so long?"

The secretary bunched his eyebrows. "Well . . . it's complicated. But I admire your directness, Mr. Tanner. And I hope we can talk again."

"Me, too," I said.

With that, the union mucks followed Slatter up the stairs with the Baldwins tagging along.

When I stuck out my hand to the captain, he gave a little start. Guess I surprised him. Said his name was Josephson.

"Is Jim Rubin in trouble?" I asked after we shook.

"That's not your concern," the captain said.

"Seems like a pretty smart guy, to me," I said. "I'd want him on my side, for sure. Guess he should have stayed on guard duty like them guys asleep under the tree, huh?"

"This isn't our affair, Alan," Lawson said.

"Okay, John," I said, turning back to the captain. "Jim Rubin's about the only outsider to give a rip about what we do up here, Mr. Captain. And he understood. It felt good to show him around. Why don't you ask him what we talked about and what he seen in that mine?"

The captain's faced reddened again. "I might do that." He put out his hand. "Good luck, Mr. Tanner. With that smart lip, you're going to need it."

I smiled and said thank-you.

The troopers ambled back to their car to wait for the state mucks.

Nick and Lawson stared at me.

"What?" I asked.

"Can't stay out of trouble, can you?" Lawson said.

I shrugged. "Shit, John, picking your nose gets you a beating. Might as well gin up some diversions."

"Just don't push your luck, ace," Lawson said. "These detectives are running short on patience and me and Nick won't always be around."

No response from me.

"You coming, Kistos?" Lawson asked.

Nick shook his head. "I will go down the hill with this criminal to scold. Pick me up on the road."

The Greek rolled a cigarette and we started walking. Said him and Cait were staying in Noble, an outlaw settlement about five miles east of Ludlow in the hills. Charlie Delveccio's cousin Leo owned a saloon and a rooming house there. Where the barkeep was getting over the beating he took from Choice Grabble.

"How is she?" I asked.

"Cait is good," Nick said. "You know her. Big plans. But Charlie is not right. I try to talk to him, but he is crazy. All he think about is killing."

"How in hell did they get out of town, Nick?" I asked.

"Wagon. Carl Abercrombie took them."

"That little suckass? Why would *he* help *them*?"

"Abercrombie is UMW," Nick said. "He take when he escape."

I shook my head. "Come on. Abercrombie has his nose stuck up the butt of ever' swell in Delagua. He's the one had the fistfight with Caitlin when she first come up here."

Nick nodded and smiled. "Abercrombie took Monroe, Charlie and Caitlin to Ludlow in the last Gestring. He was the union spy, all along, Alan. Come in as double-spotter with John Broiles, over two years ago. You know what double-spotter is?"

I didn't have the slightest idea.

"You start with two people–both union men–or doesn't have to be men. Caitlin work with John in Boulder. One guy is organizing underground, a little at a time. The other fellow has the most dangerous job. He get in real good with the company. Carl Abercrombie was the best. Even Slatter thought the clerk was a loyal suckass. Coalasses hate Abercrombie, you know."

I surely did know.

"All the while Abercrombie whisper names to the supers–names of guys who Abercrombie said was joining the union. But it really solid company men Carl tell on."

"And all three supers trusted that clerk so much, they sent 'em down?"

"Yes. Is beautiful, eh? These hard-ass company men, they so scared of union, they believe almost anything. Abercrombie get Edgerton to send Moss Browder down canyon. Moss Browder, only pit boss to survive Number 3 explosion. A word from Carl and Mr. Moss is gone. And every time a guy like Browder go down canyon a solid union man come up, looking for work. Oh, the fresh fish would tell he hate the union, but underground, he organize. One of these was Rolf Levy. Those two detectives found out."

"So you *was* using Jack's place?"

"Yes, much of the time. Paine's and Merkel's, too. But mostly McKintrick's."

"And Jack knew about all this?"

"Jack didn't care if he can make money from both sides. Do you know what become of the mayor?"

"Disappeared into thin air," I said. "We figured he burned up, but there ain't no evidence of that. Thought you might know somethin'."

Nick shook his head.

"Can't help thinkin' he might just show up. You know how Jack is." I swallowed. "Was Sid involved in this spy business, Nick?"

"No. But I think he was putting the twos together, as you say."

"Well, damn, *I* never put the twos together. I was in the dark."

"I know," Nick smiled. "Was a good plot. But them Baldwins is smart and they get Levy mad in the saloon. Rolf was a hothead and you cannot be a hothead and a good spy. Charlie and Cait was lucky to get out alive."

"How'd Abercrombie find them two?" I asked.

"He drive around in the wagon. Nobody suspect him, so nobody notice. Jack flag him down to pick up Cait and Charlie, who hid in the storeroom . . ."

"God-damn," I whispered, recalling Jack opening and closing the closet door during his search for Delveccio. He was checking to see if the wop was in there, I guess.

"Monroe wasn't part of plan. Abercrombie feel sorrow for him, roaming around." Nick smiled. "Carl tell me he pass you and Sidney, twice."

"Nick, what's gonna keep the companies from killin' us off?"

"They is desperate for coal. Even a little bit. You is here and working. Is why they ain't done nothing to you for three weeks."

"But we got no protection. We're on guard duty every night, right now. But all we got is sticks and pipes."

"Didn't companies pull back the Baldwins and let you dig with Sidney watching?"

"Yeah, but I'm still nervous."

"You can bring your mama to Noble tonight, if you want. Plenty room. Mack and Tommy will take."

"Some families are already leaving," I said. "But me and Cockeye have coal to shovel. And I can't just spring moving on Mama. It's got to be more her idea. Shit . . . I don't know what to do."

"Is a hard choice," Nick said. "The Greek say you is caught between whirlpool and rocks. How is the digging with Bastrop?"

Glanced skyward. "At least he speaks good English. Always talkin' about Barba done this, Barba done that. Him and Tostakis was at war most of the time. Now he misses him."

Nick nodded and smiled. "Look, Alan. The companies have six days to meet demands. If there is a walkout, we will have tents in Ludlow for strikers. McKintrick's wagons is at the livery for colliers to move belongings."

"But we got to go to Ludlow and get 'em, don't we?"

"Yes. But if Jack leave them here, the companies would take."

"I know that," I said. "I'm whinin', ain't I?"

Our conversation got interrupted as the two autos rumbled down the road behind us. When the troopers' car pulled even, I felt jealous 'cause Jim Rubin was driving. He steered the car so close we had to step back.

"Rot in hell, ya fucking redneck," he muttered as they coasted by.

"I'll put you there, ya goddamn college-puke," I hollered back, grinning.

Jim Rubin's hand came out the window in a secret wave goodbye.

"You two have same amount of the smart-ass, eh?" Nick asked.

"Yeah. Discovered it right quick, too," I replied. "Ain't a bad kid for a college puke."

The union car, with John at the wheel and the state mucks in back, rolled up beside us. I walked around to the passenger side with Nick.

"I know what you think, Alan. But is too late to stop, now. People cannot live and work like this. You ain't in it by yourself."

"I want to believe that, Greek."

Nick shook my hand. "I will see you another day."

CHAPTER NINETEEN
September 23, 1913

The coal companies probably figured a walkout was guff. Since most shovel jockeys were so glad to be working during hard times, only a handful of lazy gripers would leave. Besides, no real American would get mixed up with anarchist scum disguised as a union. V-A and CF&I believed, no doubt, that if they raked a few crumbs of concession off their table, the starving poor would be oh-so-grateful and steadfast. And, if all else failed, their thugs could force us to work at gunpoint.

But they were wrong. Fed-up working people had just been biding their time, waiting for someone to tell them when to go. And when Mack and Tommy brought news of the strike, the shuttles filled up fast. Me and Sid rode down to Ludlow with six other drivers and rented a Gestring with five-foot sideboards and four mules. The rigs included hobbles, feed and bags to keep the nags satisfied till we needed them. Cost: two dollars.

After me and Sid got the team, I wanted to hang around Ludlow, just to see if Nick, Cait, or Jack would show up. But there wasn't time. Didn't keep my curiosity from bubbling, though.

Mama had started packing boxes and bags when the Texans first brought word. But the morning of the walkout, our escape plan ground to a halt when she insisted on taking Grandmama's headboard, an old piece of furniture a junk dealer wouldn't give us a dollar for.

"I told you," Sidney mumbled. "Now, we're gonna have to move shit around in the wagon."

"All right," I said. "You go outside and I'll take care of Mama."

"It's freezin'," Sid said.

"Suit yourself. But if you stay in here, let me do the talking. If you two get into it, we'll never leave."

"I might as well start rearrangin'," Sidney said.

"You don't have much respect for my powers of persuasion, do you?"

"Just hurry up, scamp."

Sid went outside and I strolled into the bedroom where Mama was dusting the piece.

"You know, if we take that thing, we're gonna have to re-arrange the wagon. Barely got the last mattress in."

"I don't care, Alan, and I told you already. If you and Brother had listened to me from the start, we'd have loaded it with the beds. Where's Sidney?"

"He got tired of waitin' and left with the Bastrops a half-hour ago." I flicked a rotten place on the side and the wood crumbled. "Look here, Mama."

She swatted me. "Get your hand away from there, dumbhead. You'd just as well save your breath. The headboard and the wardrobe are all the furniture I have from Mother and Daddy's house. I can't take the wardrobe, but I'm taking that headboard."

"I'm afraid the whole thing's gonna fall apart."

Mama grabbed an end. "Pick up, Alan."

"Yes, ma'am."

We'd carried the piece into the front room just as Sidney opened the door. "Detective out here says we gotta go. We're the last ones."

"I'm well aware of that fact, Sidney. You two had to argue," Mama said. "Take this."

Brother gave me the stink-eye as replaced her, toting. I scrunched my shoulders in response.

Mama held the door and guided us through. "Don't hurt your backs, now, and mind the step-down."

Heavy slate clouds clutched the hills and a stiff, cold wind blew Mama's dress where it hung out under her overcoat.

"See, I told you we were the last ones."

"Keep chirping, Sidney," Mama said.

"That guard's gonna come up here with his pistol . . ."

"Hush, magpie!"

Sid had stacked the cage with four chickens on top of Caitlin's trunk and we slid the headboard into a sliver of space.

Sid lit on the seat. He'd spread out a portion of one of the tarps for him and Mama to sit on and left the rest to cover up with. Then he grabbed the reins. Meanwhile, Mama made a trip around the wagon to survey the load. "Is it all gonna ride like that? Looks pretty tippy."

"It's the best we can do," I said.

"Chickens are out in the weather."

"Mama . . . we got to go!" Sidney snapped.

I looked at her, then back at Brother, who was already getting down.

We rearranged the other tarp to cover the chickens.

"Okay, Your Highness, whaddaya think?" Sid asked.

"Think I reared two smart-alecky boys."

"We had a perfect role model," I said.

Mama surveyed the load. "I guess it's all right. We'll see. Goodbye, little house. Take care of yourself while we're gone."

Sidney climbed back aboard. Before I could help Mama up, she scurried back toward the house.

"What now?" Sid hollered.

"Oh, I forgot something," she called. "Won't take a minute."

I looked up at Sidney. "Don't want to leave, does she?"

"Nah."

Mama ran back, holding something wrapped in a towel. "It's our pictures." She handed them to me and climbed aboard.

"You bring the rules, too?" I asked.

"Yeah, I did. And I don't want any discussion about it, either. Can you get them inside something, so they won't get wet?"

I untied a corner of the tarp and wedged the keepsakes underneath, between the chickens and the headboard. "Anything else to put us in more danger, Your Majesty?" I asked.

"Just get moving," Mama said.

After I pulled my hat down low, tied a muffler over my ears, put on gloves and turned the collar up on my overcoat, I grabbed the lead mule's halter. "Get 'em moving, chief. I'll walk along side, at least until we're at the bottom of the big hill."

Sidney released the brake, hollered, "Up mules," and we were off.

Paper swirled in the road and between the houses. Doors flap-banged on their hinges. **UMW FOREVER** was scrawled on the side of one house and **STRIKE!** on some others. Glass had been broken out of lots of window frames.

Guess I should have felt mournful, now that the strike was on and we were leaving. But I was empty and cold as those shacks. Everything important in my life had happened here, but the word *home* wouldn't stick.

Just beyond Greektown, the road sloped as we rolled into the open.

"My God in heaven, would you look at this," Mama breathed.

Below us, hundreds of people moved past the company buildings and the ruins of the imbibery and whorehouse. Lucky ones, like us, hauled their possessions in wagons and buckboards. Others drove homemade pushcarts with bicycle tires. Lots toted belongings on their backs or carried things in their arms.

As we rolled down the hill, rain commenced in slant sheets and Mama pulled the tarp closer. I freshened my hold on the mule's halter and Sidney reined back some to slow the team. Brackish water gushed from swollen ditches and poured over the road. Had to be sure of each step so I wouldn't slip down.

The mules lumbered along. We followed the slushy ruts to the edge of town, where we took a place in the line of wagons. We'd roll forward a few feet before we had to stop. Some folks parked, seeking cover from the stinging wind and rain.

Occasionally, a Model T full of swells or detectives putted by. The road was a bog now, with water standing in spots. Mama drove while me and Sid trudged through mud up to our boot tops, pushing the wagon along as best we could.

The temperature continued to drop and, by mid-morning, the rain had turned to sleet.

CHAPTER TWENTY
September 23, 1913

A mile below Delagua, wheeled traffic stopped. Pedestrians passed on either side of the wagons and disappeared down a hill ahead.

"Somebody must be stuck," I said.

"Would you look at this guy?" Sid said. "I'll bet he's been havin' fun."

A hatless man slathered with mud hiked toward us. When he got closer, we discovered it was Cockeye.

"Hey, boy," Sid hollered. "Thought you were a mud hen. What's up?"

Cockeye wiped his eyebrows with his thumbs. "A dern mess is what. Down that hill," he pointed, "the land opens up, low, flat and wide. First time anybody could speed up and pass since we left town. The early wagons and carts got through, before the whole thing become a wallow. When I got down there, just one wagon was stuck. While we was tryin' to get them folks out, two more slid in. Total of three."

Me and Sid got tickled as Cockeye continued.

"Now, you'd think if *another* wagon-load of people rolled up on a mud hole with three wagons mired, somebody on board would say it ain't such a good idea to just pile-drive in there. But no. One at a time, three more splashed in. Total of six, turned ever-which-a-ways."

"Sounds like this could take hours," Mama moaned.

"Sure enough, Mrs. Tanner," Cockeye said. "Been down there for over an hour, already. Boneheads is muckin' around in the slop, jabberin' at each other in ten languages, like they're gonna fight right there. I told 'em to cut some pryser poles, but nobody understood. So we pushed. I went completely under, when the last one come out. I sure did. Threw my back out, too, and nobody said, 'Thank you' or 'Kiss my rear' or nothin'. I come back up here to see if I could find some loose planks, or anything, for prysing."

"Where's your wagon?" I asked.

"Everybody was in such a hurry to pass and everything, I just parked it over there." He directed us to a wagon partially hidden under a juniper. "I rigged Ida a tent so her and the kids could get out of the weather."

"That you, William Ernest?" Ida called from under the tarpaulin.

"Ya-a-s," Cockeye squawked.

"Somebody else out there?"

"The Tanners, Snowflake. Havin' a little chat. Still pretty cold and sleety. We ain't goin' nowhere, yet." Cockeye wiped his eyebrows again.

Ida backed out from under the tarp and waddled over.

"Morning, Ethel," Ida said.

Mama's "Good morning" never broke Ida's chatter.

"William Ernest been talkin' your ears off, no doubt. You can shore get the news from him, if nothin' else. He don't miss much. Can you believe tryin' to move in weather like this? Not only a rain storm, but sleet. And they say the Israelites had it bad leavin' Egypt. Was at least hot for them. If I'd a knowed it would be this bad, I woulda stayed home, I'll tell you that. Union's supposed to have tents for us, right? What if we all make it down canyon and there ain't no tents? You thought about that?"

"Lord's will be done, Ida," Mama called, with a whiff of sarcasm.

"That's the best way to look at it, ain't it?" Ida thumbed through her good book. " 'And there fell upon men a great hail out of heaven, every stone about the weight of a talent; and men blasphemed God because of the plague of hail; for the plague thereof was exceedingly great.' *Revelation* 16, Verse 21."

"Ain't nobody blasphemin', Snowflake," Cockeye called.

"Somebody was, or we wouldn't be havin' this cold snap. Just make sure it ain't you, sir," Ida responded. "We don't want to call down the wrath even more, right Ethel?"

Mama smiled weakly. I could tell she wasn't in the mood for religiosity.

I figured Sidney noticed her irritation, too, because he pulled us back to the subject at hand. "I think we can get some prysers out of those cottonwoods over yonder. If I can find the axe." He turned to the wagon.

"Might as well get the sledgehammer and the rope, too," I called. "It *was* all back left, on the bottom, Sid, before the Queen had us rearranging."

Ida turned to Mama again. "You know, Ethel, since we're stuck here, we might as well combine what we have and fix some lunch. 'Who satisfieth thy mouth with good things, so that thy youth is renewed like the eagle's.' *Psalms*, Chapter 103, Verse 5. Might even build a fire. You brought the coal oil, didn't you, William Ernest?"

"Yes, Snowflake. I'll get it for you."

Cockeye soon reappeared with his axe and a spout can, which he handed to his wife. "Be careful when you start it, now, dearie, or gettin' down canyon will be the least of our worries."

"Me and Ethel will do fine with the fire starting, William Ernest. Just make sure you don't go sneaking whisky sips with your buddies out there and cut your head off."

Like we had liquor on us. That damn woman lived to stir up trouble.

Sid brought out the hardware and me and Cockeye followed him into the cottonwood grove.

After we cut two sturdy poles and had some hot lunch, we hiked down the hill to a muddy swale. I hoped that after we'd killed all that time, there wouldn't be anybody left in the bog. But two wagons were still stuck, center of the mud puddle. Another guy had stopped a little ways up the road to let his woman and four kids climb down.

"Gettin' a team on the other side to help pull out the stranded wagons is the ticket," Cockeye said, as we walked down the hill. "The ones that got through was in too big a hurry to help stragglers." Our neighbor pointed at the knothead driving the passenger-less wagon. "Watch this."

With his family looking on from the edge of the bog, the papa whipped his mules into a running start. Obviously hoping speed and less weight would carry him through, he charged like it was a land rush across dry prairie, wide-right of the other wagons. Thought he might make it, but the mud took over. The mules bogged down, their legs churning, the papa cussing, the mama and children bawling on the bank.

Sidney whistled.

"I told you this was makin' people crazy," Cockeye said. "You got to be willin' to help each other. If we can get one rig out, we can use that team of mules to pull another."

"Well, let's get on with it," Sid said. "It ain't gettin' any drier. Or warmer."

We waded to the farthest wagon. A woman sat on the seat holding the team's reins and three young'uns huddled under a blanket next to her. Two men stood knee-deep in mud, trying to push the wagon out.

"We got some prysers, boys," Cockeye called.

The wops didn't understand anything we said, so we made motions of pushing and pulling. They joined me and Sid and Cockeye, stabbing the poles into the mud until we hit solid ground under the wagon's rear end. The sleet spattered as we worked.

The mules couldn't get any footing and the wagon kept sliding back, so Sid suggested a winch. We tied two of our ropes to the wagon's single tree and stumbled out of the swale, uncoiling the ropes as we went. While we were snubbing one rope around a cottonwood for leverage, the union roadster pulled up. Barba and John Lawson got out. They wore denim jackets and overalls with the legs stuffed into knee-high boots and both had red bandanas tied around their necks.

"Hello, Tanners, Bastrop." Barba grinned like everything was hunky-dory.

I waved, but Cockeye ignored the Greek. Still angry from that last disagreement, I reckoned.

"Is a fine muddy morning, eh?" Barba said. "You know John Lawson? He come to work, just like us."

I nodded. "We got a winch goin' here, John. Look okay to you?"

Lawson said it looked good and I slogged back out to the wagon to help with the pushing.

"We want to all be together on this, now," Sid hollered. "Up here, we're gonna pull on one rope and use the other to snub around the cottonwood, so we won't slide backward. Hey, Barba, you know how to say in wop, 'Lady, please whip the hell out of them mules'?"

Barba shrugged, turned to one of the Italian men and pointed at the woman holding the reins. "*Mamacita*, whippy *moulari*," Barba called, making a whipping motion.

"*Si*," the husband said, nodding. "*Frustare, mulas*, *Clemencia*," he called to the woman and whipped like Barba had.

Clemencia nodded and held the reins high.

The sleet clattered harder into the mud.

"Okay, everybody, '*Frustare*' is the signal," Sid hollered. "Don't let nothin' slide backward once we start. Ready? *Frustare*!"

The woman held the reins in one hand and whipped with the other. Cockeye and his wops pried. Me and the others pushed. Sidney and Lawson pulled one rope and Barba winched with the other. The wagon moved a little and we kept at it. The mules got footing and, in a great sucking and slushing, the wagon emerged. Sid commenced coughing as we waded out of the muck.

Brother's idea had done the trick and I felt like we could lick this.

* * *

We worked for two hours, while the temperature dropped and sleet and scattered snowflakes fell.

With the traffic jam dislodged at last, we brought the wagons through, one at a time, with each successful wagoneer taking his team back to the swale to help the next family. Our rig was last with Cockeye's team pulling.

Everybody got on board and the wagons were ready to leave, when I heard the gurgle of a small engine accelerating. Soon I saw a motorcycle coming up the road. When the driver got closer and slowed, I was amazed to see that it was Nick.

The motorcycle sputtered as he revved the engine and circled us. "Hey, Alan, close your mouth and tell where is John Lawson."

I pointed to the union leader who was already making his way up to us. Nick met him and delivered his message. Lawson hollered for Barba to get in the car.

When Nick came back, Cockeye asked what was going on.

"Is a problem with tents," Nick answered.

"What did I tell you?" Ida wailed, thumbing through the Bible. "What did I say? It's an omen . . . a real bad sign. And us stuck at the end of the line. Whatever you and your cronies done out there, William Ernest, you brought down the wrath."

"We didn't do nothin' except help people out, Snowflake," Cockeye said. "Couldn't move till they moved."

"You must of sinned without knowin' it, boy," Sidney hollered.

"Heed transgressions of omission as well as commission, Mr. Sidney Tanner." Ida raised her book and shouted: "Hear the word: 'Behold, the day of the Lord cometh, cruel both with wrath and fierce anger, to lay the land desolate: and he shall destroy the sinners thereof out of it.' From *Isaiah*, Chapter 13, Verse 9. The Lord sees the unseen sin and smites. Sometimes the innocent suffer as well."

"While he's got his hammer out, Cockeye ought to knock her in the head," Sid muttered.

Ida's wailing had the Bastrop kids stirred up and crying. Before he got his team moving, Cockeye hollered for everybody to shut up.

Barba cranked the engine, got in the Model T and Lawson drove them away, the tires of the automobile spinning until they got traction.

I caught hold of the mule's halter again as Nick rolled off. When he tried to speed up, the motorcycle slipped to one side and I expected him to go down. But he planted a boot in the mud, pushed forward and righted himself.

As I watched the little machine scoot down the road, I wondered if there was anything the Greek couldn't master.

CHAPTER TWENTY-ONE
September 23-26, 1913

Soaking wet and shivering, I walked all the way, holding the team in check.

Just across the railroad tracks in Ludlow, a striker was waving an American flag as big as he was. When we got closer, the joker planted the flag and ran toward us. It wasn't a guy. It was Caitlin, in fedora, jacket, trousers and boots.

Knowing now what she'd risked working for the union, what she'd hid about her past, I looked at her with fresh eyes. From that first day in Ludlow, she'd been feisty and independent–a modern woman who didn't give a damn what anybody thought of her. The raw and reckless courage that I lacked had surfaced–in Cait. I admired her and smoldered with jealousy.

"Hey, Carrot Head," I called.

Caitlin gave me a long hug. When she pulled back, her cheeks shined with tears. "You're exhausted, aren't you, Allie? We'll get some sandwiches and hot coffee in you and you'll feel better."

Sid and Mama had been trading naps, leaning against each other or back against the truck boards, but they roused when Caitlin called to them.

"Hello, Ethel, Sidney. Weather's terrible foul, isn't it? Reminds me of Wales on a summer's day."

"You gave us a fit, little girl," Mama said. "Afraid you'd been hurt."

Caitlin walked to the wagon and put her hand on Mama's knee. "Oh, Ethel, don't make me feel guilty. Things have been so hectic. I'm the official greeter for the Ludlow colony and I'd be honored to lead you into camp."

Cait came back to me, hooked my arm and kissed me on the cheek. "Me and Charlie scooted off to Noble, a little town in the Black Hills. Nick's up there, too."

"Already heard. He told me all about your unionizing. And I thought you was just a hotheaded singer."

"That, too, Allie." Cait winked. "Are the Bastrops back there?"

"Yeah, but please don't get Ida stirred up. She's been scripturizin' all the way down. That woman knows more Bible verses than a preacher. And all of 'em negative."

Caitlin snorted.

"It's the truth," I continued. "And what's worse, she quotes passages that deal with horrible things, mostly–plagues, pestilence, bad luck, punishments."

"There's no place for us to stay, is there?" Ida hollered at Cait. Our loud talk had waked her. "Ain't no tents."

Caitlin pulled me back to the Bastrop wagon. "There's fifteen tents, so far. The rest are coming. John thinks the railroad held up the shipment."

Cockeye tried to hold Ida back, calling for us to get a move-on. But it was just like I'd feared. She got cranked up again.

"Lord's will be done. No hope for us on this earth. Take this advice from *Matthew* 6: 20 : 'Lay up for yourselves treasures in heaven, where neither moth nor rust doth corrupt, and where thieves do not break through nor steal'."

I'll be damn if she hadn't hit a verse I'd heard of. Mama used to tell it to us sometimes. Always thought it was pretty good advice, until Ida proclaimed it.

Cait hoisted her flag and we walked toward Ludlow. Ida spouted a verse every so often. Everybody just let her rattle. Guess folks were afraid of going to hell if they told her to shut up.

Seemed to be two religions battling over our souls. On one side, Ida's Christianity said, "Lay up treasures in heaven," 'cause you sure won't get them here on earth. Where were the verses that said something about helping our lot, *now*? Bible verses like Ida offered gave people excuses for doing nothing.

On the other side stood the diggers' religion. The United Mine Workers was doing *something*, all right. But unionizing and this strike were bringing more misery than help.

I found no comfort in either theology that afternoon.

Where the Delagua Canyon road met the muddy Ludlow road, I saw the encampment for the first time. Caitlin said there were over a thousand people out there. Behind a barbed-wire fence on that ice-salted prairie, they milled around like cattle in a feed lot or a killing pen.

A great rumble of voice and movement rose. Babies squealed, men cursed, women laughed and cried, wagons groaned, music played and a smoky, leathery, musky smell hung about the place. Sparks from scattered fires flickered into the air, like the camp itself was giving off energy as night advanced.

A few Ludlow townspeople waved and clapped from the roadside. Some even shouted encouraging words. I figured only the promise of potential customers could have brought these strangers out in such miserable weather. But I appreciated it. Even found myself waving back and speaking a time or two.

Mama sighed again, like she had when we saw all the people leaving Delagua. But I kinda liked it. Either that old Caitlin Broiles enthusiasm had taken hold of me–or I was crazy tired–but the closer we got, the better I felt.

Inside the fence, Cissy Cuminetti rushed up to greet us. "Afraid you get lost in the mud, Ethel. I save a space for you right here next to us."

"Don't forget the Bastrops," Ida called.

Cissy pointed. "Other side of Tanners. Come on, you lazy bums, park so the women can get out of this weather."

While we steered the wagons into the spots, Cissy splashed through the puddles, pointing and clapping her hands.

"We have a neighborhood now," she said. "Right on the road so we can catch them scabs if they come in. Moraleses over here," Cissy pointed. "Giottos in between. There is sandwiches, blankets, coffee and milk in the canteen. Make yourself at home."

Cissy amazed me. I expected Baldy's death and that sorry excuse for a funeral would slow the little woman down, but she'd got stronger, more determined. Every bad thing that happened stoked the fight in her.

Tanners and Bastrops set up a shelter, stretching tarps between the Gestrings. What we didn't want soaked, like the trunks, the chickens and the headboard, we put under the wagon. Finally, we spread the remaining tarps on the ground and laid the mattresses and bedding out. Then me, Sid and Cockeye drove the mules to the livery.

By the time we got back, the sleet and rain had let up. Camp women built fires and brought us sandwiches and coffee. Sid met with Lawson on union business. After I dug out some dry clothes and changed, I found Cait and asked for a tour.

Reporters in topcoats and rubber boots tramped around, yakking and scribbling. The Greeks camped off by themselves as usual, roasting meat on a spit. They tipped ouzo and played boccie on strips of cardboard, like it was a sunny Sunday.

A stage had been built on the western edge of the camp, near the railroad tracks and a goodly number of people crouched under the platform and among them Sidney and John.

Cait introduced me to Izzy Palovich, a motorman from Hastings who played clarinet. The bohunk had already scraped together a band, with two guitar players and a violinist. Even recruited a bass fiddle man, a tailor from Ludlow. Cait said Nick joined them on occasion. The musicians were warming up under a tarp tacked to the edge of the stage and stuck over poles held up by guy lines.

I heard a motorcycle's engine accelerating and saw the union machine, now rigged with sidecar and passenger, racing up from Ludlow. It rounded the turn onto the canyon road, rumbled across the railroad tracks, entered the camp gate and rolled to a stop near the stage. Nick was driving. He got off to help an old woman out of the sidecar.

"That's Mother Jones, Alan," Cait said. "She spoke in Trinidad when we voted to strike. Bloody powerful."

"Mack and Tommy told us about her," I responded, as Sidney stepped up.

Lawson greeted the old woman, who had pulled off her motoring cap and goggles and was fluffing up her white hair. She took the strike leader's arm and let him escort her through the growing congregation. Nick walked behind them, then branched to join us in front of the stage.

As more and more strikers learned that Mother Jones had arrived, they pushed up close, cheering and shouting.

"Are you about your work, Mother?" a man called, putting out his hand as she walked by.

"I've been at it damned hard, all day, son," she called. "And how are you?"

"Tolerable, Mother, tolerable, now that you're here."

Seemed like most of the strikers had gathered by the time Lawson climbed the steps to the stage. A jaunty hop onto the icy platform sent him sliding on his back across the planks, like a ball player trying for a base.

A lot of folks tittered at John's misfortune.

Grinning and red-faced, Lawson put his hat back on, got to his feet and hollered, "If that made you feel any better, I'll do it again."

Folks chuckled and some clapped.

"My name is John Lawson, for those of you who don't already know, and I'm glad you all could make it today. We figure ninety per cent of the diggers left the camps. The UMW has set up eleven other colonies like this on the prairie. You have basically shut down the southern fields!"

Cheers.

"First, let me say how sorry we are about the tents. The railroad tricked us. But more are coming. I'll be sleeping outside until they arrive, that I can tell you. As far as I'm concerned, it's better to freeze out here in the mud than suffer one more day in sunshine under company law."

Applause.

"Before I bring Mother Jones up here, I have a few announcements.

The United Mine Workers will be paying each of you, in cash, while you're off: three dollars a week for miners, one dollar for wives and fifty cents for each child. Payday will come every Friday."

"Will our babies have to sleep out in this cold, tonight, Mr. Lawson?" Ida yelled.

"Not if we can help it. Rancher Clement Haddock is standing right over there. Wave, Mr. Haddock. He has space in his house and barn and he tells me other local families are offering places in their barns. We have some tarps. There are fifteen tents and we figure we can get at least ten squeezed into each one. Those with tents or tarps, invite in some neighbors. Leo Delveccio says if some of you want to climb the hill up to Noble, there's plenty of room up there."

"Yeah, if you don't mind gettin' stabbed," a feller called.

"Naw . . . it ain't that bad," Lawson said with a smile.

The strike leader let everyone yammer a little, then he continued. "When I was eight years old, I went to work as a breaker boy in Mount Carmel, Pennsylvania and I've fought for the union cause most of my life. I've been down to Forbes and up to Hastings, today, and I saw union strikers–men, women and children–making the best of a very bad situation. Almost nobody has tents, but we all got hope and grit. I read the weather in the *Chronicle-News*, folks, and it's not going to get any better. But if you think you've got it bad, consider the poor superintendents stuck up in the canyon, with swells and guards digging their coal. And pity those poor company women down in Trinidad, having to go out to their Tuesday night bridge parties in weather like this. Why, it's barbaric!"

I cackled at that. Throng did, too.

"We need to ask something of you this evening. It has to do with money and I know you're all low. Join the union, those of you who haven't. We've got a table down here and we're going to keep one set up in the canteen. It's a dollar a month for your voice and your organization. We want to get 100% membership this week.

"There are reporters from all over the country in every tent colony. So, let's get it right from the beginning, boys. Tell Governor Ammons, President Wilson, Mr. John D. Rockefeller, chairman of the board L.M. Bowers and, of course, our good friends, the cops in Huerfano and Las Animas Counties–I am John Lawson." He spread his arms. "And we are United Mine Workers of the United States of America. We're out here on this desolate plain in sleet and rain and snow; we're doing fine and we're staying!"

Cheers and applause.

I turned to see Caitlin's reaction, but she was talking to Nick.

"This weather *is* terrible," Lawson continued, "but it shows what you're made of. It would be easy to come out in the sunshine on a Sunday afternoon and listen to men in starched shirts, then go back to work on Monday. The owners would let us do that all year long. But it takes real citizens to leave your homes, to shake your fists in the faces of the companies, their scabs and hired thugs and say, 'We are human beings and we have rights under a higher law than state law.' "

The shouts and cheers and applause spread and I felt stirred up again. The union leader waved and stepped back to the top of the stairs.

"I got this old woman with me, today," Lawson called, amid the thunder of clapping and cheers, "and she'd be mad as hell if I didn't let her speak. Nick Kistos said he had to tie her down in the side car to keep her from trying to drive the motorcycle so they'd get here faster." Lawson waited for the merriment to ease a little. "Ladies and gentlemen, I'd like for you to meet Mother Jones!"

Lawson helped the old woman climb the steps onto the stage. She waved and the cheering increased.

"Come in close, friends, 'cause I'm about spoke out," she called in a voice so forceful, it surprised me. "I'm gonna keep this thing short because John needs to help you find a place to sleep. I know you're cold and hungry and worried. You're likely wondering why in the world you left your warm houses. Well, I'm here to tell you why. You're here because you're sick and tired and this is the only way. When Victor-American and CF&I came upon this earth, they didn't get a mortgage on it, did they? No, they did not. The earth with its coal and iron was here long before they came and it will be here when their rotten carcasses are burning up in hell."

Cheers, laugher and clapping

"I came to tell you what I told people in the other colonies who are cold and afraid like you–over twenty thousand of them, spread out from Trinidad to Walsenburg. We're gonna win!"

Hurrahs, applause

"If you organize and stick with it, you will win. I've seen it happen in West Virginia and up in Michigan. You will be free. Poverty and misery will be unknown. You will turn the jails into playgrounds for the children. You will build homes and not log kennels and shacks as you have them now. There can be no civilization as long as such conditions abound, but you men and women will have to stand and fight!"

A guy passed his red bandana up to Mother Jones and everyone roared when she tied it around her neck. "If they're gonna call us 'Rednecks,' by God, we'll be 'Rednecks' and be damned proud of it!

"Before we talk about beds for this evening, I want to bring up a true songbird who comes to us all the way from Wales, another land of coal. Our official greeter at Ludlow, Mrs. Caitlin Broiles."

Caitlin climbed the steps to cheers and clapping. Mother Jones kissed her and whispered something in her ear. Caitlin stepped out to the edge of the stage, holding her fedora against the wind. "This is a song written today, especially for this occasion," she yelled. "It's called, 'The Union Forever.' We'll sing it to the tune of 'The Battle Cry for Freedom.' I'll tell you the words for first so you can sing them with me:

We will rally from the coal mines
We will battle to the grave.
Shouting the battle cry of union.
And although we may be poor,
Not a man will be a slave.
Shouting the battle cry of union.

The union forever! Hurrah, boys, hurrah!
Down with the Baldwins, and up with the law;
For we're coming, Colorado,
We're coming all the way,
Shouting the battle cry of union,
Throughout the livelong day.

Caitlin sang the song through once before everybody joined her. By the time she'd finished, she was wiping away tears with the cuff of her jacket.

*　　　　*　　　　*

The rest of the tents arrived three days later along with the sunshine. We lined up at the depot and got the fat bundles distributed after about an hour of unnecessary train shuttling from track to track. The railroad bosses held big interests in coal mines and they were happy to have their hirelings do any little thing to irritate strikers. By the time we got back to the colony, belongings had begun to dry out and spirits were up.

Like almost everybody else, we set our tent on top of a plank platform that me and Sid built. Each tent was like a house, with its pitched roof supported by two eight-foot posts joined to a ridge-beam. The tents' sidewalls were pulled outward and staked to guy lines, four on a side. The roof had a hole for the pipe of a coal-burning Excelsior stove that sat on one wall.

By mid-afternoon, one-hundred fifty tents stood in rows across the forty-acre plot. Strikers built a bath house of corrugated tin in the southwest corner of the camp. We sank poles and strung chicken wire for a backstop and had ourselves a baseball field. The women draped American flags on the side of the stage, to attract the attention of passengers coming down from Walsenburg or up from Trinidad on the trains.

Late in the afternoon when the sun was right, Lou Dold set up his camera on an abandoned flatcar and shot three postcards, left-to-right, so he could show the whole colony. "Ludlow," he labeled the center photograph in white pen, "September 26, 1913."

CHAPTER TWENTY-TWO
September 29, 1913

According to Mama, striking offered too much temptation to get drunk and disorderly. Me and Sid knew there'd be no peace if we thought about lying around or visiting a saloon. She even frowned upon playing baseball, if we hadn't done something constructive first. So we went looking for part-time work.

Since Clement Haddock seemed sympathetic to working men, we decided to start with him. In addition to his considerable ranch and the livery, he owned the land the colony sat on and a lot of acreage in and around Ludlow. He had come out in bad weather the first night to tell families they could sleep at his place. We thought he might let us do some flunky work for him. Mama had seen to it that we were masters of flunky work.

Me and Sid were walking out the rut-road leading to the big house, joking around, enjoying the warmer morning, when a Model T swung into view. As it got closer, I could see that a woman was driving. Stopped and asked if she could help us. Looked familiar to me.

Sid told her what we wanted. She gave us the once-over. I wondered if she'd ever seen coalasses close-up.

"Clem might use you," she said. "But he'll try you out first. He's had only one full-time man in thirty years. That should tell you something. There's no point in going up to the house if you don't want to work."

"Don't we look like we want to work?" Sid asked.

"Just a warning," she said. "Others came up, stayed a day and never came back. Some only made half a day. I guess Clem wore them out."

Sid looked at me and grinned.

"Are you Mr. Haddock's wife?" I asked.

The lady cackled. "I'm his daughter. His *youngest* daughter."

I felt my face heating up. "Well, you called him Clem . . ."

"I know . . . but it's the first time anyone ever thought we were married. I run the dry goods store. You bought overalls and candy from me sometime last year."

"Yeah . . . in October. I thought I recognized you."

She nodded. "Well . . . my father and his hired man are shagging strays this morning. If you hurry up, you might catch them. If you don't catch them before they leave, you won't see them till sundown. You guys have hats?"

We shook our heads.

"Gonna need some. I sell a good hat at the store. Wide brims."

"What's your name, ma'am?" Sid asked.

"Susan Haddock," she hollered, lowering her specs and motoring down the road.

"Nice girl," Sid said, staring after her. "See how brown her face is? Bet she's no stranger to ranch work."

"I noticed her sunbeat hands that day first in the dry goods. Think you might marry her?" I joshed.

"Yeah, prob'ly." Sid snickered. "Then you and Mama can work for me."

*　　　*　　　*

The only person around the yard was an old Mexican loading hay bales onto a wagon joined to a tractor.

"*Habla* English?" Sid asked.

Said he did.

"Could you tell us where to find Mr. Haddock?"

The Mexican pointed to a johnny behind the house.

"Looks like a man of such means could afford an indoor privy," Sid observed.

"They got, but he don't like," the Mexican said. He stacked the last bales, then led a horse out of the barn. Stepped back inside for the tack and went to work saddling the nag.

Waiting for the rancher to finish his business, we leaned on the fence and watched the greaser fiddle with the rig.

"You memorizin' what that Mexican is doin' there?" I asked Sid. "Rancher's gonna give you a test, first thing."

"Oh, yeah. Nothin' to it. Just a strap and a buckle."

The door to the johnny creaked, as the old man leaned out and stepped down into the dirt. He finished hitching up his trousers, bent backwards with his hands in the small of his back. "Goddamn," he hollered, "it's hell gettin' old."

Haddock cut a pitiful figure for a rich man. His baggy pants had the knees out. He wore a threadbare tweed jacket and boots that looked like they'd been dragged through the brush, then set out to bake in the sun. His hat was an unblocked slouch, soaked through at the band. He stopped to stretch his back twice more before he reached us.

"I help you young men?" he asked. He cut a plug of tobacco and packed his jaw with it.

Sid put out his hand. "Name's Sid Tanner, Mr. Haddock, and this here's my baby brother, Alan. We heard you might have some work."

"Might. Can you ride?"

I gave Sid a sideways look. I didn't feel too comfortable mounting a bucking bronco.

The rancher glanced at his Mexican, back at us. "You boys from down at the tent colony, huh? Don't know *come here* from *sic 'em* about horses, do you?"

"Know about mules," I said. "Horses can't be that different."

"Difference between a pauper and a prince, son." Haddock spit tobacco syrup into the dirt.

"We could learn," I said.

"Oh, yeah, you could learn. That's what they all say. A monkey can learn to ride a horse. But do I want to train monkeys? That's the question. What're your names again? I'm hell with names."

Sid told him. The rancher nodded and went into the shed. Soon, he led out two huge gray horses. They were already haltered and he handed the reins to the Mexican. Then he re-entered the shed for the saddles, blankets and bridles, which he dropped in the dirt.

"Told you," I said to Sid.

"These here are drays, boys. If you can't ride them, you can't ride nothing. Let's see you saddle 'em up."

Me and Sid fumbled around, doing the best we could. The Mexican mumbled something. Haddock grinned and nodded.

"Don't know shit from *Shinola*, do you?" The old man stopped us a couple of times to stroke the animals and correct what we were doing. With a cart-load of instruction, we got the nags saddled.

"Now, get on," the rancher called.

I was about to walk behind my horse when Haddock snapped at me. "That dray'll kick the goobers right off you, Alvin. Come around front."

I told him my name was Alan and silently called myself a dumbass. I knew enough from handling mules not to walk behind one. I put my hand on the side of the horse's head and ducked under. When I lifted a foot toward the stirrup, the horse stepped forward.

"Don't let him know you're afraid of him," Haddock said.

Sid had mounted right up and walked his nag around the pen. He took the reins out left and right, leading the horse, like he was Bronco Billy or somebody. I couldn't figure out where he'd learned to do that.

"Mr. Smart-Ass Cowboy," I mumbled. My horse ambled in a circle with me holding onto the saddle and stumbling along beside him. Finally, I let go.

"That's a carnival nag I let my grandkids ride when they come visit, Alvin," Haddock called. "Steve's sittin' his horse good. What's wrong with you?"

"Horses are a nervous breed," I said. "I don't trust 'em. You might have noticed that Steve has the horse disposition. Me, I'm a mule man."

Haddock smiled. "All the mules except one is down at the livery. A hinny name of Juliet, who's good for only one thing. I seen cattle drove with mules, but they were a lot leaner and quicker than any I own. Nope. You got to ride this nag, Alvin, or you can't go with us."

I walked over to the horse again, determined to get on.

"Gather the reins and grab the horn in your left hand, back of the saddle in your right. Step up and swing your boot over before he has a chance to move. Once you start, don't hesitate."

I did like the old man told me, got my boot in the stirrup and launched myself onto the horse.

"Now loosen up, son. You look like one of them dress-dummies at the dry goods. Walk him around like Steve's doing."

I practiced some. The rancher saddled a horse akin to the Mexican's–skinnier and more muscular than our nags. Haddock and his assistant mounted and rode around me and Sid, to get their animals used to our smell, I figured.

"Yee-hah," Haddock hollered. "It's assholes and elbows out here on the great frontier, boys. You survive today and I might let you come back tomorrow. Make tomorrow and you can come back permanent. Fifty cents for every stray you bring back. We'll stay together until you see how it's done. You boys have hats?"

Admitted again we didn't.

Haddock glanced at the Mexican. He dismounted, handed his reins to the old man and stepped into the barn. When he came out, he carried two straws.

"Them flimsy things'll have to do you for today" Haddock said. "If you come back tomorrow, bring felt hats with wide brims. You don't and you'll be blistered all to hell and not worth a shit to me. Can't be a cowboy without a cowboy hat. Get 'em down at Haddock's Dry Goods, don't you know." The old man cackled. "Now, what we're lookin' for in the pastures, boys, is calves that ain't been branded or old cows we'll want to sell. Ridin' around out here lets us check on things. Me and the neighbors share fences, these days, but sometimes the wire goes down or the posts snap and the herds get mixed up. Then we have to separate their strays from ours. That's called cuttin'. I'll get Diego to show you how that's done first time we come on a doggie. You gettin' an idea of the kind of help I need?"

Sid looked at me and I nodded. "Yeah," Brother answered. "We're gettin' it."

"Good deal. You boys ever hear of a poem called 'The Shooting of Dan McGrew' by Bob Service? By god, it's bully."

Of course, me and Sid hadn't heard of it. But we were about to. The old man couldn't remember our names, but he could recite a whole poem from the back of a horse. Reminded me of Jack.

In the pasture, we spread out. I expected my horse to take off like a short fuse when he saw a cow, so I watched the sage and braced, like I was waiting for a cave-in. When it didn't happen, I relaxed some, figuring there wouldn't be any sudden outbursts from a carnival nag.

Haddock pointed out a calf off to our right, then hollered something to Diego. The Mexican spurred his horse into a gallop.

Haddock reined and lifted his hand. "Come up slow, boys. Watch and learn."

The Mexican rode ahead of the calf, turned and stopped a little ways in front of it. When the calf lunged, the horse cut it off. The calf braked and so did the Mexican. The calf hopped left, like he was about to take off, but the horse stayed with him, digging its hooves in. The horse's head dipped low, the calf bolted right, the horse drove him back. After a couple of exchanges, the calf gave up and let the greaser drop a loop of rope over its head.

"That is an old-time *vaquero* at work, right there. You boys didn't realize that, did you? Done so smooth, that little doggie just surrendered. Now, if one of you had bagged that calf, you'd have somethin' besides dirt in your pockets."

Me and Sid got our horses up to a trot and I grabbed the saddle horn to keep from falling off. Crushed sage and dust filled my nose. I sneezed and wished for a bandana. My clammy butt was getting rubbed raw by that hard saddle.

The rancher stopped on the lip of the ditch to watch us. "You'd best loosen up in that saddle, Alan. You'll crack your nuts riding stiff like that. That dray's gonna beat you to pieces."

Sid grinned and told the old man that my name was Alvin. I told Sid to shut-up.

"And one more thing," Haddock hollered, "don't never choke that saddle horn. You control the horse with them reins and your knees." The old man waited. "You hear me, Alvin?"

"Heard ya, Mr. Haddock," I called.

"Need a goddamn response when I ask a question." Haddock spit. "Okay?"

"Yessir."

"Good manners. I like that," Haddock said. "We'll ride along the edge here for a ways and see if any beeves is stuck. It's kinda nice havin' some strangers to talk to. Old Diego here lived all my good stories, didn't you, *hombre*?"

The Mexican grinned. "*Si, patron*."

As we rode along, I wondered what could be so hard about this job. Of course, we hadn't made any money yet, but we were in training. Every once in a while, Haddock would point out something and tell a little story. Everything on his property had a tale connected to it, seemed like. And his property sprawled everywhere.

We rode near a screeching windmill and Haddock cranked up. "Once upon a time, me and Diego was putting a blade on that windmill. I was forty feet up in the air, tied on, and Diego was hoisting the blade up to me. You can see into next week up there and I spotted some riders. By-and-by more appeared with lots of folks afoot. Soon this pasture was full of pitiful-looking Indians–skin-and-bone, old and young–men, women and children. Apaches, some on horseback, most on foot, their scrawny dogs sniffin' the grass or draggin' the sick along on sapling stretchers. Mixed in was cavalry, marching the Indians up the Santa Fe Trail to a reservation. Last of the wild west, boys, and it passed right through here."

When Haddock hushed, I could hear a cow bawling. The rancher and the Mexican trotted ahead and we followed. The animal was stuck in the deepest part of the ditch.

"It's that old muley, Diego," Haddock hollered. "Them drays will come in handy for this job," Haddock said, getting off his horse.

In fifteen minutes, me and Sid were knee-deep in mud–like we'd been two days before–pushing on that cow, while Haddock and Diego snubbed the ropes onto the drays above.

We worked for over an hour and were mud-covered by the time we pulled that cow out.

"You boys do stay with it, don't you?"

"Tryin' to," I hollered.

Haddock smiled. "I'd have shot that cow if you hadn't been with me. Too damned much trouble for me and Diego, by ourselves. How those backsides holdin' up?"

I'd noticed Sid lift up to rub and scratch a time or two and I figured that his tender ass was being chewed up, same as mine.

"My ass is rock hard and ready," I lied. "Looks like Steve's pillow might be lumped up, though, the way he keeps pickin' it."

"My pillow's doin' just fine, thank you," Sid said.

"Got to get 'em calloused good, don't you know. Stay loose." The old man rode around us again. "Faces are blistered, even with them straws. Wish you had some real hats, now, don't you?"

"We'll get some," Sid yelled.

We rode through the pasture like genuine cowboys. A while later, Haddock checked his pocket watch then hollered something in Spanish to Diego. The Mexican nodded, took the ropes and led cow and calf back toward the house.

The sun was almost gone by the time we got back with two more calves. We unsaddled the horses and let 'em loose in the pen, so they could walk around and dry out before they got stalled.

When the old man was out of earshot, I asked Sid if he was sore. I could barely stand up straight.

" 'Bout to die, Alvin. Somethin' about it, though, ain't there?"

"Long as we stay on the old man's good side," I said.

"He's got some ways. Bit your head off when you didn't answer him, didn't he?" Sid pointed. "Would you look at that."

The daughter was driving the tractor pulling the empty hay wagon into the yard. Diego was stretched out in the bed.

"You was right about her doin' considerable work out here," I said.

Sid nodded. "They been feedin'."

Susan had traded her dress for jeans, boots, a jacket and leather gloves. Her blond hair was stuffed under one of the felt hats from the dry goods, no doubt. Had it cinched up under her chin with a thong so it wouldn't blow off.

"Hi, sugar," Haddock said, patting his pants and coat pockets. "You ain't got two dollars on you by any chance, have you?"

"In my pocketbook at the house."

"Dang-it, anyway. Entertain these boys while I'm gone."

The woman pulled off her hat, scratched her head and raked her curls as they fell along her shoulders and back. She had thin lips, high cheekbones and her papa's nose–not exactly what I'd call pretty, like Caitlin, for example. But I could tell Sid was interested.

"Looks like you two got broken in," she said. "What'd you do, herd frogs?"

Sid dragged out the story, spicing it up with exaggerations and bits of humor. Made that girl smile.

The old man came back carrying the money. He handed us both a dollar and we thanked him. "Susan, Alvin there is a mule fancier," he said. "Why don't we show him Juliet's trick before dark?"

"I think they're ready to call it a day, Daddy."

The rancher threw up a hand. "Aw, it won't take a minute." He said something to Diego and the Mexican went in the barn. Soon he brought out an old black mule on a long lead.

Haddock took the rope. "This here's Juliet. Look at you, now, girl. Ain't you proud?"

"And handsome," I said and meant it. "Kinda small for plowing, ain't she?"

The old man stroked her flank. "Aw, she don't work, Alvin. She does one little trick and that's all. My grandkids love her."

And so do you, I thought. "What's her trick?"

"She's a jumper."

I smiled. "I seen mules do a lot of things, Mr. Haddock, but I ain't never seen one jump nothin'."

"You been around mine mules all your life, son. This here's a coon hunter." The rancher led Juliet up to the rail fence and she just stood there. He pulled the mule's head down and whispered in her ear. The old man knew how to talk to a mule up close.

Juliet turned her head and looked at Sidney.

"What'd I do?" Brother asked.

"Come on over here and quit fidgetin', Steve," Haddock said. "You're distractin' Juliet from her trick."

"I ain't fidgetin'," Sid said, but moved over by us, anyway. "Bet she heard my stomach growlin'. That mule ain't gonna jump that fence."

"Just be still, like I told you, Steve," Haddock said.

Sid straightened up some and Haddock whispered into the mule's ear again. Juliet stuck her nose over the railing and looked at the ground. She reared back on her hind legs, stood like that for a second and jumped the fence.

I whooped. "Now, that's what I call a trick. Will she do it fairly regular?"

The old man still had hold of the lead and he walked the mule back up to the fence. Juliet stood there a second, then hopped back inside the corral. Me and Sid howled and clapped.

"She just done that one day, or what?" Sid asked.

"My wife, Margaret, got her to do it," Haddock said. "She grew up in East Texas and her daddy used mules on his farm. He loved to hunt coons, but you can't hunt coons on horseback. They'll run you into tree limbs at night. But a mule is cautious and won't run into nothing. When you come to a fence, though, you have to dismount and throw a saddle blanket over, so the mule will jump it. I got Juliet in a trade one time from a teamster in Fort Worth. Margaret was always partial to her." The old man kept patting the mule. "You boys come back tomorrow and I'll show you how we feed. Round up a few more strays and we'll brand 'em. Need to do some palpatin' in the next few days. We're behind on that already." He nodded to Diego who grinned.

"What's palpatin'?" Sid asked.

"Checkin' for pregnancy. You slide your arm inside a heifer to see if she has a calf. Susan usually takes care of it, but she's been too busy at the store."

"Daddy, hush," Susan said.

"Well, somebody's gotta do it if you don't, sugar."

My stomach turned over at the thought. Sid didn't look too healthy, either.

Haddock sniggered. "You boys have took on a greenish tint."

"Don't listen to his foolishness," Susan said. "He or Diego'll palpate. They'll just need you to herd the heifers in, one at a time."

"To see if they're still heifers," Clem added with a chuckle.

"Ain't we gettin' hired to run strays?" Sid asked.

"Oh, there's always strays," Haddock said. "There's strays waitin' for you out there right now. If you had your little carbide lights, you could work tonight. And Alvin, there might even be some mule work down at the livery." Haddock looked at Susan. "I think these boys will work out fine. But they need some hats."

"Why don't I take them to the dry goods right now?"

"Could you drop us off at the colony after?" Sid asked.

Susan smiled. "Already planned on it."

CHAPTER TWENTY-THREE
October 11, 1913

A few days after Mr. Haddock gave us the privilege of feeding and chasing his cows, he let us bring our horses to the livery, so we wouldn't have to walk back and forth to work. I kept Ike, the gentle dray I rode that first day, but Sid got him a cutter named Snookers.

I bought the bare essentials of cowboy gear–a hat, bandanas and spurs–but Sid went hog-wild, with chaps, new shirts, heel boots and a fancy hat. He learned how to throw a lariat and could work a pony pretty good after just a week. And that suited Susan Haddock just fine.

Early on, Sid courted her at the dry goods, shopping for necessary pieces of his outfit. Then they started seeing each other in the evenings.

At first, I wondered how an educated, well-to-do girl like Susan could let a goozie get close to her–unless she got her kicks slumming. Then I thought about Mama and Papa's courtship. Must have been that Tanner charm.

Here it was, Saturday again, with me walking through town after I'd spent the morning mucking stalls for Gabey. The two big mountains out west–the tits of the world, the Indians called them–had a fresh dusting of snow on the nipples. The sky hung steel-blue; the grass was cornmeal yellow. Just another shitty day in paradise, as Clem would say.

Sidney had helped Haddock and Diego feed and was clerking at the store with Susan, so I stopped by for licorice and the new *Century* before heading for the colony.

The smell of fresh bread filled my nose long before I saw the loaves cooling on the table or Mama kneading dough for more. She'd fired up the Excelsior as I left that morning and the tent had got so warm, she'd rolled up the sides and opened the flaps. Last used by strikers in West Virginia, the canvas still reeked of mildew and cooking grease, making ventilation crucial.

After she put in the last loaf, Mama cooked eggs, sausage and fried potatoes. We drank several cups of coffee and ate half a loaf of bread between us, slathering on butter that Susan had given us.

The train from Trinidad whistled its approach, the afternoon so still, I could hear the whoosh of steam as she braked in the station.

I asked Mama what the date was.

"The eleventh. Why?"

"Caitlin came to Ludlow on the seventh. Just dawned on me. Day about like this one, too. Hearin' that train reminded me of the first time I saw her, in that flimsy dress and pitiful hat. I felt sorry for her. And she was comin' to help import the union." I took a sip of coffee. A lot had changed in a year. "You like prairie life, Mama?"

"If it gets you better wages and makes the job safer, then I like it. Sidney's breathing easier, so that's good. And I like getting new magazines. I long for our house, though. What about you?"

"I'd prefer diggin', but I don't miss bein' pushed around. All the union talk about conditions gets you stirred up and thinkin', but I couldn't see how bad things really were until I got away from Delagua and the mines. I just hope the negotiations do some good."

"You trust John and Nick, don't you?"

I nodded.

"Then that's all you can expect."

After lunch, I laid a pallet outside, read part of an Owen Wister story in the *Century* before nodding off.

Sid came home around two–real early for a Saturday of clerking and sparking. He plopped down on my quilt, waking me, and I could tell something was bothering him. He joked around so much of the time, when he moped, he stood out. Rubbed us all the wrong way, too, when he was somber, like entertaining was his responsibility and he wasn't entitled to ever fret or complain.

On a normal Saturday afternoon, he'd have taken special care to sneak up on Mama and scare her or spill a little water on me while I was napping. He might juggle those loaves of bread or organize a baseball game. That day, he was so blue and mournful, I feared Susan had given him the mitten.

I asked what was wrong and he said he didn't want to talk about it. I knew Sid would blab sooner or later or he wouldn't have sat down in the first place. None of us Tanners held anything in for long.

By and by, he broke. "Susan brought a picnic lunch to the store and we went into the pasture to eat. A long freight come in while we was out there. After we ate and was walking back to the store, we run into Sloan, heading for the barber shop to tell Cockeye that he'd seen some scabs gettin' off the train."

"Them kids have spotted everybody from John L. Sullivan to Woodrow Wilson gettin' off a train," I said. "I'd of took that with a grain of salt."

"What I told Susan. But the kid kept on. Said it was niggers. They'd jumped off as the train climbed the grade for the station and run into the pasture land west of town. He said a posse was on their way out the canyon road to catch 'em." Sid sat for a minute, looking into the field. "I guess it was niggers that set me off, *niggers* comin' here to get our jobs. Susan didn't want me to, but I left her and cut across Clem's pasture. By the time I got to Baca's saloon, Barba and the Greeks had 'em rounded up." Sidney looked back at me to make sure I was paying attention. "They was the most pitiful-lookin' humans I ever seen, Alan. Didn't have no socks and you could see their feet through holes in their shoes. Hair full of dust and straw, shirts and pants torn and filthy. Nobody had a coat or sweater. And their faces were scratched and swollen, like they'd already been beat up once today.

"I wanted to fight them scabs so bad. My blood was up for it. And the way the others was actin', I could tell I wasn't the only one. We longed to take all our woes out on 'em. But it woulda been like whipping bone-bare curs."

Old tender-hearted Sid was fighting a lump in his throat.

"You should have seen them boys, Allie. They hadn't ate in days, freezin' in the back of that freight."

"You talked Barba and them out of it, didn't you?"

"Didn't have to. Them niggers thought they was about to get beat and was ready to fight. But we just stood there, lookin' ignorant and shame-faced, with the steam gone right out of us."

"What'd you do?"

"I apologized, Alan, then took 'em to John. He said give 'em supper and see if somebody had any clothing to spare. He's taking them to Phelps-Dodge tomorrow."

Some of the guys from the colony were working at this non-union mine in Raton Pass. "Seems like that violates your principles, Brother," I said.

"Them boys need work same as us," Sid said. "Fucking industry in this country has us all by the short hairs. Ought to be fightin' on the same side 'stead of tryin' to kill each other."

Listening to the likes of Mother Jones, reading the screeds being passed around, Sid was sounding more and more like a radical these days. I couldn't understand getting so stirred up about shit we couldn't control. When I offered no opinions about negotiations or the evil ways of American business, it made Brother mad. He thought Jesus carried a union card.

Folks were moving toward the ball field for a game. I gave Sidney the magazine and left him alone on the pallet. Looked like his days for busting scabs had come and gone.

CHAPTER TWENTY-FOUR
October 13, 1913

The afternoon freight whistled as it rounded the curve and climbed the grade south of town. I was walking Ike near the windmill, when I spotted a calf grazing about a hundred yards farther down.

The sucker rod screeched, as the blades spun in a gust. The train whistled, again, and the calf took off. I spurred the horse, chasing the calf through the short grass while I swung my lariat free. Spun the rope, letting the loop expand. Then I flung it and missed, as usual. Ike braked to keep from getting tangled in the rope and the calf scampered away.

Wasn't good at cowboying. Only reason I kept the job was to be with Sid and rib old man Haddock. You could have the riding and roping.

I coiled my rope and went after the calf again. Was holding Ike to a canter, keeping an eye on the doggie running ahead, when I saw three wagons and some guys on horseback turning west onto the canyon road. Likely guarding company property that had come in on the freight.

Off to my right about a quarter-mile, Sid loped Snookers. He'd been working the south pasture and was coming back empty-handed. Good. For a change he hadn't bested me. Sid regularly rounded up two or three cows for every one I cornered and Clem always had some smart-ass remark about my "ineptitude."

The mill screeched again. When the wind died, a sound like paper sacks being popped came from the hills to the west. Clouds of dust kicked up in the pasture. Somebody was shooting at the wagons, with me and my brother caught in the line of fire.

I stood in the stirrups, waving my hat and hollering for Sidney to take cover. I don't know whether he saw me and misread my signal, or the horse got spooked and Sid couldn't contain him, but they took off. Maybe Brother thought he could race across a shooting gallery without being hit.

I dismounted and pulled Ike into the arroyo. Crawled back onto the flat a ways and raised up on my knees.

Smoke curled from the wagons as the guards fired back. Sidney rode low in the saddle, hatless, galloping toward me, when shots brought his horse down.

"Sidney," I hollered, crawling through the sage. "I'm comin', chief."

Seemed like it took forever to get to him, with bullets whizzing around. Sid was lying on his side a few feet in front of the horse. Snookers whinnied, kicked himself to his feet and cantered off.

"You took a hell of a fall, boy. You okay?"

"I think I'm shot," Sid muttered.

Sure enough, blood oozed from a hole under his arm. "Oh, shit. I figured it was the horse and you just fell off." I gave him my bandana to press into the wound, then gathered his head and shoulders into my lap.

"Is Snookers hurt?" he wheezed.

"He run off, Sid. I think he's okay."

"You better see about him, Alan."

"I will in good time. You just rest easy."

We sat there for a little while before Sid licked his lips and spoke again. "Feels like my arm, Allie. You can't die from that."

"That's right. They just winged you," I lied, noting the blood-soaked kerchief. "It ain't nothin'."

The shooting kept on, with bullets flaking the brush every so often. I shooed flies, not knowing whether to move Sid to the gully or wait out the gunfight.

"Don't worry. It's only my arm."

"I know. Save your breath, now, chief. I'm right here." My eyes brimmed and a hot coal lodged in my chest.

"You got any water, Allie? Mouth's dry."

"It's on Ike, Sid. Can't risk gettin' it yet."

"All right." His breathing was weak. "Ain't lost much blood. You can tell things like that."

A fist-sized spot bloomed in the dirt. "Nah, it ain't nothin'."

"Hurts funny, though."

"Imagine so. We're just waitin' out this gunfire. It's a goddamn war, ain't it? Who'd a thought? I'll get you some water as soon as the firing lets up."

Sid had closed his eyes, his face wrinkled in pain. I patted his cheek and rocked him a little. After a while, the shooting stopped. "Sid."

He opened his eyes.

"I think they quit. Gonna slide out and get the water."

"Scooter . . . ." He licked his lips. "Don't leave."

"All right, Sid. All right, now, I ain't goin' nowhere. Don't worry. You hurtin' bad?"

"Can't feel my feet."

That's when I got scared. "What do you reckon that is?" I asked.

"Heard you're about to die when you can't feel your feet."

Tears slid down my cheeks and dropped on his neck. "Naw, it ain't nothin'. Just hold on, Sid. Clem and Diego'll be along soon."

I yelled for help until I didn't have any voice left.

The only sound was that squealing windmill.

Sidney's face was chalky and damp, lips blue, eyes sunk back. There wasn't one damn thing I could do but hold on and talk to him.

"Don't leave me, now, chief," I said.

He coughed and mouthed something.

"What is it?" I put my ear down close.

"I could ride that horse," he whispered.

"You sure can, chief. 'lot better'n me."

"Would you tell Susan . . . ." The last little bit of warm breath drifted against my cheek and I raised up. His eyes and mouth were open and his head hung back.

"Goddammit . . . Sidney . . . goddammit." I hugged him and cried till I choked, sitting in that damn pasture, soaking his shirt with my tears, shooing flies.

I thought about the day he pulled me out of that air shaft. He'd watched out for me my whole life, till he got sick. Why couldn't I take care of him out here, so he'd never have to breathe coal dust again, so he could marry Susan and take over the ranch?

"Tanners? It's Clem, boys. You around?"

"Right here," I hollered and threw my hat in the air.

Haddock and Diego rode up, with Ike and Snookers trailing. Clem dismounted.

"Lord-have-mercy, sonny boy, is he shot?"

I couldn't stop crying. "Clem, he's gone."

"Oh, Lord-have-mercy, Alan. Pointless. Those guards was takin' a searchlight to Hastings and strikers bore down on 'em. Pointless, goddammit." Clem blew his nose and wiped his eyes. "Come on, now. We'll take him home."

I slid out from under Sid, then we scooped him up.

The horses shied so much because of the blood, Diego had trouble holding them.

"We'll put him on Ike," Clem said. "He's the gentlest."

We draped Sid across the saddle, then I got up behind the old man.

At the house, Clem and Diego took Sid inside and cleaned him up.

Then, they wrapped the body in a blanket and laid it in the wagon bed.

"Go wash yourself, Alan," Clem said, "and I'll telephone Susan. She'll wither when she hears." He gave me a hug. "I am so sorry, son. We were all crazy about Sidney."

Susan wanted to come to the ranch with the Ford, but Clem told her we were already loaded and heading her way.

I rode in the wagon bed, sitting next to Sid, with my hand on his chest. In Ludlow, folks lined the street, checking to see if what they'd heard was true.

Telling Mama was like being in the pasture, again, with Sid dying in my arms. She closed her eyes when she heard it and rocked forward, like she was going to fall. I pulled her down onto a chair. Her face knotted, the tendons in her neck stood out. Mama reached for me and I held on until she drew breath. When she calmed down some, she sat up straighter, wiping her eyes on her dress. "You're all right, aren't you, Allie? Your face sure is red."

"I'm okay, Mama. Clem and Susan are outside with the Ford, when you want to go look at Sid."

"Oh, me. Are a lot of people out there?"

"Yes, ma'am . . . quite a few. Should I tell 'em to go on?"

She shook her head and got up. "There's some supper under the cloth on the table, here."

"I'm not hungry, Mama. What are you doing?"

She was uncovering the food. "You need to eat something."

"I don't want anything. What are you gonna do about Sid . . . about goin' to Ludlow?"

"You eat some dinner. I have to change clothes. And clean up a little and brush my hair. I can't go view Brother like this."

"Mama, you don't have to look any special way. Clem's waitin'."

"Let him wait." She turned to wash her face. "Nobody's gonna see us falling apart."

I didn't know what to say.

"I can't abide taking on in public. We can't do anything about those people out there, but we can keep our feelings private." She took a deep breath and let it out slow. "Sid was a good brother, wasn't he?"

"Yeah, he was. The best."

Mama changed her dress, fixed her hair up, went through her pocketbook, put on her coat and a hat. Then she stepped to the table to cover up the food. "You didn't eat much. Sure you don't want to take some of this good bread with you, to eat on the way?"

I sliced a piece, just to suit her. "Come on, now. We need to go."

I was afraid that Mama had gone a little crazy talking about Sid, until I saw how everybody acted when she came out from under the tent. The neighbor ladies fought over us, pawing and weeping, like it was their kin dead.

Ida was the worst. She rushed up, tried to smother Mama with hugs and let loose a fit of versifying. Cockeye tried his best to pull her off, but she kept on about the Lord moving in mysterious ways. When she called out that Sid's death was the Lord's will being done, Mama bristled.

"If Sidney's death was the will of your God, Ida, then I don't want any part of him. The God I believe in wouldn't truck in my good son's death. I visit with my God in private. Keep your God and your verses away from me right now."

I'd never seen Ida left speechless by anything before, but she hushed. Her face was pale as a sliced potato. Mama had cut her off so short, I felt kinda sorry for her.

Nick kept a little distance, not knowing what to do or say, but sad-faced, concerned. Cait was crying, but stayed back, too. Me and Mama got into the Model T and Clem drove us to Ludlow.

Susan sat up front and I could tell she was having a hard time of it, weeping and all, but I didn't say anything to her. I couldn't say anything to anybody. All these good and concerned people made me feel worse. They were wearing me out with their advice and sympathy.

I felt like telling them to leave us alone. Shout that we didn't want to explain anything, didn't want to cry or pray over it, didn't want to drag it through the mud. But deep-down, I knew that would be ill-mannered and a waste of time.

In that drive to Ludlow, I realized that what should have been private wouldn't be private for us. Sidney was a celebrity, now–the first martyr–and, to miners on strike, more useful dead than alive.

CHAPTER TWENTY-FIVE
October 15, 1913

Sidney's burial and pension had to be dealt with. No one took the blame for the shooting, of course, and Victor-American felt no obligation to help us out. John said the UMW had a fund for strike deaths and the union made a show of putting Sid in an expensive coffin and taking him to the Knights of Pythias cemetery in Trinidad. Fanciest ride he ever got, but he had to die to get it. A swarm of strangers met us at the station and marched to the graveyard behind the wagon.

A sorry journey it was. Sid's body was something real that strikers could touch and say, "You will not do this to us. We will fight back."

Mourners sang "God Bless You Christian Martyrs" and "The Union Forever." It had sleeted all morning and Sid's gravestone was slick with ice.

" 'Woe unto the world because of offenses! for it must needs be that offenses come; but woe to the man by whom the offense commeth.' " The minister made this verse the base of his union funeral sermon and Ida Bastrop cried, "Amen." I guess the preacher wanted everyone present to heed the Good Book's warning: the woe now being visited on me and Mama and Sid's friends would come back double on the coal companies, if offenses weren't corrected.

Was this supposed to offer us comfort? Were more people going to have to die to make up for years and years of woe piled up in the camps? Were we just expected to accept death during this strike as a fact that would come to pass, sooner or later? Was this the preacher's way of urging the strikers to fight back, regardless of the cost?

Mama insisted on standing by the grave, instead of sitting in the folding chair provided her. The people filed by to pay their respects. A lot of them had never heard of Sidney Tanner until he was killed. I looked into each lined and scarred face, some still blackened from years in the slagholes, and tried to believe that Sid would have been glad to die for their benefit.

The UMW hoped that reporters and photographers would tell the world that strikers were innocent victims. But among these faces might be Sid's killer, a striker who'd taken his rifle into the hills to keep a searchlight from reaching Hastings. Any man's hand offered to Mama and me could have Sid's blood on it. Those sons of bitches were no better than the dicks who'd tortured Rolf Levy and beat Charlie senseless. No better than Delores Paul Hawkins.

About half the line of mourners had offered respects when the sleet turned to rain. Everybody got drenched as they raced for cover. Nick and John held umbrellas over Mama and me, as we walked through the cemetery gate, where the red car waited.

Back at the colony, the rain stopped just before dark and I went outside the tent for some air. The evening was cold and damp, thick with the smell of meat pies the neighbor women were baking for supper. I resented their niceness because it made us beholden.

Out west, orange and pink sundown shredded the pillows of gray cloud above the hills. I was thinking about Sidney, sealed tonight and forever in that union coffin, when a beam from high in Delagua Canyon shot out into the field east of the colony.

Addled anyway, I imagined at first that the unearthly light was a sign. The beam held steady for only a few seconds, then it began to move toward the colony, where it stopped in the tents.

Shadows scurried, flickering in and out of the cold brightness, hollering, "Searchlight" into the night air. This modern light fascinated me. Sid had died because of it.

I imagined the guards opening up on the tents, picking out targets and cutting us down like blinded animals. Half-expected shots to be fired at the beam.

The light swept across the colony, north-to-south, south-to-north–a pass every few minutes. A few people bolted.

The situation on the prairie was spinning out of control. Strikers, company swells, guards, detectives, lawmen, state and national politicians threshed in a web with the Ludlow colony at its center. One shiver here would send bigger shivers to everyone else.

Whatever the union or the companies won through negotiations, threats, or firepower would cost lives. There would be a lot more martyrs to this strike.

PART THREE

"Fly away you red-winged bird.
Leave behind you the miner's wife.
She'll dream about you when you're gone.
She'll dream about you all her life."

"Red-Winged Blackbird"
by Billy Edd Wheeler

CHAPTER TWENTY-SIX
October 20, 1913

Five days after Sid's funeral, Baldwins shot up the tent colony at Forbes. They pounced in a contraption called "Death Special," a Model T, stripped to its frame and armored with slabs of steel manufactured at the CF&I mill in Pueblo, of all places. The detectives mounted a machine gun and spotlight where the windshield had been. They tested both at the colony a few miles south of Ludlow.

Rumor had it that Forbes crawled with guns. Whether the Baldwins went down there to scare everybody into giving up their weapons without firing a shot, or they intended to shoot the place up all along was open to argument. There were as many stories about what actually happened as there were people to talk to. But it was a fact that an armored car had opened up with a machine gun on strikers who, even if they were armed, could return shots with rifles and pistols only.

When the news arrived that detectives had assaulted Forbes with such a heinous weapon, tempers ran wild. Imaginations, too. Ludlow was the biggest and most vulnerable colony, with the greatest number of Greeks and Italians. A surprise attack was on everybody's mind. If the Baldwins thought they could open fire on Forbes, what would keep them from doing the same to us?

Some lunkers had inherited eccentric old Colts or untrustworthy single-shot Savage rifles. These were no match for the light-weight Winchesters and Springfield repeaters the Baldies used. Me and Cockeye decided it was time to get armed. Neither of us had ever held a gun. Now, we planned to purchase weapons that could compete and learn to use them.

Everybody had a theory on where to get the best deal. You could buy guns in any hardware store in Trinidad, Walsenburg or Aguilar. Merchants didn't care which side you were on or what you wanted to buy, if you had cash and the smarts to come and go without getting caught. As long as the supply of guns lasted, they'd sell them.

But with citizens and cops in and out, it was a challenge for gun customers to avoid detection. Purchases in town usually involved pistols or boxes of ammunition rather than rifles or shotguns.

We decided that the least dangerous way to buy our weapons was through a gunrunner. And the most convenient gunrunner was Leo Delveccio, Charlie's cousin up in Noble. Fresh shipments of guns and ammunition arrived every few days and we intended to take advantage.

* * *

Flecks of snow swirled, as me and Cockeye snuck away from the colony and crossed the prairie. Crouching every once in a while to avoid the searchlight, we reached the arroyo a quarter mile north, near the Colorado and Southern Railroad trestle. We slid into the ditch and followed it east. Except during heavy rains, when Delagua Creek raged down canyon to cut a deeper gash into the prairie, the trench stayed dry or just-damp.

The arroyo took us beneath the Walsenburg-Trinidad Road bridge. Sure we were out of searchlight range, we climbed onto the flats and headed for the box-like shadow of the Black Hills.

A remote outpost located in a no-man's land between Huerfano and Las Animas counties, Noble was named for a trader who held off Indians for two days with only a Sharps rifle. The road up was a steep, nasty mess of chuckholes, broken paths and dead ends. Guarded on top by machine gun, rumor had it. Even the high sheriffs of the two counties balked at enduring these hazards to investigate a crime or make an arrest in Noble. And, since Leo Delveccio made healthy contributions to election funds, word circulated that policing the hideout was too damn much trouble.

I had been up there a few times to squeeze the tenderloin and knew the way through the juniper and pinyons. That night, Cockeye kept asking if *this* was the last hill before town.

"I don't want to come face-to-face with no machine gun, thank you," he said.

"That's a tall tale, Cockeye," I said as we topped the last hill. "Welcome to Noble."

"Where's it at?" Cockeye asked.

"You're lookin' at it," I answered. "Only three buildings. We're headin' for the big one that's lit up. What'd you expect?"

"I don't know," he answered, looking around. "Not this."

The street was deserted except for a lunker shambling toward us. As our distance closed, I noted a bearded man in heavy coat and fur hat. He raised his hand as he passed.

"Evenin'," I said, looking back at the traveler. "That guy look familiar to you?"

"Anarchist."

I snorted. "What makes you say that?"

"That big old coat and foreign-lookin' hat."

"Cockeye, me and you both is wearing overcoats and hats."

"Ain't carryin' a sawed-off in the lining and bombs in the pockets, though, are we? Plus, that beard. All them anarchists got scraggly beards."

"Neighbor . . . you are full of shit."

A sudden gust stirred the dust. "Dang," Cockeye said, "I need me a stove."

"We're early," I said. "You want a beer or somethin'?"

"You ain't polin' no whores, if that's what you're hintin' at by *somethin'*. I ain't allotted time for your hobbies tonight," Cockeye said.

"I ain't polin' no whore."

"That's good. I wouldn't want to wait around by myself. Place gives me the willies. A feller can get hurt in Noble."

"Aw, it ain't that bad, Cockeye," I said. "All reputation."

"Wanna bet? Furlong Carter got a piece of his ear bit off up here last month. I seen the proof. Keeps it in a matchbox."

"The guy who bit off his ear just give it back?"

"It was a *piece*, laying there, and it wadden't no good after that fight. Furlong got the best of the chomper in the end. Afterwards, he tied a kerchief around his head and went home. Wonder he didn't bleed to death."

"You seen all this happen?" I asked.

"Heard about it from a reliable source."

"Okay. We'll sit with our backs to the wall and, if I see anybody creepin' up on you from the side, I'll hit 'em with a chair."

"Suit yourself and don't take me serious, Alan. I ain't even gonna tell you what happened to One-Armed Sigrist Witherspoon."

"Much obliged."

When I opened the flimsy door to the 29th of July Saloon, the wind threw it against the inside wall with a rattling crash.

"Tear it up," Leo's wife hollered.

"Sorry. It's that wind." I retrieved the door and pushed it shut. The bar was so hot from the potbelly, my upper lip dewed. Bonita Delveccio sat at one of the tables, playing cards with Monroe Purvis. I hadn't seen the piano man since the night McKintrick's got shot up.

"Christ on a crutch, Monroe," I hollered. "You ain't tinkling keys in this rat hole, are you?"

"Nobody begged you to come up here, honeydipper," Bonita said. "My girls hate to see your skinny butt top the hill."

"Nice to see you, too, Mrs. Delveccio," I said. I took off my overcoat and laid it over a chair back. "Hotter than a whorehouse on nickel night in here. Couldn't you have got it a little warmer? My belt buckle ain't melted yet."

"You'll be standing outside looking in the window, if you don't button your lip," she tossed back.

"You mind if me and my buddy visit Monroe in private?" I asked.

She glared at me, gathered her cards and stood.

"Could you bring us a couple of whiskeys, too, please, ma'am?" Cockeye asked. "To take the chill off."

"Let me see your money, walleye," Bonita said. "I ain't takin' no scrip. Leo won't either."

"They can drink out of my bottle," Monroe said. "Just bring some glasses."

Bonita flounced over to the bar, returned with two shot glasses and left us in peace.

"I like women with fire, don't you?" Monroe said as he offered us chairs and poured drinks. Cockeye sat with his back to the wall. "To answer your earlier question, Tanner, I'm not playing anywhere right now. Been tiptoeing around my grave down at Forbes with Clara Dawes, one of Elma's whores. You remember her, don't you?"

"Hah, remember?" Cockeye chimed in. "She was his old sweetheart."

"Just shut up, bigmouth," I said. I wanted to ask all kinds of questions, but I didn't. "You got you a dangerous woman for a dangerous locale."

Monroe snickered. "It's a goddamn combat zone. The law knew guns were there. The Greeks and wops came from all over to take target practice in the hills. 'Clara,' I say, 'Moonbeam, let's move on to Noble or Walsenburg.' Clara says, 'Hell no, this is where the action is.' She's got me arranging for her out of a tent next to the one we sleep in." Monroe paused, like he'd just thought of something. "Tanner . . . I heard about your brother. My sympathies to you and your mother."

"Thank you. I'll pass on the condolences." Nose burned, eyes teared. I needed to change the subject. "I hear Charlie's in Noble."

Monroe nodded and touched his temple. "He's not right. Grabble got in some good licks before Charlie knifed him. Sorry I ran out on you, but I was scared the Baldwins were about to shoot us all. Guess I would've walked all the way to Ludlow if Abercrombie hadn't picked me up. You know he was a spy?"

"Don't get Tanner started on Abercrombie," Cockeye pleaded.

Rolled my eyes. "*El suckass pequenyo*," I added.

Monroe grinned and nodded. "Goddamn union organizing. Wouldn't you know I'd get caught in the middle of that?"

"You didn't suspect nothin' either, huh?" I asked.

Monroe shook his head. "Not a thing."

"Then I don't feel so dumb," I returned. "You spent a lot more time in McKintrick's than I did. Got any theories on Jack?"

Monroe downed his whiskey and poured another. "He's around."

"Whaddaya mean, around?" I asked. "Around where?"

"Noble," Monroe said. "In here, about half-an-hour ago. In disguise. You might have passed him and not even known it."

"We just seen an anarchist in the street," Cockeye said.

"Probably him," Monroe said.

"Well, shit, wouldn't he have said howdy?" I asked.

Monroe shook his head. "He doesn't want to visit, if you can believe that."

"We all figured he burned up," Cockeye said.

"Wanted everybody to think that," Monroe said. "Sounds like you already know about Abercrombie and the wagon. Jack helped us load Charlie at the imbibery. We tried to get him to come with us, but he was taking the rifles out. Said he wouldn't leave his Mexicans. They fought off the Baldwins till the fires started. I don't know how Jack got out of town or passed the guards in Hastings." Monroe killed his shot. "There's a lot of conjecture about that."

"Jack can bribe anybody," I said. "He'd just dish some cash and stroll away."

"Or fly," Cockeye said. "The mayor's a goldang haint."

"I know," Monroe said. "But he's not the same old Jack, now. I think he's helping Charlie cook something up." He poured us another round. "I've seen Caitlin and Kistos. They came to Forbes with Mother Jones for a rally. That Greek's the cock of the walk, now, ain't he? I remember when he couldn't say *boo* in English."

"He's the camp leader at Ludlow," I said. "Don't carry a gun, though. Caitlin calls him her 'calm warrior'."

"Alan can't stand it that she's sweet on Kistos," Cockeye said. "He'd like to be her one-and-only."

"Yeah, you could tell that in Delagua," Monroe said, grinning. "The way Tanner mooned when she sang."

I ignored this commentary, hoping it would die on its own. Which it did.

"Was you in Forbes when Death Special attacked?" Cockeye asked.

"Oh, yeah. It was drizzling rain, cold and dreary. Clara was about to give me some free pussy, when we heard little buzzing noises, like locusts caught in the pots and pans. All of a sudden, shit was flying off the table. I tell you, I lost the urge right quick. We slid under the bed and I didn't think we'd come out alive. Bastards shot up things pretty good."

"They get any weapons?" Cockeye asked.

Monroe shook his head. "Didn't even come down the hill to check. I think they just wanted to try out their machine gun. You know who I heard was in that armored car, Tanner? Our old friends Grabble, Crimmons and Hawkins. Delores Paul is supposed to have designed the damn thing." Monroe took another sip and lit a cigarette. "You guys come to make a purchase?"

I nodded.

"I've been in these camps for thirteen years and never owned a gun, even in Delagua, if you can believe that. But I'm getting some goddamned guns," Monroe said. "I'm buying a rifle and a pistol for me and a pistol for Clara. I've seen how the Baldies operate. If I keep blacksmithing for the lady, I'll need an arsenal. I'd get a fucking machine gun, if Leo could find me one."

The door flew open again and crashed against the wall, as Leo and Charlie entered.

"Say," Bonita hollered from behind the bar, "why can't men learn to open a goddamn door?"

"Hey, *bizcotecha*, is a cold, strong wind. Fix me and Charlie a meatball sandwich. We ain't had nothing since lunch."

"Say, 'Pretty please,' you son of a bitch," Bonita called, walking into the kitchen.

Charlie limped over to our table.

"Hey, boy," I said, standing and putting out my hand. "Good to see you."

Charlie looked at me like he was trying to remember who I was.

"Alan Tanner–from Delagua. How are the relatives in Italy?"

"I . . . know you . . . *buttagots*."

"Okay, Charlie," Leo said, pulling a chair out for his cousin. "You men here on business or vacation?"

"Vacation," I answered.

Leo nodded. "Cousin, sit here and have a drink with Monroe while I go out back with these guys."

We followed Leo into a dark room behind the bar. "Don't be nervous when we go outside," he said. "I got a guy on the roof with a rifle, in case anybody is followed."

I hadn't thought about being nervous until he brought it up.

A wagon sat behind the building. The wop told us to untie the tarp that covered the bed while he opened the storeroom.

"Sometime Charlie tell guys different time from me," Leo said. "Then he forget who he tell to come when. Would help to know so I don't be surprised. But Charlie lose all good sense when he get beat up. He will go for them Baldwins, if he get a chance. I feel bad, but I see him *decesso.* I seen men like that in Turin, men who carry vendettas. Their eyes is empty. You pick up some guns out of the wagon, please, and we carry inside to see."

Leo turned on an electric bulb that hung from a wire in the center of the storeroom. Me and Cockeye carried in an armload of rifles.

"Put on the floor, there. I will hide what we do not sell. Is bad you have to unload, but you choose first that way."

We'd made several trips from the wagon when Monroe and Charlie came in with Leo's sandwich. The piano man asked if they had missed the unloading.

"Only dynamite is left, sombitch," Leo said. "Cousin . . . bring in them boxes from the wagon." Leo shook his head as he watched Charlie lumber out. "Okay, look around. Ask questions. Is mostly Winchesters, but some Krag-Js, too. Four or five, I think. Them are six shot. Maybe a Springfield or two and plenty of pistols. .45 automatics. Ammunition is over there. Be sure to get bullets that match what you buy. Some guys get so excited they own a rifle, then buy bullets for a pistol. Don't figure it out till they get home."

Cockeye lifted a Winchester. "How much?"

"Thirty dollars . . ."

"Goddern, that's ten dollars more than town prices."

Leo nodded, gnawing on his sandwich. "*I* take the risk. Krag-Js is twenty-five. .45s, ten. We get all our friend in Walsenburg would sell. He is one fine businessman, you know. Selling to both sides as fast as he can."

Cockeye mumbled about having to be a rich man to buy a gun in Noble, while I pressed a Winchester's stock into my shoulder. I looked down the barrel, like I knew what I was doing. "How many shots you get from this thing?" I asked.

"That model? Seventeen," Leo said.

Monroe held an automatic in his hand like it was a dead bird.

"You got an idea what to do?" Leo asked.

The piano player looked up and shook his head.

"Give." Leo wolfed the last bite of sandwich, wiped the grease off his hand and took the weapon. "Tanner, you boys watch, too. You have a clip of bullets that go in the grip, thus." Leo turned the pistol over. He slid an empty clip half-way into the hollow handle and drove it the rest of the way in with the butt of his hand until it locked. "Okay? Holds nine rounds. Eight in clip, one in breach–inside the pistol. Comes out this way." Leo pressed a button on the side of the gun and the clip slid out. "Fill your pockets with loaded clips. When you have clip inside, you have to cock. Thus." Leo gripped the back of the pistol with his left hand and pulled. The top of the gun slid backward, exposing the barrel, then snapped back when Leo let go of it.

Cockeye whistled and smiled.

Leo pointed to the back of the pistol again. "See, the hammer cocked? Chambered first round," Leo said. "Cock once. Bang, bang, bang–nine times. Put in another clip. Clean after shooting, every time." Leo pulled the trigger and the hammer clicked.

Monroe took the pistol and snapped back the top, cocking the weapon. He aimed at a corner and pulled the trigger.

"When loaded, top snap back, chamber another round. Automatic." Leo took the weapon back from Monroe. "I don't care what you see in moving picture, you cannot shoot a man off a running horse, fifty yards away. This is a close-up weapon. Put other hand under shooting hand to steady. Sight down barrel, say a prayer. Don't just shoot as fast as you can. You waste bullets. Okay, time to choose. More customers coming soon and we don't like to sardine."

Me and Monroe bought Winchesters and automatics. Cockeye hemmed and hawed, bought a Krag-Jorgensen repeater and complained all the way back to the colony about how much he'd spent.

CHAPTER TWENTY-SEVEN
October 25, 1913

Payday dawned clear, but with a strong north wind, it changed to a gray, blustery morning. I waited in a line that dragged like a long tail out of the headquarters tent. As I inched forward, I stooped to warm my hands from braziers placed along the way.

As usual, rumors flew and there wasn't a bigger rumor-monger than Cockeye. He always swore that every bit of information he reported came "on good authority." This morning he'd heard from a reliable source that Death Special had been parked outside Baca's saloon, that guards had set up machine guns in the hills, that strikers were tearing up railroad tracks north and south of the colony to stop an attack by rail. Wanted to bet me on it.

"That's nothin', Cockeye," I said. "I heard that Delores Paul Hawkins bought an aero plane so he could drop dynamite on us."

"I wouldn't put it past him," Cockeye said.

Barba came out of the pay tent and hurried down the line, yelling that a train full of soldiers was on its way up from Trinidad. I didn't know whether to believe him or not. The line offered the best chance to scuttlebutt, so it seemed stupid to lose my place because of some wild story.

But guys *were* leaving. Some were moving their families into the arroyo or taking cover in pits they'd dug underneath the tent platforms. I knew that the Greeks would be going for their guns.

I was five back from the tent when Nick came outside to tell us the line was closing.

"I just talk to John in Forbes. He think a train of National Guards is coming from Trinidad. These soldiers will be crack shots with the best carbines. Women, children and unarmed men should take cover. If train get by Forbes, it have to change tracks to come to Ludlow. Those with rifles should go to Berwind with Barba to watch the railroad switch house.

"What are you gonna do?" I asked Nick.

"Stay in the colony, near the phone."

By the time I got back to our tent, the neighbors were bracing for attack. I pulled two loose floorboards from the tent's platform and took out my rifle, automatic and cartridge belt.

I wasn't sure what Mama would think about me getting the guns. When I came home from Noble, she wanted nothing to do with them, even though the fear of violence *had* become a part of living out here. Figured it had a lot to do with losing Sidney.

Mama's shoes scraped the platform as she came into the tent. She watched me for a little while with her arms crossed before she spoke. "You taking a blanket and food?"

Shook my head. "No time. We're tryin' to keep a train full of soldiers from attacking the colony." I stood up. Juggling the belt and Winchester, I almost dropped the .45.

"You look pretty mean with my scarf wrapped around your head like that." Mama walked to the pantry box. "Need a piece of line on that rifle so you can carry it over your back, don't you?" She cut a length of cord and tied it on the Winchester. "How long you think you'll be?"

"I . . . don't . . . know." I was having trouble buckling the cartridge belt under my overcoat.

"Some of the cloth is stuck. Here." She pulled the wad out and I tightened the belt.

"That better?"

"Yeah, I guess." I slid the .45 into a coat pocket where it hung heavy and cumbersome along with two clips. "The pistol's gonna bang on my leg."

"Stick it in your belt," Mama suggested.

I tucked the .45 under the buckle, then decided to put it back it my coat. Be just my luck to shoot off my pecker running to the fray. I needed me a holster like the Baldies wore. And a shoulder strap for the rifle.

"Take some bread and jerky. What about the canteen? You think you might want water?"

"Mama . . . I got to go!"

She filled the canteen. Dropped the food into a flour sack, rolled it in a blanket, tied it with the remaining cord and hung the bundle and the water across my back.

"You goin' down into the Bastrops' pit?" I asked.

"I expect that's the thing to do. What do you think?" Mama asked.

"It's good. You'll be safe and warm down there. Why? You're not sure?"

"It's all those kids and Ida jammed into one tight spot. I'd almost rather take my chances in the tent."

I smiled. Even though Mama had shut Ida up the day Sidney got killed, they remained neighborly. No truck in staying mad at our neighbor. Why, she had come right back to the colony that night and helped Cissy and Mrs. Giotto make meat pies for everybody. Besides, we'd owe the Bastrops forever for their help during the typhoid time. Mama and Ida did laundry and fed chickens together. Ida never stopped versifying and Mama never stopped telling her to hush.

Mama looked me over. Her eyes saddened as she patted my chest. "Don't try to be the general out there, son. Watch and learn. Use common sense."

"I will, Mama. Don't worry."

As I was on my way out, Ida came in, carrying Artesia. Colby totted along behind.

"Cockeye about ready?" I asked.

"He wanted to sit down a few minutes with Sloan, so I left. Like I told him, Mr. Tanner, and I'm gonna tell you: 'Fight the good fight of faith; lay hold on the eternal life, whereunto thou art also called and has professed a good profession before many witnesses.' That was took from *First Timothy*, 6: 12. Good luck and watch out for my William Ernest."

Goddamn, a positive verse. "Thank you, Mrs. Bastrop, I will."

Outside, I heard gunfire southwest of the colony and I hollered for Cockeye to come on. I didn't want to interrupt his time with the boy, but I didn't want to miss the fighting, either.

Cockeye came outside, wiping his eyes. "Goddern all this."

"He okay?" I asked.

"Oh, yeah. *He's* fine. Think it's games, just like all the boys. Wants me to kill everything that moves. It's *me*."

"Cockeye, nobody'd say nothin' if you just stayed here. There's others doin' it," I said. "Nick's stayin'."

"Nope. I'm gettin' my money's worth out of this gun."

We cut across Haddock's pasture, until we reached the slopes that separated the Berwind and Delagua Canyons. Topped a hill and scouted around until we saw Tostakis and the other Greeks, shooting from behind red sandstones below us.

"Barba," I hollered. "Tanner and Bastrop here." We took cover behind the rocks above them. It dawned on me that the snipers who'd fired on the searchlight wagon–the ones who might have shot Sidney–had taken positions somewhere nearby.

Puffs of smoke belched from the switch house, with bullets clipping the hillocks and bushes, whining off rocks, pelting the area so hard I was afraid to take aim.

"You think that's militiamen?" Cockeye asked.

"Ain't nobody I know can shoot like that," I said. "Goddamn . . . who needs a machine gun."

I laid there, trying to get the guts to raise up and shoot. The .45 jabbed into my leg.

I adjusted the pistol, peeped around the rock and fired at the shack. Easy enough. I shot off the magazine, pulled back and reloaded for another go-round. "You think you hit anything, Cockeye?"

"No idea. Guess this is the way it's done, though. Just rain the bullets till somebody gives or gets killed."

Both sides kept on like that until the sun went down. When the gunfire slacked off, Barba hollered for us.

"Thinks he's the biggest toad in the puddle, don't he?" Cockeye remarked.

"You guys need to call a truce," I said as we crawled down where the Greeks huddled.

Barba motioned for us to hurry. "We go down the hill and get them sombitch militias."

"I ain't," Cockeye said. "You seen the way them guys shoot. It'll be target practice for 'em."

Barba ignored his old buddy. "Tanner, if that train come here at night, we are shit. Beside, them soldiers will get away if we don't go now."

"Train might not be comin'," Cockeye said. "You ever think of that? You seen a locomotive or smoke, even? What if the guys at Forbes got the tracks tore up, like they was supposed to? Them troopers might have hiked out here on their own."

"Poosh, Bastrop . . . stay here and sit on your fist. The world stab you and you wet your pants like a girl."

"You'll get us all killed tryin' to be a hero," Cockeye said. "There's always the chance that those guys down there will retreat and we won't have to worry about gettin' shot tryin' to take that house. Them troopers know we ain't goin' nowhere tonight. I'd say we got 'em right where we want 'em."

After Cockeye and Barba argued themselves out, we decided to compromise and attack the switch house after midnight. Figured it was a good sign that those two were bickering again.

I unrolled the blanket and took out the jerky and bread. "You goozies want some supper?"

Barba stood up. "White breads love to sit and eat. Me, I go to other side of mountain. Anyone want to come?"

"And do what?" Cockeye asked, gnawing a piece of jerky.

"Shoot at searchlight. Kistos don't like, but I done it a few times. Is good practice. I show you how to use sight for long shots."

Cockeye said he wasn't missing dinner to get in some target practice, but I said I'd go. I divided the bread and jerky with my neighbor, then Barba, me and two other Greeks circled around to the side away from the switch house. We climbed to a bald knoll where we could see the searchlight when it came on.

Barba took my rifle and raised a sliver of metal on the barrel. ".30-.30 can shoot three miles with accuracy. Searchlight is up the hill behind Catholic church in Hastings. Sight about half-way up the stem. Next time you in bright daylight and shooting, watch what mark help most."

When the light came on, I knelt and fired.

"Raise the barrel little bit," Barba said.

I did and fired again. The light swung around to scan our mountain top. I flattened out and everybody poked fun.

"What, you think that light will kill you, Tanner?" Barba giggled, clattering through the rocks along the knoll. He pulled his Krag-J off his back, worked the bolt, put the rifle to his shoulder and fired. The light moved again, searching. He worked the bolt and raised the barrel like he told me to do. Just before the beam reached him, he fired again.

A flame flickered in the housing across the canyon and the searchlight went out.

"Goddamn right," Barba called.

* * *

When I got back from the ridge, I was ready to wrap up and get some sleep, but I couldn't find my blanket.

"Cockeye, where you at?"

"Right here." His hand hit my leg. "You're about to step on me. You want some blanket?"

"Damn right, I want some blanket. It's mine and I'm freezin'." I put the rifle down and slid in spoon-style behind Cockeye, who was nested in nice and warm.

"Somethin's stabbin' the back of my leg," he said.

"It's the damn .45." I pulled the pistol out and laid it next to the rifle.

"You shoot out that light?" Cockeye asked.

"Barba did. Damnedest thing I ever seen. Standing up, too."

"He fought a war with Turkey and always bragged about how he could shoot. You warm enough?"

"Uh-huh. What about you?"

"Okay. Just glad you brung a blanket. I knew it might snow, but would I bring cover? No. Had to be a hardhead, in too big a rush."

"How you know it's gonna snow?"

"Teeth hurt. Been drivin' me crazy."

I snickered. "Teeth forecastin' weather?"

"You don't believe me? Bet you two bits it's gonna snow."

"You're on."

"Alan?"

"Yeah."

"You thought much about killing somebody?"

"Yeah. Think about killing somebody all the time. Seems like the only way to get back for Sidney. There's plenty of meanness to shoot at."

"I know you got reason. But I ain't sure I can do it. Don't like being a target, neither. And what with this bad eye and Ida and the kids to take care of, I just don't know if I'll be much help."

"I told you to stay home, Cockeye."

"You know somethin' I hate, Alan? That nickname 'Cockeye.' Never said nothin' 'cause it would've just made it worse. Bill's what I'd wish for."

"That name Jack used? Fine with me. Just take some readjustment."

"Nah. It's too late. I wouldn't know who people was talkin' to now."

We laid there a while longer, before he spoke again.

"Don't say nothin' about me frettin', Alan. You know I'm a worry-wart. We'll go down there in a little while and get 'em back for Sidney."

*　　　*　　　*

The sound of the Greeks leaving woke me. Cockeye didn't budge, so I let him be. I pocketed the .45, grabbed the rifle and started down the hill.

Cockeye's teeth had been right: big snowflakes swirled in the north wind. When we reached the bottom of the hill, we fanned out.

I followed the Greeks' lead, a few at a time scampering with heads low, while the rest watched the shack.

The power of guns lured me and I began to understand what men liked about battle. Freedom. Climbing around in the rocks, shooting at the searchlight, running down the hill and across the plain with ordinary lunkers like me. Under nobody's control, doing something at last to settle the score for Sidney and make up for my cowardice.

About a hundred yards from the building, we started firing. Some knelt for shots, while others pushed on. Nobody in the shack returned fire.

Snow stuck to my eyelashes and I wiped my eyes with my coat sleeve. The pistol bounced against my thigh as I ran.

Still no shots. I gathered that the troopers had either pulled out or been killed off.

By the time I got down there, the early boys had set the switch house on fire and some were poking around. No bodies inside or out. More stragglers joined us and soon close to twenty guys ringed the shack, watching it burn. Some passed whiskey pints and blabbed about taking the fight to Berwind and Tabasco.

Scanning the circle, I spied Cockeye staring at me through the falling snow. Still wrapped in my blanket with the Krag-J barrel sticking out. He must have flown down that hill.

Cockeye held out a hand to catch a few flakes. "Old timers call this snow, Tanner," he hollered. "You owe me two bits."

I smiled and nodded. Lord's will be done.

CHAPTER TWENTY-EIGHT
October 26-30, 1913

The next afternoon, John Lawson called a meeting of everyone who'd taken part in the skirmish. Figured he was going to praise us for stopping the troopers and protecting the colony. But when his shaky hand brandished the front page of the *Chronicle-News*, I knew we were in for it.

COAL WAR!!!

Anarchists Ambush Guardsmen, Torch Switch House, Pry Up Rails, Storm Mining Camps

C.F.I., Victor-American Demand More Troops

Barba held a big loaf of Harry's bread and was tearing off chunks to share. "You say stop soldiers if they get past Forbes, John Lawson," Barba said, calm and satisfied. "That's what we done. You want bread?"

"Goddammit, I didn't say burn railroad property or assault Tabasco and Berwind," John shot back. "That could bring the whole army down on top of us. You're lucky the troopers didn't attack Ludlow."

"Them guys run like bunny rabbits," Cockeye offered around a mouthful. Everybody noisily agreed. "They weren't goin' after nobody."

"Can I see that paper, John?" I asked.

He handed it over. The jack-jawing continued while I scanned the article. "Hey," I poked Nick, "listen to this." The rumpus tapered as I read. " 'John Lawson has no control over the Greeks in the Ludlow colony. Those rebels answer to UMW organizer Barbas Kistillanos, a veteran of the bloody Balkan War. Under Kistillanos' direction, warlike Greeks have been carrying on guerilla warfare in the hills for weeks and have repeatedly declined to obey the orders of strike leaders. Military intervention is the only way to stop these belligerents!' Who's Barbas Kistillanos?"

"They confuse me and Tostakis," Nick said.

Barba held out his free hand. "Give."

I handed him the paper. Even though the rag had lots of info wrong, I felt proud reading it. We had won the first scrimmage. The strike had made news throughout the country and everybody from President Wilson to Junior Rockefeller got quoted about it. The coal shortage caused by closed mines had slowed shipping and rail traffic. And best of all, the switch house troopers who had hightailed it found out they couldn't just walk over us and go where they pleased.

"I piss on this." Barba threw the rag down.

Nick retrieved the paper, folded it and put it under his arm. "Stopping the trooper train was necessary, Barba. Burning switch house and attacking camps was mistake."

"You weren't there, Nick," I said. "You and John don't know nothin' about it."

"And now your blood is up," Nick said.

"Damn right it is. You asked us to do a job. Now, you're criticizin' how we done it."

"You don't speak for Greeks, Tanner," Barba barked.

"I'm speakin' for me, ouzo," I said. "You guys ain't the only ones in this."

Barba snorted something in Greek, then him and his cronies stomped away.

Nick shook his head and smiled.

"What?" Lawson said.

"We need them, John," Nick said.

"Well, they by-God better start thinking. I can't have a bunch of hotheads freelancing."

"I agree," Nick said. "But if we make warriors too mad, they will work against us. They carry old grudges and insults and take everything as a challenge. I have same temptation inside, so I understand both thoughts."

"They have to follow orders," John said.

"We followed orders and held 'em off pretty good the other night," I interrupted. "The troopers got more than they expected and we got respect. Why didn't you say nothin' about that?"

"Don't get cocky, sonny boy," Lawson said. "The militia can beat us with one hand behind its back."

"Aw, you're just mad 'cause the *Chronicle-News* said you'd lost control and the Greeks was in charge," I said.

Lawson's face colored. "Listen . . ."

Nick rested his hand on John's shoulder. "The Greek say, 'The hottest iron scorches the clothes.' We cool off for one day, then I find Barba to talk. If we stop talking, all is lost."

*　　　　　*　　　　　*

After a few days of whining, the company muck-a-mucks convinced Governor Ammons to send more soldiers into the strike zone to let union and management negotiations go forward. The *Chronicle-News* emphasized that these troopers were being sent to prevent violence in the strike zone—not to attack. October 30, two companies of Colorado National Guardsmen arrived in Ludlow. I wondered if Jim Rubin would come with them.

Nick woke me early to watch the militia unload. He had a white cloth star pinned to his overcoat.

"What's that?" I asked.

"I am colony marshal, as of today," Nick said. "No more confusions."

"That hanky would scare me off if I was a thug, I'll tell ya."

Nick patted the rag and grinned. "Yes. Many salute as I come here."

"What's Barba have to say about that?"

"I haven't talked to Barba," Nick said.

"Humph. Are we takin' pistols, or do you buy this bullshit about peacekeeping?" I asked.

"UMW has ordered us to believe. Besides, there will be too many troopers for us to fight."

Me and Nick joined some folks from other colonies up at Cedar Hill. We sat on the front porch of a saloon. From there we had a bird's eye view of the comings and goings.

Spirited horses, cooped up too long, kicked and whinnied as they were led down ramps. After the horses came twenty fine-looking mules, strong animals–Suffolks, like Grady–workers, for sure.

Colony girls and whores had been sashaying around in front of the saloon all morning and some of the soldiers couldn't resist coming across the tracks. Lou Dold showed up and made picture-postcards.

The National Guard boys in their dull green sweaters cocked their hats, put their arms around each other's shoulders–or around the shoulders of gals bold enough to sit on their knees–and posed for Lou.

A couple of whiskey bottles appeared and the picture-taking session got boisterous. Pretty soon, seven more soldiers crossed the tracks, three carrying rifles. I figured the festivities were about to conclude.

"Springfield repeaters" Nick said. "Six-shot, bolt-action. Accurate weapons. And lighter than a Krag-J."

I was surprised that he knew so much about guns. *Chronicle-News* had said the Greek leader had been in a war with the Turks. Could be true of him or Barba.

The soldier wearing just a sidearm–a sergeant, Nick said–and the three rifles peeled off from the group. Sidearm busted into the rabble and the rifles surrounded. In a couple of minutes, the girls scattered like quail and Lou was packing up his camera.

I sniggered. "Only the militia can scare Lou off."

Couldn't see the sergeant now, but I heard him bark. No one moved much at first. Then they backed up, right quick. Now, we could witness the action. The sergeant was standing over a kid lying in the dust. I figured he'd knocked him down.

"You men fall in," the sergeant hollered. The solders made two sloppy rows. "I'm not one goddamn bit impressed by your attitudes, gentlemen. You are presently inattentive–in your thoughts and actions, in the way you wear your uniforms, in your lack of regard for higher rank. You will not stay inattentive in this strike zone, because you will get hurt. And when you get hurt, that causes me an inordinate amount of paperwork and an inordinate amount of paperwork spoils my day. I did not come all the way down here from Denver to have my days spoiled.

"General Sisk wants soldiers out here, not a bunch of goddamned spoiled kids on a lark. I suggest that you pull your heads out of your cherry-red assholes and get attentive. If you choose to fuck with me, you will spend a lot of time on your scrawny asses–like Private Thomason, there–so you don't get yourself or somebody else killed. Do you understand me?"

A voice I recognized as Jim Rubin's spoke up from the gang of troopers. "You can't just beat us up like that . . ."

Before the kid could say another word, the sergeant knocked him down. The troopers shied away like bugged up cattle, but the rifles pushed them back.

"I want you ducks to bend your knees, squat down and put your hands behind your heads," the sergeant commanded.

Some of the troopers moaned and looked at each other, but no one squatted.

"I got all day and a strong arm, gentlemen. I'm prepared to continue this line of discipline as long as it takes for you to get right."

The troopers sank into position.

"Waddle along right here so those men on the porch can watch. And quack, goddammit!"

While the youngsters waddled and quacked, the other three guardsmen approached us. One was the captain who'd come down to guard Secretary Brake. Nick stepped off the porch and the two shook hands.

Tall, young, neat, Josephson was the softest-looking, most relaxed of the three soldiers. Like the troopers who'd bird dogged our snatch–and the ones who'd accompanied him and Jim Rubin–the captain had a smooth, cream-colored baby face that hadn't seen much sun.

"You possibly remember Alan Tanner, too?" Nick pointed at me. "The boy whose mouth runs."

The captain nodded. "I remember. That's your buddy face-down out there."

The ducks were about worn out, but the sergeant kept driving them like a farm maid.

"I seen him," I said. "Where's that old fart get off treatin' them boys like that?"

A soldier, bearing a thick mustache and mutton chops, spoke over the captain. "That's First Sergeant Perlmuter. Veteran of the Philippines. He has no patience with recalcitrants. And he hates back-talk." Mutton chops looked at the captain. "Obviously, Company K hasn't gotten the message yet. But I think you'll see that his approach gets results." The soldier put his hand out to Nick. "Major Edward Teller, battalion commander at Cedar Hill. And over here, Lieutenant McStay from Company B."

"I am Nicholas Kistos, marshal of the Ludlow colony and representative for the United Mine Workers." He shook hands with the captain, but the other trooper stood pat with hands behind his back.

"Yes, we've heard of you," the major said. He stood up so straight and paid such serious attention to everything, he didn't seem genuine to me. Trying so hard to *act* like an army man, instead of just *being* one.

But the other soldier–McStay–was different. A reddish, leathery face marked years of soldiering, outdoors. His uniform was clean and starched, but broke-in. McStay rocked forward slightly. A biggity stance for a cocky man. He was studying Nick.

Something else struck me about McStay. He wore his side-arm like Delores Paul, in an open holster slung low on his hip and strapped to his thigh, so his hand could brush across it without effort. Josephson and Teller had their revolvers buttoned-up and strapped high around their waists.

The major continued. "Governor Ammons has called upon the militia to maintain peace and order until the coal strike is resolved. General Brandon Sisk will be joining us later this afternoon to oversee the pacification of the strike zone. I assure you we're ready for whatever might happen."

"My friends and I have been discussing just that," Nick said. "It is very impressive. We appreciate your help."

The major nodded. "Just don't make the mistake of thinking we don't mean business."

"I have women, children and unarmed strikers to watch over. I know your business, Major, and I trust it is for the good. As I say, anything you can do to help get our rights, we appreciate."

"We're not here to help you get any rights, Mr. Kistos," the major said. "We're here to expedite a mission of law and order in the southern coal fields. We'll begin this morning and stay until you strikers respond to reason and return to work. The state of Colorado is losing thousands of dollars each day that these mines are closed or operating at minimum output."

"And we lose our pay, Major, every day away from the job," Nick said. "Have you been into a closed coal camp?"

"No, I haven't, Mr. Kistos."

Nick nodded. "Captain Josephson go to Delagua with Secretary Brake. Maybe I could take you for a visit to help with a different attitude."

The major traded a glance with McStay. "There are a lot of attitudes around here–most of them unacceptable. Lieutenant McStay and his men spent some time pinned down at the switch house out there–the one that is nothing but ash. His report to General Sisk is the main reason we're here."

Nick turned to the lieutenant. "You're the man who call us rebels in the newspaper for defending ourselves."

McStay spoke for the first time. "You call shooting at the state militia and destruction of private property self-defense? How do you explain that?"

"I can't," Nick said. "I wasn't there and I'm sorry about the burning."

"If you're the marshal, Kistos," Teller interrupted, "you're responsible for the actions of your men."

"I would like to see this strike settled without more incident," Nick said. "But we have needs in our camps and demands for work conditions."

"I, for one, believe that the coal companies have been too easy on you people," McStay said. "I think anarchist trash controls the UMW–trash who don't give a good goddamn about anybody's rights. Trash who'd destroy anything and anybody to bring down the government. If you know any of those men, tell 'em we're not pussy-footing around. We intend to get your guns and ammunition, one way or the other."

Nick folded his arms and stepped to one side so the sun shone right in McStay's eyes. "You are very direct, Lieutenant. Will you also take guns from scum the companies hire to shoot women and children?"

Teller saw what was developing between Nick and McStay. "We're here to disarm everyone and maintain order until grievances can be worked out. General Sisk will be coming to the colony first thing in the morning to start the process."

"I take information to John Lawson and everyone at Ludlow," Nick said, "and I make sure same information get to other colonies. We don't want bloodshed any more than you, Major. We want to go back to work."

Teller studied Nick as he shook his hand. "I'm glad we see things the same way. Understanding each other is crucial to the peaceful completion of our mission."

* * *

When me and Nick crossed the railroad tracks again, the old sergeant was marching his charges around. Jim Rubin and Private Thomason had joined the group.

"That first sergeant is hard-ass army, like McStay," Nick said. "If ordered, he will bite the head off a rat. We can learn much from Perlmuter. He has a reason for everything he does. If I was fighting anarchist trash, I would want that man on my side."

"*You're* the trash McStay was talkin' about, *Kistillanos*. You're the one everybody's watchin'."

Nick clapped me on the back. " 'The donkey call the rooster big-head.' I suppose you think that lieutenant mistook you for an ink slinger from Trinidad. You know, strikers and the soldiers tell each other one thing–smiling, nodding, shaking the hands–but we think another. All day, I worry how these guardsmen will react to men like Barba, who would start a fight with their trousers. Major Teller and Captain Josephson worry, also. But McStay, he want to fight. That's why he's here. He is the one to watch."

Me and Nick walked under the railroad bridge and climbed the grade up to where the Berwind and Ludlow roads met. A mile south of town was Water Tank Hill. At one time a big water tank sat there, so trains coming up from Trinidad could fill up. But the tank had been moved out to the steel trestle north of the colony and now Water Tank Hill was just a bald knoll.

Right on top of that knoll sat Death Special.

Three guards stood inside. Grabble and Crimmons sported carbines under their arms. A machine gun and searchlight were mounted on the dash, just like we'd heard. Delores Paul Hawkins tipped his hat to Nick. If the dick recognized me, he didn't show it.

"Goddamn, everybody is puttin' on a show for us," I said as we passed.

"All polite and kiss-ass," Nick said.

I felt mighty uncomfortable walking away from the armored car and I looked back a time or two to see if the detectives were about to shoot us in the back.

Nick chuckled. "They won't fire in daylight this time, Alan. The Baldwins make mistake at Forbes–just like Barba make mistake at the switch house. Sometimes, blunders get people to stop and think. For the first time since I come to the south fields, I believe bosses want to talk. Rockefeller and Bowers need coal dug again. No more tent colony shoot ups or switch house burnings for them, so they pull back the goons–as much as they can–and bring in the National Guard. Me and John want General to see we can pull back *our* hotheads, too."

"So you're sayin' that thugs and hotheads make for negotiation? That they let each side know the other means business?"

"Yes, they is wild cards who show how bad things can get. Negotiation is the knife edge between belligerents on both sides. Militants can serve the cause of peace, if they can be held back long enough."

"You're walking down the knife edge, ain't you, Nick?"

"And you, too, my friend. Because of all that has happened, you have found your salt."

"It felt good to fight back the other night."

"I understand, Alan. Now you must decide what kind of warrior you will be. I have told you we need men with good judgment *and* salt. A man like Barba–all salt. If I am killed, he will lead Greeks into the lion's mouth. I see same bad thing he has and I tell you, if we start killing, we lose. You should know that.

"I do."

"Victor-American and CFI might deal with a man of moderation like John Lawson. I am cushion between Lawson and hotheads. Companies know that Barba and the Baldwins–and McStay–pace in a cage, waiting for everyone to give up on talk and throw the door open. And these troopers, who have been called to take away guns and keep peace, they will find who shoots and who talks . . . on both sides."

Walking back to the colony, I thought about how the strike, Sid's death and my friendship with Nick had put me into a position I wasn't sure I wanted. I was being melted down and poured into a new mold. I'd have to live with what came out.

CHAPTER TWENTY-NINE
October 31, 1913

At nine the next morning, onlookers lined both sides of the road, from Ludlow all the way up to the colony. Mothers had dressed their kids in white and folks waved handkerchiefs and little American flags. Some even clapped as the soldiers approached.

Barba and the Greeks were back, strutting in loose shirts and pants, red scarves and skull caps.

Nick cut an odd figure for camp marshal. He wore a suit with the cloth star pinned to the lapel, but he had tied red scarves just below his knees. Instead of patrolling the colony, he was playing in Izzy's band.

Caitlin stood on the stage, flanked by the Ludlow colony flag that she'd made and the big American flag she'd waved to greet the strikers that first day. Sporting a long blue dress and high-button shoes, she'd been singing and visiting for an hour already.

When the troopers reached the turn-off for the colony, the band struck up a march. Near the front, the general rode a skittish white horse. He was followed by Major Teller, Captain Josephson and Lieutenant McStay, the only one who seemed at home in the saddle.

Perlmuter marched beside two rows of troopers armed with rifles. These guys stepped along without any hint of the smart-ass we'd seen the day before.

The soldiers spread out behind the stage and stood at rest with the sun in their eyes. Their uniforms looked fresh-ironed and their boots gleamed. Jim Rubin was on the front row.

The officers dismounted and flunkies held the reins for them. John Lawson, duded up in suit and tie, greeted the general and followed him up the steps and onto the stage. The commander of the National Guard was thin and delicate, with snow-white hair and mustache, like somebody's granddaddy. Lawson said he was an eye doctor in Denver. Caitlin shook hands with the old man. While she led us singing "The Battle Cry of Union," the geezer made a just-sucked-a-lemon face.

When the general spoke, his voice deep and commanding, the gathering settled.

"I am General Brandon Sisk, representative of the state of Colorado, empowered by Governor Elias Ammons to neutralize the strike zone and maintain law and order. Your representative, Mr. Lawson, has assured me that everyone in the Ludlow tent colony will cooperate with us. The Colorado National Guard is here for your own good. I hope you can see that. There will be no trust on either side unless you surrender your guns."

Everyone looked at each other. As far as I knew, nobody had any intention of surrendering guns. I didn't. Not only had I gone to a lot of expense buying the weapons and trouble burying them in a crate at the colony dump, I didn't want to be left unarmed. John Lawson was selling the general a bale of lint.

The old man seemed impatient. I guess he figured he could just come prancing in on his white horse, holler, "Cricket," and we'd jump.

"Get your weapons and bring them to the stage. Surrender your guns now and there will be no questions or penalties."

I caught sight of Barba and some of the Greeks moving through the horde. Nick watched, holding his lyra and smoking, as Barba stepped up to the stage and dropped a popgun at the general's feet. Each Greek walked by and added a toy gun to the pile.

People nearest the stage howled. Everyone pushed forward to see what the crazy Greeks had done this time.

The general's face turned red as Nick's scarves and he looked like he might bust a vein. He yelled at Lawson, who bent down, just as red-faced, and yelled something at Nick.

Kistos threw a hand up, as if to ask, "What the hell do you want me to do?" He handed the lyra to Izzy. As Nick hurried off to find Barba, Lawson kicked the toys off the stage.

McStay mounted up and cantered behind the troopers. You could tell he was dying to light into the Greeks.

The general glared at us like a preacher who'd discovered that some members had deposited turds in his offering plate. When he spoke his voice shook.

"It's unfortunate that you people let the action of foreigners represent the feelings of your colony. I had thought you'd take this necessity seriously, Mr. Lawson, and that your people would be reasonable."

At first, John looked like he didn't know what to say. But he defended the Greeks, sort of. "I think we'd be more reasonable, General, if the Baldwins put down their guns and stopped driving around in that armored car, scaring everyone to death."

Our shouts of agreement assaulted the old man's patience. "We know that you people are well armed and can touch your weapons whenever you like. We're here on a mission of peace, but you could force us to make war. Do you want to be the cause of a war, Mr. Lawson?"

"Well, of course not, General . . . ."

The old man turned back to us partisans. "The force of the Colorado National Guard is a fact of life in this strike zone. You might as well get used to that. If you people have *real* guns in this camp, you'd better get them. Now."

Once again, nobody said or did anything.

"I was afraid of this. Major Teller . . . ," the general hollered for his man.

"Yessir."

"You'll move Companies B and K into full bivouac just across the tracks there." The general pointed behind him at a stretch of flat grassland. "My best troopers will be your close neighbors, ladies and gentlemen. You won't sneeze without them knowing it."

The old man stomped down the steps. Perlmuter snapped his troopers to attention and the rest of the officers got back on their horses.

The general marched to his horse and jerked the reins away from the trooper who'd been holding them. He put a boot into the stirrup and stepped up. But before he could swing his other leg over the saddle, the jumpy animal bolted. The general stood like a trick rider for some seconds before he toppled. The horse had its head for the barn and galloped up the Ludlow road back toward Cedar Hill.

Perlmuter shouted an order. The troopers pulled their rifles off their shoulders and held them at ready. Who knows what would have happened if some moron had laughed or whooped.

Josephson and Teller rode out to the old man as fast as they dared and Perlmuter had some of his foot soldiers follow. I joined a few colonists running to get a better look. Sisk sat on the ground, ungeneral-like. Hatless, with grass in his hair and dirt on his uniform. The old man held his right arm in an awkward position, his face twisted in pain.

Teller had Lawson take the general to the field hospital in the union roadster. I wish I could have heard the conversation on that trip.

*　　　　*　　　　*

Turned out, Haddock owned the property across the tracks and Teller met with the rancher to discuss an encampment site. Clem drove down in the

Ford and paced the area with the major, shaking his head at the particular spot the general had designated, insisting on another farther away from our tents.

Amidst a gang of rubbernecks, me and Nick observed this powwow from our side of the tracks.

"The army can take property and use however," Nick observed.

"Clem knows that," I said. "He's jerking that dude's rope."

I hadn't seen Kistos since he'd gone after the Greeks and I asked him what had happened.

"I yell at Barba, but you never know what will stay in the head. Them popguns surprise me. The whole time they pile up, I think, 'Kistos, you should act.' But I tell you, Alan, I enjoy what I see."

Haddock and the major finally reached an agreement and shook hands. Just after three o'clock, a train packed with gear and troopers backed down from Cedar Hill. Companies B and K began unloading on a hard scrabble plot, half-way between Ludlow and the colony.

"Whaddaya think about two companies of soldiers sittin' over there?"

Nick shrugged. "Might not be bad. Josephson will be in command and he seem reasonable. Teller will stay at Cedar Hill. John say General is in strike zone for only a few days, anyway. He go sooner now, with the arm."

"That leaves McStay," I said.

"I would put that man in a sack with Delores Paul and the Baldwins and throw them in a river. He rode up while me and Barba is talking this morning. Very rude. Said he is Jesus Christ in the strike zone and we will take orders from him. McStay claim B Company will be everywhere, searching and bossing. But Josephson has rank."

"Don't you think McStay will bully him and the captain like he does Teller."

"Not with Perlmuter around. He is Josephson's right-hand, a professional. McStay won't challenge."

"Perlmuter had his troopers pull their rifles on us this morning."

"Yes. And you would too, if you was in that situation. We can't change his discipline. Him and McStay fight in Philippines. Not in the same outfit, but they was there. You've looked at both men and know they don't tolerate nonsense. After watching, Alan, which would you trust to do right?"

"The old sergeant. He's mean, but he don't want nobody killed."

Nick nodded. "The soldiers to trust are Josephson and Perlmuter. You know anything about the Philippines uprising?"

"Nope."

"Dirty, like the war between the Greeks and the Turks. Shoot and run. Women and children killed and piled up. Soldiers with their privates cut off and stuck in the mouth. . . ."

I recalled my run-in with Hawkins.

". . . War like that haunts a man, changes the way he looks at human beings, at himself. We can watch and learn from both soldiers. If ordered or forced, Perlmuter can be a quick and efficient killer. But he is not thirsty for the fight like McStay or Baldwins."

"Or like Barba?" I asked.

"Is possible. But Barba talk a lot."

"What about you, Nick? Do you thirst for it?"

"I am Ludlow marshal and must act like lawman, not warrior. If the warriors get control, everything is finished." Nick rolled a cigarette and lit it. "That your friend?"

I looked across the tracks and saw Jim Rubin unloading his bag.

"Hey, college puke," I hollered. "You too good to speak?"

Jim Rubin glanced at one of his buddies, who said something I couldn't hear as they carried their gear away.

Felt like I'd been slapped. "Fucking rude bastard."

Nick clapped me on the back. "Those boys have much on the mind, Alan. Give a little rope."

CHAPTER THIRTY
November 10, 1913

The coming of the National Guard added another odd patch to the crazy quilt being stitched. We already had our belligerent foreigners, Baldwin detectives, union organizers and gamblers. Matching swatches of whores and politicians, shopkeepers and ranchers, ink slingers and photographers. Now, soldiers were camped across the tracks.

At first, you couldn't tell the trooper companies apart. They all came on tight-ass and military, stopping men on the street, barging in to search the tents and the stores in Ludlow for guns. Before long, I realized that the only things those two companies had in common were uniforms, weapons and boredom.

Company B, McStay's outfit, was full-time army veterans. Many had been to war and had no patience with opposition. To them, strikers were redneck anarchists who deserved extermination. Company B was a uniformed version of the Baldwins and it was easy to see whose side they'd take in a fight. When Clem, Harry and some of the other merchants in Ludlow raised hell at having their stores torn up and trade disrupted, Major Teller had McStay rein in his cohorts.

On the other hand, Company K contained mostly "weekend warriors," play-acting like soldiers until Perlmuter stomped their throats to convince them that this duty could be hazardous. Josephson was in command, but Perlmuter controlled. That first day up at Cedar Hill, when the old sergeant had rounded up the strays and made 'em duck walk, I figured he'd have nothing but trouble with those spoiled brats. But he'd changed them. The way they'd marched for him the morning Sisk fell off his horse, the way they watched him and listened when he spoke, you could tell he was the officer they trusted.

Kistos and Perlmuter started meeting once a week to share concerns. "A friendship born of necessity," was how Nick put it. I actually heard them ribbing each other a time or two. Kistos said they both thought alcohol, gambling and women to be their greatest discipline threats. Temptation was everywhere. Almost every shed and outhouse had been converted into a bar, crib or dice den. Most of Company B, a few of the college pukes and plenty of strikers sampled left-handed entertainment. The men spent idle hours drinking, gambling or squeezing the tenderloin. Some soldiers bird-dogged colony girls, a fair number got caught with their pants down and had their butts kicked by papas, brothers or boyfriends. A few drifted up to the opium dens in Chinkville. Perlmuter, Josephson and Teller had their hands full with their outliers. McStay didn't give a shit about what his men did as long as they kept their weapons handy.

While the talks dragged on, a spell of warm weather cropped up. Lawson got Ludlow put on the same movie circuit as Trinidad and Walsenburg. Soon moving pictures flickered on a bed sheet outside the depot.

Thursday was movie night. Watching Keystone comedies, troopers and strikers got along pretty good. At a picture called *The Gangsters*, me and Jim Rubin had taken turns reading characters' lines in corny voices that made everybody chuckle. When Constable Fatty Arbuckle lost his pants, twice, in confrontations with the dreaded Cogley Gang, hilarity made us pals again.

Show a Bronco Billy or Tom Mix shoot-'em-up, though, and we had trouble. Strikers would sit on one side; troopers on the other. When Bronco Billy shot a crooked soldier during a two-reeler and the troopers booed, fist-fights broke out and the movie had to be stopped.

In a last-ditch effort to bring us all together, peacefully, Kistos, Perlmuter and Clem Haddock organized "The Ludlow Fair Day." Nick sweet-talked Caitlin into helping and she encouraged other women to get involved. I was glad when Mama said she'd participate and even play ball. Anything to take her mind off Sidney.

Mack and Tommy made a banner announcing a softball game, a barbecue and a dance. Clem and Diego started cooking sides of beef the day before and the smell of meat barbecuing filled the air.

I was amazed to see the thing come together. Unarmed strikers, troopers and even a few Baldwins mingled and relaxed. First, Izzy's band played. They'd learned the newest dance tunes and had gotten so popular, some mothers quarantined their daughters, fearing they'd get overcome with "tango madness" and lift their skirts for a college puke.

The Haddocks brought Juliet and four ponies over. The donkey leapt the camp fence for our amusement. Clem gave the kids horseback rides, while Diego tended the fire.

A little after noon, troopers and strikers drifted out to the ball field east of the colony for the game. Under the watchful eyes of four troopers, all the men piled up their coats and jackets to show they weren't armed.

Those not playing ball spread quilts and a few spectators brought in folding chairs. Dressed in their red exercise bloomers and plims, Cait, Mama and some of the other camp girls greeted everybody. The college pukes hooted when they caught sight of that garb. Killing time, shagging flies and skinners, the troopers hotdogged and chitter-chattered like pros expecting to dump a case of whip-ass on us indigents.

Surprise was about to descend. We could hit, we had speed and we could field. Plus, we had our ringer, Ethel Tanner.

Mama didn't show "The Windmill" during our warm-up, choosing instead to sand-bag the pukes by lobbing rainbows that a baby could hit. To establish her ineptitude, she dropped the ball a time or two when I threw it back to her and even let one toss sail over her head.

Clem had bought caps for us and had the letter *L* for Ludlow sewn on the front.

"That stand for 'Losers'?" one of the pukes hollered as we took the field.

"Wait and see," Mama came back with a fake look of concern.

Before the game began, Ida stood and read: " 'Order ye the buckler and shield, and draw near to battle. Harness the horses and get up, ye horsemen, and stand forth with your helmets, furnish the spears, and put on the brigandines." From *Jeremiah* 46, Verses 3 and 4. Good luck to all involved." She received light applause for her effort.

Mama unleashed "The Windmill" right off, striking out the first two batters with six pitches. As catcher, I witnessed the shock on their faces when those rockets zipped in. "Fucking unfair," out two shouted, beating the ground with his bat. Howls of agreement rose from the pukes' bench as Perlmuter strode up.

The sergeant had shucked his army shirt and cap, pushed up the sleeves on his long johns and grabbed a bat. Mama uncorked two "Windmills" for two strikes. Seemed like she took a little off the next pitch and he smacked a long fly, which Nick dropped. Perlmuter could run pretty damn fast for a big man and he rounded the bases for a home run. The next guy struck out to retire the side.

As the pukes took the field, Ida rose again. " 'Know that I am the Lord'," she shouted. " 'With the staff in my hand I will strike the water of the Nile and it will be changed to blood.' *Exodus*, 7: 17. Batter up." More applause and even laughter this time.

Jim Rubin pitched and Perlmuter caught him. You could tell the puke had some experience. He threw hard, but in a more normal way than Mama. Our first two batters struck out and the pukes cackled and preened.

When I came up, I nodded to Rubin, but he didn't respond. I couldn't figure the kid out. That day at Number 6 and later at the moving picture, he'd seemed like a regular guy with my sense of humor. Kinda reminded me of Sid. But he was snooty, on fair day, same as he'd been the day they set up camp across from the colony.

Perlmuter pattered to break my concentration. "Hey-hey, Mule Man." I had no idea how he knew I was partial to mules. "How-ya-doin'-Mule-Man-waste-of-time-tryin'-to-hit-my-pitcher-now-throws-comets-okay-here-she-comes-batter-batter-batter-batter . . . swing, batter."

To humor him and Jim Rubin, I spun around like a pinhead, red-faced and grunting, as the ball popped Perlmuter's mitt, twice.

"Oh, that's two strikes, ain't it, Mule Man? Might-as-well-quit-can't-hit-a lightning-bolt-batter-batter-batter-batter . . . swing . . . ."

The ball sailed in knee-high and I drove it over the second baseman's outstretched glove for one bag.

Cheers and applause

Mama came up. The outfielders moved closer. "Loser," a puke hollered. "Easy out."

Mama took two practice swings then stepped in. Jim Rubin unleashed his hardest pitch. Mama blistered it so far into left field we had to stop the game to look for the ball.

From all the cheering, you'd have thought the strike demands had been met and John D. himself was coming to Ludlow.

Cockeye, wearing an eye-patch, batted next.

"William Ernest," Ida called, " 'Do your best to present yourself to God as one approved, a worker who has no need to be ashamed, rightly handling the word of truth.' *Second Timothy*, Chapter 2, Verse 15. Now, be a hitter."

Everyone cackled when Cockeye tipped his cap and hollered, "Yes ma'am."

I'd been playing ball with Bastrop for a long time and it still seemed like a miracle he could even see the ball, much less hit it. First pitch he swung at, the bat flew out of his hand and propellered toward first. Fortunately, no one was hit. Jim Rubin got another strike on him before Cockeye slammed a two-bagger.

Clem joined the onlookers just as Susan blooped a single. With runners on first and third, Nick hit a triple.

Perlmuter walked out to calm down his pitcher.

Ricky Morales came up. Jim Rubin got two strikes on him when the Mexican dribbled a grounder to the third baseman. The puke fielded the ball and zinged it to Perlmuter who crouched at home, waiting for Nick.

The Greek hit the sergeant like a ram butting a stump. Perlmuter toppled onto his back, a whoosh of wind busting out of him. Kistos glanced off the hind catcher and skidded on his side over home plate. A gasp exploded from the fans.

Nick rolled onto his back, sat up and looked around. Still resting, Perlmuter raised his hand and showed everyone the ball. The Greek was out.

Score after one inning: Coalasses 4, Pukes 1.

As we took the field, Ida stood. " 'Do nothin' in rivalry or conceit, but in humility count others more significant than your selves. Let each of you look not only to his own interests, but also the interest of others.' *Philippians* 2, Verses 3 and 4. Get three, Ludlow."

Widespread applause, some cheers. I was amazed at Ida's good reception.

Caitlin and Susan waggled their cute little bloomer-covered fannies around, as we took the field. Just before the first batter came up, Clem called out, "Pig in a poke, pork off the rind . . . look on your scorecard and see who's behind."

Our pluck and Mama's pitching had embarrassed the pukes so much they bore down. Their first two batters homered. The third singled. I ran out to talk to my pitcher.

"What's up?" I asked. "These boys shouldn't be hittin'."

Mama looked at her feet, evading my question. "Arm's sore."

"It's never got sore before," I said. "You feelin' sorry for these kids?"

"You just go on back to catching, Alan, and let me do my job."

The next batter, Jim Rubin, got two strikes on him, then punched a skinner to Ricky, who flipped the ball to Mack, covering second. The puke running from first slid outside the base path to break up a possible double-play. Mack dragged his foot across the bag just as the kid toppled him.

As Mack and the runner wrestled, both sides flooded the field. Nick and Perlmuter separated the combatants, then stood between us and the troopers.

"AT EASE," the sergeant hollered and everybody shut-up. He pointed at the slider, who was standing now. "You're spoiling my fun and begging for an ass-whipping, son. All you men come here." The pukes gathered round.

While the troopers confabbed, Ida rose. " 'Two are better than one because they have a good reward for their toil. For if they fall, one will lift up his fellow. But woe to him who is alone and has not another to lift him up!' *Ecclesiastes*, 4, Verses 8 through 12. Let us lift each other up and not the other way around."

The crowd clapped while Perlmuter and the pukes finished their talk.

Glad to avoid a beating from his sergeant, the slider apologized to Mack. They shook hands and we started back where we left off. Score: Coalasses 4, Pukes 3.

I couldn't believe it, but the fracas seemed to calm everybody down instead of stir them up. During their team meeting, Perlmuter must have reminded his charges of why we were playing baseball together.

The pukes' next batter flied out to Caitlin for the third out. On her way off the field, she lobbed the ball to Mama, turned a cartwheel, then caught the ball when it was tossed back. The crowd roared. Found out later they'd practiced that.

We booted the bottom of the third, three-up, three-down.

It was past four o'clock and the sun had set. The pukes scored another run before we retired 'em.

With the score tied 4-4, I came up. It was getting dark now and the ball came in like a spook. But I got lucky and smacked a long, high fly. I trotted to first, thinking the fielder would catch it. As long as the ball climbed, he could follow it. But when it fell, he lost sight and it dropped into darkness behind him. I rounded the bases for a homer.

The knotheads hoisted me on their shoulders, shouting "Hip-hip-hurrah."

Ida gave her final oration, from memory.

" 'I have fought a good fight, I have finished my course, I have kept the faith: henceforth there is laid up for me a crown of righteousness, which the Lord, the righteous judge, shall give me at that day: and not to me only, but unto all them also that love his appearin'.' That verse come from *Second Timothy*, Chapter 4, Verses 7 and 8. Final score: Ludlow 5, Company K, 4. Let's eat."

The fans clapped once more and we all went to dinner.

* * *

I couldn't recall ever seeing this much pep in folks who hadn't been drinking. As we walked back to the colony, me and Mama accepted lots of compliments, even from the pukes.

I got myself a pail of beer, but before I could take much more than a sip, Mama stole it for herself. By the time I'd returned with another, Perlmuter had come up and was chatting with Mama. Guess the sergeant could be interested in her. We each got a plate of beef, red beans and bread. Me and Mama sat on the ground and Perlmuter squatted on his heels, goo-goo-style.

Some of the girls lit paper lanterns and hung them from poles nailed to the corners of the stage. It was good dark now with reds, yellows and oranges flooding the platform. Izzy and Nick set up the band and, after tuning up, played a waltz.

I pointed at couples moving around the stage. "You talk about bored. These mole rats have learned to dance. They ain't gonna be worth squat when we get back to the mine."

"You dance?" Perlmuter asked.

"Too busy for that," I said.

"Good way to meet the ladies," Perlmuter said.

"Lets you get close without much risk," Mama said and winked. She was a little tipsy. "Are you boys finished with your plates? I'm going for another beer and I might as well take them."

Perlmuter watched her walk away. "She's crackerjack, ain't she? I never saw a woman hit a ball like that. And that one pitch. My God in heaven."

I laughed. "She was a star in high school. We play catch sometimes, but it's been a while since I seen her in a game. She ain't played since my brother died. Today was good."

When the waltz ended, Nick got the band to play a tango so he and Cait could dance. When he stepped toward her, she threw her head back, like she was going to fall, and he caught her. Then they reversed and she came at him fast, her legs matching his backward steps. They kept it up like that for the whole tune.

Perlmuter pointed at Nick. "You his deputy?"

"What makes you think that?"

"The way he watches you, brings you along when he's got something hard to consider–like that first morning at Cedar Hill. He values your judgment."

I didn't know what to say. All this personal talk might just be a smoke screen to get the scoop on Nick.

"Me and Kistos dug coal together at Delagua, since he first come up. He saved my life, more than once. There ain't nothin' I wouldn't do for him."

"He's a good leader, but he's got his hands full with hotheads. Not sure every one of your boys takes him serious." Perlmuter swigged his beer. "You think the negotiations are doing any good?"

"Yeah, I guess. It's hard to tell."

"Well, your people better hurry up and decide what they can live with, because vacation's about over. The strike's costing the state too much and the college kids didn't plan on bein' out here this long. They got school or jobs, you know, and the lark's gettin' old. When the state cuts funds, Company K will be the first to go. That'll leave the hard core. And it'll be nut-cuttin' time."

"If Company K goes, you'll go, too, I guess?"

"Yeah. I'm Captain Josephson's first sergeant. But I get on with Teller and he commands the big show. We'll just have to see." Perlmuter drained the last of his beer as Mama returned with two more pails.

"One of you want this?" she asked.

Perlmuter chuckled. "Let's split it," he said, pouring beer into my pail.

"You know how to polka, don't you, Toby?" Mama said.

Toby? Where had she gotten that?

"My people are all square heads," the sergeant answered. "I can hop with the best of 'em."

"Okay. I'll go ask," Mama said, stepping up to Izzy.

"Good talking to you, Tanner," Perlmuter said. "You know to watch out for McStay, don't you? He's got it in for Kistos. Lookin' for any little excuse to come down on this colony. Plus, he's a mean, careless drunk. You could catch a stray bullet, if you aren't careful."

"Good advice," I said, as Mama came back. When the band kicked up her request, she and Perlmuter joined the dancers.

After they played two polkas, I asked Izzy for another waltz. Then I climbed the stairs and stepped up to Cait and Nick. The pail-and-a-half of beer had made me bold. If I couldn't ask her to dance now, I never would.

Nick smiled and bowed. "Ah, Tanner, be my guest. Caitlin is an excellent teacher. She'll show you everything."

She grinned and put her arm around my shoulder. "I knew you were a warrior, but I didn't know you were a dancer, too."

"I ain't no warrior and I never danced a step in my life," I said, looking at our feet as the music commenced. "But I'm turnin' into a fiend for reckless activity."

Even with the band playing, I could hear insults spilling out of the yahoos below, as Caitlin guided me around the platform. Our feet got tangled up a few times, but I eventually smoothed out enough for her to tilt her head against mine and hum the tune.

Being close to Cait again brought back that queasy feeling I used to get in Delagua. Her hair and skin smelled of tang, soap and toilet water. Her tits pressed my chest, her belly rubbed mine. No way I could hide my woody. Wondered what she thought of that.

When the waltz ended, Caitlin called for a tango. She tried to get me to stay, but that dance risked more than I was up to.

As I was going down the stairs, Jim Rubin was coming up. Said, "Good game," as he passed. Walked straight to Caitlin and started talking. Figured he was asking her to dance. Coulda been my imagination, but she looked pleased.

As the music started, I joined Nick below the stage.

"You did good, Alan." He laughed as he clapped me on the back. "A little stiff, but good."

Caitlin and Jim Rubin drifted across the floorboards like they'd made up the dance in the first place.

"Goddamn guys, think they can just come down here and take over," I said.

"Is just a dance, Alan," Nick said.

"Looks like more than that to me."

Nick snickered. "With you, was a dance. With the private, is a proposal?"

"Don't her flirtin' bother you?" I asked.

"Not like you," Nick said.

"Shit, I don't care. Figured *you* would."

Nick shook his head. "Her boldness make you nervous, eh? Same with the Greeks. Barba would slap a curfew on her. She threaten his manhood."

"So, you don't care if she fools around, right in front of you?"

"Would it matter if I did?" Nick smiled.

"What if you lose her?"

Nick shrugged. "Was alone before she come up. Papa would say, 'Nicholas, dance by yourself and you can jump as high as you want.' "

"Don't you love her?"

"I love Cait and admire. But I don't own her. She marry early and is managed by John Broiles. Now, *she* manage. You know from that waltz." Nick grinned. "The barber in my village, when he have trouble with his wife or *gomena*, he say, 'Aye, a woman's pube can tow a ship.' My friend, Caitlin could pull the navy."

A north wind laced with mist picked up. Some of the lanterns blew down and caught fire. Nick's cap took flight like a scared bird and he ran to fetch it. When he returned, he took out the lyra and joined the band.

I got another pail of beer. Izzie had a little accordion now and he and Nick offered the most mournful tune I'd ever heard. Those left on the stage stopped to listen. It was too sad to dance to.

At first, the lyra floated under the accordion, supporting Izzie's version of the melody. When the bohunk faded into the background, Nick brought his strings to command. The Greek scrunched his eyes and mouth, like each note was being ripped from deep inside. When Izzie came back full-force, he and Kistos sparred until the tune ended.

After resting his bow on the strings for a few seconds, Nick relaxed. Everybody seemed too stunned to clap. He and Izzie lit cigarettes and struck up a livelier tune.

With the weather changing, people started drifting off to their tents. But Jim Rubin and Cait stayed with it until Izzie said he was too cold to keep playing.

When the last song ended, the flirt and the trooper walked down the steps together. Kistos smoked and visited, with his back to the stage. Before Caitlin joined the Greek, Jim Rubin kissed her. She didn't put her arms around him, or anything, but she didn't slap shit out of him either. I was burning up.

Wobbly from drink, I followed him a short way. In the light of a remaining lantern, I called to him.

Jim Rubin turned.

"You think you're better than me?" I asked.

He didn't answer.

"I asked you a question, sonny."

"Why don't you just hit me and get it over with," Jim Rubin said.

I stepped in close, my beer courage raging. "You and them college pukes figure you're better than us, don't you? Come down here, think you're somethin', sparkin' our girls. Tell you what: you ain't nothin', college boy. I shit better turds than you."

I took a drunken swing at him, which he stepped away from. He shoved me and I went down. Sat there a little dazed.

Jim Rubin pulled something out of his pocket and tossed it in my lap. "If we get an order, I'll have to fire on you. We can't be pals, dumbass. Thought you'd figure that out."

The private walked away.

When my head cleared, I felt around for the thing he had dropped. From a crease in my trousers fell the chunk of coal Jim Rubin had taken as a souvenir from Number 6. He'd been carrying it all that time.

CHAPTER THIRTY-ONE
December 21-31, 1913

Snow had fallen for ten days, piling around the tents and sheet metal buildings. The clouds sagging above the prairie could drop as much as a foot in one night. It never warmed up much during the day and, with the snow so heavy, most folks stayed under cover, trying to keep warm. Christmas Eve, John had brought a carload of candy and fruit for the kids and some of the women made rag dolls. Only a few got out to claim their gifts.

When the blizzard commenced, I thought lying around might be all right. But that feeling drained the first day I spent inside, listening to the wind blow snow against the tent.

The worst part was having no one except Mama to talk to. Every conversation turned to Sid. I tried to get her to do some of Caitlin's exercises or at least play cards. But if we weren't talking about Sid, all she wanted to do was read, cook a little and sleep.

Sid. Sid. Sid. Grief and a guilty conscience over his death took ghostly form for me. Shadows became my brother; gusts of wind, his coughing. He haunted my dreams. During the day, I'd sit in a chair by the stove, try to read and nod off. At night, I lay wide-awake, running things through my head.

Like every other morning lately, I stayed in bed until it was light enough to see, then wrapped up in my blanket to start a fire. When I had the juniper going good, I added three lumps of coal–half of what we had left.

I pushed on the underside of the tent roof to knock off fresh snow –something we had to do constantly to keep the shelter from collapsing. Then I slipped back in bed to let the fire warm the tent.

A gun went off. Sid came through the tent flaps, blood-soaked, his face half-eaten away. He stumbled to my cot, shook me, hollered to wake up.

"Let me alone," I screamed, but he jerked my hand. When I wouldn't come around, he dragged me onto the floor.

Cockeye still had ahold and I pulled away. Mama sat on the edge of the bed with her overcoat on.

"You were out of your head, son, hollering and fighting. Mr. Bastrop woke you up. What was pestering you so?"

"Just a bad dream, Mama." I couldn't tell her it was about Sid.

Cockeye shook his head as he stepped over to the stove. He pulled open its door and knelt to mess with the fire.

"Let that alone, nosey," I said. "We don't have enough coal to be stoking."

"Shut-up, Alan. I brung you some more and you want to fight."

I grabbed a boot and pulled it on. "Where'd you get coal?"

"Train hauled some down from Tabasco this morning. Me and Sloan got the allotment for us and you."

"Well . . . thank you." I tried to shake the creepy feeling from my dream. So real, like Sid could be nearby, waiting to take me away. I finished lacing the boot and pulled on the other. "Cockeye, that was the weirdest fit. Dreamed I heard a gunshot."

"There was one. Come from out in the tents, someplace."

"This blizzard is driving everybody crazy," Mama said.

"Sure is," Cockeye said. "All cooped up like this, I can see how you could hurt somebody. I was ready to strangle my kids this morning. Of all the things they could play with, they got into Ida's sewin' basket. Artesia stabbed Colby with a needle. I had to get outside, even if it meant freezin'. You want to see about the shooting?"

"I sure do." Got up off the floor, stomped into the boots, put on my hat, tied the muffler around it, grabbed gloves and coat. "You comin', Mama?"

She shook her head. "The neighbor women are cooking a New Year's soup and Ida wants me to bake bread," she said. "What business is it of yours, that shooting?"

Me and Cockeye looked at each other. "Mama, if I don't get out of this tent, I'm gonna go nuts. You have to understand."

She nodded.

When we left, Mama was mixing batter.

Outdoors, I surveyed the sky. The storm eased up every so often, giving us a little time to shovel the paths. Dirty, frozen snow lay piled as high as five feet in spots. "Looks like it might clear to me."

"I bet you two bits it starts again before noon," Cockeye said.

"Teeth hurtin', huh?"

"A little."

I smiled. "I'll take that bet, anyway."

Wound our way through the maze, until we reached the northeast corner, where Cockeye thought the shot had come from.

Lunkers had gathered outside one tent. Barba stood near the flaps and

Cait waited over to one side. We walked up just in time to see Nick come out with a Greek kid everybody called Little Deke.

"Where you take him, Kistos?" Barba asked.

"If you want to talk, walk along," Nick said.

"No . . . you wait. You take him to train yard captain, ain't you? I wipe my ass on that man."

Cockeye shook his head. "I've had enough of his bull-hockey, Alan. I'll see you later."

Barba pressed closer to Nick. "You cannot give up Little Deke."

"He killed Tharmas," Kistos said. "I don't have to explain the rule to you."

"I shit on that rule. You shouldn't turn Greek over for a trooper rule. He don't know what is happening."

The kid did look pitiful, white-faced and damp, even in the cold weather. His jacket was thrown over his slumping shoulders and his cap rested crooked on his head. He didn't struggle or argue. I felt kind of sorry for him.

The Greeks kept grumbling about the arrest. When Nick was leaving with the kid, Barba caught Nick's sleeve.

Kistos didn't pull away. "What are you grabbing, Barba? Say now."

Barba didn't speak.

"Either hit or let go of my coat."

Barba glanced at the other Greeks then dropped his hand.

Nick nodded. "The troopers would like to sit in their camp while we kill each other. You speak of *leventis*, of being proud. At home men use their head first. Now, Barba, because of you and men like you, the Greek is known as one who fights before thinking. Attacking out of rage would be as effective as popguns against canons. And when friends are dead and you stand alone, proud and haughty with your popgun belligerence, Major Teller will cut you down like a lonesome reed."

"And you would kiss butts and make deals until we on our knees again," Barba said. "I will die on the feet, Kistos."

"Greek, we have agreement to stay away from guns here. I say this to you and to all these heroes: if you have to shoot your friends to be a man, go far away from this camp to do that."

It had been a long time since I'd seen Nick take starch out of the Greeks. Barba and his buddies looked like kids who'd been spanked by their mamas in public.

"Now, show Anglo-Saxons the pride of our fathers and bring out your dead countryman," Nick said. "And let us act like people who can keep a promise and not people who look for first chance to break one. Go into the tent, get Milos and take to undertaker."

Nick took Little Deke's arm and led him away. And Barba and three of the Greeks went into the tent to get the body.

* * *

The sun came out and water dripped off the icicles that clung to the edges of the tents. I took the long way back, strolling through the slush with Cait.

"I don't know how much longer Nick can get away with that," she said.

"Barba's a hothead, but I don't disagree with him altogether. I don't know whether to trust the soldiers and I feel like a sittin' duck out here. Does Nick own a pistol, Cait? I'm just curious."

"Not that I know of. I do, though. A little revolver that Johnny bought me."

"You keep it with you all the time?" I asked.

"No. It's hidden in the tent," she said. "Guess I should start carrying it."

"At least yours is close. My guns are at the dump in a crate."

"The sun is glorious, isn't it?" Cait slid her hand under my arm. "What do you think, Alan? Nick and I are going into Ludlow tonight. Why don't you join us? We'll get supper and drink some wine. Have something to take the chill off."

"Mama ain't doin' too good, Cait. I don't know if I can leave her. She's bakin' bread to go with a neighborhood soup right now, but I never know when the miseries are comin' on. Sid's death is still knockin' her down."

"How about you? How are you feeling?"

"Okay, I guess. Stayin' in that tent all the time makes everything worse. I heard it's the snowiest winter in thirty years. Cissy measured a seven-foot drift against the north side of the latrine."

"I don't mean about the blizzard. I mean about Sidney."

Thought I might cry if I told her how much I suffered. "Miss him. I go a while without rememberin', then I see Susan, or smell horses, or see Sid in a nightmare, like this morning, and I feel terrible again."

Caitlin squeezed my arm. "I miss him, too. We all do."

"This winter would have been real hard on his cough. I wish he'd had a chance to do somethin' different than mining. He woulda made a good rancher. Him and Susan might have got married." Wiped my eyes on my sleeve, right quick. "He was sweet on her."

"I know." Caitlin sniffed and hugged me. "Will you come with us tonight? We haven't all been out in a long time."

"You sure you don't mind me taggin' along?"

Caitlin slapped my arm. "Go on. Next to Kistos, you are my best beau, Allie."

"I'd like to believe that," I said and kissed a corner of her open mouth.

She turned to face me, blinked, licked her lips and grinned. "You missed, scooter." Cait put her hands on my cheeks and gave me a sure-nuff smacker. She'd had a slug of whiskey and I tasted that. When she pulled back, she was smiling.

Without a care for who saw, I kissed her again.

CHAPTER THIRTY-TWO
December 31, 1913-January 1, 1914

The three of us walked arm-in-arm up the Ludlow road, Caitlin and me sharing a bottle of whiskey and enjoying stars we hadn't seen in weeks. Nick was in a good mood, considering the day he'd had. In one hand he carried his lyra case; in the other, a big flashlight that he shined across the guardsmen's tents like it was a searchlight.

Couldn't stop thinking about kissing Cait and what it meant. Was she tired of Nick and looking for a replacement? Had she been going around behind his back? Was she just a prick-teaser? No. I convinced myself that she'd been falling in love with me for a long time, waiting for some gesture of affection on my part. What would we tell Kistos?

When the beam from Nick's light caught two troopers on horseback and another driving a team of mules out of the encampment, I hailed them. "That the way you guys celebrate New Year's up in Denver, skinning mules?"

"We've got an automobile slid off in a ditch about a mile north of the colony," one of the guys called out. "Coming back from Aguilar with medical supplies."

"You want some help?" Nick asked.

"Keep your nose in your business, Kistos," someone else answered. "We'll take care of our affairs."

"Well, that was bleeding rude," Caitlin hollered. "He was just being nice."

"Hush now," Nick said and pulled her along. "Let's not call the militia down on us tonight."

"Yeah, Caitlin," I said, "I'd like to pass the evening without gettin' shot at or called any names, if you don't mind. You two ain't the safest people to be traveling with, you know."

Cait giggled. "But we are the most exciting."

Nick insisted on going to Pagonia's, a favorite Greek hangout. I wasn't sure what kind of reception we'd get. The baker and some of his customers might object to the way Nick had handled Little Deke. Besides, like Barba,

Harry made public his dislike for company swells, detectives and National Guardsmen so loud and often his place was always watched and searched.

When Harry saw us enter, he came to the door.

"So here is the big marshal with his white bread friends. You come to eat with countrymen?" He slapped Nick on the back.

Nick nodded. "Give us a table."

"Take one by the window. That way, if a son of a bitch put a machine gun in my street, you will be first to see it."

"And first to get shot. How about the one in the back?"

Harry led us through the pack. Some spoke to Nick; some ignored him. "Do not worry, Kistos. Only half these Greeks want your head," Harry said.

Nick held the chair for Caitlin. "Which half for you, Harry?"

"I stand with you, marshal. You catch a killer without firing a shot and . . . ," the baker leaned over, "you put Tostakis in his place, too. Barba . . . that one is slave to the temper."

"You think he will still be my friend?" Nick asked.

"I believe so," Harry answered. "He need you. This little girl want more drink, don't she?"

"Sure do," Cait said.

Harry stepped away and returned with a bottle and three little glasses. "You white breads should beware for ouzo. Is very strong and make you big with love."

Cait raised her eyebrows and grinned. "Leave the bottle," she said. "We'll have a contest."

She was shameless.

The baker poured himself a shot. "To my balls," he called and kicked back the liquor.

We cackled while he filled glasses for me and Cait.

"I see you bring the lyra, Kistos," Harry said. "To play later?"

"We'll see," Nick said. "What excuse you have for a meal?"

"Chips of beef cooked in olive oil with peppers and onions, served on rice. I baked baklava this morning and bread. Sorry, no lamb. But I have better surprise: Calamata olives."

Nick closed his eyes and smiled.

"I will bring you a plate of them."

When the olives arrived, I tried one. Too bitter and slimy for me. Plus, I bit down hard on the pit and nearly busted a tooth. Nick ate them like candy, rolling them around in his mouth, chewing the meat slow, sucking the pits. Cait liked them, too.

Nick licked the oil from his fingertips, "Is fresh taste of old country. I breathe the Calamata and I am home."

He put another olive into his mouth, chewed and stared across the room for a few seconds. "I will tell a story. I come from Loutra, a farming village on island of Crete. We have a grove of two hundred olive trees, some very, very old. In the U.S.A., they call us 'olive pickers' to insult, but I am proud. I pick and press olives with Mama until the fingers turn green. Papa was mayor. Giant man with great mustache and booming voice. From him I learn the lyra, Cait. We hear that Turks rip apart other islands and I pray they would not come to mine.

"One morning we wake to a sky of black smoke. Papa run to town. The Turks set fire to houses, hack and shoot my neighbors. I smell the olive trees burning. Mama and me put wet blankets over our heads and escape through flames, but Papa stay behind. We ran to another village and warn of attack. That day 500 Cretans die.

"I find out, they hang my father by his ankles from a carob tree and cut his throat. The blood make a pond in the square."

Cait touched his arm.

"Many Greeks carry only fire and blood, Alan. *Leventis*–all passion. The *andarte*–the real warrior–has a Loutra of blooming olive trees and a Loutra of throats cut in his mind and heart. *Andarte* struggle with visions in conflict when he has decision."

Now I knew what Nick meant when he said I'd have to choose what kind of warrior I'd be.

Harry brought the plates of food. After we ate, Kistos played all the sad songs the Greeks asked for.

About eleven, Talleo Zarias stuck his head around the corner of the backroom doorway and motioned for Nick.

Cait took the lyra and bow. "Set the case on the table, Alan. He won't be playing anymore, tonight. Something's up or they'd leave him be."

"They who?"

"Men he has watching."

Nick disappeared into the back room. After a few minutes, he returned.

"Josephson want me. That trooper we see on horseback earlier, leaving the camp–his horse get tangled in barbed wire when they try to pull automobile from snow."

"Are you responsible for everything now?" Cait asked.

"Somebody strung wire and that boy get hurt. I am marshal. Lawson has gone to Denver. Who else would they ask? I will meet captain at depot."

"You sure Zarias talked to Josephson and not McStay?" I asked. "You know Jake's looking for any excuse to get you."

Kistos nodded. "Talleo bring message straight from captain. Everything is fine with Josephson and Perlmuter there. The depot has light and space. Nothing will happen."

Caitlin grabbed the handle of the case and stood. "Okay. Let's go."

For a second, the Greek looked like he might argue, then thought better. "We pass through the back," Nick said.

Harry waited at the door. Before he opened it, the baker mumbled something to Nick, who smiled and nodded as we stepped outside. I jumped when two men came up on either side of us.

Nick snickered. "Is Talleo and Gus Felix."

The men wore overcoats and fedoras. I imagined them holding pistols inside their big pockets.

"Why don't you give a feller some warning?" I whispered to Nick.

"They need comedy, Alan."

We came around to the front of the building with no trouble. A swirl of snow blew against our legs as we crossed the street.

"I ain't tryin' to be nosey, Nick, but what did Harry tell you just before we come out?" I asked.

"Is old Greek saying: 'In baiting the mousetrap with cheese, always leave room for mouse.' "

"What's that mean?" I asked.

"You will see," Nick answered.

Our bodyguards slid into the shadows when we climbed the steps. Lights beamed through the depot's frosted windows. From the porch I could see three troopers warming themselves before a pot-bellied stove–Josephson, Perlmuter and McStay.

"All right, listen now and follow direction–both of you," Nick said before we went inside. "I draw McStay out. Nothing bad will happen with sergeant there."

"But what if Perlmuter's not quick enough and you get shot," Cait protested.

"I talk and you do nothing, Caitlin," Nick said. "Only me, no matter how mad you get. Understand?"

Caitlin agreed, but I could tell she wasn't happy about it.

Nick nodded to Gus and Talleo, then opened the door and we stepped inside. Nick wished the officers and the ticket seller in his cage a happy New Year. I exchanged nods with Perlmuter. McStay shifted about. His face was redder than usual, eyes bloodshot and he reeked of booze. I wondered why the captain had brought him.

"Good evening, Kistos," Josephson said. "I'll get right to it. You know we had a man injured tonight."

"I heard and am very sorry. He is at hospital?"

"Yes, in Trinidad. Major Teller asked us to find you."

"I am here. What can I do?"

"We want you to help . . ."

"You'll tell us who put that goddamned wire out there," McStay interrupted.

"I don't know, Lieutenant. Why do I want to hurt a man who does nothing to me? I will ask my men about."

Josephson held a gloved hand against McStay's coat. "I want you to calm down or leave, Jake. We discussed this."

"It's just one lie after another with these people," McStay said. "Kistos will lick your boots up here, while his spies pick us off, one-by-one, in the dark. Our boys wouldn't be out in the snow in the first place, if it wasn't for these goddamn olive pickers. If you let 'em get by with something like this, they'll take over."

"No one's getting by with anything," Josephson said. "If you'll let me question this man . . ."

"Goddamn olive pickers in pup tents don't run the United States."

Nick stepped closer to McStay. "And who does, Jacob? You and the hoodlums? Only with guns do men like you control anything. Men who would shoot innocents down in the snow. Cowardly trash, with no upbringing . . . ."

Kistos got what he'd come for. McStay's big fist came around in a punch that sent Kistos sprawling. You'd really have to believe in something to stand flat-footed and take a punch like that, knowing it was coming.

"Hold-up," Perlmuter said, jabbing his pistol barrel between McStay's ribs. "I'll take that."

McStay's hand rested on his revolver and the sergeant took it.

Josephson's voice shook when he spoke. "Well, goddamn, Jake, what was coming next? Were you going to shoot this man?"

"No fucking olive picker is gonna talk to me like that."

"We're taking this matter to Cedar Hill tonight, Lieutenant," the captain said. "As far as I'm concerned, you can stay up there until the strike is over. If I had my way, they'd send you back to Denver."

Nick was out cold on the floor, with Cait kneeling over him, patting his face and trying to wake him. As usual, I didn't know what to do and just stood there like a bump. When Nick came around, I helped Cait get him to his feet.

"We'll talk about his tomorrow, Kistos," Josephson said. "Be where I can find you."

* * *

The next morning me and Cockeye went to the well for our usual buckets of water. I told him how Nick had outsmarted Jake McStay.

I felt proud, but nervous, too, seeing everything up close. Being friends with Nick and witnessing so much was becoming more and more risky. I'd kidded about it with him and Cait, but it was no joke.

When we got to the well, a few dumbbells were standing around griping. They couldn't get any water because something was caught in the shaft.

"I bet it's ice," I said.

"It's never been froze before," Mack said.

"Been ice-cold, though," Tommy added.

"I'll bet anybody two bits it's somethin' else," Cockeye said. "If we want water, somebody's gonna have to go down in there and see what it is."

We all stared at Cockeye. "How bad you want to win that bet?" a lumpie asked.

"Okay . . . all right . . . I'll go, since nobody else is volunteerin'. Seems like I have to do ever'thing." Cockeye tied a rope around his ankles, then we lowered him into the hole. Almost as soon as he disappeared, he hollered for us to pull him up.

"It's barbed wire," Cockeye said when he reappeared. "A bunch of it."

"Couldn't you grab it and pull it out?" I asked.

"I tried to, but it's stuck. Have to cut it."

Mack went for his pliers, then we lowered Cockeye back into the well.

Nick showed up with Lou Dold and a reporter from *The Sentinel*, a Walsenburg newspaper willing to print our side. The Greek looked like he had a tire patch on his face where McStay had punched him.

By the time Cockeye had cut the wire so we could haul it out, the photographer was ready to make pictures.

Cockeye tried to pose, but was so woozy from hanging upside-down, he almost fell. Guys caught him and made him sit.

"Okay, Kistos," Lou said, "you get in there. Nobody's gonna believe this if we don't get a photograph."

Nick tipped his hat back and rested his hand on the bucket housing. Loose coils of wire sprang up to his chin. Lou took the picture.

"Who'd do something like that?" the reporter asked.

"Jacob McStay and D.P. Hawkins," I hollered, before Nick could answer. "It's their guarantee."

PART FOUR

"Oh, can't you see that pretty little bird,
Singing with all of his heart and soul?
He's got a blood-red spot on his wing,
And all the rest of him is black as coal."

"Red-Winged Blackbird"
by Billy Edd Wheeler

CHAPTER THIRTY-THREE
April 18, 1914

I sat in the rocks high in the Black Hills, hoping another hen would show, so I'd have three birds to take home with the two rabbits I'd shot. None came. I was shivering and decided to call it a day. Wanted to get the game cleaned and on the stove before it got too late and I was an hour's walk from the tents. I crossed the plain, keeping on course with the flickering lights and fires from the colony.

Josephson, Perlmuter, Jim Rubin and Company K had gone back to Denver on April 1st. Like the old sergeant had predicted, the state ran out of strike money and pulled the college boys. What had begun as an adventure for them turned into week after week of wet and frozen drudgery. Toward the end of their stint they weren't in much better shape than most of us. Their uniforms and boots were worn, their tempers short. Wages had been held up and they'd been forced to hunt game for food. Unlike us, though, they didn't have to hike out of earshot to do their hunting. And they could go home.

Jim Rubin came to our tent before his train left. Wished me and Mama luck. Said he'd be honored if I'd come visit him in Denver.

I took his coal chip out of my pocket and dropped it in his hand. "You got dust in your pockets, Jim Rubin," I said. "It won't ever come out."

"I know," he said and we shook.

K's exit left a lot of mining property unprotected and the companies got nervous. On April 18, over 130 concerned citizens–laid-off pit bosses, mine foremen, engineers, clerks, sheriff's deputies and local thugs–congregated at the National Guard armory in Trinidad to form "Company A" as replacements for the pukes. A similar gaggle was organized in Walsenburg. The state sent these rag-tags to the strike zone without training, disciplinary instruction or uniforms. Jacob McStay swore them in.

When I reached the camp dump, I uncovered the crate me and Cockeye had pilfered and pried open the lid. I pulled back a corner of the tarp and nestled the rifle among the other weapons.

My .45 rested in its new holster with the full cartridge belt wrapped around it. I considered taking the pistol back with me. With Company K gone, I figured McStay's troopers or the Baldwins would be coming back to the colony. And it wouldn't be a social call.

Then I thought about the promises Nick had made, about him risking his life to avoid gunplay, so the talks would continue. As far as I knew, he didn't carry a gun. For now, anyway, I'd leave my weapons where they lay. I tucked the wrapper around the guns, nailed the crate shut and covered it.

When I got back to our tent, I draped the game over a mound of dirt and went inside. Mama sat on the bed, huddled under a blanket, leaning toward the stove. The orange light from the open grate colored her face, the tent ceiling and walls.

"I burned the headboard and the chairs," she said. "Mr. Bastrop helped me break them up."

I took off a glove and put my hand in front of the coals and barely felt any heat at all. "What happened to the coal allotment?"

"Victor-American held up the train, again. Lawson brought some down in the Ford, but he could only let us have a few handfuls. I saved a little for tonight. Mr. Bastrop came by twice this afternoon. Said he needed to talk to you."

"He'll be back. Let's get supper ready here. Stoke the fire and throw on the rest of the coal." I put my hand on her arm. "Come on, now, Mama, you got to move around."

I took out the butcher knife and stew pot. "I've got two chickens and two rabbits–enough for a banquet."

Lit one of the lanterns and went outside. I plucked one chicken, gutted it, cut it up and dropped bones and all into the pot. Was about to start on the second, when I saw Cockeye standing by the fence, motioning for me.

To hell with secrecy. "Come here. I'm tryin' to start supper. Mama's about froze."

He walked over. "I know. We give away all the coal we could spare. Everybody's burnin' their furniture. I burned the handles out of my tools. 'Cept for my hammer." Cockeye crouched beside me. "Charlie Delveccio is dead, Alan."

I looked up.

"He killed Choice Grabble comin' out of Maybes last night. Willy Crimmons shot Charlie and Jack got Crimmons."

"Where'd you hear that?"

"I was in Ludlow this afternoon with John, seein' about the coal shipment, and we heard it from Mack and Tommy. They was gettin' off the train from Trinidad. Said Jack was in it with Charlie, like Monroe figured."

I started skinning a rabbit. "Here, pluck this chicken while you're yammerin'."

Cockeye went to work.

"How'd Mack and Tommy know all this?" I asked.

"Seen it happen. They was havin' a beer at Masterson's. Unbeknownst to them, Crimmons and Grabble were across the street. When the detectives finished up and stepped onto Maybes' porch, Charlie was waitin' in the street with a .45 and cut loose. Mack said him and Tommy heard shots, hit the floor and crawled up to the doorway in time to see Jack step out of the shadows and plug Crimmons in the stomach, like Crimmons done Rolf Levy."

I'd finished the skinning and was slicing meat away from the bones. "How'd they know it was Jack?" I asked.

"Shouted out some poetry just before he fired. They recognized his voice."

"I'm sad to hear about Charlie. But I ain't surprised."

"Me, neither."

"Where'd Jack go?" I asked.

"Walked into Maybes just before the coppers come."

"To see his nieces, no doubt," I said.

"No doubt. You don't think Jack would come here, do you? I figure he'd hightail it to Denver."

"No reason for him to come to this colony. I bet he'll hang around, though. That's a shit-load of info, boy."

"Had it on good authority," Cockeye said. "Thought you'd want to know."

"What'd Lawson say?"

"For us to sit still and do nothin' stupid. Him and Kistos have went up to Cedar Hill to see Teller. What in the world are they thinkin', leavin' us alone like this? You know McStay and the Baldwins is lookin' for any excuse to get at us now with the college pukes and Perlmuter gone."

"Guess Lawson figures we can handle it," I said. "Him and Nick can't nursemaid us all the time."

"Wonder if we ought to get the guns?"

I thought about my hesitation at the dump. "If we had a for-sure tip-off that the Baldwins was plannin' a sneak attack, like they done at Forbes, I'd say yeah. But if they just search the camp, I'd say no. Somebody'd get hurt if there's guns here. Best thing to do is sit tight like John said and be patient." I tossed the rest of the rabbit meat and the carcass into the pot and started gutting the plucked chicken. "You already eat?"

"Kids and Ida did. I ain't had no appetite, worryin' about all this."

"I've got more than enough for us here. Take this other rabbit."

Cockeye stood.

"Man, I got these chickens, too. Take a goddamn rabbit for your kids." I held up the animal. "I ain't skinnin' it, though."

Cockeye took the rabbit. "Thank you, Alan," he said and went to his tent.

After me and Mama started the stew, we sat on the bed. I told her about the shoot-out in Trinidad. "That could mean trouble for us," I said. "Me and Cockeye decided not to go for the guns, though." I watched the fire. "I wonder if it *was* Jack that helped Charlie."

"Sounds like something he would do," Mama said. "I was too judgmental, Alan. Looking back, he did a lot for us."

"Yeah. I liked Jack, but he was a rogue, like you always said." I smiled. "You know all those stories he told about doin' this and that? We thought they were flim-flam. Turned out, most were true. It's amazing how many people I met who vouched for him."

"Knew more about Emily than I do," Mama said. "I was floored."

"He ever get you that book?" I asked.

"Oh, goodness. I imagine he forgot about that the minute he said it."

"I wouldn't be so sure. Jack thought of you as a fine lady. And when he says he's gonna do somethin', he does it. Come to think of it, you've had a bird dog or two sniffing around lately, haven't you? Think Toby will keep in touch?"

"Check the stove, scallywag."

I did, then went back to questioning. "Let me ask you somethin'. Did you go easy on those college boys when you were pitching?"

Mama smiled. "Maybe, a little. Didn't hurt to make it more even, now, did it? Your pal Jim pitched pretty well and they could hit. But I knew we'd win."

"I just got a lucky hit," I said.

With the stew ready at last, we ate, cleaned up and went to bed. I hadn't been asleep long when a gunshot woke me. I popped up and stuck my head through the tent flaps. Two more shots went off. A new Hastings searchlight was holding steady in the center of the colony and I could see people moving around in the stage area.

"What's happening, Allie?" Mama asked, sitting up.

I pulled my trousers on. "Guys lookin' for guns, I imagine. Just stay in bed. If things turn bad, go to Ida's cellar."

I was putting on my shirt when I heard footsteps coming up quick on our tent.

"Alan Tanner?"

"Yes, it's me," I called, trying to get a boot on. "Who wants to know? Get under the bed, Mama, right now," I whispered.

Before either of us could do anything, the tent flap was jerked back and a man came inside. Two more stood in the opening, one shining a flashlight on us. These guys weren't wearing uniforms: they were either Baldwins or rag-tag.

"Get up," the inside man said, sticking a pistol barrel into my face.

"Whoa . . . hold on," I hollered, throwing my hands up. "I ain't armed."

"That's what we're here to see about," Flashlight said. "You two get out here."

"I only got one boot on," I said, stalling long enough to pull on the other. Pistol jerked me up before I had time to tie either. My pants were falling down, too. Hoisted my suspenders as Pistol shoved me outside.

The dick without the light started to enter the tent when Mama stepped out, wearing her overcoat over her nightgown. "There are no weapons in this tent, sir. You may search, but we're going to watch. And if you damage anything, I'll report you to Major Teller."

Flashlight chuckled. "Major Teller? That's rich."

"Let's go," Pistol said. "The both of you."

"You don't need my mother," I said. "Just take me."

The flashlight came down on the back of my head, knocking me into the cold mud. When I tried to get up, I caught another blow on my cheek. Mama yelled and tried to get between us, but they pulled her away.

"Don't mess with him too much, Jessup," Pistol said. "D.P. wants that fucker for his own self, 'cause he's so special."

They pulled me to my feet and I stumbled along with Mama's help. Babies cried and dogs barked. Families in gowns and nightshirts got rounded up, while scum went through their belongings. No troopers were around.

"Oh, Ethel," I heard Ida cry. Mama disappeared and two of the Baldwins shoved me closer to the stage, where everybody had been herded. In the light I saw Barba, kneeling with his head down. Cockeye lay beside him. Couldn't tell if he was alive or dead.

A gloved hand clutched my neck and forced me to my knees next to the Greek.

Somebody stepped up behind. "We ain't fuckin' with you rednecks anymore." It was Hawkins. "I want to know right now who put Charlie Delveccio up to shootin' my men last night. It was a union thing, wasn't it, Tanner?"

My mouth was so dry I had to swallow before I could speak. "You can't do this, Hawkins."

"Goddammit, peckerwood, I'm doin' it right now, ain't I?"

"What about Bastrop there?" I asked, looking back at the dick. "You already kill him?"

A boot kicked my butt. "You ain't asking questions," Hawkins squealed. "*I'm* asking questions and you're gonna give up some answers. You two pissants get on your feet."

Barba and me were jerked up. The spotlight was a cold sun in my eyes.

"Give 'em both a shovel," Hawkins said, still behind, barking orders. "Dig deep, 'less you want to lie in shallow graves."

I could hear Mama screams above all others. Heart kicked; stomach ached. I shivered, with sweat running into my eyes and down my face. Afraid to take a swing at the dicks with our shovels or try to make a run for it, me and Barba scratched the hard ground.

"I want to know who was in on it with Delveccio," Hawkins hissed, "or I'm gonna blow your fuckin' heads apart."

A revolver cocked behind me.

"Come shoot me in the chest like a man, you shit," Barba said.

The gun fired. I flinched, dropping the shovel, my hands flying up to my ears. Smoke from the shot drifted into the light.

Barba fell forward into the mud.

Whoever held the gun had fired between Tostakis and me and somebody had shoved the Greek down.

Hawkins stepped around and stood in front, his revolver raised. "Okay, fuckhead, who was in cahoots with Charlie?"

"I don't know nothin' about that," I answered.

"How many guns you got?"

I looked into the broad face of the detective, my ears still ringing from the blast. "I don't own a gun. Don't none of us own guns."

Delores Paul swung his pistol and, before I could put my hands up, the ground smacked me.

In the slush, half-conscious, freezing, burning, bleeding, boot toes buried in my side, the iron taste of blood.

Hands lifting. Mama crying. Brain dreaming black and white movement. Body floating down a muddy path. Voice saying all right. All right.

I woke in bed, way in the night, with Mama sleeping next to me in overcoat and muffler. A candle guttered on the table and the wind whirled outside.

CHAPTER THIRTY-FOUR
April 20, 1914

I heard the scrape of Mama setting the kettle for the wash on the stove. As far back as I could remember, she'd done laundry on Monday. Boiled things in a tub, wrung them out and hung them on the line. And cold weather, or the miseries, or me having knots on my head wasn't going to sidetrack her.

The Baldwins had raided the camp on Saturday night. Unless Mama had moved her wash day up, I'd slept Sunday away.

"You don't have to be so quiet," I said. "I'm awake."

She stepped over, sat on the bed and laid her hand on my forehead. "How do you feel, sonny boy?"

"A little sore. Headache. Side ache. Guess my hard head's not so hard after all."

"Let me put some fresh salve on your places."

"Not right now." I sat up and moved my head from side to side. "Did I sleep all day yesterday?"

"Hardly moved a muscle. Everybody looked in on you. Caitlin stayed most of the afternoon. Greeks celebrated their Easter."

"And the Baldwins didn't come back?"

Mama shook her head. "Cait said the major had them barred from the colony." She stepped back to her wash tub. "How's this gonna end, Allie? We have no protection."

"I reckon Nick and John will come up with something."

"They'd better." She stirred the laundry with a sawed-off broom handle. "I can't forget it, Alan, them making you dig, then beating you like that." She wiped her eyes and nose on the back of her hand.

"Mama . . . is Cockeye dead?"

"No. Just roughed up, like you. I visited him yesterday." She shook her head. "What's next, Alan?"

"Don't know. Not retreat or surrender, I'm sure."

She nodded. "Give me that union suit."

I stripped off the underwear under the covers and tossed it into the pile of dirty clothes. Mama threw a clean suit on the bed. I put the long johns on and got up. Was sore all over, like I'd been thrown off a horse and dragged around.

"Where'd you get enough coal for the washin'?" I asked.

"Nick brought some yesterday." Mama stirred her load. "You're down to skin and bones, son. I can fix you some griddle cakes."

"Maybe later. I got to go to the johnny first." I pulled on overalls, socks and boots, put on my hat and went outside.

The sun hung in a pale blue sky with only a tuft of cloud here and there. I hoped the day would be warm enough to melt the rest of the snow and dry things out some.

The colony was awful still. Couldn't tell if it was sleeping-quiet or getting-ready-to-fight-quiet.

I pondered going to the dump for my guns. I wanted to torture all the rag-tag, slow and painful, the Greek way. Tie 'em to a fence post, gut 'em, make jokes while they bled to death. If *I* was thinking like this, Barba was probably making bombs. I needed to talk to him.

On my way to the latrine, I saw two troopers on horseback waiting outside the headquarters tent. One held the reins of a third horse.

Colonists had gathered to watch and speculate. I figured the soldiers had come over to investigate the raid.

When I came outside, Cait was waiting.

"You walked by so fast, I couldn't stop you." She hugged me. "Your cheek looks awful. Are you all right?"

"I'm okay, Caitlin. How about you?"

"Just ashamed, hiding in the cellar under the floorboards. Nick and I agreed about what the Baldwins would do if they caught me alone. The bastards tore our tent apart while I listened to them doing it. You were up here getting your head bashed in and I cowered in the dark with my little gun cocked."

"You did the right thing. I would have put Mama in Bastrops' cellar if they hadn't grabbed me so quick. Now she's doing laundry, like every Monday of her life. I feel bad because I couldn't do nothin' to protect her. Thanks for comin' by yesterday."

Cait nodded.

The trooper in the headquarters tent came out, mounted his horse and the three men rode off.

"What happened Saturday night was the last straw for Nick and John," Cait said. "They think Teller and McStay tricked them into being gone so the

Baldwins could jump us."

"I'd agree with that. Sure weren't no troopers around to stop the mayhem."

When Nick stepped outside, he had on his jacket with the cloth star pinned to it and his plaid motoring cap. He'd also tied a red bandana around his neck and red scarves below the knees.

He came over and shook my hand. "You got bad bruises, Alan. They hurt?"

"Some."

"Your first battle wounds." Nick smiled weakly and lit a cigarette.

"Them guys investigatin' the raid?" I asked.

Nick shook his head. "The Guard decide it was Abercrombie who help Charlie and they think we hide him. They want to search the colony. I say no."

"Worthless cocksuckers." I saw no point in spilling what Cockeye had revealed about McKintrick. "Abercrombie ain't in the colony, Nick. If he was, the Baldwins woulda found him Saturday night."

"I told them, Alan."

"Ain't gettin' shit on no more," I said.

"At long last, you reach the boiling point, eh? Don't let the hot head get you killed."

Cait laid her hand on my arm, but I shook it off.

"Listen, Nick, while you and John was socializin' at Cedar Hill, the Baldwins knocked Bastrop out and had me and Barba dig our own graves. How you think that felt?"

Nick's face reddened. "I know all this. You think I'm not sorry? That I'm not working in your interest?" He threw his hand up. "I will go find Barba."

Caitlin studied Nick as he walked away. "I've never seen Kistos mad or scared. He's always believed that everything could be reasoned out. But things are different, now, aren't they?" She looked back at me. "I know how you are, Alan. Be careful, today."

Hoped for a kiss, but none came.

On my way back to the tent, I met Mama carrying the laundry basket to the clothesline near the stage. "There's gonna be trouble, Mama. Forget the washing and go to the cellar."

"I got to hang out these clothes, son, or they'll mildew."

I pulled the basket out of her hands and dropped it. When she stooped to pick up what had spilled, I grabbed under an arm and drew her up.

"You're gonna get in Bastrops' cellar and leave those clothes alone. Now, come on."

At the tents, I turned Mama over to Ida. After I put on a shirt and grabbed my overcoat, me and Cockeye parleyed. While I explained what was going on, we noticed movement on Water Tank Hill. I ducked into the tent and grabbed the binoculars Nick had given me.

"Troopers unloading somethin' from a wagon," I said. "It's a goddamned machine gun, Cockeye. Them guys are about to open up on us. Time to go to the dump."

* * *

We dug up our weapons and ammunition and I strapped on my pistol. We'd almost made it back to the neighborhood when a gang of strikers scampered out of the camp, heading east.

"What are they doin'?" Cockeye asked.

Looked through the binoculars. "It's Tostakis and the Greeks, headin' for the railroad swale, looks like. Nick's standin' inside the fence waving his arm. He must of given the order. You in it?"

"Well . . . yeah . . . I guess I am. Let's get the families under cover before we head out, though."

Mama wasn't in the cellar or our tent.

"Slipped off, Mr. Tanner," Ida said. "You know how she is when her mind's set."

"She's gone after that damn washing." As I ran to find her, I saw Nick dart across the camp.

While the Ludlow colony girded for attack, my mama pinned sheets to the clothesline. As strikers dashed along the railroad tracks up toward the steel trestle, she lifted a pair of overalls.

"Put down that washing and come on with me."

"I can't just leave our clothes out here, Alan."

Suddenly, gunfire erupted.

"I guess you'll come now, dammit. Keep your head down."

Nick ran up to us.

"Who's shooting?" Mama asked.

"Greeks in railroad cut," he huffed. "Militia on the hill firing back with machine gun." I saw despair his eyes for the first time. "I cannot stop this, Alan"

Strikers appeared behind the corners of the latrine, knelt and started shooting at the encampment across the tracks. "Hold up," Nick hollered, moving toward the lumpies. "You draw fire into this colony."

"Come on, Mama," I said, hurrying us along, but not sure where to go.

"What about the neighbors?"

"They'll get in the cellar, where I wanted you. Let's go around by the headquarters tent."

Center of the colony, people swarming, rattling around inside their shelters, steeling for what we'd all feared. A tent flap blew up to show a woman stuffing her kids under their bed. The last one, a little girl, turned to us and reached out a hand, her face bunched and red with sobbing.

"Poor darling." Mama stopped and stepped toward the child.

"Come on," I hollered and pulled her away.

Farther along, we met Caitlin coming out of a tent. She wore a white shirt with red crosses sewed to it and held a crying baby. A woman following carried another kid, bawling and squirming.

"Where you goin'?" I asked.

"Taking them to the arroyo," Cait said. "Lawson's on his way from Aguilar with ammunition. Nick tried to call Major Teller but couldn't get through."

"We just saw him at the latrine," Mama said. "You're not gettin' in your cellar?"

"Not right now. I'm needed up here," Cait said.

"Ain't you afraid of gettin' shot?" I asked her.

"They won't fire on these red crosses."

"I wouldn't be so sure," I said, having a look through the binoculars at the militia's encampment. Appeared to be deserted. But the dregs could have taken cover in the weeds and were biding their time before firing.

I looked at Mama. "I think it's best if we go with Cait. Better ways to escape in the arroyo."

More women and children joined us as we worked our way up to the northern fence line. Caitlin stopped the group at the corner tent. "We'll climb through the fence and run along the railroad track here. Keep your heads down and hurry."

It was at least fifty yards to the gully. We were about half-way, hurrying along the gravel slope beside the tracks, when shots kicked up from Haddock's pasture. Strikers on the trestle ahead fired back. Figured they saw the women and kids coming and climbed up to cover them. Bullets pinged off rails and rock and the women and children ducked into the sage.

I pulled the Winchester off my back, knelt and returned fire while the party crawled to the arroyo. I'd shot up half a magazine by the time Cait came back, no longer wearing her red crosses.

"Those bastards," she screamed. "They were using the crosses as a target. When we took cover in the brush, the firing let up. Everyone is safe, by the grace of God."

"Be careful," I called to her, as she ran back to the tents.

I crawled through the sage and, when I reached the ditch, slid down the muddy bank. Strikers were still firing from the arms of the trestle, their shell casings dropping into the slop below. Mama held a baby now, trying to keep it calm.

More armed strikers moved up and down the muddy bed and someone hollered for the women and children to get out of there.

I hurried over to Mama. "Give the kid back. We're goin' to the Haddocks'."

CHAPTER THIRTY-FIVE
April 20, 1914

Haddocks had a yard-full of refugees to feed and care for again and Mama went right to work helping out. Clem said when the shooting started, he had tried to call Major Teller at Cedar Hill, but the lines were down. Concern that rag-tags might attack the family for sympathizing with the strikers sent Clem for his rifle. Diego perched atop the barn, keeping watch with a carbine.

By the time I got back to the colony, the sun had set and it was chilly. You could measure the battle by the sound of machine gun and rifle fire, or the lack of it. The opening flurry of panicky excitement had evaporated into a game of planned shots and observation.

I was walking down the trench, when the machine gun opened up again, then got louder, faster. "TACK-TACK-TACK-TACK, like a treadle sewing machine. Two guns firing at the tents. I climbed the bank and took out the binoculars. Death Special sat just east of Water Tank Hill.

Suddenly, yellow flashed, black smoke curled and a tent burst into flame. With the west wind, the fire swirled through the tents nearest me. Soaked with cooking grease, they smelled like bacon frying and burned quick, leaving only the stoves upright.

A rag-tag carried a flaming broom through the colony, setting more fires. When I shot the bastard, he fell into the tent he'd just torched.

Greeks had congregated along the bank farther down the arroyo and I heard Barba yapping at them. When he'd finished giving instructions and his men had hurried past me, I walked over.

"Baldwins is burning everything," Tostakis said. "Shooting dogs, looting tents."

"I know. Is Cockeye with you? He run to the railroad cut a little later than you guys."

"He's dead, Tanner. I seen him coming out to us this morning. He never fire one shot before the machine gun catch him. I bring his body and give it to Lawson after he come with ammunition."

I felt my heart crack. Cockeye hadn't wanted to fight. He never would have bought a gun if it hadn't been for me.

"How about Cait or Nick?" I asked.

"Ain't seen them. But if they is in that colony, you can say goodbye. 'When the horse is dead, get off,' Tanner. Things is finished here."

"Not for me, if Nick and Cait is in them tents. You'd desert your own mama, wouldn't you, Barba?"

Bullets clinked the arms of the bridge. Under the trestle, men were snatching ammunition from crates lying in the mud.

I grabbed two boxes of cartridges and moved to a spot along the north bank. Had loaded the Winchester and was filling the loops on my belt, when Tostakis joined me.

"You don't know, Tanner. We fight the trooper machine gun all day. They can't run us off. But Death Special is too much. If the Baldwins drive that car up to the tents here, Barba get. Detectives think they is bomb-proof and the dumb redneck can't outsmart. But I already send Greek to Noble for Leo's dynamite. We light and throw when detectives drive by. I get for countrymen who die today and for Bastrop."

"You didn't give a shit about Cockeye, Barba."

"Tanner, you don't know nothing. I could leave in that field, but I brung him here on my back. If I say he was a friend and I will get blood for him, that word is law."

I needed to pay my respects to Cockeye, but I was nervous. Remembered what it was like to hold Sidney and I hated to relive that.

When I'd finished loading the belt, I moved farther down the arroyo and peered over the lip of the embankment. The searchlight beam jerked around the colony. The machine gun and rifle fire became scattered, unpredictable.

Lawson joined me. He'd slung a Krag-J over one shoulder and wore an ammo belt. First time I'd seen him armed.

"Want some bread?" John asked.

I wolfed down a piece and he gave me another.

"You see about Bastrop?" I asked.

"Got him covered and laying beside the Ford."

The shooting stopped for a little while and I heard cries coming from the tents. "This is misery, John. We got to do somethin'."

"You want to get shot, jump out there." Lawson said, chewing. "Evening train from Walsenburg will be along any time. When it stops at the station, we'll go in."

"And the scum will move up the tracks toward us."

"Probably so," John said. "We'll be waiting."

All of sudden, a woman with dress and hair ablaze sprang out of a flaming tent.

"Lady . . . drop down," I hollered. She couldn't hear, so I laid the rifle down and crawled onto the plain. The woman staggered toward me, slapping her back and chest. Suddenly she twisted and dropped into the grass. When I reached her, I rolled her around to put out the flames. That's when I saw the bullet hole in her side. Smoke and a greasy smell of charred skin rose from the body. I leaned over her face, but felt no breath against my cheek. Laid my head on her chest. No heartbeat either.

A train's whistle sounded and the big headlight flashed across the plain to the north. I grabbed the woman's hands and pulled her toward Lawson.

With John's help, I backed into the ditch, dragging the body in behind me. "You see that goddamned train? Poor lady needed just ten more minutes."

Lawson knelt beside the body.

"She's dead," I said. "Shot. Either side could have done it. Just like Sidney."

I slung my rifle and we carried the body through the blackness and laid it under the trestle. Two women met us.

The whistle screamed. The ground shook. The headlight, bearing down, caught strikers jumping away from the bridge. The locomotive roared across the trestle, belching smoke, flinging cinders. Wheels clicking over the rail couplings, sound-no-sound, sound-no-sound. Lit-up windows blurred against dark metal.

The whistle wailed again, as a string of cars rumbled over us. Then the bridge was empty with the stench of coal smoke settling around us.

What a black joke. Here were these passengers, who probably didn't even know a strike was going on, taking a quiet night ride to Trinidad and stopping in the middle of a slaughter. Hearing the shooting and screams, they had to be scared shitless, hugging the floor while window glasses exploded, wondering, "What in hell have we run up on?"

When the train stopped, a bunch of us raced into the colony, hollering for everyone to get out. Didn't have to coax. Folks popped out from unburned tents, from behind stoves, from cellars. I went farther in, past the flaming stage, the hospital tent and latrine. Smelled like suppers had burned and somebody had just opened the oven doors.

The machine guns had stopped. I tried to get up to the front row to see about my neighbors, but the fire was too much.

I covered my nose and mouth with my coat sleeve and backed up. When I could get full breaths again, I laid down and checked the encampment.

Sure enough, rag-tags were sneaking back in. I shot two before the rest took cover and I kept firing until the engine groaned and lurched forward. Then I sprinted across the open space near the stage. The train had pulled away by the time I reached the trestle and the machine gun and rifle fire intensified once more.

A flash-flood of people surged through the arroyo, screaming and crying, fighting, knocking each other down, while gunfire splintered the water tank and pinged the bridge.

John stood in the muddy bed, shining his flashlight, turning people back, yelling for them to head east down the ditch toward Noble. In the flickering beam, I saw Nick kneeling over someone. He had his back to me, but I recognized the plaid cap and red scarves.

I slid down the bank.

Nick was wrapping a cloth around Caitlin's left arm. When he had finished, he pulled her shirt sleeve down and draped her overcoat around her shoulders. He whispered something and she reached up to hug him.

I called to them and ran over. A bullet had grazed Caitlin. She leaned against the dirt wall as Nick stood.

He shook my hand. "It didn't go so good, today, did it?" He spoke soft and tired. "If you'll mind Caitlin, I'll go see Major Teller."

"That guy ain't nothin', Kistos. It's goddamn McStay. He's waitin' for you over there. Ain't it a little late for chit-chat?"

"No, no. Never too late to talk. Will you straighten the star?"

"What goddamn difference does that thing make now?" Yellowed from smoke and soot, streaked with Caitlin's blood, the little rag hung on his lapel like a wilted flower.

"Please fix, Alan," Nick said.

I smoothed the material and repinned it.

"Let me go with you, Nick," I said.

"Who would take care of our girls? You stay." He took off his bandana and tied it around my neck. "You is only one can tell the story, Alan. Ever since that day at Number 3, when you show me how to work, every time I look up, you watch over me."

Strange that he thought *I'd* been watching over *him.* Wonder if he meant that. "Afraid you was gonna slit my throat," I said. "You grease bags didn't arrive with the best reputations."

Nick chuckled. "I just think about the night Caitlin teach you to waltz. Look like wrestling." Laughter chopped up his words. "Like . . . you had . . . three feet."

"And you was about the worst fielder I ever seen. Couldn't catch a fly in a barrel."

"We have fun, don't we?"

"Yeah, Nick, we do."

He pulled me into a quick, tight hug and kissed me on each cheek. "I will see you another day, my friend, and on that day I teach you the tango."

I nodded and we shook hands. No use arguing with him.

Nick hollered at Lawson, who was heading up the arroyo toward the trestle. Planning to greet the marauders, no doubt. He and Kistos yakked for a few minutes and I could tell by the way John's light jerked around that he *was* arguing with Nick. Directly the beam dropped into the dirt, lighting up the men's legs just enough for me to see them shake hands.

The Greek called instructions to the trestle boys then climbed onto the prairie. Lawson scrabbled up the bank and ran to the bridge. Figured he was going to cover Nick's surrender.

I squatted beside Caitlin.

"Dumb bleeder thinks he can talk his way out of any mess. Using my handkerchief as a flag of truce. A stupid goddamned handkerchief, for Christ's sake." She sighed. "Would you hand me a fag, Alan? Left pocket of my coat there."

I stuck a smoke between her lips, put a match to it. "That's your last one."

"Criminey," she said, blowing smoke out.

"Arm hurtin' much?" I asked.

"It stings. Guess you could say I was lucky, huh?"

"Yeah. Where you been all afternoon?"

"After I was wounded, we got in our cellar. The tent never caught fire, but I still had trouble breathing, with all the smoke. Nick kept petting me and wiping my face with that wet handkerchief." Wiped her eyes on her cuff. "He wanted to surrender earlier, but stayed for me."

"You heard anything about my neighbors?"

"No one could get to them," Cait said. "Tents up front caught the shots from the machine guns and most of them were on fire. It would be a miracle if anybody survived."

"Even if they was in their cellars?"

Caitlin didn't answer. "You take your mother to Noble?" she asked.

"No, out to Haddocks'. Mama's stiff-neck saved her. If I'd had my way, she'd of been in Ida's pit."

Rifle fire had slowed to scattered pops and the machine guns had quit altogether. When the rag-tags cheered, we heard them plainly.

"Bastards. They're so glad to have him," Cait said.

"I'm gonna see if I can get a better look," I said. "Will you be okay?"

Said she would.

I crawled onto the prairie and was sprinting for the trestle when I heard a volley of shots across the tracks. Wouldn't let myself ponder what that meant.

Found Lawson on the bridge with Mack, Tommy and a brace of lumpies.

"You seen anything?" I asked.

"Rag-tags leaving," John said. A few bodies. None his, that I can tell."

"They captured Kistos right out there," Mack pointed. "He was waving this white rag and the scumbitches come out of them willows when he hollered out his name."

"Could have shot 'em all dead when they popped up, but Kistos told us to hold our fire," Tommy said. "Unless they shot *him*. Then he said we could open up."

"Scumbitches got pretty damn close to this ditch," Mack said.

"Shouted, 'We got Nick the Greek.' Then they all disappeared," Tommy added. "How's your mama doin'?"

Took me by surprise. "Well . . . all right, as far as I know. She's at Haddocks'. Thanks for askin'."

"Yessir," the lumpie returned, without Mack's prompting. "I been thinkin' about her.

We stared at the train yard for a while in silence, waiting for something to show.

"Figure they're taking him to Cedar Hill," Lawson said. "Rag-tag woulda been on us if Kistos hadn't surrendered."

"Most likely," I said. "What were them last shots about, Mack?"

"Couldn't tell. Was a while after they vanished."

"We ain't got no bi-nocs," Tommy tacked on. "Got our suspicions, though."

I climbed onto the trestle arm and scanned the train yard, backlit by the spotlight. No living troopers around; no Kistos.

"I know what you're thinking, Tanner," John called. "But we're not going over there tonight and stir up trouble. I just got the stragglers out of that ditch. We can't stand another skirmish."

I stepped down. "Same as always," I said. "Nothin' we can do."

"Not tonight, anyway," John returned. "We'll have a good look in the morning."

Back in the arroyo, I sat beside Cait and put my arm around her. She rested her head on my shoulder.

"You see anything?" she asked.

"Dead troopers and rag-tag." I stroked her hair and petted her. "Lunkers on the bridge said the dregs almost made it to the arroyo, Cait. Nick stopped them."

"You heard those gun shots, Alan. You know what happened." She sniffed and spit.

"We don't know anything, Caitlin, 'cept that he stopped the attack."

"Stupid bleeding hero," she whispered and started to cry.

CHAPTER THIRTY-SIX
April 20-21, 1914

The last little bit of fight trickled out of everybody when Nick turned himself in. Barba was right–the thing was finished. A few burning tents still crackled and a ceiling of black smoke hung over the colony. Bodiless voices shouting from the darkness softened as they moved on. Mothers beckoned their kids. Friends swore vengeance. One feller called his dog. Another sang a piece of some old song.

Lawson had parked the Ford in a depression north of the arroyo. Cockeye's body lay next to the burned woman on a tarp that John had spread near the car.

From the bandana around my neck, I caught a whiff of the bay rum Nick fancied. Those gunshots needled me and I prayed he was okay.

"You two cold?" Lawson asked. "There's blankets in the car."

"I'm fine right now, thank you," Cait said. "Looky there."

Southeast of the colony two headlamps and a spotlight had come on and slender red-orange dashes flashed across the prairie, seconds before the stitching of the machine gun.

"Death Special," John said. "Using tracer bullets."

I found the armored car in the binoculars.

"Guess the Baldwins didn't get the message about Nickie's surrender," Cait said. "They're coming up here to finish us off."

Lawson stood. "Well, they'll have to do it without lights. We'll go for the spot first, Tanner. Let's separate in case we don't get it right off. I'll holler when I'm set."

John disappeared into the darkness to my right.

"Get behind the car and lay down flat, Caitlin," I called. "Soon as we fire, that light and gun'll turn this way."

I jogged far left until Lawson yelled, then I sat in the dirt. Hefted the Winchester, rested elbows on my knees and started firing.

The spotlight swung toward us and the machine gun fired a burst just as we shot out the light.

"Headlight on the left," I hollered. Got it with my second shot. Then we both fired at the right. Don't know which of us got it.

Seconds later, sparklers arced into the car, then boomeranged out. Happened again. The Greeks were lobbing Leo's dynamite sticks into Death Special and the Baldwins were flinging them overboard. Explosions surrounded the vehicle and, in flashes, I saw the battle. The car sped up, lurched sideways, jerked to a stop. Meanwhile, the dicks abandoned the machine gun, firing their pistols while trying to eject the explosives.

Finally the Baldwins got overwhelmed and "Death Special" smithereened.

* * *

Lawson had laid the flashlight on the hood of the Ford and I used the beam as a beacon to get back. I found him and Cait pulling out blankets.

John had just noted how quiet it was when the screaming started. The sound carried so far it was like the suffering joker lay right next to us.

"Is that a Baldwin from the armored car?" I asked. "How could anybody survive that blast?"

Neither answered.

"Is you, Delores Paul Hawkins?" somebody hollered. "You hurt, cocksucker?"

"That's Barba," Cait said.

"Shoot me. I got . . . no . . . legs." Screaming again.

"No legs would hurt," the Greek called. "You will die soon."

"SHOOT ME." Sobbing and pleading, then a gunshot.

"Was close?" Barba again.

"HERE, MOTHERFUCKER." Long scream for location, another shot and all was silent.

"Well . . . that cut *his* water off," I said.

"Best thing I've seen all day," Caitlin added.

We wrapped up in blankets, sat on the ground and leaned against the car. I was startled when Cait scooted back between my legs and rested her back against my chest.

"Lean forward a second, sweetie," I said. I unbuckled the gun belt and laid it over the Winchester next to me. "Okay." Wrapped us in my blanket and put my arms around her.

"Mind my arm, love," she said. "And . . . could you take off his bandana?"

I did. We shared a bottle of *Yukon Jack* and watched the fires till we fell asleep.

*　　　　*　　　　*

Middle of the night, someone whispered, "Alan."

Heard myself mumble.

"Alan . . . love me."

"Do," I stammered, half-asleep.

"Alan . . ." little bit stronger, louder. "Love me now."

I opened my eyes. Caitlin lips touched mine and pulled back. "I need you to love me right now, Alan."

She ran my hand under her shirt where I found pebble-hard nipples.

"Mmm, sweet," she whispered and sniffed. "I'm lonely, Alan. Could you love me just for tonight?"

"Well . . . yeah, of course," I said.

"Let's go into the field a little ways," she said and stood.

I grabbed my blanket and followed. The colony still smoldered with tiny fires cropping up.

Cait sat on her blanket. "I'll need your help."

"Okay. Sure." I knelt, untied her boots and removed them.

She unbuttoned her trousers, laid back and I pulled them off. Her nickers had slid half-way down and I got rid of those with a tug.

"Don't worry with your boots, honey," she said, lying back. "Just come here."

I stood, took off my coat and shirt, peeled my pants and long johns to my boot tops, dropped to my knees and eased myself between her legs.

"Mind my arm now," she said, guiding me. I slipped inside and started pumping.

"Not so fast, love. Can't you wait a bit?"

"Yeah . . . I guess."

"Just let me feel you in me." Cait moved her hips up and down real slow. "Hold me tight now."

I kissed her and rubbed her tits until she hunched faster, harder.

"Oh . . . you feel good, love. Hold off, long as you can . . . please." She raised her knees along my sides and bucked, moaning soft at first, then louder. I matched her thrusts. Finally, she arched her back and yipped. I hollered, spunked and we relaxed.

Still inside, I lay atop her, running my fingers through her hair, kissing her. After a while, she moved my hips to one side and slid out from under me. I pulled the blanket and coat around us as best I could and folded her pants and my coat into a pillow. She nestled in, rubbing the hair on my stomach.

"You cold?" I asked.

"I'm fine. You're like a furnace. Breathing hard, too."

"You 'bout wore me out. Ain't never held out that long. Arm hurt?"

"It's all right. Wish I had a smoke, though."

"Caitlin?"

"Uh-huh." Sounded groggy.

"What was that about?"

"You didn't enjoy it?"

"It was great. I been wonderin' what that would be like for a long time. Took me by surprise, though. Feel a little guilty, I guess."

"I know." She yawned. "I got so blue after he was gone . . . figured you did, too. Thought we could make each other feel better."

"Did it help?"

"Oh, yes, love. I'm so glad you were here." She nuzzled against my shoulder and fell dead asleep, her lips touching my chest.

I was wide awake, hard again, running over every tiny detail of what just happened. The parts and play I'd always paid for seemed like a crude mocking, now that I'd had Cait. I would need a whole new vocabulary and outlook for the can of worms we'd just opened.

* * *

When I woke, smoky light touched the hills. Cait snored softly against my neck. I rubbed her tits, slid my hand down her belly and slipped my fingers between her legs. She let me linger inside for a few seconds before rolling away. She cried out a little when she put weight on her bad arm, but fell back asleep.

After I tucked the blanket and coat around her and kissed her neck, I pulled up my long johns and pants, put on my shirt, overcoat and hat and walked back to the Ford. John was covered up on the ground, snoring like he was sleeping in a hotel bed. I strapped on the gun belt, leaned the Winchester against the side of the car and climbed onto the trestle to get a look through the binoculars.

Only thing moving was some dogs, sniffing the dead. Scanning the area, I spotted three bodies that hadn't been there the night before. One, lying face-down, had red scarves tied below the knees. Had to be a Greek.

Lowered the glasses, wiped my eyes, looked again. Felt dizzy, like I was gonna puke. Drew some deep breaths and took off down the tracks.

Whiskey bottles lay scattered around and I kept the pistol ready, in case the turds in the yard was just dead-drunk instead of dead. Nothing to worry about on that score. Throats had been cut.

I turned to Nick. Three holes punctured the back of his coat. He'd already begun to stiffen when I rolled him over. Somebody had stomped a boot print on his face, breaking his nose. He still clutched Caitlin's handkerchief.

Kistos had been courting death since he lit in Delagua, riling the bosses, pecking at the detectives and McStay, strutting around with his cloth badge and no weapon. He'd watched his union dreams torched and shot at Ludlow, then gave himself up so the rest of us could escape. Only a few minutes before he surrendered, the Greek wanted to laugh. That's how I'd remember him.

I sat next to him and cried, which made me mad. After Sid, I swore I'd never grieve that hard again.

When somebody you love dies, you think you won't get over it. Your arms will always hold their twitching bodies. Their crying will wake you, their flesh and blood will ooze out through your pores.

I'd lost my papa and sisters, my brother, my best friends. I'd heard women and children begging for help, smelled them burning up and couldn't do one thing to stop it. All my belongings had gone up in flames. God himself wept. How could anybody forget that?

But when your head clears, you realize that people are moving on and they think you should, too. "Somebody's name is gonna hang on the station hook again, Tanner," they'd say. "It might as well be yours."

I had tricked myself into thinking, next time, I wouldn't feel it when folks I knew died. Dangerous work costs lives. Nick had come to Delagua with guns already pointed at him. Cockeye couldn't keep his mouth shut and his head down. Why should I shed tears for them?

But about the time I considered myself good and numb, the memory vultures wheeled overhead. They smelled my guilty heart, stinking below, lit and ripped me open. So I cried.

"Nicholas Kistos," I whispered. Sounded like poetry, his name. "Nicholas Kistos, twenty-seven years."

I holstered the automatic, pulled Nick's arms over my shoulders and tried to hoist him onto my back. No go–he was too heavy.

"You need help?"

I fumbled for the pistol.

"Is Barba, coalass."

Wiped my eyes on my sleeve. "Goddammit, where'd you come from?"

"Back there. I figure you will be here this morning and I make sure no one take Kistos before you." He pointed at the dead rag-tags nearby. "They was dragging him away. Barba get."

I nodded. "Got Death Special, too, didn't you?"

"Yes." He cackled. "You should see Baldwins scramble for dynamite sticks."

"That was Hawkins screamin' in the field, wasn't it?"

"Yes. Barba get."

"We heard that," I said. "Bully the way you pinpointed his location. How'd he survive that explosion?"

"Jump out as last stick go off and catch only part of blast. You shoot out them lights?"

"Yeah. Me and John."

"Took eleven shots," Barba said. "I could get with three."

I looked back at Nick. "You see what they done to him? He wasn't carrying a gun."

"I see. We take Kistos to union car?"

"Yeah."

"Okay." Barba knelt beside the body and picked the dirt and grass from Nick's face. He straightened the dead man's tie, dusted off his coat, rearranged the damn star. "Nicholas was a good man with much *ethos*. But he fly too close to sun, with wax wings."

"What's that mean?"

Barba stood, dusting his hands. "Is old Greek story about too much . . . *ambition*. In English, is *ambition,* yes*?*"

"Yes."

Barba smiled and nodded. "On Crete, where Kistos was born, a papa and son is in prison. The papa make wings for escape and stick on son's arms with wax. Papa say fly to freedom, but don't get too close to sun. The boy go over walls. He sail. He dive and climb. He love to fly so much, he forget papa's warning. Go higher and higher, too close to sun. The wax melt and, soon, he flap only arms. He fall into sea and drown."

"But he got out of prison and flew," I said. "Maybe that was worth dying for."

Barba grabbed Nick under the arms. "His papa didn't think so."

I got his feet and we carried him out of the yard.

Lawson and Cait met us near the trestle. "Christ Jesus," she muttered when she saw his face. "Lay him down a minute." She knelt, laid her hand against his cheek, bent to kiss his lips. "All right. He's yours." Cheeks slick with tears, she stood and walked up the tracks.

Barba pointed. "Now she is yours?"

I shook my head. "She ain't nobody's, Barba. Never was nor will be. I know what you guys think of her. Kistos told me."

The Greek scratched his throat. " 'Outside a doll, inside the plague,' " he said and hiked toward her.

"That guy's hard to figure, ain't he?" John said, helping me tote the body the rest of the way.

"Yeah. I bad-mouthed him for not caring about nobody, then he brung Cockeye back and kept watch over Nick."

"I still don't trust him. He's a loose canon."

"Ain't we all." I sighed. "There's loyalty under that arrogance. I want him on my side."

After wrapping Nick in John's blanket, we loaded him, Cockeye and the woman into the Ford. The bodies reeked.

"Bettin' it was McStay shot Kistos in the back, John. I'm gonna get that son of a bitch."

"You think killing McStay will make up for Nick's death?"

"Course not. It's what he's owed, though," I said.

"I agree he deserves to die. But what if he didn't do it? What if you waste years chasing him down and shoot the wrong man? You heard all those gunshots, same as me. Any of those assholes could have shot him."

"Nobody hated Kistos like McStay. Nick made that guy crazy."

"Still doesn't mean he was the one. No way to be certain who did it. You don't even know who was over there."

So . . . what? You're sayin' do nothin' as usual?"

"Hell, no. I'm saying do the thing that'll accomplish the most. Work smart and you can get the militia *and* the companies. When word gets out about the Ludlow colony, you'll have an army at your fingertips. All you have to do is get 'em organized."

"I ain't no organizer, John."

"You can be, if you want the revenge you're entitled. Count your losses, man–your brother, Bastrop, Kistos . . ."

"Goddamn, I been doin' that. You don't have to remind me."

"Why waste your time on McStay? Everybody's got their private grudges, but you've lost the most. You're the one to get these men focused. The UMW is a righteous army, waiting for a general."

"You're the general."

Lawson shook his head. "I'll always be the outside agitator from goddamn Pennsylvania, Tanner. You're home-grown, one of them. Barba could have got Nick's body, but he saved it for you. Like it or not, you're the one."

"Settin' me up, ain't you, John?"

"Tanner, you've spent years setting yourself up."

I looked at the colony through the glasses. Three-fourths of the tents had burned and the ground smoked in spots. Broken ridge beams smoldered amid buckets, dishes, kettles, bedsprings, sheets of tin, fallen smokestacks.

"Where you plan to take these bodies, John?"

"Trinidad will be best, if I can get through. We want to give proper union burials."

"Oh, yeah, by all means." I recalled the proper union burial Sid had got and felt sick. But how else would you bury Nick Kistos?

When Cait and Barba came back, she said nothing to John or me–just got into the automobile and fell asleep, head thrown back against the seat.

Could still smell her on my fingers. I wanted to kiss and hold her, but I stayed back.

The last I saw of Barba that day, he was hiking toward the train yard. Had henchmen hidden in the pasture, I figured.

I cranked the Ford, got in and John pulled away. We passed a chunk of the armored car's frame and what looked like a fender lying in the grass. A circle of black craters marked the spot where Death Special had been surrounded. The vehicle got closer than I'd figured.

"Over there," I pointed to a mess of vultures.

When John eased the Ford up to the body, the birds hopped away. They'd taken the eyes and most of the face already, but I knew it was Delores Paul Hawkins. Legless, with only one hand and Barba's bullet hole center of his chest.

I started to wake Cait, then thought better. "Would you drop us off at Haddocks'? I want to see about my mother."

Lawson pulled away. "Then what?"

"Don't know. I *would* like to make the bastards say, 'Give,' just once."

"I'll help all I can," Lawson said.

I looked out the window, listening to Cait's heavy breathing, feeling her weight against my side. Nick did this. When he said I was the only one who could tell the whole story, he cursed me. Sealed it with a kiss, too.

CHAPTER THIRTY-SEVEN
April 23, 1914

In the pit where I'd wanted Mama to go, eleven children and two women suffocated. I found out when Susan woke me. The three Bastrop kids, the two Costas, the six I didn't know–candles snuffed out. Clem and Diego had gone back to the site. First, they discovered Ida and Cissy roaming around, blathering out of their minds. Later, they found the hole where the dead lay. After they brought the two women to the house, Clem went to Cedar Hill. Guess the bodies would have rotted if the rancher hadn't made Teller take them out.

Clem drove Ida and Cissy to Trinidad to be with their dead children. Mama and Cait went along to caretake.

Children smothering in darkness hounded me. Brought back the fire in Number 3, the insulting panic from no air.

Imagine an earthen cellar under the floorboards of your tent. Even in the daytime, it's dark, musty, scary. Bugs crawl across the walls, rats on the floor. Your mama takes you and your sisters down there because bad men are shooting at your tent. Everything will be okay, she says; your papa dug the hole in case something like this happened. Neighbors join you and soon fourteen are canned like potted meat. Hot and sweaty from bodies wedged, you're lumpies trapped in a room with little air. The attack lasts for over eight hours. By-and-by, smoke seeps in. It gets hotter. The tent is on fire. You try to climb out, but the guns drive you back. YOU CAN'T BREATHE. Sisters stop squirming . . . crying. Eyes close . . . terror dissolves. You are dead.

Two days later, over 100 armed miners seeped through the pinyons above the mines in Delagua, with me among them. I didn't give a damn about organization or mission. Each thing I could tear up or burn, each swell I could torture would ease *my* pain a little. I didn't have to wait for the lead of a warrior. I knew the way back home. And I had scores to settle.

In a clearing in front of Number 10 mine, we opened up. Guards returned fire and two strikers fell. Finally, the firing from the mine entry ceased.

I worked my way through the pinyons and stumbled down a slope. At the bottom I knelt behind a slag heap where strikers were firing on three shacks.

One shooter turned to me. "Ben always had to be first." He pointed at a body on the porch. "Somebody in there shot him."

I helped them riddle the flimsy dwelling, breaking windows, splintering the plank sidings. Porch rounds fractured and a corner of the roof caved in.

Certain that nothing would be firing back from that house, I walked up to the building with the other lunkers.

On the dirt floor lay three Jap scabs, one still breathing. The tiny room reeked of onions and grease. Bricks supported a screen over a smudge pot and steam rose from three blackened and battered pots. Two of the dead held old revolvers, which strikers kicked away.

"Surprised they knew which end to point," one of the men said.

"Looks like we come on 'em just before breakfast," another threw in. "Fuckers live like rats."

"Formidable resistance," I said.

As I stepped outside, a pistol shot echoed in the shack.

I glanced up the street just as a loose black shirt and pants sneaked out of a shack. Might be armed. I tracked with the Winchester and brought him down on the run. He sailed into the dust like a slender bird. I slung the rifle and pulled the .45, creeping behind the houses, peering inside each one before I passed, just in case an ambush awaited.

The scab I'd shot was just a kid. He lay on his side, with blood oozing from a hole in his back. In one hand, he clutched a few lines of scrip.

His watery, yellow eye stared at me. I wouldn't have known he lived if he hadn't blinked. My face and throat caught fire, gall filled my mouth and I felt like puking.

Here was my righteous retribution, close-up: a scrawny, unarmed Jap kid, suckered into digging Victor-American's bloody coal for worthless pieces of paper. And he needed mercy.

I whispered curses and pawed the ground, a loony arguing with his pants. "Put him down," I whispered over and over. I cocked the .45, put the muzzle to the boy's chest, closed my eyes and fired twice. Then I went to the nearest tool cubby, got a pick and shovel and dug him a shallow grave.

* * *

At the pluck-me, goozies were streaming out with their arms full of loot. On the porch, a man, naked from the waist down except for his boots, stopped long enough to pull on a new pair of pants.

Inside, the front room was a free-for-all. The tables had collapsed and lunkers wrestled for the remaining overalls and jackets. One striker cold-cocked another with an axe handle to get at a jar of hard candy. The ceiling rumbled from the pilfering in the superintendent's apartment upstairs.

A fat sausage had rolled under a table. I picked it up and walked toward the back of the store. Behind a drape was a narrow storage room full of the burning-meat smell of death. Light came through a shaded window on the far wall. Shelves with sliding ladders reached to the ceiling on either side of the room.

I was ready to leave. Instead of fighting my way through the front-room bedlam, I'd climb out the window. I stepped around empty boxes and crates that had been dragged from the shelves. When I pulled the shade, the fresh light showed a surprise. In the corner near the shelving, a striker lay face-up with an automatic in his hand. The guy's jacket was open, his belly stained with blood.

His wasn't the only body. Under the bottom shelf was a Vic. Looked like the striker with the automatic had discovered him and a quick exchange of shots had killed them both. The planks above the swell were splintered where the striker must have fired again as he fell.

It was funny, in a way, this lumpie checking the canned goods and getting the jolt of his life. Could have been me lying there, dead from curiosity. Next time I'd have my pistol ready and creep in.

The company man had been shot below the eye and a mess of blood and brains pillowed his head. Most likely a clerk heading for this same exit window when the striker broke in. Had run out of time for escape and was forced to find a hiding place.

By chance, I patted the swell's waist and felt a bulge. Under his shirt was a money belt. I checked behind me, in case somebody else had stumbled in. Smoke crept under the drape, but all was quiet.

I raised the window before unbuckling the dead man's belt and pulling it out. The compartment was packed with bills–not scrip, but currency. I fastened the belt around my waist, lowered the rifle, squeezed through the window and dropped into the alley.

Explosions boomed from the west end of town and the rank smell of dynamite filled the air. Strikers blowing up the mines.

A canyon-long cloud of dust and smoke from fires and blasting hung so thick and low I saw only pieces of sky. Stores, houses, company buildings coughed flames.

Delagua had fallen and I had a belt full of jack out of it. But I was sweat-soaked, thinking about the boy I'd killed.

"Hey, Tanner." Lou Dold sat on Paine's front steps.

Glad for some conversation to still my conscience, I walked over. A bottle of *Yukon Jack* stood on the floorboards within easy reach.

"How'd you wind up here?" I asked.

"Automobile. Rode up this morning with a reporter from Walsenburg. Fitting it should end in the canyons. Feel good seeing this place burn?"

"To tell you the truth, I don't feel much one way or another. When I got here, I wanted to tear up everything. Now, I just want to get out."

Dold swigged from the bottle and handed it to me. "You want some poison?"

I took a drink, wheezed and set the bottle on the porch. "That shit ain't improved with age."

Dold laughed. "President Wilson is sending federal troops, under the command of General Sisk. Got yourself a civil war down here."

Gunfire popped in the hills above town.

"Somebody's got into a hornet's nest," I said.

"Tostakis and his Greeks, up at Number 11," Dold said. "You going?"

"Directly. Why ain't you up there takin' pictures?"

"I got to be more careful than usual. The *New York Times* wouldn't want its special correspondent to stop a bullet."

"*New York Times*, huh? Big britches."

"Yeah, big britches. One of my photographs from the 'Death Pit' is on the front page of today's paper."

"What 'Death Pit'?"

"The one under the Bastrops' tent. You haven't heard?"

"I heard about the dead." I sat on the porch. "Nobody was calling it the 'Death Pit' when I left Ludlow." I took another drink. "Guess you were right there with your camera, huh?"

"Something wrong with that?"

"It's stealin' private grief, is what," I answered.

"Look, those two women were yammering for all to hear. What's private in that? I've been trying to tell the real story up here for two years, haven't I?"

"Yeah, I guess you have."

"Nobody would have known, much less cared, about you and your families if *I* hadn't showed dead kids being pulled out of that hole. Those pictures roused more sympathy than all my others put together."

"It's mean business, Lou. You ought to see that."

"I see it, Tanner. But you got to realize how big this thing is, now. Ever heard of John Reed or Upton Sinclair?"

"Nope."

"World-famous writers, breaking their necks to get to the strike zone. But *I'm* already here. I've been here. You think I'm gonna let Johnny-come-latelies tell this story? Kiss my ass." Dold took a sip. "You remember that picture of you and your brother I took right up there, just after you escaped from Number 3? Both green as peas. I still have the plate. I got a lot of pictures of Nick and John Lawson. Some of Caitlin. You'll all be famous."

"That's what I'm talkin' about, right there, Lou. I'm so sick of people makin' a name for theirselves off our misery. Let me ask you something: does lookin' through that camera keep you from having feelings?"

"I got feelings, Tanner. Why do you think I've been hanging around this pisspot? If I recall what I've seen, I'd probably stop taking pictures. But who'd know about all this? Right now, you're news and the rubes can't get enough."

"But you're gettin' money for it."

"What . . . I'm supposed to *give* my work away? I don't care how much something means to you, it's not important until somebody pays to know about it."

"That's stone-cold, Lou."

"Goddamn, Tanner, that's the way the world works. Haven't you learned anything?"

The Jap kid blinked again. I'd kept on until Dold asked the question I couldn't answer.

The shooting picked up with a fury in the hills.

"Duty calls," I said.

"Yeah," Dold snorted. "Shoot one for me."

I left the photographer to his drinking, grabbed my rifle and headed for Number 11.

CHAPTER THIRTY-EIGHT

April 23, 1914

At the edge of town, I cut through Suckass Row to pick up the Number 11 rails. The company employees' shacks weren't much better than ours and had given way to easy looting. Several houses smoldered where strikers had torched them, but I didn't see any bodies. Most likely the haphazard attack at the other end of town had given the company men enough time to escape to Number 11.

Peering through the binoculars, I spied bodies lying along the tracks approaching the portal. The guys inside the mine had clear shots down the hill and they peppered the slag heaps and coal cars below, where Barba and his boys had taken cover.

Two strikers climbed high in the rocks far to the left, out of sight of the riflemen in the mine. The lunkers disappeared into the pinyons. In a few minutes, I heard a muffled explosion, with debris and rock shooting skyward. Sounded like the guys had dropped dynamite down an air shaft and the kick-up was the wrecked fan house flying apart.

Poor swells, believing working men wouldn't harm innocents.

Two more strikers loped up the tracks, but the gunners inside Number 11 dropped one of them before he had run ten feet.

I took cover behind a pile of timbers, raised the site on the Winchester and aimed at the mine's entry. The death smell hit and I saw the Jap, sprawled in the dirt, blinking.

My rifle came down and I sat back, wiping my mouth on my sleeve. Killing a man close-up had turned me yellow. If I couldn't beat back hesitation, I was as good as dead, myself.

When the firing let up, I hollered for Barba.

"Who is it?"

"Tanner. In the willows behind you."

"Moving here," Barba called. "Needing cover."

The strikers fired and soon the Greek crawled through the trees.

His men kept shooting. "Is enough, goddammit." Barba shook his head. "Stupid idiots. We don't have much ammunition. Come on these people by accident–pow, pow, pow. We cannot blast out with dynamite even."

I pulled out the sausage and my knife. "Eleven's got the strongest tunnels in the canyon. I never heard of a single station caving in up there." I sliced two pieces and tapped the knife blade on a rock between us. "Thick granite between coal seams."

Barba ate the sausage and I cut him two more hunks.

"You think Slatter is up there?" I asked.

"I hope so."

I looked through the binoculars just as one of the air shaft blasters came out of the pinyons above the mine. "Your shotfirer is up there again, wavin' his arms not to shoot."

The man climbed down the steep embankment to the edge of the cliff above the mine's entrance.

"He's throwin' a stick of dynamite."

The blast a few seconds later spewed rocks down the hill and smoke blew out of the hole. The entry was still open when the smoke cleared, but the shooting had ceased.

"That should finish it," I said.

"I wouldn't charge yet," Barba said, chewing the sausage. "When they see sparklers, could have run. Come back to shoot when smoke clears."

"We'll see," I said.

All of a sudden, one of the Greeks ran into the open and sprinted up the tracks. Shots from the entrance nailed him. The firing picked up again as two strikers crawled up to the wounded man.

"Goddamn," Barba said, "I never seen such a sturdy mine."

I rolled onto my back, stretching my leg out to stave off a charley horse. "How much time you plan to spend on this piece of property?"

"I stay until they come out or start stinking. They have to eat and get water. I shoot when they show faces."

Black smoke plumed farther down the canyon. At first, I thought Hastings might be on fire. Then I noticed the concentration and steady movement of the cloud.

I looked through the binoculars. "Train comin'. Could pen us in up here."

"You don't want to stay and get them back for Kistos? Go on Tanner. *Analatos*, like I always say."

"Yeah, okay, Barba." I cut the sausage in two and left half for him. "You chip Mr. Slatter's teeth for me."

I traversed the hill, moving away from the mine, until I came to a long ravine cut into the hillside. I'd go as far as I could up the gully, wait until dark and crawl out. Then I'd climb over the hill and leave Delagua the way I'd come in, walking just below the ridgeline. The sun had set, but I didn't want to risk silhouetting myself, cresting the hill in twilight.

I climbed up the ditch, sidestepping the stinking puddles of coal drainage. When I could see the railroad tracks below and the ridgeline above, I hunkered down, rested the Winchester across my lap and waited.

The train rolled through town, made the turn-around and stopped near the tipple. I pondered why no one got off. Guardsmen or detectives must have been sent to save property and rescue employees. Or the train could be a decoy and somewhere along the north or south ridges rag-tags were creeping around the pinyons, hoping to surprise lunkers like me. That fight would be close-up and sudden, with little time or space for a rifle.

I checked the ridgeline again just as two troopers came over the hill. I leaned back into the roots and moist dirt and held my breath. My coat and pants were dark, the shadows deep and the men had no idea I was there. But my face and hands stood out like spotlights.

The men ran right by the gully, on down the hill and out of sight. Relieved, I scooped a handful of coal mud and blackened my face and hands. I slung the rifle, pulled out the .45 and cocked it.

Six troopers scooted by.

Heart throbbed like a piston trying to bust out of my chest. I considered picking off the next batch, just to get the tension over with. Fool idea, of course.

When I looked up again, a lone trooper walked along the crust of the ditch, so close to the rim that pebbles and dirt hailed down. He stopped, squatted on his boot tops, goo-goo-style, unbuttoned a shirt pocket, pulled out a whiskey pint, drained the contents and flung it into the ravine.

Jacob McStay crouched twenty feet away, with no idea that justice hid in the darkness below him. Held his rifle across his lap and stared down the hill where the others had gone.

All the evil in my shitty little world perched above. Fate had delivered the lieutenant to me and she begged for action. I raised the pistol.

What happened next came in a blur of crumbling earth and falling man. I guess the souse miscalculated how close he was to the gully, because when he stood and stumbled into a little balancing side-step, he went over the edge.

McStay plummeted into the coal slop like the heavy sack of shit he was. He landed full-force on his right shoulder and side of his head. Unconscious, maybe dead.

God's will be done; no shots required.

I laid the Winchester down and plunged into the mud puddle, covering the trooper with the .45 as I drew near. His right arm was jack-knifed behind his back. He'd dropped his rifle, but his hand gripped the revolver.

Even stumbling drunk and falling, the fucker had drawn his side arm. I didn't let myself marvel at this feat until I'd snatched the gun away and stuck it in my belt. McStay must have seen me out of the corner of his eye and just couldn't twist enough to get off a shot. It was almost worth what I'd gone through to see it happen. The guy was a goddamn rattler.

The most dangerous man I'd ever come across had just proved to be the biggest fool. I intended to take advantage.

I slung both rifles, unloaded the revolver and flung it out of the gulley. Gunfire kicked up down the hill. The troopers must have stumbled onto the Greeks at Number 11.

Time to go. In the last little bit of light, I climbed onto the slope and crawled up to a juniper, twenty feet away. I pulled my rifle, checking the clump of trees behind me, in case some of the troopers were coming back. Nobody. I looked up the hill where fence posts marked the company perimeter.

Wormed into the open just as two rag-tags appeared at the fence. One bent to pull up the bottom strand of wire so the other could duck under.

I fired into the dark shapes until they fell. Counted to sixty and aimed three shots into the clump of trees down the hill then took off across the clearing as fast as my jack rabbit legs would carry me.

I crested the hill and dropped down a little ways on the other side to pick my way along. I hadn't gone very far when a pinyon branch swished just ahead. I dropped to the ground, drew the pistol and was about to fire when a mule lumbered out from behind the tree.

Even in the dark I could tell it was Grady.

"Look at you," I said, approaching. "Where in the world have you been?"

The mule let me love on him, not a bit skitterish. His coat was dusty, his ears full of burrs. Living off the land since the night of the troubles. Another miracle for the magic mule.

"Will you let me take you home, fella?"

Grady nodded and we set out.

CHAPTER THIRTY-NINE
April 26, 1914

I found Mama in the backyard at Blackmur's Rooming House in Trinidad. She sat in a folding chair, reading the newspaper. Looked like a girl from behind. Her dark hair, gathered with a bow, fell loose and long down her back. I watched while she did a typical Mama-thing, creasing the paper into a quarter-page section, resting it in her lap. She paused every so often to stare at something. One time, she took off her glasses, laid them on the paper and wiped her eyes with a handkerchief.

So I wouldn't scare her, I called out as I approached.

She dropped the paper and turned. "Oh, sweet boy. Come here."

Mama rose and hugged me so tight that it made me uneasy. Like she had cracked.

I patted and rubbed her back. "I'm all right."

She let go and wiped her eyes. "Sorry, Allie. I been so afraid you'd get killed and now here you are. It's a shock."

"I know, Mama." I gave her another little hug. "You okay?"

She nodded. When she sat again, I noticed a new book lying on the ground next to her chair. *Poems of Emily Dickinson, Third Series.* Before I could ask about it, she started talking again.

"Clem bring you to town?"

"Naw, I didn't want to impose. Took the train. Guess what, Mama? You remember old Grady, don't you?"

"Yeah. The mule that saved you and Sidney. Burned up the night of the troubles. Why?"

"Well, he's not dead. He's been living wild in the hills. Don't ask me how. I was leavin' Delagua over the ridgeline when he stepped out from behind a tree. Let me walk him to Ludlow where he's liveried at Gabey's."

Mama drew a deep breath and smiled. "Strange what survives, isn't it? Is Ludlow full of soldiers again?"

"Yeah, some."

"President Wilson's called out federal troops," Mama said. "General

Sisk is supposed to arrive sometime today to take charge. You still have your guns?"

"Left them with Gabey. Said he'd give them to Clem for safe keeping till I could pick 'em up. Livery man couldn't quit talkin' about the massacre and how strikers had stormed the county seat and took over."

Mama snickered. "There was no storming, Alan. The sheriff and his people cleared out. Mayor resigned. Armory is empty. Police are still around and some thugs, of course. But no real resistance. Didn't even get stopped on our drive from the Haddocks'."

"Lots of people for the strikers now," I said. "Train conductor wouldn't take my fare."

Mama tapped the newspaper. "Well, the *Chronicle-News* isn't for the strikers. There's one tiny story about the colony funerals, hidden four pages back into the paper, while this piece about a boy in Philadelphia whose neck was run over by an automobile got the front page. Course, there's nothing about union occupation. If the paper doesn't report it, it didn't happen, I guess." Her lip quivered. She shut her eyes and took a deep breath, trying to hold in the tears, but some squeezed out, all the same. She dabbed them with the handkerchief and blew her nose. "I've about worn out this hanky." She smiled, pulling at the cloth. "Old Iron Ethel, blubbering like a baby when I got so much to be thankful for, with you back."

I took her hand and sat on the ground. "If you'd done what I said and not gone back for the laundry, you'd have been in that pit. Dumb luck saved us."

"Tanner luck and my hard head. You were just telling me to do what you thought was right." Mama sniffed and a sob coughed out. "Ida and Cissy were the only ones to get out of the cellar alive."

I rubbed her back. "I know, Mama."

"They climbed over their dead children to get some air. Can you imagine what that was like? Ida's sharing the room with me and it's been awful. She doesn't sleep. Cries and prays, worse than ever." Mama blew her nose again. "Caitlin and Mother Jones have taken Ida and Cissy to Denver to meet with the governor. They're coming back early tomorrow."

"Have they buried Nick and Cockeye yet?"

"Buried everybody but Mr. Kistos yesterday. About two hours before the funerals, there was a fire at MacMahon's Mortuary and the thirteen coffins from the pit, plus Nick, Mr. Bastrop and the woman you pulled out of the field had to be carried into the street. Had the ceremonies right there for all but Mr. Kistos. These days, you think things can't get any worse right before they do. Ida prophesied that Blackmur's roof would fall in on us next." Mama smiled.

"Caitlin is bringing a Greek Orthodox minister back from Denver for Nick. His body was moved to Dingle's Funeral Home. You can view him there."

"How is she, Mama?"

"Cait? You know her. Stays busy, so it's hard to tell. Frets in private, like me." Mama swept a leaf out of her lap with the back of one hand then smoothed her dress. "She had big plans for all of us. And she loved Kistos."

My stomach knotted. "She talk about Nick a lot?"

"Not a great deal. But you can sense she misses him," she said.

"So do I. How's her arm?"

"Far as I can tell, she's all right. Never saw a doctor. I've helped her change the bandage and clean the wound. She's tough as a boot."

So blue after he was gone . . . thought we might make each other feel better. I smiled weakly. "She's not too tough."

Mama shrugged and didn't argue. "You see about our house?"

"Got in too big a hurry to leave. I found some money, Mama. Just over five hundred dollars, cash."

"Found it where?"

"In a zipper belt I took off a dead clerk at the pluck-me. I'm gettin' a suit and you some new clothes. We're gonna look like something for Nick's funeral. We'll get a better place to stay, if you like. I'm gonna have a bath in a real tub. You can even give me a shave afterwards. And I want to buy Caitlin a dress. We'll go back to that shop you got thrown out of."

Mama smiled. "That sounds nice." She picked up the new Emily and handed it to me.

"I was gonna ask about this. Where'd it come from?"

"Can't you guess? Look inside."

I did. "To Ethel, with warmest regards. A. J. McKintrick." I handed the book back. "What'd he have to say?"

"Didn't talk to him," she answered. "He came while I was at the funerals and left the book and letters for Ida and Cissy with Mr. Blackmur. Brought you something, too." She picked up her newspaper. "Come on."

I followed Mama inside the house to her room. On the chest-of-drawers sat a softball.

Mama handed me a postcard showing the dead detectives from Maybes. "That was inside the new Emily," she said.

"Young Tanner," it read, "Here's your homerun ball that won the game. A tragedy things turned out as they did. Griffith wired me to come to Hollywood and shoot a film. See you on the silver screen. Jack."

"How'd he get that?" Mama asked.

I rubbed the ball, tossed and caught it. "How does Jack do anything?

Cockeye thought he might be a phantom." I smiled. "Who's Griffith?"

"A movie director," Mama said, leafing through the newspaper. "His latest picture, *Judith of Bethulia,* is showing at the West Theater. It's an hour long."

I looked over the advertisement. "Aren't you afraid of hurtin' your eyes?"

"I'd take the risk to see that picture," she answered.

"Then we should go."

*   *   *

Lawson stood on the sidewalk outside Dingle's, giving directions to mourners filing in to see Nick's body. When I stepped up, he shook my hand.

"You could pass for the undertaker in that suit, John," I remarked.

He smiled and rubbed his fingers on the lapel of my new coat. "Talk about me? This is fine cloth. You buy it today?"

"Yeah. First suit I ever owned. Mama helped pick it out. No dust in the pockets."

"Looks good. I'd have bought a derby instead of that fedora, though. That's a derby suit."

"Fedora's more . . . mysterious." I smiled, running my thumb under the brim, detective-style. "Sounds like it was a cake-walk comin' into Trinidad, John. What happened to the militia?"

"Teller didn't have enough men to go around, so he ordered the armory cleaned out and called the troopers here back to headquarters. The major didn't expect canyon attacks and was caught short-handed. He kept a small force with him at Cedar Hill. Sent some men to Forbes and Berwind. The rest went with McStay to Delagua. You know the lieutenant got hurt up there?"

"I heard," I said.

"The street says he's got a concussion and a broken everything–ribs, shoulder, arm," Lawson said. "Nearly died. They took him to Walsenburg on the train."

"Couldn't have happened to a nicer guy," I said, smiling. "Heard General Sisk is comin' back. Didn't get enough abuse the last time, I guess."

Lawson gripped my arm and led me along. "The truce agreement won't allow him to come to Trinidad."

"You think a truce will keep the militia from goin' where it wants?" I asked.

"Actually, it looks like lumpies scared the companies into submission.

President Wilson wants to get this settled. You guys did a good thing."

No opinion on that. "Glad Cait's bringin' the minister for Kistos," I said. "These people need that funeral."

Lawson nodded. "I wish you'd been here a little while ago. Four Greeks–warriors from Forbes, you know, all decked out in the regalia–came in to view the body. They banged their stocks four times on the floor in there."

"What for?" I asked.

"A vow to avenge Nick," Lawson answered. "I watched it through the windows."

"And the struggle continues," I said, stepping onto the porch. Two more guys went inside as the Haddocks and Diego stepped out. I took off my hat and spoke. Clem and the Mexican shook my hand and Susan gave me a long hug. She looked like a different person in her black dress and high buttons. We blocked the door for a few seconds until Susan pulled us to one side.

"Nice of you to come see Kistos," I said. "*Muchas gracias para* Nicholas, *amigo*."

Diego nodded and stepped into the yard.

"That Kistos was right as a trivet," Clem said, turning his hat in his hand. The old man wore a suit and his sandy hair was plastered with sweat. "A rip-snorter. It was a privilege knowin' him."

I smiled and nodded. "Bravest I'll ever come across. We kinda ruined your property, didn't we?"

"Alan . . . ," Clem started, coughed, cleared his throat. His eyes watered. "Alan . . . if you . . . aw, goddammit-all-to-hell."

I patted his lapel. "My sentiments exactly, Clem. Goddammit-all-to-hell."

Susan put her hand on my arm. "We'd like for you to come work with us, Alan. You and Ethel. Come live."

"Could do whatever . . . goddamn it," Clem said. "Could do nothin' but play with the mule, far as I'm concerned. You wouldn't have to go back up there anymore."

"Would you teach me that long poem?" I asked.

"What . . . 'Dan McGrew'? Course."

I smiled. "I'll probably go back to the mines. It's what I do. I ain't much of a rancher, you know."

"You don't have to decide right now," Susan said.

"Or next month even," Clem added. "Just want you to know you're welcome."

I nodded. "I do have a favor to ask. You remember Grady, that old blind mule I told you about?"

"Gabey said you found him roamin' in the hills," Clem said.

"Yeah. I don't know what he survived on, but there he was. In pretty good shape, too. I wondered if you'd stable him with Juliet. Can't imagine a better place for a mule of his caliber to finish up."

"You bring him tomorrow," Clem said.

"The funeral, Daddy," Susan said. "You and Ethel come on Tuesday. We'll have lunch."

"Okay," I said.

"I moved the other things you left with Gabey out to the house," Clem said. "Had a goddamn arsenal, didn't you? I'll clean 'em for you."

"Thanks," I said.

Susan gave me a kiss on the cheek and a hug. "Tell Mama we said hello. You both come any time for as long as you like."

"Thank you. Is there anything special to do when I go in?" I asked.

"Touch his forehead and offer a prayer," Susan said. "That's what the countrymen said to do."

"Sidney loved you, Susan," I blurted. "Guess you heard him say it, but I wanted to say it, too."

She sniffed. "I loved him, Alan. He knew it."

Clem put his arm around her. "We'll see you tomorrow at the funeral and for lunch on Tuesday. I'll tell Juliet Romeo's comin'."

"Bye-bye, Alan," Susan said, taking her papa's arm as they stepped off the porch.

I started for the back of the line, when a joker called my name. I turned. The mourners had removed their hats and were watching.

"Step in right here," another stranger said. "You was at the front, already."

"Obliged," I said. "I'll just go on back there."

"Nobody's goin' in till you're done, Mr. Tanner," first mourner said. "You might as well come on now, 'cause we ain't movin'."

I shook hands with the feller and stepped in. Nick was laid out in the front room, lit only by tall, white candles. I waited in the hall until the last few men passed by the coffin and went outside. I walked into the room, alone with my friend.

Kistos' face was bloated and, in spite of the heavy paint job, I could still see scratches from the boot prints. The lyra lay beside him in the coffin.

Through tears, I watched my fingers touch his forehead and heard myself say: "I will see you another day, my friend."

When I came outside, John Lawson was yakking with a guy in line. I stepped into the yard, thinking I'd say goodbye. But the union man was lost in talk. I respected Lawson, but I could never care about him like I did Nick. John showed only one side. Like McStay, who was all-militia, and Hawkins all-Baldwin, Lawson was all-union. Wouldn't let anybody get close enough to really know him.

I took a last look at the lumpies still waiting on the porch and caught my reflection in Dingle's window. Costumed in suit and fedora, I didn't altogether recognize myself. Images of the mourners inside mingled with my likeness and I found it impossible to say whether I was one of them or some stranger dissolving in the fading light.

When the intruder disappeared, I strolled into the street and headed toward tomorrow.

CHAPTER FORTY
April 27, 1914

The electric lamps flickered in their globes as me and Caitlin turned onto Main Street. She had taken my arm as we walked back from the funeral, neither of us saying a word.

Two columns of people, over a mile long, had followed the coach that carried Nick down Main Street and onto Commercial. Greeks in their blouses and leggings marched right behind the coffin, Barba and Harry among them. Strikers stood at attention with their hats off, their rifles at their sides, as the coach rumbled by. Curious townspeople, some holding little American flags, lined the streets like it was a parade. Automobile and wagon traffic held up. If troopers or detectives were around, I didn't see them.

We crossed the Purgatoire and climbed the hill to the Knights of Pythias cemetery, where Sid was buried. Over five hundred people prayed over Nick's fresh grave and the graves of the others who'd died at the colony.

The Greek Orthodox priest swung a lantern and called to the Lord: "Give rest to the soul of thy departed servant, Nicholas, in a place of brightness, a place of verdure, a place of repose, whence all sickness, pain and sorrow have fled away."

Before leaving, we visited Sid's grave. Afterwards, I asked Mama to eat dinner with us, but she wanted to go back to Blackmur's with Ida and Cissy.

As we strolled, Caitlin brushed my cheek with her fingertips. "Don't let me be blue, Allie. Tonight, I'm a fine lady in Swansea, out with my beau. We've come from a music hall and you're taking me to a swanky restaurant."

I patted her hand. "May I recommend Masterson's, madam?"

"Ah, yes. Top drawer, I hear."

Turning onto Church, I pointed out a sign propped in the street before Maybes.

VISIT THE MURDER PORCH HERE!
STAND WHERE OFFICERS OF THE LAW
WERE MERCILESSLY GUNNED DOWN!
TOUCH BLOOD STAINS!
SEE ACTUAL BULLET HOLES!
POST CARDS OF FALLEN HEROES ON SALE INSIDE!

"That's the place where Crimmons and Grabble got the chop," I said. "You want to touch some blood stains and see real bullet holes?"

"Oh, could I?" Cait laughed. "Not right now, love. Might get me a post card later. I need a picture of those dead bastards."

When I opened the door to Masterson's, I knew I wouldn't be having a steak. In fact, with the odor of meat cooking, I wasn't sure I'd eat anything at all. Just couldn't get the rankness out of my nose.

I asked the waiter for a table by the window where I could watch the street. Caitlin took off her hat and lit a cigarette. She looked so pretty in the dress I'd bought. Didn't think I'd ever seen her look better. She had twisted her hair on top of her head and, as usual, a few unruly strands coiled down.

I ordered two beers and two shots of whiskey.

Caitlin checked me out. "You look spiffy in that suit and fedora. And I love my dress. Some big spender you are, all of a sudden. Might take your hat off at the table, though."

I smiled and removed my lid. "John said I needed a derby for this suit, but Mama and I thought a fedora looked better." Even though I'd been inside her, I couldn't figure out how to approach this woman who wouldn't be pushed or owned. "I came into my inheritance in Delagua, Caitlin. I have . . . enough."

"For tickets to take us all north," I wanted to say. Waiting for the train to Trinidad, I'd seen a railroad flyer advertising cheap land near Alamosa. "Richest soil in Colorado," I could tell Caitlin. "They're practically givin' it away to people who want to farm. We could make a go of it up there."

"Your pa hated everything about farming," I imagined her saying. "It would chain you down, same as mining."

"At least we'd be above ground," I'd reply.

On Maybes' porch, Mack and Tommy were posing for a photograph. Tipped their hats at various angles and looked to each other for approval. I smiled, but my thoughts veered to the dead.

"Ethel looked pretty today," Cait said.

"Still turns heads. Watched it all my life. Drove Papa crazy."

"She has no interest in marriage?"

"Don't know, really. Sergeant Perlmuter took a shine to her and McKintrick had poetic interests."

She grinned.

"You know, Caitlin, it's funny how much you lose and how fast you lose it when all you're interested in is gettin' even. Shoot, I can't figure out what even is anymore."

Her smile faded. Should have shut up right then, but I couldn't.

"We stopped the companies' operations and burned up their property. We got a union and our rights. Made 'em say, 'Give.' So what? Our friends are dead; our jobs blown up. After the colony fire, we don't have a pot to piss in. I don't have enough years left to get even for what's happened. Barba was willing to die rather than let the swells come out of Number 11. Me, I was ready to quit."

She punched her cigarette at me, agitated. "Well, I'm not ready to quit. Mother Jones told Governor Ammons the fight was just beginning and I'm with her. I heard people crying for mercy in the colony all afternoon on Monday. So did you. Ida said they kept trying to get out of the pit, but the machine guns wouldn't let up on those front tents." Caitlin mashed the cigarette in a bowl. "The UMW wants to send me, Cissy and Ida around the country to stir up sympathy for the cause."

There it was, just like I figured–another plan and it didn't include me. "You'd be interested in doing that, huh, puttin' up with a screamer and a sermonizer? Seems like that would drive *you* crazy. It would me."

"I'd tour this country on the United Mine Workers' dime in a New York minute, Alan."

I cleared my throat. "What if I wanted to talk about somethin' different for us?"

She narrowed her eyes, cocked her head. "Who's *us*?"

"You and me. And Mama."

"Doing what?"

"I got some ideas. Something that doesn't involve guns or unions. Something that'd make us both happy. Like the other night."

Caitlin leaned forward. "Just because you parked your mule in my stall doesn't make you the skinner."

"I'm not trying to be the skinner, damn it, Cait. I'm askin' for your opinion about the future."

"I just told you about the future," she said.

"You already made a firm commitment?" I asked.

"I'm not saying."

A woman's pube can tow a ship. "Would you just think about it?"

"Don't know whether I will or I won't."

"Might your stall be available later?"

She slapped my arm. "You'll be lucky if you ever see my stall again, son."

I grinned and ran my fingers along the brim of my good-looking hat. While we waited for another round of drinks, I told her about my run-in with McStay.

"He was out cold, almost dead. All twisted and broken up, holding his pistol. I weighed taking advantage of that gift, doing somethin' to give deserts at last. Could have done anything I wanted, too. Could have shot him in the back and stomped *his* face, the way he did Nick. Could have carved him up. But a little voice inside said, 'You don't *have* to do *anything*.' And I was free."

Cait fidgeted, lit another cigarette, sipped her beer. I really didn't care if I was making her uncomfortable. *She* had other plans.

"For a long time I been tryin' to figure out a way to be, so certain people would notice and I'd get respect. Deep-down I burned to be a cold-blooded, efficient fighter like Barba or McStay . . . or Jack, even–somebody who didn't give a shit and enjoyed his treats wherever he found 'em. Well, I got my cold-blooded wish. I killed an unarmed Jap scab, a *kid* in Delagua." Goddamned tears brimmed. I bowed my head, but I knew she saw 'em. "You know what I found out, Cait? Gettin' even wears you out." I went ahead and wiped my eyes on my coat sleeve. "Instead of figuring out how to be, I discovered how *not* to be."

My hands lay palm-up on the table and Caitlin covered them with her own. "Enough of this for now, all right, love?"

I nodded.

"All of it will get sorted out," she said.

The feller who came to play the piano was none other than Monroe Purvis. Guess living with Clara in Forbes had aged the music man or something, because I didn't recognize him at first. But Caitlin knew right off.

"Let's go talk," she said, rising.

When he saw us coming, Purvis stood, kissed Caitlin and held her hands.

"You turn up in more places than a wild hog, Monroe," I said. "You give up on Forbes? I hear that's where the action is right now."

"Oh, I been gone from out there for over a month. Clara took off with a Baldwin. I suppose they'll be sharing our wealth throughout the East."

Caitlin was kneeling in front of the piano bench, rifling the sheet music in the compartment under the seat. Monroe asked if she'd consider singing something.

She stood and handed him a piece. "I see you have 'Lazy Moon'. Always the newest things for you, I swear. I might sing that later. We haven't eaten."

Monroe smiled and nodded. "Well, if you get the urge, I know you still have lots of admirers. Nice to see you, Tanner."

Turned out, Cait didn't want steak, either. We poked around, instead, at cheese enchiladas and fried potatoes and kept drinking. We were having slices of lemon pie when Mack and Tommy, Barba, Harry and some of the Greeks came in. They dragged up chairs and ordered drinks. Like the old days, everybody started griping and speculating.

I knew it was just a matter of time before Caitlin got up to sing. Monroe accompanied her on "Lazy Moon," then she sang "Cockles and Muscles" by herself.

I was drunk and fretful, not getting proper attention from the girl I loved. Thought a dance might warm her up. "Hey, Monroe," I hollered. "You know any tango songs?"

"Sure. You like this . . . ?" He rolled out a bit of tune. "Or this?"

"That last one," I said. "Play it fast and loud, the way Kistos favored." I stepped up to Caitlin and bowed. "Could I have the pleasure?"

She grinned. "A tango? Why, I'd be honored."

I grabbed her hand. "Lead me off, sweetie, and I'll do the best I can to hang on."

I tried to relax and let her teach me like she'd done with the waltz. My three feet stumbled around some. Pretty soon, though, I got the hang of it and I was pushing her back and pulling her, feeling the rhythm and turning, dizzy from drink and the sorrow down deep.

The lights of Masterson's streamed around us. Faces blurred. And with Caitlin's white throat before me, I danced.

ACKNOWLEDGMENTS

The Red-Winged Blackbird represents a long, meandering labor of love to vivify a crucial but little known historical event using tools that only fiction provides. I could never have completed this task without much help and encouragement. Two books opened the story of the Ludlow Massacre for me and became the historical underpinnings for the novel. The first, *The Great Coalfield War* by George S. McGovern and Leonard F. Guttridge recounted the saga and its importance in stark detail. The second, *Buried Unsung* by Zeese Papanikolas is a remarkable biography of strike leader Louis Tikas.

I would like to recognize the kind assistance of librarians at the Andrew Carnegie Library in Trinidad, Colorado, who helped me find newspaper accounts of the strike on microfiche (yes, alas, I've been working on this project that long!) and made photocopies for me. I would also like to thank the curator of the State Historical Society in Denver who allowed me to don white gloves and hold the actual photos of the tumult preserved in the Louis Dold collection.

I greatly appreciate the suggestions and words of encouragement offered by members of the Dallas-Ft. Worth Writers Group, who listened attentively to the novel during its early iterations. I would also like to thank the creative writing classes at R.L. Paschal High School in Ft. Worth for their critiques as part of our class. We learned a great deal from each other.

Nashville Songwriters Hall of Fame member Billy Edd Wheeler allowed me to use the title and lyrics to his powerful lament "Red-Winged Blackbird." The only payment he requested was a copy of the novel. Thank you, Mr. Wheeler.

Thanks to David Alan Hall, Kevin Coffee, Mark Dilworth, Jim Woodson and Jim Beckman for reading early drafts. Thanks especially to Metaxia White who put a critical eye on the dialogue and behavior of my Greeks and Italians.

Kudos to my old friend Jim Galloway for the great photo shoot and to my brother-in-law Walter Webb for the cover design and formatting assistance.

And most of all, thank-you, thank-you, thank-you to my wife Sandra, who edited countless drafts, asked the right questions and made the best recommendations a writer could ask for. I love you, darling.

The Red-Winged Blackbird is available at www.createspace.com/3947028.

Made in the USA
San Bernardino, CA
04 May 2014